SHADOW OF THE WIRE

C M Mawing

CHAPTER 1

Claire was lost. Not physically, as she had made this walk several times in the last two years since her parents accident, but emotionally. She moved slowly down the long, narrow hallway that led to her high school guidance counselor's office. With a little luck, this could be her last visit to Mrs. Stone, but she wasn't feeling good about her chances. She had been unable to come up with a satisfactory course of action for what her future was to entail, and in fact, she had not even been able to fake a plan. There was no place she could picture herself once high school was over, and every recommendation to her had been readily rejected. She shuffled forward, trying to ignore the walls of the hall which were lined with inspirational photos and quotes; the kind that showed somebody doing something of great achievement or importance....motivation, dedication, perseverance, and about a dozen others. Looking at them made Claire feel even worse about herself, as it would seem she lacked all of those characteristics that were supposed to make for a great and successful human being.

She dropped her backpack carelessly on the dirty, perpetually scuffed tile floor, and sat down in one of the cheap plastic chairs placed outside of counselor Stone's office, briefly thinking about how much money the school spent on their athletic programs every year, but couldn't afford to put more comfortable chairs out for those people who were waiting to be told that they would never amount to anything unless they drastically changed the current course of their life. Maybe that was the point.

The conversation with Mrs. Stone played out in her head, and she knew exactly how it was going to go: No, she hadn't filled out her college applications, no she hadn't decided what she wanted to be when she grew up, yes she realized that she would be a disappointment to her parents, even though her father was dead, and her mother couldn't even remember her name. She supposed that she shouldn't feel so resentful, but Mrs. Stone seemed to have a knack for bringing peoples inadequacies to the forefront of the conversations. Until she had met her, Claire was under the impression that counselors were supposed to guide and support. A concept that was clearly lost on this school's counselor, as she seemed to thrive on shaming people into making choices for their future, whether they were the right choices or not.

With still a few minutes before her scheduled appointment, Claire let her thoughts wander to the only thing that really ever kept her attention, and that was the horses. She couldn't wait to get out of school and get to the barn. It was the only place that she truly felt alive and at home. Although she no longer owned a horse of her own, the stable where she rode always had something for her to ride. She worked weekends cleaning stalls in exchange for lessons. Her work was conditional; she had to keep her grades up in order to keep her job at the barn, but she managed. School was not one of her strengths. It is not that she struggled, she just failed to see the point in all of it, especially when she knew that college was going to be out of the question. She reached into her backpack for a book, pushing her short, blonde hair back behind her ear, for the hundredth time that day. Her hair was in the growing out phase, she had cut it short on an impulse, and decided almost immediately that she didn't like it. Just one more thing to add to the list of poor decisions she'd made in the last few years.

She was just starting to get comfortable with her book when the door to the counselor's office opened and Mrs. Stone poked her head out.

"Miss Durham, you may come in now," she said, in her usual, haughty tone.

Claire picked up her backpack and made her way into the office. Mrs. Stone's office was small, an oversized desk sat right in the center, taking up the majority of the space in the already tight quarters. Floor to ceiling bookshelves stood against the walls on one side of the desk and behind the counselor's chair. Claire glanced at some of the book titles, most of them involving child psychology, with a few textbooks on random subjects scattered through in no particular order. The desk was old, although not quite as old as it's owner Claire thought, and held pictures of what were assumed to be Mrs. Stone's grandchildren. The tiny office had no windows, which was probably for a reason. Undoubtedly, Mrs. Stone didn't want anybody daydreaming out the window when she was lecturing them on their future, or lack thereof.

"How have you been, Claire?" asked Mrs. Stone, as usual, peering over the top of her glasses. Claire didn't know if she actually used the glasses, or if they were just part of the costume that made Counselor Stone.

"Fine," she mumbled.

"Of course you are fine, young people are always 'fine'." There was no effort to hide the sarcasm. Claire raised her eyes to look at her counselor. If there was ever a stereotypical guidance counselor, Mrs. Stone was it with her steely gray hair, cut short and suffering the effects of too many permanents. She was tall and thin, almost to a point of being gaunt, and the way her blue eyes always seemed to look over the top of her glasses, but down her sharply pointed nose, gave her the appearance of a crane.

"Have you filled out any of your college applications yet, or given any additional thought to your future?"

Here we go, Claire thought. Time for the lecture, so she might as well just get it over with. "I don't think that I'm going to fill out any applications," she said, flatly.

"And why not?"

"I don't want to go to college. My grades are average, and there is no way I'm getting a scholarship anywhere. My family doesn't have the money for me to go, so I thought I'd be better off just getting a job."

Mrs. Stone sighed, and rubbed the bridge of her nose with her thumb and index finger. That was practically a scripted move for her, an indication that she just didn't understand why the youth of today had to make her job so difficult.

"Claire, you really need to give some thought to your family. Do you really think that getting a minimum wage job right out of high school is going to provide the money that you're going to need for your mother's continued long term care? Your brother graduates from Syracuse in the spring, and he will most certainly get a job right away, but you can't expect him to be footing the bills."

Claire knew that her brother, Colin, would be brought up in this conversation. Colin, the great student, who went on to Syracuse with a full scholarship, on the verge of graduating at the top of his class with a major in education and a minor in math. He was everything that Claire was not; self-motivated, self sufficient and always driven to be just a little bit better. Even with everybody comparing them and her always coming out the lesser of the two, she loved him more than anything in the world, and no matter how bad she felt things were, he always could brighten her outlook.

"I don't expect Colin to take care of everything," she said, "but I just don't see how my going away to college is going to make things better for us."

"It won't make things better right away, but you need to think about the long term," Mrs. Stone's face softened slightly. "Your mother could still live for a very long time, and the life insurance and long term care insurance is not going to last forever."

The anger began to brew inside her. Ever since her parent's accident, the school has had its nose in Claire's home life, as well as at school. Part of her knew they were just trying to protect her, but she felt the involvement of the school in her family's private life had gone beyond the boundaries of simply looking out for the students and stepped into the complete invasion of privacy. Her parent's wills and insurance policies were nobody else's business.

"I will be 18 in March, and then you guys can't be sticking your nose in my business anymore, can you?" Claire asked coldly.

Mrs. Stone was unfazed. "That is right, but you have to understand Claire, I am not trying to be nosy or pushy. What happened to your parents was a tragedy no child should have to deal with, and the staff at the school is just trying to do what we can to help you through what has to be an extremely difficult situation. I know you young people don't believe we understand any of what you deal with on a day-to-day basis, but we try to do the best we can for each one of you individually. Your case is particularly hard, and I can't pretend to know how you feel, but that is why I'm here. It is my job to guide you and assist in the decision making process for your future."

"And you do that by telling me any decision I make is the wrong one? As far as you're concerned, the only 'right' decision is for me to go to college, everything else would be the wrong decision," Claire snapped.

"Watch your tone young lady," Mrs. Stone said sharply.

It was Claire's turn to sigh. She had always been told that she needed to think before she spoke and someday her mouth was going to get her into trouble. That was something she knew she needed to work on, but she decided it was easier said than done. She shuffled her feet on the dirty tile floor, and gazed around the room, trying to think of something she could say that could get her out of Mrs. Stone's office in the quickest way possible. Her eyes caught on a picture on the wall, and she couldn't believe she'd never noticed it before. It was another motivational photograph with a quote beneath...a picture of a racehorse, taken with a slow shutter speed, so it gave the perception of extreme speed. The quote beneath the picture was blurred by the glare on the glass from the fluorescent lights on the ceiling above, but Claire suddenly felt inspired, and saw her escape.

"I am going to be a jockey," she said.

"Excuse me?" Mrs. Stone said, now obviously taken aback.

"I'm going to be a jockey." Suddenly, Claire felt excited. She had the build to be a jockey, being barely five feet tall, and about 95 pounds soaking wet. The fact that it had never crossed her mind before was what she found the most surprising.

"Well, I should have seen this coming," Mrs. Stone said. "You need to be realistic, Claire. Horse racing is an incredibly dangerous sport, and I think given your current family situation, you should be thinking about getting a real job."

"Since when is being a jockey not a real job?" Claire demanded.

"I just don't see how you think you can be successful in a career that is dominated by men, and there are very few women jockey's of note. Do you know anything at all about the race track?"

Claire had to admit she didn't know much at all about horse racing. She had spent all her life around horses, but never gave a second thought to what was beyond the doors of the barn where she rode.

"I know I'm the right size to be a jockey, and I am a more than capable rider. Why shouldn't I try?"

"I think it's a little girl's dream Claire. Every girl wants to ride horses, but it doesn't pay the bills. You need to be more realistic with your goals." Mrs. Stone looked as though she would rather be done for the day, but Claire just derailed her plans for a short meeting and a quick escape.

Claire continued to push. "If I could make a living as a jockey, couldn't it be a career for me? I know it would mean I don't go to college right away, but maybe I could make enough money that I could go to college down the road." She knew if she ever wanted to get out of this meeting, she would have to start to play to Mrs. Stone's college driven sensibilities.

"I really don't believe you're thinking this through properly. You have more responsibilities than your average high school senior, and you cannot afford to be impulsive and fanciful."

Claire slid her chair back, preparing to stand up and leave the office. She was obviously getting nowhere with Mrs. Stone, and any more time spent in here was going to be a waste. Her head was swimming with ideas about horse racing. Maybe she could win the Kentucky Derby! At that time, she didn't realize the challenges that would lie ahead if she decided to embark on the path of becoming a professional jockey, but it didn't matter, the seed had been planted, and the dream was in motion.

"May I go now?" she asked, trying to be polite.

"No Claire, I don't think that our conversation is finished, do you?"

She sat back down heavily, and waited for more.

"Don't you want to do something that would make your parents proud?"

Stunned, and furious, her emotions threatened to boil over. How dare Mrs. Stone presume her wanting to be a jockey wouldn't make her parents proud. "My parents always told me to do what made me happy. Shouldn't that count for something?" Claire could feel her throat begin to tighten. She refused to cry in front of Mrs. Stone, but couldn't help but think about the fact that she did seem to be failing her parents.

"Of course it counts, but what if you fail? Can you come back home five years down the road with no money and no education and expect everything to work out for the better? You have to have some sort of plan."

"I have a plan, and this meeting is over," she said, picking up her backpack, tossing it over her shoulder as she hurried out the door, letting it slam behind her just a little bit harder than she should have. Her eyes were filling with tears, and she fought them back as she walked quickly down the hall. She could hear Mrs. Stone calling her, but she ignored the counselor, picking up her pace as she headed out of the corridor, making a sharp left turn past one of the many long rows of lockers on her way out the front door. She hurried to her car, got in quickly, and then started to cry.

That late November afternoon in upstate New York was cold and still. Claire wiped the tears from her eyes and started her car, an older model, light blue Honda that her parents bought for her as a Christmas present, the week before their accident. She sat for a few moments while the car began to warm up, trying to decide what to do next. She didn't want to go home, so she put the car in drive, and headed to the only place she could think to go, the lake. The trip was short, and when she arrived, she grabbed her hat and scarf out of her backpack and headed to her favorite place.

In the summertime, the lake was bustling with people, swimmers, boaters, and sunbathers, all taking advantage of the cool water on a hot day. The nearby playground was always teeming with children playing mindless games and screeching in merriment. Families sat at the tables with their picnic lunches, while boats peppered the lake. Fishermen idled, waiting for that tiny nibble, as water skiers zigzagged up and down the expanse of water. Summers on Canandaigua Lake were beautiful and busy, but Claire's favorite time of year was the fall. Things quieted down to a snails pace, and on this particular day, there was not another person to be seen.

She sat down on the small stonewall that ran along the shoreline, and gazed out into the gray. In typical late November fashion, the afternoon sky was cloudy. The lake itself was completely still and the color of steel while still reflecting the afternoon clouds. Claire pulled her hat down over her ears, her short, blonde hair just skimming out from underneath. She wrapped her scarf around her neck and recalled the many times she came with her family to this exact place, and her thoughts began to drift back to that night that changed her entire life.

It had been New Years Eve, nearly two years ago. Claire was a sophomore in high school, and Colin had been home for the holiday break. Their parents, Cora and Robert Durham, were going to a New Years party, and left Claire and her brother to celebrate on their own at home. They had pizza for dinner and played video games for a while. Claire had been tired, but she forced herself to stay awake for the ball drop in Times Square. They toasted in the New Year with sparkling apple cider and Claire went to bed shortly thereafter. She was awakened at 3am by the doorbell ringing. Her thoughts immediately went to worst case scenario, but she met her brother in the hallway, and he said it was probably just her parents wanting to wake them up to say Happy New Year. She allowed herself to think positively for a few seconds, until Colin opened the door to two police officers. Immediately, she knew that things were bad, but it wasn't until they came inside and sat both of the kids down, that Claire understood the full tragedy of the situation. Colin held on to her hand as the officer told them that their parents had been involved in an accident and their father had been killed. It had been snowing when they left that evening, but Claire hadn't even realized it had become a full-blown blizzard by midnight. Apparently, her father had been driving and lost control of the car, hitting a semi truck head on. He was pronounced dead at the scene, but her mother survived the accident and was taken to the local hospital where she was in critical condition. Claire and Colin dressed hurriedly, and drove at a snails pace, through the blizzard, with a police escort to the hospital. They were given very little information when they arrived, except that their mother had sustained serious injuries, the worst of all being a head injury, and her chances for recovery were slim. The days stretched into weeks. It was discovered, not to anybody's surprise, that their father had been drinking, although his blood alcohol level was only slightly above the legal limit. There had clearly been several contributing factors to the accident, and Colin believed it probably would have happened even if their dad hadn't had a drop to drink, but Claire was unconvinced. For as much as she was devastated by the loss of her father, she still wanted to blame him for the accident. They buried their dad, and waited every day, hoping for their mother's recovery. In a way, she did recover somewhat. Her bodily injuries healed, but her head injury left her in a semi-vegetative state. The doctors told them her condition was most likely permanent, and she would require 24 hour care for the rest of her life, however long that may be. It was by the good grace of Claire's aunt Robyn, that their mother could receive her care at home, rather than at a nursing facility. Robyn was Cora's older sister, and she'd left her life in Indiana to move in with the Durham's. She was a registered nurse, and had worked in a long-term care facility in Indianapolis, giving her the skills she needed to tend to Cora's needs. Putting her own life aside, she assumed custody of Claire, who was still a minor, and, given the situation, Claire didn't know what would have happened to them if Robyn hadn't come to stay.

Claire turned her attention to her surroundings again. The temperature seemed to have dropped drastically in the 30 minutes or so she had been sitting there, and she shivered against the cold, wishing she hadn't forgotten her gloves. There were small snowflakes beginning to fall, and although they were few and far between, Claire knew that this could mean an accumulation on the ground by morning.

She thought about her announcement to Mrs. Stone about wanting to be a jockey, and she thought about what it would take to get there. Horse racing was never even a consideration for her growing up. She had always ridden for pleasure, partaking in shows during the summer and fall, and working for lessons in the off-season. Since the accident, she had to sell her own horse, as it was a luxury their finances would no longer allow, but, thanks to her instructor, Jürgen, she was still able to ride whenever she wanted. The idea of making a living doing what she loved was certainly appealing, but she had no idea where to start.

The first thing that she needed to do was talk to her brother. He would know what to do, and he would either talk her out of it, telling her she was crazy, or he would point her in the right direction. She swung her legs back over the wall and stood up, giving her rear end a few seconds to wake up, before she headed to her car. If she were going to make the drive to Syracuse that evening, she had better get home and get a few things packed. The weather was questionable, and she didn't want to be stuck in her brother's apartment for who knows how long without at least a toothbrush and a change of underwear.

She called Colin on her short drive home to let him know she was coming, and would be there in a couple of hours. He had a hockey game that evening, but she could go straight to the rink and they could go eat when the game was over. Claire was actually happy. Her brother was a natural on the ice, and she loved watching him skate. There weren't many opportunities for her to see him play, so she looked forward to sitting in the bleachers at the ice rink and watching him perform one of his many talents.

When she arrived home, she parked on the street, as the handicapped van was parked in its usual place in the driveway. It was a great, white ugly thing, but it was decked out with all of the necessary accessories and the lift to accommodate Claire's mother's wheelchair. For all its lack of style, she couldn't complain too much. The van had been purchased on their behalf by the engineering firm where her father had worked. That kind of vehicle didn't come cheap, and the family was grateful.

She cut across the grass that was turning to its winter brown, and around the giant oak tree that dominated the entire front yard. They hadn't lived in this house for very long, but she already loved the tree. It was always so splendid, regardless of the season. She noticed that the sky was no longer spitting snow. The drive to Syracuse might be pretty fast after all, and maybe she would only have to stay one night.

Claire let herself in the house, and headed straight into the living room, where she knew her mother would be sitting, with some mindless network movie on the TV while Aunt Robyn prepared dinner.

"Hi, Mom," she bent to give her mother a kiss as she was removing her scarf and coat.

Cora remained motionless, her vacant eyes simply staring at the television. Claire sighed, hoping maybe, someday, her mother would show some sign that acknowledged her presence. She dropped her backpack on the floor, knowing her aunt would scold her and she would have to take it to her room, but it was fine where it was for the time being. Looking around the living room, she realized she still wasn't used to calling this place home. They had moved into the smaller, single level home after the accident, in order to accommodate her mother's wheelchair. It was about half the size of the home where Claire and Colin grew up, and she had a very hard time adjusting.

"Hi Aunt Robyn," Claire said, as she entered the kitchen.

"Hey there," Robyn said, "how was your meeting?" Her aunt was bustling about the kitchen, bouncing from the fridge, to the sink to the stove and back. She was a woman of endless energy, and Claire couldn't help but think of her mother every time she saw her. All of the women in the family were built the same...petite yet strong. Cora Durham had been a college gymnast, and the electric blue eyes were a genetic trait that both Claire and her brother got from their mom's side of the family.

"It was okay," Claire replied. "I think I'm going to go spend the night with Colin, if that's fine with you?"

Robyn glanced up from cutting the onion she had in her hand, taking the time to wipe away the onion tears. "Things didn't go well with Mrs. Stone, I take it?"

"Yes and no. I know that I am not going to go to college, but I think I know what I want to do with my life. The problem is, Mrs. Stone didn't approve, and she said I would let down my family if I tried and failed."

"That doesn't seem like something a counselor should say, but what's your idea?" Robyn inquired, continuing to chop the onion.

"I think that I want to be a jockey." Claire waited for some sort of reprimand for being foolish, but her aunt surprised her.

"It's about time you came up with that!" Robyn laughed. "I only wonder why it took you this long?"

"You think I should try?"

"Of course! I don't know much about horses or racing," Robyn said, "but I do know you're a talented rider, and you are the right size. It would seem like you have things in your favor if you wanted to give it a shot. Is this why you want to go talk to Colin?"

Claire nodded. Robyn understood her connection to her brother, and how their parent's accident brought them even closer together. "I guess I am most afraid that I won't be able to do well enough to provide for you and mom. At least not in the same way that Colin will."

Robyn put down the knife and went to the sink to wash her hands. When she was finished, she sat down at the table across from Claire. "I want you to know that no matter what happens, we'll be fine. The money is always a concern, but we'll make do. You need to do what you feel is right in your heart, what makes you happy. Do you think being a jockey will make you happy?"

"I honestly don't know," Claire replied. "But I won't know until I try, will I?"

"You're exactly right," Robyn paused for a moment. "It is one thing to try and fail, but it is another thing to not even try. Life is too short for regret."

Claire looked into her aunt's eyes, which were also her mother's eyes. "Do you think mom is in there somewhere?" Claire asked, changing the subject. "I mean, do you think there's some part of her that knows what is going on, even if she can't show us?"

Robyn nodded. "I do," she jumped up suddenly, startling Claire. "You'd better get going if you want to get to Syracuse in a decent time."

"Right," Claire hurried to her room to gather a few things she would need for an overnight stay.

Her room was that of a typical teenage, horse loving girl. She had ribbons of all colors lining the walls, and trophies from significant wins sitting on the top of her dresser. She quickly grabbed a small duffle bag from the closet and yanked a shirt off the hanger and had to jump to pull a pair of sweats off the shelf that always seemed to be just out of reach for her meager 5 feet of height. She got a change of underwear out of the dresser drawer, and headed across the hallway to the bathroom to get her toothbrush. She went back into her room and grabbed her book off of the nightstand, then pulled the bedroom door closed behind her. Before she left, she stopped to quickly kiss her mother good-bye.

"Bye mom, I love you," she said quietly. "Bye Aunt Robyn," she called into the kitchen.

"Bye to you. Drive safe!"

Claire replied she would and headed out the door to get back in her car for the 90-minute drive east.

CHAPTER 2

The drive to Syracuse was uneventful. Claire had made that drive so many times in the last four years, first with her parents, and then on her own, she was nearly on autopilot. Ninety minutes after leaving home, she pulled into the parking lot of the campus skating rink, where her brother was probably just getting on the ice for his intramural hockey game.

She grabbed the blanket she kept in the trunk, as she knew it was bound to be cold in the rink, and hurried across the parking lot towards the entrance of the arena. When she opened the doors, she was immediately greeted by the chatter of people, students mostly, who were using the hockey game as one more excuse to socialize. Claire climbed the bleacher steps and found herself a seat higher up, away from the immediate noise of the more rowdy spectators, to a place where she could see all of the ice, and sit alone. She spotted Colin on the ice, standing by the team's bench, receiving instructions from one of his teammates. He glanced up at her and tipped his stick to his helmet in acknowledgement. She smiled and waved and then settled herself into her blanket to watch her brother play.

Colin was a natural on the ice. He never ceased to amaze her with his skill. Most of it probably had to do with the fact that Claire could barely stand upright on skates, much less do the things that seemed to come naturally to him. She compared it to watching a Grand Prix level dressage horse; pure poetry in motion and every movement was perfectly choreographed and executed with precision. As far as Claire was concerned, he should have been on the college team, but he was satisfied with playing intramural and focusing on his studies. His goal was to be a high school teacher and hockey coach. She had no doubt he would do exactly that, not only do it, but be better than everybody else at the same time. At times, she thought he should have set his sights a bit higher, but he knew exactly what he wanted, what would make him happy, and that is what he was going to do. Claire couldn't help but envy him a little. Until that day, she hadn't had the faintest idea as to where she was going with her life. At least Colin had a plan.

She watched him zig and zag across the ice, moving the puck with such ease and grace, passing and shooting...going from a complete standstill to full speed down the length of the rink. The sound that the skates made on the ice was something that she would never get tired of hearing. The metal of the skate blades cutting through the surface of the ice made a sound that was impossible to describe, but was one you could never mistake.

The game ended with Colin's team winning, as usual. Claire wasn't the only person who thought that he should have played at the competitive college level. He was clearly the star of his team, and every team in the entire intramural league knew what they were in for when they played against him.

Descending the steps of the bleachers, she went to wait for her brother in the main lobby of the arena. It would take him a few minutes to shower and get dressed. In the mean time, she meandered around the building, looking at the cases of trophies and photographs of the school's athletic stars. She glanced at the cork bulletin board, observing flyers for everything from roommates wanted to music lessons, yoga instruction and the occasional lost pet.

"Claire!" she heard Colin call her name.

"Colin!" she ran to greet him as he dropped his bag of hockey gear and sticks on the ground and grabbed her in a huge bear hug.

Claire never quite could come to grips with how handsome her brother was. His dark hair was always a bit untidy, and he had a day's growth of facial hair that just made him look even more ruggedly handsome. They shared the same brilliant blue eyes, but it was Colin's perfect smile that usually sealed the deal. His look was effortless, and it seemed like he always had a group of female followers.

"How was your drive?" he asked as he lowered her back to the floor. At six feet tall, any hug from her brother lifted her off her feet.

"It was fine," she said. "Boring as usual."

Colin laughed. "You could have waited. You know I am going to be home next week for Thanksgiving."

"I know, but I just had one of those days, and I wanted to see my big brother."

He reached to ruffle her hair, but she pulled away. "You know I hate it when you do that!" she exclaimed, exasperated.

"That is why I do it!" he laughed, and she couldn't help but laugh as well. "Are you hungry?"

"Starving," Claire said. "I haven't eaten anything since lunch."

Colin picked up his gear and headed for the door. "Do you want to go out for something, or should we just grab a pizza?"

"Pizza sounds good. I just want to sit down for a while. I have some things that I need to talk to you about, and I would rather do it at your place."

"Uh, oh," Colin gave her a look of feigned concern. "Boy trouble?"

"Please. I wish it were that simple. Do you really think I'd drive for an hour and a half just to talk about some stupid boy?"

"I could only hope. I know all there is to know about stupid boys, being one myself and all," Colin joked. "I think I could offer some quality insight."

Claire smiled. "I'm sure you could, but unfortunately this is more complicated."

"Well, hold that thought, I will meet you at my place," Colin said.

Colin's apartment was only a few blocks away from the arena. He was technically off campus, but everything was still fairly close. Claire found a parking spot on the street, not far from the entrance to the building. The apartment complex was an old, brick building, which housed about eight apartments, four on the main floor and four on the second floor. She grabbed her overnight bag out of the trunk and headed towards the building where Colin was waiting for her by the door. They walked up the stairs and into her brother's one bedroom unit. Inside, the apartment was exactly what one would expect from a 22 year old college male. Decorations were sparse, and all he had were the essentials.

Claire tossed her overnight bag down next to the futon, and then plopped down on it herself next to Ed, Colin's cat. Ed was a fat, nondescript solid gray cat with absolutely no redeeming features Claire could see, but her brother loved that stupid feline. In typical cat fashion, Ed hopped off the futon indignantly and stalked into the kitchen.

"Long day?" Colin asked, as he dropped his hockey gear by the bedroom door and took off his coat.

"Yes, but I don't want to talk about it right now, can we eat first?"

"Yep. Pizza should be here in about 10 minutes. Do you want to hear my news?"

Claire perked up. Colin wasn't usually one to carry on about his personal life, so this sounded like it might be interesting. "You have news? This doesn't sound like you just wanting to talk about the guy in your psych class who refuses to bathe as part of his sociology 'experiment'."

"It's not. And that guy still hasn't bathed, by the way. People keep sitting further and further away from him. He is probably going to ace his project," Colin grinned. "No. I met someone."

Claire was surprised. Colin was a catch for sure, and he never had to actively look for a date, but he had never given any indication that he was serious about anybody. "Wow. You mean like an actual girl?" Claire jested.

"Yes, an actual girl. Her name is Emily, and I think I might really like her."

"Wow. You THINK you MIGHT like her. That's the most commitment I have ever heard from you. Is she pretty?" Claire asked, then hesitated. "Of course she is pretty. You can have any girl you want, so I'm sure you wouldn't go for an ugly one."

Colin laughed, his blue eyes sparkling. "Yeah, she's pretty."

"Where did you meet? I want to hear a story!" Claire wiggled excitedly on the futon.

"We met at the vet. Ed had some digestive issues, so I took him in, and she was working in the office. She's a biology student, and wants to go to vet school. We kind of hit it off." Colin 's look got dreamy, maybe this was the real thing, Claire thought.

"Ok, so how is Ed now?" Claire winked at her brother. "Did his digestive issues get fixed, or did he have to go back in for more treatments?"

"I only took him back once!" Colin said defensively, then laughed. "I got her number the second time."

"I'm astounded. That's got to be some kind of record...it usually only takes you about two minutes to get a girl's number, this one made you wait two whole trips! She is already making a better impression than some of the others," Claire paused as she listened to Ed munching on his food in the kitchen. "I suppose the vet told you that Ed needed to go on a diet." Claire said as she watched the cat amble back into the living room and flop down on the floor as if he were unable to take another step.

"Yeah, I have to put him on diet cat food. Do you have any idea how hard it is to put a cat on a diet? He hates the new food!" Colin was exasperated as he sat down on the floor next to Ed and proceeded to rub his belly. Ed purred like a rusty motor.

"I think you and that cat have an unhealthy relationship," Claire laughed. "But at least he found you a girlfriend!"

At that moment, the doorbell rang. The pizza had arrived, and not a moment too soon as Claire was absolutely famished.

Colin took the pizza into the kitchen and began to get out the plates. Claire made to get up and help, but he waved her back.

"You just sit...you had a long drive. What do you want to drink?"

"Just some water," Claire really wanted a Coke, but she knew that even one would keep her up half the night. Caffeine seemed to hit her hard, even in small amounts. She figured it was probably because of her size. It seemed like anything that would mildly affect another person, always hit her twice as hard.

"You sure?" Colin asked from the kitchen. "Water with pizza doesn't sound very exciting."

"I'm sure. You know how I am with caffeine...I would never get to sleep!"

Colin laughed. "Ugh, I forgot what a lightweight you are."

He returned to the living room and gave Claire her plate of pizza and an ice water and then went back into the kitchen for his own plate. Claire was shoving pizza into her mouth when Colin returned to the futon with his pizza and a beer in hand. She nearly choked as she stared at his choice of beverage.

"You're drinking a beer?" she said around a mouthful of food.

"Yes, is there a problem?" Colin responded, without looking her in the eye.

"Is there a problem?" Claire repeated, coldly. "Of course there's a problem!" her voice began to rise, and she was getting angry. "Our father is dead and our mother's a vegetable because dad had been drinking. Does that not mean anything to you? Do you simply pretend the alcohol had nothing to do with it? Do you want to end up like dad?"

Colin swallowed his pizza and took a drink of his beer. He then turned to Claire, slightly irritated. "I am having ONE beer with my dinner in the comfort of my own home. I'm not going anywhere tonight. I have no plans of driving or operating heavy machinery. I am of legal age, and if I want to enjoy the taste of a single Corona with my pizza, I am well within my legal rights to do so. You're acting like I am on the road to becoming a raging alcoholic."

"But after what happened to our parents, I can't believe you would even consider taking a drink," Claire said quietly.

Colin looked at her, and realized he didn't fully understand how their parent's accident had affected his sister. He'd been able to come back to the university and escape from everything, but she was at home, seeing their mother in her unresponsive state, every single day. He was still frustrated with her. "You are acting like dad was a falling down drunk who never should have gotten behind the wheel of a car. Did you forget that there was a blizzard that night? Did you forget that there were literally dozens of car accidents reported due to the driving conditions alone, three of them resulting in fatalities?"

Claire looked down at her feet. "I know all of that, but the truth is, dad had been drinking. Who's to say that the accident wouldn't have happened if he hadn't?"

"His blood alcohol was only slightly over the legal limit," Colin said, but Claire interjected.

"It was still OVER the legal limit! That's why it is called the legal limit. He was intoxicated,

and he died because of it... and look at what he did to Mom!"

Colin sighed. "Claire, you need to stop trying to demonize Dad. He was a good person. He did everything for us, supporting us in all of our crazy endeavors. You know he was a good man...a good man who made a bad decision that unfortunately cost him his life. Do you want to know what I think?" he said, grabbing her hand.

Claire shook her head, not wanting to look her brother in the eye.

"I'm going to tell you anyway," Colin said. "I think Mom and Dad just wanted to get home that night. They went to the party and probably both had a glass of champagne or two. The weather started to get bad, and they decided they needed to get home...to us. I know Dad drove because he knew how much Mom hated driving in the snow. What gets me through the toughest moments is the belief that the accident would have happened anyway. The weather was terrible; nobody should have been out driving. That's what the police told us, and it's what I believe. You can blame Dad all you want, but it won't bring him back. It won't make Mom better."

"I know," Claire resigned. "It's just easier to blame somebody, or something, rather than to think our parents are gone because of some random, stupid accident."

Colin let go of her hand and went for his pizza. "At least we still have each other," he said. "Don't be so cheesy," Claire poked at him.

"Well, we do!" he said. "Call me cheesy, but you are my baby sister, and believe it or not, you were the only thing that kept me going in the months after the accident. I wanted to protect you, but I also needed to keep my focus on school. Every day, I thought I needed to get through school so I could look after you."

"You don't think that anymore?" Claire asked.

"I still do. It's different though. As time has passed, and you've grown up, I realized you don't need a protector so much as a sounding board. Aunt Robyn has done a good job in making sure you have everything you need, but I think it's our phone calls, and nights like tonight, that are best for both of us."

Claire looked up at her brother and realized she didn't really lose all of her dad. "You are a lot like him you know...dad I mean."

"How so?"

"He was a hopeless romantic, and all about the cheesy cliché's," she said. "You're just like him."

Colin looked at her and smiled. "I suppose there are worse things to be."

"My pizza is cold, and I am still hungry," Claire said as she got up. "I'm going to get another piece, do you want one?"

"Sure," Colin said, relieved for the distraction. The conversation was getting far too heavy for his liking.

Claire returned with more pizza for the both of them, and they finished their meal in silence, with Ed periodically sniffing around for a possible handout. Claire was content. She did really love this time she was able to spend with her brother. She thought about the possibility of him having a serious girlfriend, and couldn't help but feel pangs of jealousy, not sure whether or not she could share the most important man in her life with another woman.

They finished eating, and Claire took the dishes to the kitchen. She wanted to talk to Colin about her plans, but she didn't know the best way to approach it. Blurting out that she wanted to be a jockey probably wasn't the best idea, so she decided to take the round about way of getting there.

"So, how's work going?" she asked casually, knowing that working freight at the local super hardware store wasn't exactly stimulating.

"It's work. It pays the rent, if that's what you mean, although I have had to cut my hours because of my student teaching."

"How's that going?"

"I love it. I can't wait to graduate. I know the job market right now is tough, but I think my being able to be a hockey coach will make me a bit more desirable in a high school. Hopefully I can find something in the Rochester area, so I can be close to you and Mom," Colin paused, and glanced at Claire. "But that isn't what you want to talk about, is it? You didn't drive for an hour and a half to talk about Mom and Dad and ask me about my work. You could've done that over the phone."

Claire shook her head. Her brother knew her far too well. "No, I guess I didn't. I had my meeting with Mrs. Stone today, and I told her I wasn't going to college," she waited for some sort of exclamation from Colin, but he just nodded. "She basically told me I was throwing my life away and would be forcing you to carry the financial burdens of Mom's care."

Colin looked at her for a moment. "You have a plan," he stated plainly.

"Yes, but I don't know what you'll think about it. I don't even know if it is the right thing to do, but I think I should try."

"Well, girl, don't keep me waiting. What is it?"

"I want to try and become a jockey," she said, again waiting for the reprimand.

Colin looked at her for a moment, and then a huge smile spread across his face. "I knew it!" he practically shouted. "You would be fantastic. You are an amazing rider, and obviously the right size, so what's the problem?"

"The problem is, I don't know the first thing about horse racing. I know horses, and I am a good rider on jumpers and dressage horses, but I wouldn't even know where to begin with the racing."

"Have you done any research? There has got to be tons of info on the online. What do you know so far?" Colin asked, immediately slipping into teacher mode.

"I only made the decision this afternoon, I haven't had much time to research things," Claire thought for a moment. "I know that a lot of the jumper people at the barn are a little snide when talking about the race-track, like it is an undesirable place to be, but I think they are probably just snobs anyway."

"Well, maybe you should take some time to do some research and ask questions. Why don't you talk to Jürgen about it?"

Claire immediately wanted to kick herself. Of course her riding instructor would probably be an excellent place to start. "I didn't even think about that. I guess I never thought he'd have any insight into the racing. I don't know how much he knows, but he might be able to put me in contact with somebody in the business."

"Exactly," Colin grinned. "You know, sometimes you're a real blonde!"

Claire punched him jokingly and he put his arm around her. "Just imagine," he said, "Claire Durham, first female jockey to win the Kentucky Derby."

Claire pulled away from him. "Do you really think I could do it? Mrs. Stone said I'd probably fail, and then what would Mom and Dad think?"

"Mrs. Stone can take her wire rimmed glasses and stick them up her ass," Colin said. "What would make Mom and Dad the most happy is for you to do what you love, regardless of what it is. I know I'm never going to be a millionaire teaching math and coaching hockey, but I can guarantee that I am going to go to bed every night loving what I do, and being proud of my own accomplishments. I would like to think somehow Mom, and even Dad, wherever he may be, are happy that I'll be happy."

"You always have a way of putting a positive spin on things, dear brother," Claire smiled. "I guess when I go home tomorrow I will start doing some research. I'm going to wait until I turn 18 anyway, but March would probably be a good time to get started. It'll give me some time to figure things out and try to come up with a five year plan."

"Claire, there's no such thing as a five year plan. Plan all you want, but life is day to day, you of all people should know that. You have the right idea. Go home and do some research. Talk to Jürgen and see what you have to do and then do it. I'll help you as much as I can, and once I graduate this spring I'll be around more to help with Mom also. Just go for it."

She smiled at her brother. It had been the right decision to come here for the night. He always said and did the right things...the things that made her believe that she might someday amount to something. At that moment, Colin's phone rang. He picked it up and smiled slightly.

"Emily?" Claire asked with a smile.

"Yep. I am going to take it in my room, if that's fine with you."

"Ooohh," Claire jibbed. "Colin has a girlfriend, Colin has a girlfriend," she chanted.

"Grow up," Colin said as he stood up and threw a pillow at her. She laughed, dodging it easily.

Claire decided to take that time to get herself ready to go to bed. She dug out her toothbrush and pajamas, and went into the bathroom. When she was finished, she took her book out of her bag and sat herself down to read. She could hear her brother's voice from his room, but she couldn't make out any of the conversation. He really did seem happy, with every aspect of his life, so she supposed she should be happy for him as well. She just didn't think she was ready to meet Emily yet.

Ed jumped up on the futon next to Claire, and tried to make himself comfortable without actually appearing like he wanted any attention. She really never considered herself a cat person. Ed only solidified that belief, since their relationship was one of mere tolerance, both knowing that the other wasn't going anywhere as long as Colin had anything to say about it.

"You know I don't like you very much," she said to the cat. Ed ignored her, and started grooming himself. "I don't understand you cats. All you do is eat and sleep. Tell me what's to like?" Again, Ed ignored her, still washing. Claire sighed. Obviously this conversation was going nowhere. She picked up her book and started to read, but her mind began to wander. Her parents never really understood her passion for horses. Neither of them had ever grown up with horses, or had any contact whatsoever, so her love of those four-legged creatures had put them at a loss. They supported her regardless, coming to every show she ever rode in, cheering her on wholeheartedly, but that was as far as it went. Occasionally, her dad would make mention of how much it cost, but he would never hesitate to provide her with money for entry fees and any extra equipment she needed. Claire thought her mom had been afraid to watch her jump. It was just too scary. Cora had a flair for the dramatic, and would always imagine the worst possible thing happening in the jumping arena or on the cross-country course. Her father said that watching dressage was like watching grass grow, but in spite of their complaining, they were proud of her. Would she ever see that look of pride from her mother again? Probably not, she thought, but she had to try. Maybe being a successful jockey could fill the void that was left inside of her after the accident. Maybe knowing that she had gone on to do what made her happy might make her feel like she would be less of a failure, even if her parents weren't really there to see it. Only time would tell.

Colin came out of the bedroom, his conversation finished.

Claire looked up from her book, and Colin was smiling, still obviously thinking about the phone call.

"I think I really like her, Claire," he got a dreamy, far away look in his eyes. "She's smart and beautiful and we have a lot in common. Oh, and Ed loves her."

"Boy, that was like taking a bullet," Claire glared at the cat. "He hates me, but he just loves the new girlfriend."

"He doesn't hate you, he just knows you aren't a cat person," Colin bent to scratch Ed between the ears.

"I suppose Emily is a cat person," Claire muttered.

Colin realized there might be some jealousy on the part of his sister. "I think you and Emily will get along. She loves horses, and is also a rider, although not as serious as you are. She wants to open her own veterinary practice and work on both large and small animals."

Claire remained unconvinced as she put her book back in her bag.

"Come on, Claire," Colin said, reaching over to muss up her hair, "you know you are my best girl, and you know I'd never get serious about someone who I didn't think you would get along with, or who couldn't accept our family as it is."

"How did Emily react when you told her about Mom and Dad?" Claire knew the answer to that question would say a lot about her character.

"Well, she didn't head for the hills, if that's what you mean. I didn't keep anything from her, but we also haven't been seeing each other for very long. I told her the whole story and she was understanding, but not overly sympathetic. She knows I don't want her to feel sorry for me and this is my life. She seemed pretty cool with it all. If things continue to go well, I'll probably take her to meet Mom after the holidays. She'll be going home for the break anyway."

"Where is she from?" Claire asked, wanting to seem more interested than she really was. "Detroit."

"Ugh," Claire groaned. "A Red Wings fan. The relationship is doomed to fail! Does she know you're a die hard Penguins guy?"

Colin laughed. "Not yet."

"I'm tired," Claire stated bluntly. "I think I'm going to bed."

"Alright sis. See you in the morning. Sweet dreams."

Colin headed into the bathroom, and Claire pulled out the futon and made it up with the blankets and pillow that her brother had set out for her, and climbed in bed. Her head was filled with thoughts of horse racing and she fell asleep imagining what it would be like to lay the garland of roses over her own Kentucky Derby winner.

CHAPTER 3

March in upstate New York was really anybody's guess. One day the weather is beautiful, and there's a blizzard the next. Claire's birthday dawned with the promise of a beautiful, early spring day, and she was excited to get to the barn and do her work so she could have her lesson. She quietly and hurriedly got dressed, pulling on her riding breeches and boots and her orange, Syracuse sweatshirt. Getting out of the house quietly, without waking her aunt or mother was usually pretty easy, but she was always cautious, tiptoeing down the hall and out the front door without so much as a floorboard squeak.

Once outside, Claire paused to take a deep breath, relishing the cold morning air, and knowing that this was going to be an absolutely gorgeous day. It would be the perfect day for riding, and the perfect day for having her conversation with Jürgen about her hopes to become a jockey. The past three months had found Claire in front of the computer every opportunity she got, researching the racing industry the best she could. Unfortunately, there was not a lot to go on. She was able to study various tracks and entries and results from those tracks, but when it came right down to getting into the business, the internet proved pretty useless.

The drive to the barn was about seven miles, and she could have done it with her eyes closed. She had been traveling that road, since she was eight years old. Claire made the right hand turn into the drive that lead to the barn. She passed the larger parking area that, by afternoon would be filled with trucks and trailers belonging to students who were having lessons throughout the day. She pulled into a smaller parking area, grabbed her helmet off of the passengers seat and headed into the barn.

Jürgen's barn was large, housing a full size indoor riding arena. Set on the right side of the arena was an aisle flanked on both sides by stalls for boarded horses and farm horses. There were 24 stalls total, 12 on each side of the large center aisle. At the end of the rows of stalls were four grooming stalls, which were enclosed on two sides by a short wall where there were several saddles set. Baskets full of various grooming tools were hung from the wall, and at the back of the grooming stalls were racks of horse blankets in all colors, styles and sizes. The indoor entrance of the arena was next to the grooming stalls, and further down the aisle, near the back exit, were two tack rooms and Jürgen's office. Both tack rooms were full to capacity, one with farm saddles, bridles and all the necessary extras, and the other with the tack of the students of the barn who boarded their horses, or like Claire, rode the farm horses.

Claire got started with her chores, first feeding, and then going on to the stall cleaning. As she worked, she thought about how much she loved being in the barn. The sights, smells and sounds were things she had loved since childhood. Robyn always told her that she stunk like a barn when she would come home, but as far as Claire was concerned, there was no better smell in the world. The mix of alfalfa and manure, leather and horses, was a stimulation to her senses that only another horse lover could truly appreciate. She worked on the stalls, getting them done one by one, checking the levels of the automatic water tanks as she went, and always pausing to visit with the occupant of each stall. Mostly the horses ignored her, as they would not be distracted from their breakfast, but occasionally, one would take a break from their meal to nuzzle her pockets, looking for an extra sweet snack. Claire tried not to carry carrots, since if she gave one to one horse, she would have to give to them all, and she quickly found out that buying carrots for the entire barn everyday was a bit cost prohibitive.

Things began to wake up, as the activity level in the barn began to increase. Students started coming in, getting their horses ready for lessons. Claire still had work to do before she would have her lesson, so she headed into the tack room to get food for the barn cats, and then decided to track down Jürgen to see whom her mount would be for her lesson that morning.

She found her instructor in his office, going over the day's schedule. "Morning Jürgen," Claire said enthusiastically.

"Good morning Claire," he responded, looking up from his schedule book.

The man was a life long horseman, and she couldn't help but admire him. She didn't know for sure how old he was, but he had to be in his 60's. He was weathered from years of riding and working in the elements, and his thinning gray hair was always tucked under a roadster style cap or riding helmet. She had never seen him in anything other than riding breeches and boots, with only his outerwear changing, depending on the seasons. He had been Claire's riding instructor since she was eight years old, and even after a decade, she found that she really didn't know much about Jürgen Peters. She knew he had immigrated from Germany in his twenties, and that he had been riding horses his entire life, but other than that, she knew surprisingly little about the man in whose company she spent every weekend. What she did know is that he was one of the best horseman and riders she had ever seen. His long, lean frame seemed to be made to sit on a horse, and every time she watched him ride, she was awestruck. The horses responded to his invisible cues, and he could make even the most difficult horse bend to his commands with the softest touch. She had never seen him get abusive or aggressive with the horses, and in her mind, if ever there was a horse whisperer, it was Jürgen. She had become a highly skilled horsewoman herself under his tutelage. He was not free with compliments, but he never yelled. He was encouraging to his students without creating any false assumptions about their individual skill, and he never condescended. Claire had taken clinics and lessons with other instructors, and in her own, slightly biased opinion, Jürgen was still the best.

"Who am I riding today?" she asked, hoping for one of her favorites.

"Fred," Jürgen responded.

Claire deflated. That was not the birthday lesson she wanted.

"I hate Fred," Claire said, not even trying to hide her disappointment.

"Everybody hates Fred, but Fred makes you a better rider."

Claire couldn't argue, so she left the office, slightly sulky, and went to get her nemesis from his stall.

Fred was an absolutely gorgeous horse, and his physical appearance was his only redeeming feature. He was about 16 hands and of slightly undetermined breeding. The consensus was that he had some kind of Warmblood in there somewhere, as well as some Thoroughbred. His gorgeous, dark bay coat always shone, and he would dapple beautifully when he shed his winter coat in the spring. He had a couple of short white socks on his hind legs, and a unique star and stripe marking on his face. To look at him, he was striking, and people fell in love with him just walking by his stall, but that is where Fred's charm ended. Under saddle, the horse became Claire's interpretation of pure evil. Every move he made seemed to be a deliberate attempt to make his rider look bad. He was never dangerous, just calculatingly difficult. His behavior went against everything Claire had ever believed about horses. Any other horse she rode at least tried to please. They would make an effort to do her bidding, perhaps not always getting it right, but at least trying. Not Fred. If he did well, it was because he wanted to, but mostly, an hour lesson was an hour-long battle of the minds, and Claire often felt like she lost. Her sessions usually ended with her in a foul mood, and she swore if horses could smile, Fred would be grinning from ear to ear. Happy Birthday to me, Claire thought.

Fred's stall was about halfway down the row. She grabbed his halter off of the door and let herself in. From the ground, the horse was kind, almost sweet. He put his head down into the halter, making it easier for her to reach. She led him down the aisle to the grooming stall and got started brushing. The horse wasn't too big, but she still needed a stepping stool to reach his back in order to get him tacked up and ready for her lesson. She quietly hoped that he would be in a forgiving mood today, and her lesson would go off without a hitch, but she knew she wouldn't get that lucky. She led Fred into the indoor riding arena and took him to the mounting block, where she would need all three steps to get her foot into the stirrup to mount. In typical fashion, Fred sidestepped the mounting block, forcing her to circle him around two more times before he stood for her to get into the saddle. She already knew how this lesson was going to go, and she sighed and began her warm-up. Jürgen came into the arena and the session began.

For Claire, it was an hour of pure torture. Fred was more obstinate than usual, and she ended the hour feeling tired and deflated. Leave it to Fred to make her feel like a completely incompetent rider. Jürgen was encouraging, and she did get a moment or two of compliance from the horse, but overall, she was unhappy with her lesson.

Once her session was finished, she cooled the horse down for about ten minutes before dismounting and taking him back to the grooming stall to get him untacked and brushed before putting him away. Fred was back to his usual charming self once Claire was off of his back, and he began nosing her pockets for any potential snacks.

"You don't deserve any snacks," Claire said to the horse, who pricked his ears at her and gave her his usual puppy dog look.

Claire took off the saddle, and brushed him down. She knew she was a sucker, but couldn't help it, and gave her nemesis a carrot before leading him back into his stall. For as difficult as he was, she still loved him, if only for the fact that he was a big, beautiful horse. In his stall, she took off his halter, allowing him to rub his head on her back for a few moments before she closed the door behind her.

Today was the day she was going to talk to Jürgen about her hopes to become a jockey, and now was the ideal time, as he would be breaking for lunch before his next lesson. She found him in his office and knocked quietly on the door before going in.

"Ah, Claire, Happy Birthday!" Jürgen said as she entered the small room.

"Thanks. That was a great birthday present," Claire said with a touch of sarcasm in her voice. "You mean Fred?" Jürgen smiled.

"Yes."

"Well, you're welcome. I know you don't like him much, but you do better with him than any of the other students. I thought you had a great lesson today. He seemed to be responding better than usual," Jürgen chuckled to himself. "That horse really seems to like you."

"You've got to be kidding," Claire said as she flopped down in the chair next to her trainer's desk. "He's horrid. I can't get him to do anything I ask, and here you are telling me I had a good lesson. What was good about it? The fact that he didn't dump me on my butt?"

"You don't give yourself enough credit," Jürgen looked at her seriously. "Every time you ride that horse, you both get a little better. You can't expect perfection from Fred, it just isn't going to happen, he is not like other horses, but what you get from him is always earned. Every lesson on that horse is different, and as a rider, you learn something new every time you get on his back. He's going to make you work harder than you want to for an hour, but at the end of the session, I can guarantee that you have done a little bit more, and he is a little bit better than the last time. If you want to improve as a rider, it is important that you ride the horses that give you that opportunity."

Claire nodded sulkily. "You can make Fred do anything," she said, immediately regretting she had said anything at all.

"Yes, but I have been riding horses for 50 years, and I have been riding Fred consistently for the last six. There's something to be said for having my experience, and that horse and I respect each other. That is the key with Fred. You have to earn his respect, and you get a little more every time you get on his back."

"Humph," Claire grunted. "I think it is going to take me a lot longer than six years to get him doing what I want him to do."

"Maybe," Jürgen said. "But if you keep after it, you'll get there."

Claire looked around the room. It was small, and the floor was always dirty from people tracking in and out from the arena and outdoors. One of the barn cats was curled up on the old sofa that had certainly seen better days. The cushions were flat and uncomfortable, and it was in desperate need of some new upholstery, but its primary purpose seemed to be a nap site for any one of the numerous cats that patrolled the grounds. The walls were covered with pictures, many of them in black and white, of Jürgen in his younger years. There were photos of him doing dressage, and jumping huge fences. Claire's favorite was one of him jumping what looked to be an absolutely huge wall, completely bareback. Even with no saddle, he looked perfect on the horse he was riding. She couldn't tell if the horse was bay or chestnut due to the black and white of the picture, but it didn't matter, it was gorgeous.

Now was as good a time as any. "Jürgen, I wanted to talk to you about something, and I was hoping you'd be able to help me out."

"What's on your mind?" he asked, giving Claire his full attention.

"You know that I am going to be graduating this spring, and since I know I am not college bound, I am going to have to find a job."

Jürgen nodded, still curious.

"I've given it a lot of thought, and I've done quite a bit of research, and I was thinking about becoming a jockey. What do you think?" Claire prepared to cringe, waiting for a scolding, but what she got was a surprise.

"Why not?" Jürgen said and shrugged. "You know you're the right size, and you're an extremely talented rider. What did you find out in your research?"

Claire looked up at him, realizing he was serious. "Well, I know that there are not a lot of women jockeys, and no woman has ever won the Kentucky Derby, although there have been a few successful woman jockeys who have won several big races like the Belmont Stakes, some Breeder's Cup races, and lots of graded stakes races. I've learned the difference between maiden, claiming, allowance and stakes races. I've watched races on TV, and I've learned about different surfaces and distances."

Jürgen never took his eyes off of her as she was reciting her newfound education, but he still shook his head when she drew a breath. "What?" she inquired.

"What do you really know about the racetrack Claire? You've told me things that anybody can find online, but what do you really know? Were you just planning on walking into Finger Lakes and saying 'here I am, put me on a horse'?"

"I don't know," Claire said, clearly a little flustered.

Jürgen continued. "Do you have any idea how difficult it is to get started? How dangerous it is? Do you know how many jockeys are killed or permanently disabled in racing accidents every year? Do you know how many horse are lost due to catastrophic injuries incurred during the races?"

Claire shook her head again.

"I am not trying to scare you Claire, but those are the things you have to be aware of if you decide to pursue a career as a jockey. It's not a profession to be taken lightly, and the amount of dedication and commitment that it takes every single day, is a lot to ask of anybody. Early mornings, afternoon races, watching your weight, dealing with ignorant people. There's drugs, alcohol, people assuming that you have to have sex for mounts. It can be a pretty scary environment, and if you're not properly prepared, you can get swept up in the hustle, and before you know it, you don't even remember the person that you used to be. Are you prepared to deal with all of those things?"

Claire was flabbergasted. The Internet didn't tell her those things. "I don't really know. I just thought that it would be something I'd be good at. I can ride, you said yourself that I am one of the best riders that you have instructed, and I know horses. I guess I just thought I could earn some money while doing something that I love."

"You're an incredibly talented rider. You have an excellent seat, and the quietest hands of anybody that I have seen, and I am not just talking about my other students. You could go as far as you wanted if you decided to pursue the eventing and jumping or dressage, but I also understand it's very expensive, and your situation just won't allow for that right now," he paused, allowing Claire to absorb some of what he had said, and then he continued. "Being a jockey is a logical choice, but you need to know everything, and I mean everything, if you want to go that route. It's incredibly demanding physically as well as emotionally, and it's not always roses and mint juleps. The majority of jockeys out there are making enough money to pay the mortgage and put food on the table, and that's it. These jockeys that you see in the big races are the exception, not the rule. What happens if you get hurt? Have you thought about what would happen if you couldn't make it, and you had to come back? What would you do for money?"

Claire was starting to get angry. "No!" she almost shouted, "I don't know what I would do! In one breath you tell me that I could be a good jockey, and then you spend the next 10 minutes telling me how horrible it is and that I won't make it? What's the deal? I came to you for some advice and all you do is tell me how terrible it is! I don't get it."

Jürgen smiled, amused at Claire's outburst. "Claire, calm down. I'm merely playing devil's advocate. I think you could be a great jockey, but you cannot be naive going into that business. It is a business, and you need to know your stuff, or you'll get taken advantage of in a heartbeat."

"So you are saying I should do it?" Claire asked, still slightly peeved.

"What I am saying is that if you want to do it, you need to get with the right people to teach you what you need to know before you head to the track."

Claire sighed. "I don't know anybody at the race track. I've asked people around here, but most of the responses are snooty, saying that the track is no place to be."

Jürgen laughed. "They can be snooty all they want, but where do you suppose all those fancy event horses came from? Some of the greatest equine athletes, event horses, show jumpers and the like are ex-racehorses," Claire nodded, and he continued. "Isn't that why you came to me? To find out if I had any contacts at the race track?"

Claire startled. Of course that is what she wanted, but she had been so side tracked by Jürgen's diatribe about racing that she had forgotten. "Yes, I guess that's what I really want."

"Well, you're in luck. Have you ever met Mandy Zakarian?"

Claire shook her head. She'd heard the name, but never actually met her.

"Mandy and her husband Kelly run a training facility about 20 minutes from here. Kelly is one of the top trainers at Finger Lakes, and they have a sizable stable at both places. During the racing season, Kelly has the two year olds at the farm, as well as older horses who have been laid up for a time and are just returning to training. This time of year is extremely busy for them, but I bet Mandy would be willing to let you come out and spend some time with them in the mornings."

"You really think so?" Claire asked, clearly excited.

"I know they would. The Zakarian's are great people, and true horse people. Mandy is around here quite a bit. She is always looking to re-home retired racehorses, and between she and I, we usually can find good homes for them all. I usually take a couple myself every year, but as you can see, I am getting older, and I am not sure that I have many more years of getting on kooky Thoroughbreds who only know how to turn left!" Jürgen laughed, but for a moment, Claire did notice the signs of age on his face. It never really occurred to her that Jürgen would ever be too old to ride and train, but it became clear at that moment that he was in fact getting older, and he may not want to take the risks.

"When do you think I can meet her?" Claire asked, referring to Mandy.

"I'll call her this evening, and then I'll let you know. If you really think you want to be a jockey, the sooner you get learning, the better. Kelly used to ride, but he got too big too fast, and he just couldn't keep his weight under control. He was a great jockey, and he is still an excellent horseman. Anything you want to know about the business, he'll tell you. He can probably also tell you a bunch of things you don't want to know, but I trust him, and I think he'd be the right person to get you started."

Claire couldn't contain her excitement, and she squealed as she jumped up from the chair, scaring off the cat that was resting on the ratty sofa.

"Do you really think that I could do it? Do you really think that I could be a good jockey?"

Claire bounced as she asked her instructor the question which she guessed she already knew the answer.

"Yes, I really think you can do it. Just promise me one thing."

"Anything," Claire said, nodding.

"Promise me that you won't lose yourself out there. Don't compromise your principles to get ahead, do it on your own merits and skills. You are a beautiful and wonderful human being, and I would hate for you to lose that," Jürgen was sincere.

Claire was taken aback. In all the years that she had known Jürgen, he had complimented her riding, but never said anything personal. She felt honored by his trust and sincerity, and she answered from her heart. "I promise I won't lose myself."

Jürgen smiled at her. "Go then, be a jockey. I expect to see you in the Kentucky Derby some year."

"You got it," Claire said as she left his office.

Driving home, Colin called, wishing Claire a happy birthday. She spent most of the drive telling her brother about her conversation with Jürgen and the prospect of having a contact at the racetrack. Colin made her promise to call as soon as she spoke to Mandy, and he wanted updates on everything.

Claire pulled into her parking place in front of her house and went inside. "Happy 18th Birthday!" Robyn yelled as she walked through the front door.

"Thanks," Claire said, smiling. "How's mom?"

"She is good today. We've been watching the home and garden network. We decided we want a grand staircase," Robyn laughed and winked at her sister. Cora remained motionless.

Claire went over to her mother and kissed the top of her head.

"How was the barn?" Robyn asked.

"Good. I had a lesson."

"And?" Robyn pushed suggestively, knowing what Claire's plans were for the day.

"And....Jürgen is going to put me in touch with his contact in the racing business, and said I should go for it," she said, unable to keep the smile off of her face.

Robyn was giddy with excitement. Claire thought her aunt was more excited than she was. "Here, Happy Birthday," Robyn said as she handed Claire a wrapped box that she had pulled out from underneath her mother's wheelchair.

"You didn't have to get me anything Aunt Robyn, you know that."

"I know, but I saw it, and I just had to get it."

Claire tore off the wrapping paper and opened the box. Inside the box was a framed photograph of John Henry, who was Claire's favorite race-horse. "Wow, it is beautiful. How did you know that I love John Henry?" Claire asked, since she was sure she'd never said anything to her aunt about that particular thing.

Robyn smiled. "I remember your mom telling me how enamored you were when you saw him on your vacation to Kentucky. She said you guys toured that entire horse park, and all you wanted to do was go back and see John Henry. Your mom didn't understand. She didn't think the horse was particularly attractive, not compared to some of the other horses that you had seen that day, but you were in love."

Claire remembered that trip. She had been 11 years old, and the family went to Lexington that summer for a vacation. It was mostly for Claire, as her parents never really got the horses, and Colin was 15 and could care less. They had done the entire tour of the Kentucky Horse Park, and when they went through the hall of champions, Claire was im-mediately drawn to John Henry. He was not much to look at, small and plain, and not particularly well put together, but it was his attitude that Claire loved. Even in his advanced years, he was an ornery thing, nipping at his handlers, and prancing into his paddock like he was a three year old on the racetrack. He had an air about him that said champion, and she learned that on the racetrack, he was all heart and hated to lose. She didn't realize that it had made such an impression on her mother, certainly not to a point she would pass the information on to her sister, whom she didn't speak to that often.

"Thank you," Claire said, choking up slightly.

"You're welcome," Robyn smiled. "I was thinking about ordering some Chinese for dinner. What do you think, it is your birthday?"

"Sounds perfect," Claire said, smiling, and thinking this birthday turned out to be pretty great. Her new life was about to begin and she was ready to take up the reins.

CHAPTER 4

Claire got a phone call from Mandy the following afternoon, and they arranged for her to come to the farm the following Saturday morning. She was told to be there by 7AM, as they needed to wait for some daylight, but by summer, work would start at 6AM. Claire would have to get used to early mornings. The week seemed to drag by, and she struggled to focus on her schoolwork. She had to force herself to pay attention in class and do her homework every night. It was hard to find the motivation towards school at all, but her brother had told her that she only had a couple more months, and she could get through it. Besides, all the next week was spring break, and she was hoping she would be able to spend every morning at the farm.

Saturday finally arrived, and Claire dressed hurriedly, glancing out the window to try and get a gauge of the weather. It was probably cold, but at least it wasn't snowing. Even that late in March, the periodic snowfall wasn't uncommon, and she didn't want her first day at the farm to be hampered by a springtime blizzard. She snuck quietly out of the house, glad that she decided on gloves and a heavy coat, as it was quite cold, and she had no idea what the morning was going to bring. The drive to the farm was longer than her drive to Jürgen's, but she didn't mind. Her thoughts were racing as she imagined what might be in store for her that day. When she arrived at the entrance of the farm, she immediately caught her breath. She recalled driving past the place once in a while, not realizing who the grand expanse of ground belonged to, but pulling into the driveway, she knew that this was the real deal. There had to be a hundred acres of land. Most of it being white fenced pasture that reminded Claire of her trip to Kentucky, and the beauty and vastness of the Thoroughbred farms. The driveway was at least a quarter of a mile long, flanked on both sides by the four rail, white vinyl fence. Large leafless trees, probably maples, were perfectly spaced along the length of grassy area between the pavement of the driveway and the fence line. Claire imagined how beautiful it must be in the summer with the trees offering shade from their full crown of foliage. As she drove further down the driveway, she glanced out into one of the pastures that abutted the lane. She saw about 10 young horses, probably yearlings frolicking in the pale light of the early morning. They looked to be enjoying themselves, playing amongst each other as they fended off the chill of the early morning air. She was told to park at barn B, which was clearly marked above the double doors, and come inside. Mandy said she or Kelly would be there, more than likely tacking up a horse for the track.

Claire got out of her car and paused to look at her surroundings. The place was so incredible, it put Jürgen's barn to shame. She was overcome with the desire to get back in the car and go home, forgetting that she ever wanted to be a jockey in the first place, knowing she didn't belong. Instead, she gathered her courage and walked into the barn. Upon entering, she inhaled the familiar scent of horses. It seemed no matter how fancy the facility, they all still smelled the same, and it calmed her a bit. She continued down the aisle, admiring the spotless floor, and the polished brass plates on both the stall doors and the leather halters that hung from them. At the end of the aisle, she saw several grooming stalls, similar to those of Jürgen's barn. There were horses occupying three of the five stalls, and she instinctively headed in their direction, as she didn't imme-diately see anybody to guide her anywhere else. The first horse she came to didn't look like much of a racehorse. It was a large, stocky chestnut with a big white blaze and a right knee that was about twice the size it was supposed to be. She held her hand up to the horses nose and allowed him to sniff her. He gave a bored sigh, and let Claire examine his knee. It was certainly ugly looking, and judging by the fact that the horse was sporting a Western saddle, she guessed that he must be a pony horse who just acted as a calming companion for the more high-strung racehorses.

"You must be Claire."

Claire startled as she heard the voice and turned to see who it belonged to. She was greeted by a woman in her late twenties to early thirties, who was a bit taller than she. The woman was wearing a riding helmet, and seemed to be bundled in several layers of clothing. Claire quickly found her voice. "Yes," she said, holding out her hand.

"Nice to meet you, I'm Mandy," the other woman said, shaking Claire's hand firmly. "Kelly should be here any minute, he had to see to a horse outside."

Claire nodded, not really knowing what to say.

"Well, let's have a look at you," Mandy said bluntly, taking a couple of steps backward to get a full visual of her newest help.

Claire couldn't help but feel a little self conscious as this stranger looked her up and down like she were a horse in a sale.

Mandy nodded her head in approval. "You certainly have the build to be a rider...how much do you weigh?" she asked, without any hesitation.

"About 95 pounds," Claire replied, blushing slightly.

Mandy shook her head. "We'll have to get a bit of weight on you. You don't want to have to pack lead every time you ride. It shouldn't be too hard. Be grateful that you won't ever have to worry about your weight."

Claire liked Mandy. In spite of her small build, and girlish looks, she was direct, and Claire didn't doubt that she was tough as nails. She took a moment to study the woman whom she hoped would become her new boss, as she went to the second horse in the line and was fiddling with something on the bridle. Mandy was about 5 foot 5, and had a solid frame, although it was difficult to tell under the layers of clothing. There was a spattering of freckles on her nose, and she had what appeared to be medium length, curly brown hair that was pulled back in a ponytail and partially stuffed under her helmet. Her actions around the horses were effortless and precise. She made adjustments in the equipment quickly, while speaking softly to the horse that she would be riding.

The stocky chestnut in the adjacent stall sneezed, and Claire walked over to give him a pat. "I see you have met William," Mandy said, smiling.

"Yes, he seems sweet, but he doesn't look like much of a racehorse," Claire responded while stroking his nose.

Mandy laughed. "No, he's one of our ponies. He's the old man of the farm and has been a pony horse for years."

"What happened to his knee?" Claire asked, genuinely curious.

"He hyperextended it as a youngster and ended up with some hardware in there, about 4 screws I think. He was actually supposed to be a show horse, but after his injury, he would never make it in the arena, so we bought him super cheap, and he has been the best pony we've ever had. He's very patient with the babies, and big enough to give the older ones a push back if they get to be bullies."

Claire smiled. She already liked the horse. "How old is he?"

"Seventeen," Mandy answered. "He probably doesn't have many more years left to be babysitting these guys, but we'll go as long as he can, and then he will have earned himself a nice cushy retirement in one of the big pastures. He's our baby, so he isn't going anywhere."

Claire's opinion of the Zakarian's just jumped a notch or two. It was clear they loved and cared for their horses like they were their own children. She was impressed.

"Has he ever had any soundness issues with that knee?" she asked.

"Nope. He doesn't have full flexion, and the shoer has to work a little bit harder since he can't bend all the way, but he has never been the least bit gimpy. Here's Kelly," Mandy stated, turning to greet the man entering the barn with another horse under western tack.

"Morning, you're Claire." It was more of a statement than a question, and Claire nodded at the man who was Mandy's husband.

"She looks good, doesn't she?" Mandy said, again as if Claire was a horse to be looked over.

Kelly scrutinized her as well and then nodded his apparent approval. He was an average looking man, also probably in his early thirties. He donned a baseball cap and a puffy down coat, and while he wasn't overly large, Claire could see how he would have struggled with his weight in his days as a jockey.

"Jürgen told me you were a good rider," Kelly stated.

Claire shrugged. She had a feeling that the kind of riding that she had been doing wasn't going to amount to much here.

"Alright. If you want to learn, the best thing to do is come out and watch. We'll start you off slow, and once you get fit, it'll be easier, and you can start doing some real galloping."

"I'm fit," she said indignantly.

Kelly laughed. "No, you're not."

Claire thought that was a bit rude, but she held her tongue and waited for some instructions while Kelly got his wife legged up onto the Thoroughbred she would be riding.

"Claire, why don't you jump up on William and come out with me. We can watch Mandy gallop this one, and I'll give you some pointers."

She was happy with that instruction and smiled to herself as she led the old pony horse out of the barn to where she could mount. William stood quietly as she adjusted the stirrups, which were far too long, and it took her longer than usual since she wasn't used to the western saddle. Finishing her adjustments, she climbed up onto the big chestnut's back and headed him towards where Kelly was waiting on his pony with Mandy's horse on a lead next to him. They walked as a trio down a long, sandy lane that led to the one-mile oval racetrack. Claire admired her surroundings, taking in the sights and sounds of the beautiful farm. The first robins of spring were flitting about in the grass along the fences of the pastures and she listened to their song while breathing in the cool, clean morning air.

At that moment, life just couldn't get any better. She was curious to see what the morning would bring, but in that minute, she didn't care. Life was good.

Kelly broke the silence. "I didn't mean to offend you when I said you were unfit, but the plain fact is, you are about to see how tough it is to gallop these horses. You're lean, and I'm sure you can ride, but an hour or two in a dressage lesson doesn't equate to anything out here on the racetrack."

Claire looked at him, trying not to be offended by his disregard for what she had been doing the last 12 years of her life. "Alright," she responded plainly.

"I'm serious," Kelly said. "You watch Mandy as she gallops this horse. He's an older horse, and he knows his business. He's going to go out there and pull her guts out, and she has to prevent him from running off. You may think that galloping a racehorse means you just get up and let them go, but that is far from fact. If you let them run off every time they are on the track, they're going to get hurt. They need controlled gallops for conditioning, the speed works are done about once a week, and those are timed over specific distances. That's to build up their cardio, just like a human runner," he paused for a moment to let Mandy and her horse go on the track, and then they walked their ponies to a good vantage point, near the finish line, so they could see her entire circuit. "Now, she's going to backtrack down to just before the turn, and then she will turn him around and begin the gallop."

Claire watched Mandy jog the horse along the outside fence of the track, heading down the stretch in the opposite direction, from which the horses would run, which she guessed is what backtracking meant, since the horses ran on the track turning to the left. Mandy was standing, not posting the trot, and she was bent at the waist so her hands rested on the horse's withers. Already, Claire was beginning to realize that this was going to be a different style from what she was used to.

Kelly spoke again. "Now watch when she turns. Bubba there is going to take a hold of the bit and start to pick up speed. She will have to hold him for about a mile and a half, as she will take him all the way around, and then end over there on the backside," he pointed across the infield of the track across from where they were standing.

Claire watched Mandy turn the horse around, and immediately saw what Kelly was talking about. The horse, whose name was apparently Bubba, took off into a gallop almost instantly. Mandy had a tight hold of the reins, and the horse had his neck bowed to such an extreme that his chin was almost touching his chest. "Oh my God," she said, unable to contain her amazement.

Kelly smiled and continued her education. "Have a look at the position of Mandy's feet. You see how she has got them shoved way forward? How she is leaning back against the reins, all the while keeping her butt off the horse's back?"

"Yes," Claire could plainly see, as the duo galloped past them for the first time, that Mandy had her hands full, and was using every ounce of strength that she had to keep the horse contained.

"That's called having your feet on the dashboard," Kelly explained. "You will see jockeys doing it in races sometimes, usually on frontrunners, as they are trying to keep the horse from going too fast too soon. Out here during training, it usually means that your gallop boy or girl is on a super tough one."

"Wow. I guess I have a lot to learn."

"Don't worry about it. It seems like a lot to absorb right now, but if you're serious about riding and learning, pretty soon it'll all make sense. Before you know it, all of the little things will just come naturally, but yeah, you have a long ways to go." Kelly shielded his eyes from the morning sunrise that was blinding both of them from seeing Mandy on the far side of the racetrack. "Just wait till you get to work one. You'll be hooked!"

Claire was confused. "What do you mean 'work'?"

"Full speed, near race speed for anywhere from three to seven furlongs. Your first work is a rush like no other. You'll get to watch Mandy work a couple this morning, and you'll see what I mean."

Her stomach was starting to churn. At least she knew that a furlong was an eighth of a mile. She realized there was so much more to the racetrack than she could even comprehend. "I'm never going to figure it all out."

"Of course you will," Kelly said, without taking his eyes off his wife and her mount heading towards them for the second time. "You have only been here for a half an hour. Nobody expects you to know everything. I'm guessing you'll be ready to ride by the first of the year though, if you stick with it."

"The first of the year, next year?" Claire asked, clearly thinking that it shouldn't take 8 months for her to become a jockey.

"Yes," Kelly replied. "I know it seems like a long time, but believe me, you are going to need every minute of it. You have to allow yourself at least 2 months to get riding fit, and I mean you need to be fit enough to gallop 10 to 15 horses a morning, no matter how tough they are. You'll need to be working horses regularly, and working fitness is different than just galloping. You need to break from the gate, work from the gate, work in company, work in company from the gate. The list goes on and on. Even if you are ready in 6 months, it doesn't make any sense to start your bug before the first of the year."

"Bug?" Claire asked, feeling more and more like a complete idiot.

"Your apprenticeship," Kelly stated.

"Ok, why did you call it a bug?"

"That is what apprentice riders are called. In racing forms and pro-grams, and apprentice's name is followed by an asterisk, looks like a bug on the paper, hence the term 'bug'," Kelly laughed. "You'll have to get used to being called a 'bug girl'."

Claire was mortified. She thought that sounded incredibly degrading, but she just kept her mouth shut as she watched Mandy jog back with Bubba.

"He looked good," Kelly said to his wife, as she pulled up to a walk and joined them to head back to the barn.

Mandy was breathing hard as she kicked her feet out of the stirrups, which Claire thought were incredibly short, and shook her left arm in an effort to loosen it up slightly. "He was tough today...nearly pulled my arms out of the sockets," she laughed, as she gave the horse a pat on the neck. "I think he'll be ready to work a half this week."

"Good," Kelly nodded in agreement.

Claire guessed that meant he would work a half a mile. She wanted to see that, as the excitement of her surroundings was building, and she knew she wanted to learn everything there was to know.

They returned to the barn and all dismounted their horses. A young Hispanic man showed up, seemingly out of nowhere, to hold Bubba, while Mandy took off his saddle and bridle. Kelly said something to him in perfect Spanish, and the young man nodded and took his charge over to the mechanical hot walking machine. Claire had seen the hot walkers before. They were a large, mechanical walking machine that had four arms extending from the center post unit where the motor for the walker was held. Each arm attachment had a heavy rope hanging at the end that clipped to the horse's halter, enabling the horse to cool off after exercise while allowing the grooms and trainers to move on to other jobs. After putting Bubba on the walker, the young man, who's name Claire learned, was Juan, went back into the barn and brought out another horse for Mandy. Kelly legged her up effortlessly, and he and Claire got back on their ponies and headed back to the track.

"Now you will get to see one work," Kelly said to Claire.

Claire nodded as she watched Mandy shortening her stirrups even further.

"What on earth are you doing?" she asked in astonishment, as she was sure nobody could ride with their stirrups that short and still stay on the horse.

"I have got to shorten myself up a couple of notches for the work," Mandy responded casually. "You'll see. If you want to be a jockey, you're going to have to crank them way up. Besides, it is easier on the tough ones, as it gives you a bit more leverage. For the workers, you want to have your center of gravity where it needs to be in order to cause the least amount of interference with your horse. The works are fast, but controlled and you never, ever want to get in your horses way by hitting his mouth or bouncing on his back. Let him do the work, you are just there as a guide. The good ones know what they're doing, and I tell you, there's no better feeling than dropping down to the rail on a horse that knows his business, and just letting him take you along."

Claire started to feel butterflies of excitement in her stomach, which she thought was crazy, since she was only watching. They reached the track again, and Kelly let Mandy go.

"Just do an easy half," he said, as she was gathering herself for the job. She nodded, and headed at a jog up the stretch, away from the pair of ponies. Kelly pulled out his stopwatch, and got in position near the finish line.

"Where is she going to start from?" asked Claire, wondering how Mandy knew where a half-mile would begin.

"You see that red and white pole, across from us?" Kelly was pointing across the infield of the track.

"Yes."

"That is the half mile pole. She'll want to start dropping down to the rail before she gets there, as she wants to be into the work at the pole, for a full half-mile. If you look, you will see other poles around the track as well. Those are your three eighths, five eights, three quarters and seven eighths poles. You will learn those as you begin works."

"What do you mean by 'dropping down'?" Claire asked, figuring she might as well keep the questions coming.

Kelly kept his eyes on Mandy, who had just begun as easy gallop past them. "When a horse works, you want to put them as close to the rail as possible. That is basic geometry....the further off the rail you are, the further your horse has to travel to get to the finish. Works are done on the rail; gallops are done more toward the center of the track. It is basic race-track etiquette. Never gallop on the rail, or you're bound to get screamed at by someone trying to work. Let's watch this," he got his watch ready, as Claire watched the horse and rider across the track.

To Claire, the scene that unfolded was breathtaking. Mandy and her filly looked as one as she sped down the track, with Mandy sitting motionless, as the filly continued to stride along, covering the ground with a stride that was pure poetry. Claire watched as they made their way through the turn and straightened for home, the filly changing leads smoothly and leveling off for the stretch. The duo crossed the finish line and Kelly hit his watch.

"Forty nine flat," he said, nodding. "That's exactly what we want."

Claire was silent as she watched Mandy pull up from the work and make her way back.

"Check this out," Kelly said, in a voice that indicated that Claire was about to be impressed by something yet again.

"How fast did you go?" he asked Mandy as she eased up to them. Claire noticed a sly little wink when asked the question.

"Forty nine flat," Mandy responded confidently.

Claire was shocked. "Did you have a watch on you?"

Kelly pointed to his head, but Claire still didn't get it. "Mandy's clock is in her head," he stated. "She has a better clock than most jocks out there."

"You know how fast you were going, just in your head?" Claire was blown away.

"Yep," Mandy replied as she again kicked her feet out of the stirrups while they walked back toward the barn. "You will too. It takes lots of practice, but once you do it enough you get a feel for it. It isn't as hard as it may seem."

Claire was sure she would never be able to have a clock in her head like Mandy, but she kept that to herself. They arrived back at the barn, and Juan came out again to take Mandy's mount. Kelly spoke to him briefly in Spanish, and once again he nodded and took the filly to the hot walker.

Mandy spoke up, obviously understanding what Kelly had said to the young groom. "Maybe we should put Claire on Max, and I can go out with her on Belle. They'll both go pretty easy, and I can help her out if I need."

"You're the boss," he said, winking at his wife. Their relationship was one to be admired. They operated like a couple who'd been together for a long time, doing the thing they loved to do. There was an unspoken communication between them that Claire knew was what happened with married couples who truly loved each other and had been together for a long time. Her parents had been the same.

Realizing that they were talking about her, Claire suddenly panicked. "What do you mean, 'put me on Max'?"

"You want to ride don't you? Isn't that why you're here?" Kelly said inquisitively.

"Well yes, but I didn't think that I was going to...." Claire trailed off, knowing there wasn't anything she could say that wouldn't make her sound like she wasn't committed to riding.

Kelly finished her sentence for her. "You didn't think you were going to jump right on and start galloping."

She nodded silently.

"Did you bring your helmet?"

"Yes."

"Then why not get started. There's no time like the present. Don't worry, I'm only going to put you on one or two today, and the first guy is pretty easy. Mandy will be out there with you, and if you are as good as Jürgen says you are, you should have no problem at all."

Claire felt a surge of confidence in knowing Jürgen had spoken so highly of her, but it was immediately followed by pure terror. After watching Mandy, she didn't know if she was ready.

Mandy seemed to read her mind. "You'll be fine. Max is a big puppy dog. You just set your cross on his neck and he lopes around like a gentleman."

"Set my cross?" Claire questioned, again, feeling like she didn't know this foreign language.

Mandy waved dismissively as Juan brought out yet another horse for her to get on. "I'll show you. I know all of this is different from what you are used to, but don't worry. I will walk you through everything, and before you know it, it'll all be second nature."

She was not sure about anything, but she climbed back up on William and headed to the track for the third time that morning.

"I want to get Mandy to work a couple more, and then I'll have Juan get your two ready to go." Kelly said, sensing her anxiety.

"Okay," Claire replied, not sure whether she was more excited or nervous. She looked around casually, realizing that for such a huge facility, it was awfully quiet. The horses that Mandy was on were the only ones on the track. She thought that there should be more activity. "This seems like an awfully big set-up, where are all the other horses?" Claire asked, hoping she didn't sound like too much of an idiot.

"You're perceptive," Kelly said. "Yes, it is quiet, but you should have seen it here last week. We just shipped everything over to the track at Finger Lakes, so it is quiet for a week or so before we start getting all the two year olds in. For a couple of weeks every March, it is quiet like this, and then the babies come and it gets crazy. Once the race meet starts at the main track, we will be getting a lot more horses through as some need time off due to injury, some just need a freshening away from the hustle of the big track. Some horses, like Max for example, only go to Finger Lakes to run. We ship him in on a race day, he runs his race and then comes home."

"Why do you do that?" Claire asked. "Wouldn't it be easier to just keep him over there all the time?"

"Ideally, yes, but we found out fairly early on that Max just gets too stressed out over there. He prefers the peace and quiet of the farm, and he runs much better if we just keep him here to train."

"How many horses do you have?"

Kelly let Mandy go as they reached the track before he answered. "Between the farm and the track, we have about 150 horses."

Claire gasped. "Holy cow! You own that many horses?"

Kelly laughed. "Hell no! Those are the horses that we are training. Most of them are owned by other people. The owners are the ones that pay the bills. This farm, meaning my dad, Mandy and I, personally own about 25, but the rest belong to several various owners."

Claire continued with her questions. "And you know all 150 horses?"

"Of course, that's my job," Kelly responded a bit more seriously. "I don't see every horse every day, my dad is in and out at the main track, so he oversees them some of the time, but I do know them all. They also come and go. Some get sold or claimed, owners buy or claim horses and we get new ones. It's a business, and I need to know as much as I can about the horses so I can relay the necessary information to the owners."

Claire sighed. "I am never going to learn everything."

"Of course you will. And you'll learn it a lot faster than you think," Kelly said, trying to ease her apprehensions.

They watched Mandy work another two horses and Claire continued to ask questions as she thought of them. Before she knew it, it was time for her to get on her first racehorse.

When the time came, she waited outside of the barn, her helmet secure and her hands shaking slightly. She knew she could not be afraid, as Max would immediately sense it, but she still had a hard time controlling the butterflies.

"Here is your guy," Kelly said to her, and she looked up at the horse being led out of the barn. Her stomach did a summersault and she thought it was a good thing she hadn't eaten breakfast that morning, or it would have come right back up.

Max was the biggest horse that Claire had ever seen, and she worked in a barn full of Warmbloods and Thoroughbreds alike. He was chestnut in color, and had to be well over 17 hands.

"Oh my God," she said, unable to contain the awe in her voice. "This is what I am riding?" she said, to no one in particular.

Mandy giggled as she came over to rub Max's head. "Don't worry, he's a gentle giant."

"Giant is right. How am I supposed to get up there?" she asked.

"Here, I got you," Kelly said, approaching her to give her a leg up. Even with the significant push that Kelly gave, she still felt like she had to pull herself the rest of the way into the saddle.

Once up on his back, Claire felt surprisingly at ease. He was, after all, just a horse, and she was a rider, and she would make this work. She found her stirrups and tightened her girth, while Max waited patiently as Kelly mounted his pony. Claire was unsure what to do with herself, as Mandy seemed busy on her mount, doing things with her reins and adjusting her stirrups. They began their walk toward the track, and once she was set, she turned in her saddle to check out Claire.

"Alright," she said with a getting down to business tone. "The first thing you want to do when you get on is tie your reins. Having a knot in your reins keeps them more manageable and prevents them from flapping around while you are galloping."

Mandy showed her how to tie off her reins, and Claire paid careful attention, copying what her fellow rider had done, with her own reins.

"Good, now I am going to show you how to set your cross before we get going, so that you have that control right away."

"Okay," Claire said, still not having a clue as to what that meant.

Mandy proceeded in a professional tone. "All a cross means is that you cross your reins so that they overlap in your hands. You will actually be holding both reins in each hand. It is like making a bridge with your reins. The last thing you want to be doing out there on the track is constantly readjusting your grip on the reins. On a horse like Max, that isn't a big deal, but for horses like Bubba, it becomes incredibly important. If you have to move your hands for a second, he will grab the bit and take off. By setting your cross, and keeping your hands at the base of the horse's neck, you maintain the maximum amount of control and you don't have to worry about changing your grip. It's also easier on you as a rider when you are on a tough horse. Rather than pulling directly against you, if your hands are low, and the bridge of your reins is over the horse's neck, the horse himself will absorb some of the pull. You won't get that with Max, but you'll get a feel for what I am talking about anyway." Claire could only nod, as she watched Mandy show her how it was done.

"Next, shorten your stirrups.... about 5 holes," Mandy said, bluntly.

Claire did as she was told, immediately conscious of the fact that she had never had her stirrups even close to that short in her entire life, and she wondered how it was going to work.

Mandy sensed her apprehension. "You will be fine. It's all about being as little of a hindrance to your horse as possible while being able to maintain balance and control. It may seem strange at first, but once you get strong, it'll come easy."

"I'm not totally sure I believe you," Claire laughed nervously. "But I'll take your word for it." "Good to know," Mandy laughed in response.

Claire was envious. Mandy looked so comfortable on her horses. Every movement was fluid and she knew every horse's actions and personality so well that she could adjust herself accordingly.

They reached the track and pushed their horses into an easy jog. Claire imitated Mandy, standing in her stirrups, instead of posting the trot and they headed up the stretch towards the turn. She was immediately impressed with Max. He had a huge, floating trot, and she thought that if he were ever to retire from racing, he would make a fantastic event horse. They reached the turn and stopped for a moment.

"Max likes to stand here for a few minutes before he gets going," Mandy said, as her mount started to get fussy. "We'll give him a minute to sightsee...he'll let you know when he's ready."

Claire thought this was interesting. Yet another horse's quirk that Mandy knew by heart.

As Mandy had predicted, Max got started on his own. Claire stood up in her irons, keeping her hands quietly set the way Mandy had shown her, and let the big horse begin to gallop. Mandy was right next to her, watching her every move, all the while keeping her own mount under control. "Let him out a bit more," she called to Claire. "This isn't the dressage arena.... think more about your speed on the cross country course, and then go faster."

Claire smooched to Max who immediately responded, lengthening his stride even further. It seemed as though they were flying, and Claire began to focus on what was happening. She could feel the big horse move underneath of her, as smooth as glass, his long strides eating up the ground. She felt the wind in her face and his gentle pull on her arms, and in that moment, she knew she was doing the right thing.

"Bring him back a bit," Mandy called to Claire.

Claire did as she was told, tightening her grip on the reins, asking Max to slow down slightly. He responded, but not without giving her a bit of a pull. They were coming out of the turn and down the stretch for the second time when Claire began to realize she was getting tired. Her legs were burning, her back was beginning to ache, and she could definitely feel the pressure on her arms. Once on the backstretch, Max eased himself down to a jog, then a walk.

"How was that?" Mandy asked, smiling.

"Unbelievable!" Claire exclaimed between breaths. She was surprised to find that she was so winded after a simple mile and a half gallop, and began to realize that Kelly was right about her not being fit.

"You looked great. You really have a natural balance on a horse. You'll be galloping 10 a day before you know it."

Claire beamed at the compliment. All of her fears and apprehensions had vanished, and she suddenly felt like superwoman. "Thanks."

They began their jog back to where Kelly was waiting. Max just dropped his head and trotted back on a loose rein, calm and relaxed, and Claire allowed herself to relax as well, posting the trot instead of standing as they approached Kelly and his pony.

"How'd it go?" he asked Claire.

"Awesome!" she said. Talking was a bit easier now that she had her air back.

"You looked really good. I like that you have nice quiet hands. Max likes that too," Kelly said as he looked at the big horse.

"Thanks. You were right about me not being fit. I had no idea."

"I know. It's going to take you about a month to 6 weeks to get strong enough that you feel you can hold anything, but you'll get there. I'd like you to get on one more if you want."

Claire agreed, excited now rather than nervous.

When they reached the barn, Juan came out and grabbed Max's bridle so Claire could dismount. She jumped off, and her knees buckled, almost giving way completely. She held herself up, embarrassed, and got her horse unsaddled. Her legs were feeling like Jell-O, but she didn't want to say anything. She had always considered herself fairly fit, running and doing some minor weightlifting on her own time, but this was a whole other level of fitness, and one that she felt she was a long ways away from attaining.

Her next mount was brought out, a smallish dark bay mare they called Melody. Kelly legged her up again and she once more followed Mandy's lead in tying her reins and shortening her stirrups.

"Melody's good, though she isn't as smooth as Max, and she is probably going to pull a bit harder, but it shouldn't be anything you can't handle. She is a nice little filly, but don't let down your guard on the jog back. She looks for things to spook at, and if you give her head, she'll duck out from under you in a heartbeat," Mandy warned.

"Okay," Claire was glad for the heads up, but she wasn't concerned. Nothing could be as bad as Fred when it came to finding spooky things.

They began their jog, and she noticed right away that this mare was nothing like Max. The filly was light and lithe, and her stride was short, almost choppy. They stopped and turned, and Claire felt the mare immediately take a hold of the bit. She focused on setting her hands properly and letting the mare pull against the cross of her reins. Mandy was right next to her as they made their way around the track, stride for stride. Melody was pulling, but Claire held her, aware of the burning in her arms and legs, realizing that this was going to be much harder than she had anticipated. With half a mile to go, Claire began to worry that she wouldn't be able to hold the mare, as her arms became numb and her back began to cramp. The end of the gallop came none too soon, and Melody, like Max, pulled herself up. The horses seemed to know the routine and Claire was grateful, as she didn't know if she would have been able to actually pull the horse to a stop.

Mandy came up next to her as they began their jog back. Claire kept her reins tight and her legs firm, not wanting to be dumped on her first day.

"How was that one?" Mandy asked.

"I can't feel my arms," Claire responded.

Mandy laughed. "You think you are sore now, just wait until tomorrow!"

Claire had no doubt, as she returned her focus to her mount who she could feel was tensing for a spook. As soon as Melody felt that Claire was prepared, she relaxed and jogged back with no problems. They reached Kelly and he leaned over and clipped a lead rope onto Melody's bit.

"Go ahead and relax," he told Claire. "I've got her."

Claire was grateful as she kicked her feet out of the stirrups and untied the knot from her reins. Thankfully, Melody wasn't that tall, so the dismount shouldn't be as awkward as it was from Max. She knew that her legs would not cooperate, and a shorter distance to the ground would be welcomed.

"How'd you feel?" Kelly asked.

"Good, but she did pull a bit. My arms are going to be sore tomorrow."

"You're whole body is going to be sore tomorrow," Kelly laughed as they stopped at the barn.

Once again, Juan came out dutifully and took the horses. Claire was becoming more and more aware of the fact that her entire body was shaking and exhausted.

"What else would you like me to do?" Claire asked Kelly.

"Nothing, you can go home and recover."

"Are you sure? No stalls or grooming or anything?"

Kelly looked at her and smiled. "You're a gallop girl now Claire, not a groom. I pay somebody else to groom and muck stalls. Your job is to come here and gallop horses. When you're done, you go home."

Claire was unsure of herself. At Jürgen's barn she cleaned stalls, groomed horses and got her own mounts saddled, unsaddled and cooled off all on her own. She wasn't sure what to think about having somebody else taking care of her horses for her. "I feel guilty though, not taking care of my own horses."

"Don't feel guilty, you'll get to a point where you ride several horses a day, and there just isn't time. It's more efficient to have the horses ready so you can just jump on and go. While you're out, Juan gets the next one ready and so on. I pay him to groom and tack, I pay you to ride. Speaking of," Kelly paused and reached into his pocket. "Here's for today. The going rate is $12 per gallop. I'll put you on two more tomorrow, and then you can have a day off to recover," he said, handing her some cash.

"Thank you," she said politely, taking the money. "Same time tomorrow?"

"Yep. Go home and get some rest," Kelly said.

"Ok, see you in the morning," Claire said as she headed down the aisle of the barn. She wished she could say goodbye to Mandy, but she was already headed to the track on another horse.

As she got into her car, she became fully aware of how weak her body felt. Her legs, arms and back all felt wobbly and she became aware, now that the adrenaline of the morning was wearing off, just how tired she was. The drive home seemed to take forever, and she pulled up to her house feeling like she could barely keep her eyes open.

She went inside, taking off her coat as she walked in the door.

"Morning Claire!" Robyn said in her usual cheerful tone. "How'd it go?"

Claire barely looked up as she removed her boots, struggling to stand up straight when she was done. "Great, but I am going to bed."

"What's wrong? Did something happen, are you okay?" Robyn jumped up from the sofa in full hover mode.

"I'm fine, but I need to sleep. It was great, and I'll tell you all about it when I wake up." Claire staggered down the hall to her room. She closed the blinds and fell onto the bed, not even bothering to get under the blankets, and in a matter of seconds she was sleeping like the dead.

CHAPTER 5

Claire woke about 3 hours later, feeling like she had been run over by a very large truck. Her aunt had obviously been in, as she was covered with a blanket, but she had no recollection. She gingerly pushed herself up to a sitting position and tried to figure out how she was going to get out of bed and make it to the bathroom without assistance. Every muscle in her body was sore, and while she was no stranger to periodic muscle soreness, this was pain on a whole different level. She didn't think that there was a single part of her body that didn't hurt. Her arms, legs, back, and hips were in agony. Even her hands hurt from maintaining such a tight grip on the thick racing reins. She gingerly set her feet on the floor and slowly raised herself off of the bed. The trip to the bathroom seemed like a mile and sitting down on the toilet was going to present a whole new set of problems.

She finished in the bathroom and hobbled down the hall to the living room where she knew her mother would be sitting. Her aunt and mom were by the sofa; Robyn was brushing her sister's hair lovingly as they watched something uninteresting on television.

"What on earth happened to you?" Robyn asked, concerned.

Claire winced as she slowly lowered herself into the recliner. "Nothing terrible. In fact, it was incredible, I just wasn't prepared."

Her aunt raised an eyebrow at her. "Do elaborate."

"Well," Claire began. "I galloped two horses at the farm today. I know that doesn't sound like much, and it isn't, but I'm not fit. It takes a strength that I don't think I'll ever have. My whole body is sore and I am supposed to go back and get on two more tomorrow morning. I don't know how I'm going to do it."

"You only rode two?" Robyn questioned. "You're right, that doesn't seem like much. What's the difference between that and the riding you've been doing?"

Claire shook her head as she didn't even know where to begin in trying to explain to her aunt how vastly different race track riding was compared to the dressage and jumping she'd been doing for most of her life. She managed what she hoped was a satisfactory explanation, and her aunt smiled with some amazement.

"Wow. I never realized," Robyn said finally.

"Neither did I," Claire sighed.

Robyn looked at her for a moment and then spoke again. "It probably wasn't a good idea for you to come home and go straight to sleep. You should have stayed up and moving instead of letting your body shut down. It's going to be really hard for you to get sufficiently mobile for tomorrow's rides if you can't even walk right now."

"I know, but I was just so tired."

"I'm going to make you some tea and something for lunch. In the mean time, you need to start trying to move. Just do some mild stretches, and tonight, after dinner, you will soak in a nice hot Epsom salts bath so hopefully you will be semi-functional tomorrow," Robyn was in full nurse mode now, but if anybody knew how to help her, it would be her aunt.

"You don't need to take care of me," Claire said without much conviction. The truth was, she was grateful for her aunt's assistance.

Robyn waved a dismissive hand and grunted some response as she went into the kitchen to get lunch things ready.

Claire sat in the chair and thought about her morning. She thought about the horses that she had ridden and her new bosses, Mandy and Kelly. They appeared to Claire to be honest and hard working people who took their job very seriously, and loved what they did. There was a passion for the horses and the life Claire knew she shared, and she could see that the information that she would get from them would be of great value. Her thoughts drifted to her parting with Kelly and she remembered the $24 that she had in her coat pocket. It wasn't much, but the idea of getting paid to ride horses was mind blowing. She did some quick calculations in her head. If she was ever fit enough, Kelly mentioned that she could get on around ten horses a day. Ten horses at $12 per mount was $120 a day! Multiply that by six days a week, and she was making real money. She would never make that kind of money flipping burgers or waiting tables she thought, and there was the potential to save a significant amount. She could certainly be more help around the house by providing some extra cash for things.

She looked over at her mother, who was gazing blankly at the television, as usual. The thought of getting up out of her current position was daunting, so she decided to stay put. She would talk to her mom later. It was unknown to Claire whether or not her mom ever understood, but she talked anyway. The one sided conversations were cathartic, and she hoped that there was some part of her mom that understood, even if she was unable to communicate.

Robyn returned with a cup of steaming hot tea and set it on the end table next to Claire, making sure to scoot the coaster close enough that Claire wouldn't have to reach too far. "Here you go. I'm making you some chicken noodle soup and a grilled cheese sandwich. You need to nourish your body if you hope to recover."

"Yes, doctor," Claire joked.

"It's nurse to you," Robyn poked back. "And you better eat it all!"

Claire sat, sipping her tea as the smells from the kitchen drifted towards her. She suddenly realized how hungry she was. Breakfast had been skipped in her nervous rush out the door that morning and her stomach growled as she thought about the food that was coming.

Robyn came back to set up a tray at Claire's chair. It was the same tray that she used for Cora's meals, and Claire laughed out loud.

"What is so funny?" Robyn asked.

"Did you ever think that you would be taking care of two invalids?" Claire said, regaining her composure.

"No, but your condition is only temporary. Just don't ask me to feed you!"

Claire laughed again. The fact that her aunt had to feed her mother three meals a day was not lost on her, but in their situation, sometimes it was better to laugh, just so you didn't cry.

Robyn returned with Claire's food and she ate heartily, finishing every last crumb. She had always had a healthy appetite, and she was amazed that she managed to maintain such a lean figure. It would probably catch up to her someday, but right now, she didn't care. "That was excellent," she said to her aunt. "Thank you."

"You're welcome," Robyn said, looking at her knowingly.

When Claire finished, her aunt cleared her tray and then came back into the living room, returning to her place on the sofa. "What's the plan?" she asked Claire plainly.

"What do you mean?"

"I mean, what's your plan. Spring break is next week, but then you go back to school. How are planning on working and finishing school?"

Claire had been thinking about that too, and fortunately she had, what she thought, was a satisfactory answer, assuming that Kelly and Mandy would be willing to work with it. "I'm going to work this week, but it will probably only amount to a couple of horses a day, at least until I get stronger. Once break is over, I'll go ride in the mornings before school. I have a free first period anyway, so if I start right at six, I should be able to get on a few horses before I have to go to school. I can just have a change of clothes in the car so I can just go straight to class."

"Do you think that it is a good idea? Judging by the way you came home today, I wouldn't want

you falling asleep at your desk every day."

"It'll get easier," Claire said, hoping she sounded convincing. She wasn't sure herself if she would be able to do it, but she had to try.

"I certainly hope so. Your brother would be extremely disappointed if your grades took a dive with only two months left before graduation," Robyn was sly.

Claire caught on instantly. "Nice. Using the thought of disappointing Colin to guilt me into promising that my grades won't fall, and I will graduate with my standing 3.0 GPA."

"Whatever works," Robyn said, grinning.

Claire smiled back. She knew that she had an extremely difficult road ahead of her for the next couple of months, but she would make it work. She had to.

That evening, she did exactly as her aunt suggested; a nice hot bath followed by a couple of ibuprofen and an early bedtime, taking some time to stretch the best that she could before she fell into bed. She didn't know if she would be able to sleep considering that she had slept for 3 hours earlier in the day, but she was asleep when her head hit the pillow.

Claire was awake before her alarm the next morning, excited to get to the farm. Her body was sore, but manageable and she rushed quietly out the door.

When she reached the barn, she saw William in the cross ties again, saddled and ready to go. Juan was busy tacking up one of the Thoroughbreds as Claire approached, stopping to greet the pony horse, and nodding a hello to the groom.

Kelly entered the barn and spoke briefly to Juan before greeting Claire. "Morning, Claire. How are you feeling today?" he said with a slightly evil grin.

Claire decided it best to tell the truth. "I have never been so sore in my life. I suddenly have a new respect for jockeys. And Mandy....that woman is amazing."

Kelly laughed. "Yep, she is pretty amazing. And you can now say with certainty that jockeys are in fact athletes."

"There is no doubt in my mind. Every single muscle in my body hurts."

"Well, let's not waste time, Mandy's waiting. Why don't you jump on William again and you can come out and watch some more works before you get on yours," Kelly directed, already heading out of the barn with his pony.

Claire grabbed William and headed out of the barn where Kelly and Mandy were both waiting.

Mandy looked at Claire walking gingerly and smiled. "Kelly tells me you are a little sore today."

"You have no idea."

"Actually, I do. You think you're sore now, wait until tomorrow. It will make today's soreness feel like a minor ache." Mandy and Kelly both laughed, but Claire didn't find it all that funny. She had never felt that kind of soreness in her life, and now she finds out it's only going to get worse.

Kelly held William as Claire clambered her way onto his back. Her muscles not allowing her to mount with any grace. "Just so you know, I'm giving you tomorrow off. You're going to need it, but you need to be ready to ride on Tuesday," he said.

"Okay. I'll be ready," she said, hoping her voice contained the confidence that her body currently lacked.

They began their walk down the path to the track. In spite of her sore muscles, Claire was happy to be on horseback. It was always her favorite place, and she had the feeling that she was going to love her early mornings with the horses, and the fact she was making some money while doing it was even better.

That trip to the track was very similar to the previous morning as they watched Mandy gallop around. The time was spent in silence as Claire noticed a light snow was starting to fall. It was cold and still, and a typical March morning in upstate New York. Tomorrow would probably be sunny and warm.

"Are you having second thoughts?" Kelly asked, breaking the silence.

"No. I want to ride," Claire said, "I'm just worried that I'll never be strong enough."

"You'll get there, don't worry. You'll have that moment where everything comes together and you suddenly realize that you can ride anything. Your body will begin to change and you will notice muscles that you never thought you had. Check out Mandy's arms some day. Talk about guns!" Kelly laughed, but couldn't keep the admiration out of his voice.

Mandy returned to them, and they headed as a group back to the barn. Kelly spoke again. "Hey love, I was just telling Claire that she should check out your arms. She doesn't think she'll get strong."

Mandy didn't hesitate. "Kelly's right," she said to Claire. "You will have an absolutely fantastic physique, and you won't have to pick up a dumbbell. Nothing like looking like a million bucks and not even trying."

Claire smiled slightly, not sure whether she believed Mandy or not as she had yet to see her boss in anything but a down coat.

They arrived at the barn and Juan appeared as usual to tend to Mandy's mount. Kelly told Claire to give William to Mandy and get ready for her first mount of the morning. Claire guessed that meant she would be out on the track on her own, which didn't bother her too much. She thought it would be nice to have the entire track completely to herself.

Juan came out of the barn with pretty dapple-gray whose name, Kelly said, was Wolf. Claire was legged up and began to go through the motions of tying her reins and adjusting her stirrups as Kelly and Mandy flanked her on the two ponies. Kelly explained that Wolf was a fairly easy horse to gallop, but he got too competitive when there was company around, which is why she was on her own. Claire gathered herself together and broke off from her companions as they reached the track. Wolf was pleasant enough, responding to Claire's cues as they stopped and turned to begin. He picked up the bit and broke into an easy gallop. Claire found her position, and immediately was aware of how much her body hurt. She tried to block out the agony of her muscles by focusing on the horse beneath her. The sound of his rhythmic snorting in conjunction with his hoof beats lulled Claire into a zone of pure exhilaration as the horse moved effortlessly over the fine dirt of the track. The snow had begun to fall harder, and in spite of her sore body, Claire relished the moment. She was alone on the track. The only sound was Wolf's breathing, and the fat, wet spring snowflakes were settling on her eyelashes as the duo made their way around the turn and headed down the stretch for the second time. Claire became more aware that her strength was waning, and she was grateful when, like the others, Wolf pulled himself up on the backstretch. They jogged back quietly, Claire's body was screaming and she couldn't help but drop her stirrups and her reins when she reached Kelly as he grabbed Wolf's bridle.

"You looked great," he said, without hesitation.

"Thanks, but I don't have a whole lot left," Claire responded.

"No worries. You can take Max next and then be done."

Claire knew Max was easy, but she wasn't confident that her body would cooperate.

Mandy spoke up next. "You have a really great style. Jürgen wasn't kidding when he said you could ride. You'd never know that you were so sore just by watching you. You look like you've been doing it for a while."

Claire blushed slightly, but said thank you just the same.

Mandy continued. "You have fantastic hands. Jürgen also said that you had the quietest hands he had seen in a long time. I think you will make a great jockey. The horses respond to you, and you seem to calm them. I didn't want to say anything before, but Wolf can tend to be a bit squirrelly, and he never turned a hair. Your quietness transferred to him and he did beautifully for you. I can't wait to see you start to work these horses." Mandy truly sounded excited and Kelly nodded in agreement.

This time, Claire simply beamed. That kind of a compliment, coming from Mandy, was enough to make her day. These two people whom she already admired and respected had confidence in her abilities and thought she would be successful. She almost forgot about her pain, until she had to dismount and she did so awkwardly, as her body just wouldn't cooperate.

In typical spring fashion, the snow had tapered off as she took the saddle and bridle off of Wolf and put them on the rack that sat near the barn door, knowing that Juan would take care of it after he put the gray horse on the hot walker. She waited a moment or two and then Juan came out with Max.

She still couldn't believe how big the chestnut horse was, and had no idea how she was going to get on him, even with Kelly's help. He legged her up, doing most of the work, and she readied herself for one more gallop. Kelly and Mandy flanked her again on their way down to the track and she headed off on the big, red horse.

Max was as quiet as he had been the day before, for which Claire was grateful. She was gaining more confidence in her position on the horse, but her strength was gone and she just allowed Max to gallop along at his own pace, which was comfortable and not too fast. When they finished and returned back to Kelly and Mandy, Claire's entire body was shaking. She was feeling physically ill, but she didn't want to let on to her new bosses that she was having such a struggle. They walked quietly back to the barn and she dismounted, her knees buckled and she crumbled to the ground.

"Crap!" Mandy said and reached over to grab Claire's arm. "Are you alright?"

Claire was embarrassed, but allowed herself to be helped to her feet. "I'm okay. I can't believe how physically exhausted I am."

"Why don't you come into the office and have a seat for a few minutes. You did great by the way," Mandy said.

Claire didn't have the energy to speak, so she let herself be led into the office where she sat in the chair closest to the door.

Kelly came in as Mandy went out. They exchanged words about the next gallop, and then Kelly sat down in the chair behind the metal desk. "I guess I don't need to ask how you feel," Kelly said, not really joking.

"I think you have a pretty good idea," Claire responded. "I'm mortified, but my body just won't work."

"Okay, so physically, you are exhausted, but how are you doing mentally?" Kelly questioned.

"What do you mean?"

"Are you ready to commit to becoming a jockey? Because if you are, Mandy and I are prepared to help you as much as possible. You have a ton of natural talent, and I think you could do very well, but you have to be 100% sure."

"I'm sure. If I can get through these next couple of days of pain, I'm sure," Claire said.

Kelly smiled at her. "Good. Go home and take care of yourself, and we will see you at the same time on Tuesday morning." He held out his hand to help her to her feet, and she took it, gratefully, easing herself into a standing position. "I have got to go check on some horses, so I'll see you later."

"Thanks...see you," Claire said as she shuffled out of the office and down the barn isle.

The drive home felt far too long, even though it was only about 15 minutes. Once again, she went home and went straight to bed, knowing that she probably wouldn't be able to stand when she awoke, but she had no choice. She was completely exhausted.

*

Claire was awakened by a knock on her door. She looked at the clock and realized that she had been sleeping for nearly four hours.

"Come in," she said groggily.

To her surprise, Colin walked into her room carrying a cup of hot tea. "Robyn told me you weren't doing too well, so I thought I'd come see what she was talking about."

Claire tried to push herself into a sitting position, but her body hurt so badly that she quickly gave up. "I have never hurt so badly in my life," she said, trying to smile at her brother. "The sick thing is, I did this willingly."

Colin looked at her and shook his head. "Are you sure you want to do this?"

"Yes. I just need to get through this week, and things will get better. Kelly said that it would take me a while to get fit, but like any new activity, I am going to be sore for a while just starting out. I just never imagined that I would hurt this badly," she paused for a moment. "I really need to pee, but I don't think I can get up myself. Will you help me up?"

Colin stood and put his arms around her, helping her to her feet as she tried to straighten her legs. He kept his arm around her to the bathroom and she went in on her own, using the counter for support. When she was done, she came back out and Colin was waiting by the door to take her back to her room.

"Are you sure you are alright?" he asked. "I don't think this is normal muscle soreness."

"It's not normal, but I'll be fine. Just give me some ibuprofen and let me go back to bed.

"Oh, no. You're not going back to sleep. You need to get up and move around or you may never walk again." He steered her down the hall to the living room where she sat back in the recliner while he went back to her room to get her tea. Claire looked around, realizing that the house was empty aside from her and her brother. She couldn't remember her aunt saying she had anywhere to go, but the last two days had been such a blur that had probably just forgotten. Colin returned with her tea and dropped himself heavily onto the overstuffed sofa.

"Where's Mom and Aunt Robyn?" Claire asked.

"Mom had a doctor's appointment. Nothing major. Didn't Robyn tell you?"

"I don't remember," Claire admitted.

Colin asked her about her new job at the racetrack, and she filled him in on all the details, telling him about each horse that she rode, and the horses that Mandy rode. She told him all about her new bosses and the fact that they both said she had great potential as a jockey and they would be willing to help her along the way.

Her aunt and mother came home a couple of hours later and they all enjoyed dinner, which Colin cooked, displaying one more of his many talents. Robyn helped Claire with some stretches to try and loosen up her body, and she repeated the Epsom salts bath and an early evening to bed. She was exhausted but the happiest she had been since before her parent's accident. She eagerly anticipated the weeks to come, wondering what exciting events the future would hold in her efforts to become a jockey.

CHAPTER 6

In the six weeks following her first trip to the farm, each day seemed to be harder than the one before. Claire felt she would never get strong. She was up to riding 5 or 6 horses a day, but she still didn't feel like she had it right. She still struggled to hold the tough ones, and she was beginning to feel disheartened, as it didn't seem like she was making the progress that she had hoped.

The first Saturday in May dawned with the promise of a beautiful day, and Claire was thrilled. She had 7 gallops on the morning schedule, and then she was going to spend the afternoon with Kelly and Mandy and watch the Kentucky Derby from their home. The Derby was, of course, something she had seen on television many times before, but this would be the first time she would watch it in the company of people who really knew the game. Claire hoped that it would be a good learning experience. She'd been studying the horses in the race, and chosen her favorite, but she still didn't really understand how to read the racing form and the past performances of the individual horses in the race. Kelly was going to have a form available, and he promised to walk her through it, line by line, as he said it was vital for a jockey to be able to read and understand the form, not only for his or her own horse, but for every horse in the race.

He had told her that the form was critical for developing racing strategy and studying the competition. When all was said and done, it was still a horse race, and anything could happen, but it is always helpful to go in with a plan.

In the past month, Claire's relationship with Kelly and Mandy had blossomed from boss and employee to friends. She had become comfortable with them both, and while Kelly spent a lot of time running the stable at Finger Lakes, Mandy was almost always at the farm and she and Claire had formed a very close bond. Their first love was the horses, Mandy joked that Kelly was a close second. They spent the mornings galloping their respective horses, and when they were finished, they often just sat in the office and talked. Claire talked about her family and her parents, about school and life in general. Mandy asked about any potential love interests, and Claire was not the least bit embarrassed to say that she just didn't have time for a relationship. Besides, the boys at her school were idiots.

That Saturday morning, Claire's first mount was a horse by the name of Blue. He was a mid- sized, well built, chestnut gelding who she had been struggling with since she had started riding him a couple of weeks prior. He was tough, and she always felt like she was one false move away from being on a complete runaway. She wasn't thrilled about having to ride him again, and couldn't decide whether or not it was best to ride him first and get him out of the way, or ride him last and be done completely.

She jogged him up the stretch, comfortable enough now with her short stirrups and the different riding style. Blue was the opposite of Max in that he didn't like to wait around to start his gallop. Once she reached the turning point, she readied herself and the horse turned and was into a gallop immediately. Blue began to pick up speed. She prepared herself for the pull and began to let her body do the work. The horse began to pull harder, and Claire resigned herself to the fact that this was going to be another tough gallop, but then she had a thought, easing up on her grip slightly, letting Blue pick up his pace. He lengthened his stride to where he was in a strong gallop, but not too fast and suddenly he stopped pulling so hard. Claire allowed him to cruise comfortably and suddenly she felt like super woman. She was hit with a strength and confidence that she didn't ever think she would achieve, and realized that this was the 'aha' moment that Kelly had told her about. Blue made his way around the track in what was the easiest gallop that Claire had ever had on him, pulling himself up on the backside and trotting back comfortably. Claire couldn't wait to tell Mandy, but she knew that she wouldn't have time, as there were still six more horses to get on before they had their morning coffee and chat session.

She had the best morning yet, galloping all of her favorites, Max, Wolf, Melody and others. With her newly discovered confidence, she was letting the horses gallop stronger than she ever thought she would have. The real test would be whether or not she could hold Bubba. She thought she would ask Mandy about riding him one of these days, as she felt her skills were up to par.

When she untacked her last mount for the morning, she went into the barn to find Mandy, and found her standing outside the stall about halfway down the aisle. She was all ready to tell her boss about her break-through morning when she looked into the stall and immediately caught her breath. The horse in the stall was unreal.

"Nice, isn't he?" Mandy said, before Claire even had the chance.

Claire could only nod, as she was speechless at the sight before her. In the stall was a giant of a horse, at least as tall as Max, but he had a look in his eye that was seductively frightening. His blood bay coat shone in the morning light as it streamed into the barn, and he stood in the back corner of the stall, staring outside at something neither woman understood. What surprised Claire the most was the metal contraption that covered his nose and attached to either side of the halter he was wearing.

"Is that a muzzle?" Claire asked, knowing the answer, but never having seen one on a horse before, she felt she had to confirm.

"Yep," Mandy said, never taking her eyes off the animal in the stall. "This guy just came in this morning. I guess he's pretty incredible on the track, but the previous trainer said he's impossible to gallop and the meanest horse he'd ever seen. I was told to keep the muzzle on him at all times unless we had a stall with a barred door."

"Why did you get him?" Claire asked, not believing that Mandy would willingly agree to such a charge.

"I don't know. One of Kelly's hair brained ideas. I swear that guy sometimes does things just to make my life difficult...typical man," Mandy was shaking her head, but smiling. "Kelly's a fantastic horseman, and has a great eye. I guess he saw something in this one that he liked, although I don't know why you would buy a five year old non-three."

Claire understood that meant that the horse had never won three races in his life, and for a five year old, that wasn't a good sign. "I thought you said he was 'incredible' on the track? Only two career wins doesn't seem that incredible to me."

Mandy just shook her head again. "That's what Kelly said. He also told me that the horse's previous trainer said he was a constant runoff, and they ended up doing his conditioning just with a pony, and only working him under a rider....Kelly seems to think he'll be able to gallop him, so he can be my guest. I just hope our insurance is paid up!" she laughed briefly and then turned her attention to Claire as they headed back toward the office. "How'd everybody go this morning?"

Claire had momentarily forgotten that she had a break out day, but her excitement returned as she told Mandy all about her gallop on Blue and the rest of her mornings successes. "I can't believe it just happened!" she exclaimed. "It was like one minute I was afraid I couldn't hold him, and the next, we were cruising along and I felt like I could have held a freight train. On every horse after that, I felt fantastic, like I could've ridden ten more!"

"I knew you'd get there. I guess it is time for you to ride Bubba," Mandy smiled slyly.

Claire grinned; she was amazed at her boss's ability to read her mind when it came to the horses. "I think I'm ready," she said.

"You're probably ready for a 3/8 work as well. I'll look at the schedule and see if we can get a set out so I can work with you and give you some tips."

"Great!" Claire was genuinely excited. A real work, at full speed! She knew the day wouldn't come soon enough.

Mandy went on to see to the horses on the walker, before they were put in their stalls. She was diligent about checking legs and overall well-being of every single horse that had trained each morning. Claire had some time to kill, so she headed back to where the new horse was stalled.

As she approached, she could see him getting restless, pacing back and forth in the confined quarters of the 14x14 stall, which seemed small, considering his size. She approached the entrance of the stall, in which there was not an actual door, but a nylon stall guard clipped to eyehooks on each side of the doorframe. Not the most secure looking set up for a horse who was supposedly so aggressive, but she guessed that they had their reasons for not banishing him to the jail type confines of a fully barred door.

She stood a few feet away from the stall guard, looking in at the magnificent animal. He stayed in the farthest corner, but watched her every move. She clucked softly to the horse and he responded by pinning his ears and shaking his head at her. Smiling slightly, she took a step toward the guard and the big horse reacted by charging the guard, ears pinned and teeth grinding. Rather than stepping back, which is what most would do, Claire stood her ground, somewhat amused by the horse's behavior, but mostly wondering what had been done to him to cause such aggression. The big horse immediately stopped his charge and looked at her, seemingly confused. She spoke softly, and reached out her hand, something she probably wouldn't have done if he hadn't been wearing the muzzle. He took one cautious step toward her, then another. In a second, he was close enough for her to touch. She allowed him to sniff her hand, then reached up to scratch the big white star on his forehead. To her utter surprise, the horse lowered his massive head and allowed her to scratch all over, leaning into her as she scratched behind his ears. He even went so far as to grunt with pleasure as she began to scratch him with a little more force. In that moment, the big bay horse was kind, clearly enjoying the attention that he was getting, and showing no signs of the meanness that he was purported to have.

"What in the name of God are you doing?" Kelly said, in not quite a shout, as he came into the barn. "Do you want to get your arm taken off?!"

"I think you got the wrong horse," Claire said, smiling. "This guy's a puppy dog."

Kelly stopped abruptly and simply stared. "I have seen that horse in full killer mode. I know I got the right horse, but this isn't what he was like when I saw him at the track yesterday. What'd you do to him?"

"Nothing," Claire responded. "I just stopped to pay attention to him. Has anybody ever paid any attention to him other than to train?"

Kelly thought for a minute, and then he had a look of enlightenment. "No. I don't think ever. He was stabled at the end of the row, completely isolated. Nobody ever walked by his stall, and if they did, they always carried a whip to swing his direction if he charged the door. I don't believe that he was hit; it was just used to back him off. It took two grooms to tack him up, and the muzzle wasn't removed until the last minute for his bridle or for his meals," Kelly began to laugh heartily. "I think you just discovered the secret to Reggie."

"What is that?" Claire asked, amused.

"He is just an attention whore who wasn't getting any attention! I would still be on my guard though," he said. "And, you have a new job."

Claire raised a quizzical eyebrow. "What's that?"

"You are to spend some time with him every day. Give him a carrot, brush him in his stall, or just stand there and scratch his head, I don't care as long as he is happy."

Claire couldn't help but smile as she nodded in agreement. Reggie was her new favorite, and in spite of everything she was told about not getting too attached to the horses, she knew she was smitten. She also found that she was in awe of Kelly's skill as a horseman. In a matter of seconds, he diagnosed the problem with the horse and knew the fix. There was no guarantee it was going to work, but she had obviously established a bond with the big bay, and he knew how to use that to the fullest extent.

"I have some things to do before we head to the house, so you can hang out here with him for a while. I don't know that I would take the muzzle off just yet, but I think we'll soon enough. I'll come get you when it is time to go." Kelly headed toward the office, leaving Claire with her new best friend.

Claire hung out with Reggie until Kelly and Mandy were done and they headed up the hill to the house. She was surprised by the modest look of the home, considering how huge and immaculate the barns and pastures were, she expected a house of equal elegance. What she saw was almost completely the opposite of her expectations. The small, ranch style home was nestled amongst some large oak trees, well hidden from the training and stabling facilities. The lilac bushes were beginning to bloom, and haphazardly planted around the perimeter of the home. Claire decided that her favorite part of the house was the view from the front door. She could see the entire track from her vantage point, and she thought about how she would love to have a place like that of her own someday.

The trio entered the home through the front door, and Claire glanced around at her surroundings, noticing that the home, while small, was clean and tidy with win photos of some of the farm's better horses occupying every visible wall. Right as they entered, there was a large glass cabinet that held numerous racing trophies. Some were classic style trophies with horses on top, others were silver platters or crystal bowls with engraving of the particular race in which the prize was awarded. The curio was absolutely bursting with accolades, and Claire guessed that they might need more space, sooner rather than later.

Kelly motioned Claire to the sofa while Mandy headed into the kitchen to prepare some lunch for all of them. Claire took her place on the sofa, noticing that the television was significantly too large for the space that it occupied. Kelly turned it on the Derby pre-race festivities as well as races on the day's undercard and settled next to Claire with the racing form in hand. He wasn't going to waste any time chatting before educating her on the nuances of reading the form, so they got right to it.

Claire learned that every single line on the past performance of a horse gave an immense amount of detail. One line of past performance contained the date and location of the horse's last race, as well as the number of horses in the race, what kind of race it was, who was riding, where the horse was positioned at each call of the race from start to finish, their odds at post time the finish time of the race as well as the top three finishers with a few words description of what occurred for that particular horse during the race. The horse information also gave the owner and trainer's names, jockey's name, age, sex and color of the horse as well as the horse's breeding.

Claire was confused at first, trying to understand how one line of type could contain so much information, but Kelly walked her through it several times, and she gradually began to understand.

Mandy had excused herself momentarily to take a shower, and when she returned, Claire's mouth dropped open in amazement. Her boss entered the room wearing a light, feminine, pale pink tank, and denim Capri pants. It was a look far from what Claire was used to seeing at the barn.

"You have fantastic arms!" She said, gathering her composure. "I have never seen you in anything but coats and sweaters. I didn't know you had such an amazing physique."

Mandy replied, not the least bit self-conscious. "Thanks. It comes from holding all those crazy, tough horses. You have been riding for about 6 weeks now, haven't you?" she asked Claire.

Claire nodded, not sure what she was after.

"Have you taken a look at yourself in the mirror recently?" Mandy continued.

"No." Claire hadn't even thought about it. She was so busy every day, between morning gallops, school and homework, and falling into bed by 8pm every night, she had never really paused to look in the mirror.

Mandy grabbed her suddenly and hauled her down the hall. "Where are you two going?" Kelly called.

"Girl time," his wife said in reply, as they went into the main bedroom. "Take off your shirt," Mandy said, boldly.

Claire hesitated for a moment, but then decided that there was nothing to be ashamed of, except the fact that she didn't have the other woman's uber toned arms and torso. She proceeded to remove her shirt, standing there in her bra, which wasn't holding up much anyway.

"Look in the mirror," Mandy said, smiling.

She did as she was told, looking in the mirror that stood on the large maple dresser. She had to take a couple of steps back in order to see herself from the waist up, but when she did, she couldn't help but grin at the reflection looking back at her. Her shoulders were nicely muscled, lines of definition detailing the smaller muscle groups. She noticed that her triceps were actually noticeable, and her forearms were vascular and defined. Mandy turned her around and she looked at her back. It was the back of a figure model with beautiful definition and tone. As she moved her arms, she could actually see the muscles ripple under her fair skin.

"Damn," She whispered. "That's freaking awesome!"

Mandy laughed and handed her shirt back to her. "It's only been 6 weeks. You're going to get stronger and look better."

Claire couldn't stop smiling. She always wanted to look strong and defined, but she hated the gym. Her mother always had a very toned physique that she had maintained after her college gymnastics career was over. Claire knew she had the genes to look good and strong, but she didn't think she had the desire. Galloping horses was, in her opinion, the best physical conditioning she had ever done, and it was certainly the most fun. She got the figure of an athlete, and she never had to set foot in the gym. What's more, she was getting paid for it, which made it even sweeter.

The two women made their way back into the living room and sat down with Kelly, turning their attention to the horses racing at Churchill Downs. Claire watched with the mentality of a student, asking questions as they arose, and learning everything she possibly could about the horses, jockeys and trainers that were involved in each race. Kelly talked about the different scenarios that could occur during the races, and broke each race down frame by frame for her to watch and learn what to do and what not to do. She listened to the post race interviews intently; paying attention to what both the jockeys and trainers had to say about their horse's performance in the race, and pretty soon, it was time for the big race, the Kentucky Derby.

She had always loved watching the Derby on TV, but this time was different. Her brain was like a sponge, as she absorbed every little nuance of the pre-race activities, the saddling paddock and the actions of the riders and everybody else involved in each individual entrant. There were 20 horses in the race and it was hard for her to keep from jumbling things together. Claire was sitting on the edge of her seat, completely entranced by the picture on the big screen. The horses made their way onto the racetrack, and she immediately welled up, as 'My Old Kentucky Home' began to play. Her thoughts drifted. What if she could be there someday?

What if she could have her own mount, and be there, riding through the post parade, listening to the traditional song of the Derby playing, and the people singing in the stands? The thought sent a chill through her body, and she knew right then and there that someday she would have a mount in the Derby. There was no question in her mind.

The three of them sat silently, watching the horses prepare to enter the starting gate. They each had their own picks, although Claire didn't have much confidence in her skills as a handicapper. Once the gates opened, the silence was broken, and Kelly immediately started cheering on his pick. Claire had to giggle as he got more and more excited, yelling at the TV, mostly yelling at the jockey on his selected horse. As the horses entered the stretch, all three of them were on their feet, cheering on their favorites. When it was over, as it turned out, none of them had picked the winner, but it was still a thrill. The post race excitement was creating a buzz around the winning connections of the horse, and reporters were interviewing the owners and trainer. Claire was eagerly awaiting the interview with the winning jockey, and when she saw him on the screen, she quickly shushed Kelly and Mandy so she could hear what he had to say.

The interview with winning jockey, Ryan Valentin, was short, but Claire was impressed. "I like him," she said, thinking about the incredibly attractive, well spoken man she had just seen, unaware that, in a year's time, he would be the one person who would make her life a little bit of heaven, and yet a living hell.

"Why?" Mandy asked, somewhat amused.

"He's the first jockey I have seen interviewed all day who can complete a sentence without saying 'you know'. He doesn't sound ignorant."

Kelly piped in. "You're right about that. He's based in southern California, and he has been the top rider in the country for several years now. He's comfortable in an interview and takes his job very seriously. I rode against him a few times. He's an incredible rider, but kind of an ass."

"Hmm," Claire muttered. "I want to meet him someday."

"I bet you will, if you do as well as I think you will, you'll be there in So Cal, kicking around with the best of them," Kelly said confidently.

Mandy smiled slyly. "I think it is more than that," she said. "I think Claire might have a little crush. He isn't too hard on the eyes anyway."

Claire blushed and shook her head. "No, I just respect him is all. I could probably learn a lot from him."

"Probably you could," Kelly answered, "but one piece of advice...don't ever date anybody on the racetrack...it can become a nightmare."

Mandy nodded, but Claire was confused. "Didn't you two meet on the racetrack?"

"Yes," Mandy said, "but I was just there to look at some horses. I was 18, and looking for some jumping prospects. I met him at his dad's barn one morning, back when he was actively riding, and it was love at first sight, sort of. The point is, I didn't come to the track until after we met, and most of my work has been done here. I only go to the track if I have to, and to watch my babies race."

Claire nodded, and Kelly continued. "You'll learn that the racetrack backside is a small community, and like any small town, people gossip. They don't have anything better to do. The best thing for you, if you're serious about making it big in this industry, is to keep your nose clean and mind your own business. If you get caught up with the wrong people, it can seriously screw up your career," Kelly's mood changed drastically, and he suddenly looked almost angry. "Stay away from the shit...drugs, booze, sex, everything, and you'll be fine." He stood and headed out the front door.

Claire was taken aback, but Mandy looked at her, offering only a few words of explanation. "Kelly lost a close friend at the track, another jockey. It was a horrible situation and he took it pretty hard," that was all Mandy cared to share, as she walked out to her husband.

A few days later, Kelly agreed that Claire was ready for a work, and, as Claire had hoped, Max was going to be her first worker. Mandy was going out on Bubba, and they were going to work the two geldings 3/8 of a mile. Kelly went out with William and said he wanted them pretty fast, around 36 seconds flat. Claire knew she would have to rely on Mandy's clock for that, but she wasn't concerned. She shortened her stirrups a couple more holes, and got herself ready, unsure of what to expect, but she was excited and not the least bit nervous. Max was a pro, and he would take care of her, even if she completely screwed up. They began their easy gallop down the stretch for the first time. Claire felt good, and Max was relaxed, but Mandy had her hands full. Bubba was pulling harder than Claire had ever seen, and Mandy was constantly moving the bit, forcing him to turn his head from one direction to the other, as for him not to grab the bit and go.

"He gets even tougher when he has company," Mandy said, obviously struggling with the big gelding. "That's why he always gallops alone, I couldn't do this every day!"

They made their way around the turn and into the backstretch. Mandy had Bubba placed on Claire's outside, and as they headed down the stretch, she told her to start dropping down to the rail. Claire got a visual on where the 3/8ths pole was, and began easing Max over to the fence. He knew immediately what was happening, and automatically began to lengthen his stride. Mandy released her stranglehold on Bubba, and the horses began to increase their speed, matching strides as they hit the turn and the post where the clock would start. Claire sat as still as a statue, trying to emulate what she had seen jockey's do on television, and what she had seen Mandy do several times in the past weeks. The duo sped through the turn, and Claire was hit with a surge of adrenaline as she felt the power of the massive horse, pushing to keep his head in front of his opponent.

"Pick it up down the lane," Mandy called, the wind whipping the words out of her mouth as she spoke.

Claire smooched to Max as they came out of the turn. He switched to his right lead, smooth as glass, and flattened himself down for a drive to the finish. Mandy and Bubba were right next to them as both horses surged to the wire. Claire passed the finish line, and only then did she realize how tired she was. The shorter stirrups, and the different position in the saddle were something that her body was not yet used to, and she was winded, even after such a short work.

The horses pulled up on the backside, and as they turned to jog back, Mandy was grinning as she looked at Claire. "Pretty amazing, isn't it?" she said.

Claire couldn't stop smiling, responding between breaths. "What a rush!"

Mandy laughed, and they finished the jog back in silence. Claire was floating on air. She didn't think she would ever come down from the high of that speed. Nothing she had ever done on horseback before that moment could compare to the sensation she had while flying down the lane on the big chestnut gelding. She knew that no matter how well she did as a jockey, she would never forget that first work.

"How'd I do?" she asked Kelly, before she was even close enough to him to slow down to a walk.

Kelly sensed her excitement. "You did great, and you looked like a pro. I like your style...you don't interfere with the horse; you just let him do his job. It helps that you're so light Max probably didn't even realize you were up there!"

Claire relished the compliment, as they headed back to the barn. As usual, Mandy's clock was right on, and Claire understood what she meant about getting a sense of timing. She knew she was a ways away from having that kind of clock, but she no longer thought of it as a foreign concept.

At the barn, they all dismounted their horses, and the two Thoroughbreds were put on the hot walker. Kelly handed William to Claire and told her to mount up. She looked at him quizzically.

"I am going to take out your baby," Kelly said. "I thought you might want to watch his gallop."

Claire realized what he was talking about as Juan led Reggie out of the barn. The massive gelding's bay coat shone in the morning sunlight as he pranced in a circle around his handler. He didn't look aggressive, just excited. The big gelding hadn't been out to the track since his arrival on Derby day, and his body was quivering with pent up energy.

Juan gave Kelly a leg up and they headed to the track. Reggie towered over William, but he seemed to relax in the presence of the old Quarter Horse. Claire was interested in this gallop. She was eager to see Reggie train, but she was also looking forward to seeing Kelly ride something other than a pony horse.

Kelly started at a jog up the stretch, and Claire positioned herself opposite the finish line, which was the best vantage point for the entire track.

The big bay turned and was instantly in a fast gallop. Claire watched Kelly intently, as he positioned himself to have the most leverage against the monster underneath of him. Reggie continued to pick up speed, and Claire thought he was going a bit fast, but she figured Kelly knew what he was doing. By the time they were about halfway down the backstretch, Reggie was absolutely flying, and Claire knew something was wrong. Kelly had said nothing about working the horse, and his position indicated this was not planned. She watched them pass her, and noticed, while Kelly was cursing under his breath and pulling with all his strength, he wasn't panicking. Claire had assumed, that like the other horses, Reggie would just allow himself to be pulled up after a lap around, but she was wrong. He kept going, maintaining his speed, and while Kelly kept his cool, Claire could tell that the rider was going to tire well before the horse.

As they came into the stretch for the third time, she heard Kelly yell. "Grab me, Claire!"

Without hesitation, she kicked William forward, and he was in a canter almost immediately. She positioned the pony close to the rail and held him controlled, watching as Kelly approached. William began to pick up speed, and as Reggie came up on them, the pony put forth a burst of speed, maintaining pace with the Thoroughbred and allowing Claire to reach down and grab Reggie's bridle. Once he was held, the horse slowed with the pony and they pulled up on the backside. Oddly enough, the big bay didn't seem much the worse for wear after nearly working for a full two miles.

"Thanks," Kelly said, trying to catch his breath.

He didn't talk much on the way back to the barn, sometimes muttering an expletive or two about his mount when Reggie would shake his head. They got back to the barn and Mandy came out to grab the horse. "How did he go?" she asked her husband.

"Son of a bitch ran off with me," Kelly grumbled as he took the saddle off the horse.

Mandy tried not to smile, but she couldn't help it. "When was the last time you were run of with?" she asked him innocently.

"When I was a frigging bug," Kelly snapped, as he stalked into the barn.

"What happened?" she asked Claire, once Kelly was safely out of earshot.

"I am not really sure," Claire explained. "From the get go, Reggie was going fast, and then all of a sudden it looked like he was in an all out work. The only thing is, he didn't pull up, he just kept going. I think he worked about two miles, and then Kelly yelled for me to pull him up and I did."

Mandy put the bay gelding on the walker and watched him for a moment before speaking. "He certainly doesn't act like he just ran off for two miles. Maybe we should take him out again!" she laughed, then came back to where Claire was standing with William.

"Good old William," Mandy said, rubbing the old gelding's forehead. "He's still got it, doesn't he?"

Claire felt guilty. She was so worried about Kelly and Reggie that she had forgotten about her dear pony's stellar performance in picking up the runaway. He had acted quickly, knowing what was expected of him, enabling her to do what she needed to do without worrying about her mount. It occurred to her that he was more than just a companion, and while his job was mostly to just walk back and forth to the track with the flighty Thoroughbreds, those few times he needed to really work, he was always ready.

She wrapped her arms around his neck, giving the horse a big hug, hoping it would make up for her lack of acknowledgement immediately after the incident. William nuzzled her briefly, then began to rub his head on her shoulder, clearly wanting to be rid of the bridle so he could have a proper head scratching.

Claire was in a hurry, as she had to get to school, but she was thrilled. She had no idea how she was going to focus on a day of school after the day's events. Her first work and a runaway made for an adrenaline packed morning, and she was grateful there was only a couple more weeks before graduation. Once school was done, she could focus all of her energies on her work, and the dream of becoming a jockey would be that much closer to becoming a reality.

CHAPTER 7

The next couple of weeks seemed to drag by. Claire was eager for graduation, but she also was looking forward to her brother's graduation from Syracuse, knowing that after, Colin would move back home while he waited on news of where he would be working in the fall.

The weekend before her own graduation, she and Robyn loaded her mother into the van, and made the drive to Syracuse to watch Colin's ceremony. The day was pleasant, and the outdoor commencement was beautiful. Colin graduated with honors and Claire and Robyn yelled the loudest of anybody when his name was called. Claire had looked at her mother while Colin took the stage, but she was greeted with the same blank expression as always. Her brother had always been mom's favorite, and she had hoped this event would draw some expression of recognition, but still nothing. She was beginning to think there really was nothing there, and her mother was just a shell, with a mind no longer cognizant of what happened around her. Claire often thought about what it would be like to have every single memory that you had completely obliterated, and it was something she couldn't even imagine. She felt bitter about her mother's physical losses, but not as much as the fact that there was no longer life in Cora's eyes. Those brilliant blue eyes that Claire and Colin both shared, were an empty pool. There was no depth or motion, just flat.

They returned home that evening, and she couldn't wait until morning when she would be back on horses. Mandy was working Reggie the next morning, and Claire was more excited about watching the work than she was about her own mounts for the day. She hoped that she could get her jockey's license in time to ride Reggie in a race, but Kelly was insistent that she wait until fall before she even apply. Mostly, she was eager to get to Finger Lakes and begin learning about real track life. The sheltered life on the farm was doing nothing to prepare her for the realities of the racetrack, and she felt the sooner she could see what she was really in for, the better she could prepare for life as a jockey.

Sunday morning dawned with the threat of rain, and Claire hoped that it would hold off until she was finished, as she didn't care for galloping in the rain. When she arrived in the barn, she was greeted by Mandy, whose hand was bandaged.

"What happened?" Claire asked, concerned.

Mandy shook her head as she answered. "I was stupid. I got too close to Reggie yesterday when I put him on the hot walker. He kicked out and grazed my hand. I didn't break anything, but it's swollen and still hurts like hell. You're going to have to take over these horses this week."

Claire felt terrible for Mandy, but this provided her with a great opportunity. "I can handle it," she said confidently before she remembered that she still had one week of school. "But I still have to go to school in the mornings. I can't ditch classes in the last week."

"And I don't expect you to," Mandy smiled. "If you can get here a half hour earlier in the morning, we could get out a couple more and we will work it so you get on the most important ones, and anything that can wait will just have to go another time. Kelly can take what you don't get when he gets back from the track."

"Okay," Claire agreed. Getting up early in the morning had become easy, and she didn't figure an extra half an hour was going to be a big deal.

Mandy brought William out, and Claire got ready to get on her first of the day. She was surprised when she saw Juan bring out Reggie.

"I'm riding Reggie?" Claire asked, both excited and a little nervous.

Mandy nodded. "He really needs to work 5/8, and I can't do it. I will break you off with William, and then I'll pick you up when you are done. All you need to do is hang on and let him do the rest."

"What about your hand?"

"William will work fine off of leg cues, so I only need to hold the reins with my left hand, he won't pull me, and my right hand is fine, I should be able to pick you up with no problem."

Claire was uncertain, but she allowed Juan to leg her up anyway, and the pair headed toward the track. Immediately, she became aware of the massive horse under her. Sitting on Reggie made Max feel like a pony, and the big bay obviously had the desire to run that Max sometimes lacked. As they jogged up the stretch, Claire noticed that Mandy was hiding the pain in her hand, trying not to wince as she held William's reins while Reggie pulled against both of the women. She readied herself for the work as Mandy let her go before she reached the five-furlong pole. Reggie instantly was into a full work, and the force of forward surge took Claire by surprise. She gathered herself and just sat, letting the herculean horse do his thing. He was so powerful, with a stride that positively ate up the ground; Claire couldn't help but feel like she was moving faster than the world. The horse was still pulling against the bridle, and she let him out another notch, not knowing how fast she should be going, but not really caring. In that minute, she was invincible. Reggie rolled down the stretch; his stride increasing even more and Claire understood what it felt like to ride a truly classy horse. She guessed that the rush of coming down the stretch in the Kentucky Derby could compare to the feeling she was having at that moment. As they passed the finish line, she stood and began to try to pull Reggie up before she reached Mandy, in hopes of saving her hand some of the pain. Her mount immediately took a hold of the bit again, and began to pull against her. After that 5/8 work, she knew she didn't have the strength to get in a tug of war with him, so rather than just pulling, she wiggled the bit in his mouth and began to talk to him.

"Easy there, big guy. Can you please come back to me?" she whispered as she continued to work the bit. "Please come back.....atta boy," Claire was surprised as Reggie began to slow himself down. He didn't make it easy for her, she had to work every second, but he was responding.

She managed to pull him up before they reached Mandy, and her boss was obviously impressed with Claire's handling of the monster horse.

"Wow!" Mandy exclaimed. "What did you do to him? I didn't think you would be able to pull him up...Kelly can't even pull him up. That work didn't seem to take much out of him, so what's your secret?"

Claire shook her head, because she wasn't sure if what she had done was anything special. "I'm not sure. When I started to pull him up, he started to pull back, so I just asked him nicely to come back to me, and he did."

"You asked him nicely? What, he needs his riders to be polite?"

Claire smiled as she replied. "I don't know. I just know that I am not strong enough to fight him, so I just asked him with my voice and my hands, and he responded. It wasn't easy, he still made me work, but he did come back."

Mandy clipped the lead rope to Reggie's bit as they walked back down the track towards the barn. "Impressive," she said. "You really seem to have a connection with this horse. I'll pass that onto Kelly. He might want you to start galloping him regularly."

Claire was flying high. With the combination of the adrenaline of the work, and the complements of her boss, the day couldn't get any better. She finished her morning rides and headed home. There were a few last minute projects to do for the last week of school, and she didn't want anything to interfere with her work at the farm. Things were finally rolling, and this final week of school was a necessary annoyance.

As Claire was driving home, she began to think about what was going to happen once school was finally over for good. She had a ton of questions about her future, but not enough answers. Her bank account was no longer empty, but she knew she would need that money down the road. Where was she going to ride? When was she going to ride? How much more did she have to do before she was going to be able to ride? These were all things that she was concerned about, but she would be able to get the answers she needed after graduation.

*

Her high school graduation was uneventful, and in truth, she would have preferred to not be there at all, going through the motions as necessary, but her mind was elsewhere.

After the ceremony, she went home with her family and Colin prepared a hugely elaborate dinner consisting of all of Claire's favorites: spaghetti with homemade sauce and meatballs, fresh garlic bread and sautéed asparagus, cooked to perfection, being crisp and flavorful. Her brother was an excellent cook, and she looked forward to a summer of his fantastic meals. That particular trait was one that he had picked up from their father. Robert had been an amazing cook, and Colin was always tagging along in the kitchen and out on the barbecue, learning everything he could from their dad. Claire didn't have the patience or the flair for the culinary arts. Her idea of cooking was heating up a can of soup.

They ate dinner and chatted about the day's events. Claire was grateful that everything was done, and she could now focus on riding full time. The next day was Saturday, and Claire was going to Finger Lakes for the first time. Several of her regular mounts were scheduled to run that day, and she was thrilled to be able to watch the fruits of her labor the last couple of months as they performed on the racetrack. Colin was going as well, so it was a doubly exciting day. Her brother would finally see what all the hype was about. She hoped he would come to the farm someday to watch her gallop. Her skills had developed significantly, and it would be nice to have somebody to show them off to, other than Mandy and Kelly.

As they finished their meal, the conversation turned toward the possibilities of the following day.

"So, tell me about these horses that are running tomorrow," Colin said to Claire as they were filling the dishwasher. "Are any of them worth betting on?"

Claire shrugged. "I think so, but I don't think you should be betting all your money on a horse race."

"I am not planning on betting all my money, but a couple bucks to win on something isn't going to hurt my bottom line," Colin joked.

"Well, in that case, I think that Max has a good shot, but he can be lazy sometimes. Bubba's race is pretty tough, Wolf should win for fun, and Melody looks good in hers too," Claire rattled, hardly containing her excitement.

Colin looked at his sister lovingly. "I don't know what any of that means. You might as well be speaking a foreign language."

Claire laughed. "I have the form in my room. After we are done here, I'll show you what it all means," she was pleased at the prospect of teaching somebody what she had learned. Her form reading was still a bit shaky, but she knew if she were to teach somebody else, it would further build her confidence.

When they were finished clearing the dinner dishes, Claire and her brother sat on the sofa studying the form. She taught her brother everything Kelly had told her, and a few things she had learned along the way. Colin asked the appropriate questions, and was a fast learner.

After she had sufficiently educated him, he sat back, smiling. "I'm excited to see these horses of yours. I honestly didn't know if you would be able to stick with it, after I saw you that first time you had galloped, but I am glad you did. I think you're going to be a great jockey," Colin reached over to ruffle his sister's hair, and Claire pulled away as usual, although quietly beaming inside. Granted, her brother didn't know much about horses or racing, but she could always count on his support.

*

Saturday morning was clear, with no threat of rain, which was nice. Claire was at the farm at her usual time to gallop her horses for the day, and then she headed home to get herself cleaned up and head to the track for the day's races. She and Colin arrived plenty early, as Claire didn't want to miss a minute of the action and Max was in the first race of the day. They found a place near the fence of the saddling paddock and waited for the horses. Claire was nervous, which she thought was silly, considering she was neither the owner nor trainer of these horses; she was just the gallop girl at this point.

Finally, Max made his entrance into the paddock, led by Mandy, with Kelly following behind, carrying a few pieces of equipment that Max would need. She watched as Kelly put the tiny jockey saddle on the big red horse and he pulled the girth tight. He was being assisted by the jockey's valet, who had brought out the yellow number four saddlecloth and a leather bridle number that he hooked to the right side of Max's bridle when he finished helping Kelly saddle the horse. Mandy lead Max out of the small saddling stall and around the circle of the paddock as they waited for the jockeys. As the riders emerged, Claire took notice of how light and agile the jockeys were, springing up easily up onto their horse's backs. Max's rider looked relaxed and confident as his mount was led out to the track to the bugler's call to post. Mandy and Kelly came out of the paddock and met up with Claire and Colin to watch the race.

"He looks great," Claire said, to nobody in particular.

Mandy spoke up. "Yes, he does. I just hope he runs as good as he looks!"

Kelly remained silent. Mandy had told her that he gets so focused on the horses before the races you might just as well not even try to speak to him.

Claire's eyes tracked the field of horses warming up with their ponies to the backside of the track. This race for Max was six and a half furlongs. That distance was a bit short for him, but it was what was available, and Kelly wanted to get him in a race sooner rather than later. There would be longer races down the road, and this would be more of a conditioning race.

The field arrived at the gate, and although Claire couldn't see much, she listened to the track announcer as he called the loading of the horses. The field was in, and Claire was on edge as the horses were off and running. She couldn't see anything, so she just listened, Max was toward the rear, he didn't break very sharp.

"Don't worry," Mandy said, "he tends to break slow, and then make a run from behind."

The horses were heading into the turn and into Claire's line of sight. She could see Max's yellow saddlecloth, still at the back of the pack halfway through the turn. As the field began to straighten into the home stretch, the jockey gave his horse a crack with the whip and the big chestnut began to pick up his pace, passing rivals as they were surging to the wire. He just wasn't getting their fast enough! The four of them were all screaming as he came to the finish, but his late run just wasn't enough. Max finished third, closing on the front-runners with every stride.

"He did great!" Mandy beamed as they walked toward the track where they would pick up the horse when his rider brought him back. "Just needs a bit more distance. He should win next time."

Claire nodded as Kelly went to get Max and return him to the barn area where he would be getting Bubba ready next. Mandy turned to Claire. "It is time for you to get licensed," she said.

Claire looked at her questioningly. "What do you mean?"

"Well, if you are going to be hanging out at the racetrack, you need a license. Come with me, and we will get you licensed so you can come to the backside, and you'll be able to come in when you start working here in the mornings."

"Okay. I guess I'll be back," she said to her brother. He shrugged, and said he was going to get something to eat and he would meet her when she was done.

Mandy led Claire into the main grandstand area where they went into the licensing office. The pleasant looking, plump woman at the desk handed Claire a form that she had to fill in, so she pulled up one of the cheap plastic chairs to the small round table in the corner of the office and began to supply her vital information. Mandy was having a discussion with the woman, they obviously knew each other well and were speaking animatedly about the races and the people. The conversation turned to Claire, and she began to feel mildly uncomfortable as she listened to the chatter. Mandy was telling the woman that Claire was going to be big name to come out of the region, and to keep a watchful eye on her career as she was sure to be a success. When she was finished filling out the paperwork, she approached the counter and handed the clipboard to the woman, whose name was Donna.

"All finished?" Donna asked, as she took the clipboard from Claire.

"Yep."

"Alright then, come over here and let's get your fingerprints taken." Donna said as she stood with what seemed to be great effort.

"Fingerprints?" Claire questioned.

"It's the law. If you are going to be licensed, you have to have your fingerprints submitted. You're not a felon are you?" Donna laughed.

Claire giggled. "No. Not last time I checked."

Claire did as she was instructed and got her fingerprints taken. After that, she stood for her photograph, and a few moments later, Donna handed her a professional, laminated racetrack license, stating that Claire Durham was an exercise rider at Finger Lakes racetrack. She was absolutely bursting as she looked at her photo.

"You're official," Mandy said as they left the office, thanking Donna for her services and promising to come back and visit when they had time.

"Awesome!"

"You're a step closer to getting your jocks license, but remember, every track has different rules for licensing, and every track requires a license. Don't forget, or you won't be allowed to ride," Mandy warned.

"There is so much to remember!" Claire said, exasperated.

"You hang out here long enough, and it will become second nature," her boss said reassuringly, as they headed out to find Colin.

They found her brother near the fence by the finish line. Mandy excused herself to go back to the barn area, and Claire decided to stay with her brother and make her first excursion to the backside at another time.

Bubba's race was next, and Claire and Colin headed to the paddock again.

They watched the bay gelding get saddled, in the same process as Max except that Bubba wore the blue, number three saddle cloth. The horses headed to the track again and the same routine was followed.

Colin spoke to Mandy when she came out of the paddock. "Is he worth a bet?" he asked.

"I think so," she said. "He's on his toes, and he looks fantastic."

"Alright," Colin replied heading to the betting window.

Mandy turned to Claire. "Quiz time. What do you expect to happen in this race, based on the form?"

Claire had memorized every detail of each horse they had running that day, so she told Mandy everything she could think. "Well, this race is

6 furlongs, which is Bubba's favorite distance. He has proven that he is a sprinter. He likes to go straight to the front and go as fast as he can for as far as he can. Sometimes that works and sometimes it doesn't. He hasn't had a race since December, so he might come up a bit short, and this is a tough field, but there is no other speed in the race, so he might just be able to carry it all the way."

"Good," Mandy said. "Now what do you think personally, knowing the horse like you do?"

"I think he's ready," Claire responded.

"Me too. I might just go have a bet on him. He is about 10 to 1 right now, which are great betting odds."

Mandy headed off to follow Colin, and Claire stood by the fence, deciding to keep her money in her pocket. They returned, just in time, as the horses were loading into the gate at the far side of the track again. The announcer gave his familiar call as the gates sprung open, and Claire heard that Bubba had broken sharply and was in the lead heading down the backstretch. She watched the field come into the turn with Bubba about three lengths clear of the field. As the horse rounded the turn and straightened for home, Bubba was maintaining his lead, but Claire could see the jockey going to the whip, trying to encourage the horse to hang on for the final furlong. Again, they were all screaming as the horses were coming to the finish, the field closing the distance on Bubba. Claire was sure that he was going to get caught, as one of his rivals was rapidly closing ground, coming to even terms as they crossed the finish line.

"Did he get it?" Claire asked Mandy, once they stopped screaming.

"I don't know. That was awfully close."

They all waited anxiously for the results of the photo finish, and when the announcer called that Bubba had in fact held on for the win, they erupted with cheers.

The jockey brought the bay horse back to the winner's circle, and Kelly went to grab the horse's bridle and circle him so that Mandy,

Claire and Colin could get into the win photo. After the picture was taken, Kelly headed back to the barns with Bubba. Mandy followed, as she wanted to help get Wolf ready and Claire and Colin headed to cash Colin's ticket.

"How much did you get?" Claire asked as her brother walked back to her, grinning from ear to ear.

"Enough to buy us dinner," Colin said, still grinning.

Claire wasn't satisfied. "How much did you bet?"

"Ten dollars to win at odds of 11 to 1."

Claire did some calculations in her head. "You made over $100!"

Colin just smiled. "I'm going to put another $10 on Wolf, and then I'm done for the day. I know how to quit while I am ahead."

They wandered around the grandstand area, killing time before Wolf's race. Colin was on a high from his winnings, and Claire was on a high from watching her favorite horses run. The conversation was animated, and they discussed fanciful scenarios about Claire becoming a jockey and winning the Triple Crown. She felt like anything was possible as she absorbed the electric atmosphere of the racetrack and what it felt like to win, even if she was only watching the win. Certainly the sensation of riding down the stretch and crossing the finish line in first would be the rush of a lifetime.

As they headed to the paddock to watch Wolf be readied for his race, they were quiet. Claire studied the big gray horse, his dapples shimmering silver in the afternoon sun, and thought that he couldn't look any better. She had learned that Wolf was one of the top older horses at the racetrack, and this race was going to be a prep for the stakes races for older horses that would start in another month.

The horses went through the post parade, and Mandy hurried back to the barn, as Melody was in the next race, and she wanted to bring her up so Kelly could watch Wolf, although he was clearly nervous about the race. It was the most important of the day, and he hoped for a good performance. Colin headed off to place his bet, and Claire stood by herself, watching the horses move into the starting gate, which was placed near the fence where she was standing as a one mile race would be the full circuit of the track. Claire was intrigued by the loading process, watching the men on the ground, called the gate crew, expertly handling the horses, bringing them into the gate and keeping them quiet while the field loaded. The gates sprung open, and Claire was hit with the surge of power as the full field of 10 horses broke from the gate in unison and worked their way into positions on the course. Wolf was relaxed, sitting about mid-pack going into the first turn. Along the backside she noticed his jockey had a tight hold on the reins, and Wolf was pulling, eager to pass rivals. Going into the far turn, the jockey had the big gray horse sitting in third position, right on the rail, and as the horses came out of the turn into the stretch, the leaders drifted out wide, and Wolf shot through on the rail, his stride lengthening with every step as he pulled away from his competition, winning the race by about 5 lengths in the end.

Claire and Colin were jumping up and down, and ran to the winner's circle to get their picture taken again. Claire spoke briefly to Kelly as they waited for Wolf to return. "That was pretty amazing!" She said, out of breath from all the yelling.

"He ran a good race. I'm glad his jock was patient enough to wait for that hole to open up, although if it hadn't he might have been in trouble. It was a good win though, and he will be tough in the stakes series this summer, assuming he stays sound."

Claire watched Kelly head out onto the track to pick up the horse and she found her place in the winner's circle for the photo. After the picture, Colin went and cashed his ticket, which was substantially smaller than his winnings with Bubba, and met Claire back at the paddock for the last race of the day, which, as it would happen, would be the last race of Melody's life.

The plain little filly was antsy and on her toes, but her dark bay coat shone like mahogany in the sun and her feminine head tossed playfully as they went through the post parade.

Claire and Colin took their places on the rail near the start of this next mile race, and Mandy joined them. "Last one," she said, sounding tired and relieved. "She should run well, although I am not expecting a win. Top three would be nice."

Within moments, the field was off. Melody was sitting about mid-field, looking good and moving easily. The field made their way towards the far turn and suddenly something was off. The filly's jockey was standing in his irons, trying to pull her up, and then she fell, sending her rider flying over her neck and into the paths of the horses behind. Mandy began to scream, and Claire was frozen, stunned. Neither horse nor rider was standing and Claire's stomach dropped. The rest of the field managed to avoid the fallen pair, but she didn't know what was wrong.

"Claire! Come with me!" Mandy screamed and they ran to the gate crew's truck that had been parked by the fence. The rest of the horses crossed the finish line as Claire and Mandy sat in the back of the speeding truck heading for the fallen horse and rider. Claire saw the ambulance stopped, tending to the rider, and the track vet, who was riding in the ambulance, was at Melody's head. They jumped out of the truck before it had come to a stop and ran to the aid of the filly.

Claire's stomach lurched when she took in the gruesome scene before her. Melody was flat on her side, her breath coming in short, deep rasps and her left front leg was hanging at a grotesque angle.

It had been snapped in two, and was only being held together by fragments of skin. Claire took a step backward, afraid she was going to vomit, as Mandy sat in the dirt of the track and held the filly's head in her lap, stroking her face and speaking softly while tears streamed down her cheeks. The track vet spoke to Mandy, but Claire couldn't hear what had been said. She saw her nod and the vet immediately returned to the ambulance to retrieve the things that would be needed.

The vet worked quickly and quietly. Melody would be euthanized right there on the track. Her injury was so catastrophic that it was not worth prolonging the filly's suffering. Mandy held Melody's head while the vet placed the injection, and within moments, the filly took her last breath in the arms of her master. After a few moments, Mandy stood, her body shaking with sorrow and exhaustion. Melody's body would have to be loaded onto the trailer and other people had to do their jobs. Claire approached her boss, but stopped short, not knowing what to say. Melody's jockey had come to Mandy's side. He took her hand in his and very quietly said. "I'm so sorry," he then got into the ambulance and rode back to the jock's room.

Claire began to sob hysterically, and Mandy came and put her arms around her, hugging her tightly while trying to control her own tears.

"Come on," she said, pulling Claire away from the scene and towards the barn area. "We don't need to stay any longer."

Claire nodded and allowed herself to be led away.

They went to Kelly's barn and straight into the tack room. Kelly was sitting at the desk and looked up at them as they entered, his eyes glistening with tears. He stood and hugged them both and for a moment they were all three locked in an embrace of sorrow.

Kelly was the first to speak. "It's my fault. I shouldn't have sent her out today. I should have noticed that something was wrong."

Mandy shook her head. "Nothing was wrong. She was perfect going into that race. She must have taken a bad step."

Claire looked at them both. She didn't know if the question she was about to ask was appropriate, considering the circumstances, but she felt she had to ask it anyway. "What happened? Did the jockey make a mistake?"

Mandy shook her head again, taking a deep breath in order to control her emotions as she spoke. "It wasn't his fault. It wasn't anybody's fault. Maybe we overlooked something, but I don't think so. She was right as rain going into the race. Did you ever feel that she was off during her gallops or works?" She asked, looking at Claire.

"No. Never."

"Well then, it was just an accident. We'll probably never know exactly why it happened, but I can tell you that she was sound. We would never send out a horse we had any concerns about."

Kelly looked hard at Claire. "This is racing Claire, and it is something you just learned the hard way. You can experience the highest of highs and the lowest of lows in a matter of minutes. You'd better grow some thick skin if you want to succeed in this business."

Claire was shocked by his coldness, and she didn't think about her next words as they fell out of her mouth. "Don't you care about what just happened? How can you just shrug it off so quickly? Did that filly mean so little to you?"

Kelly was angry, and Claire instantly regretted what she had said. "Do you really think that I don't care about my horses? Is that what you have learned in these last few months you've been with us?"

Claire shook her head hard. She knew that Kelly and Mandy cared more about their horses than most people, and she could feel her throat tightening. She didn't want to cry again, but she didn't know what to say.

Kelly continued. "In the ten years that I have been training horses, I have only ever lost three. I took every one personally, and spent the days following trying to figure out what I could have done differently, blaming myself for whatever happened and swearing it would never happen again. But the plain fact is, it happens. It sucks, but it happens, and if you think you're going to go through your career as a jockey and never be on a breakdown, you have another thing coming. It happens to everybody, jockeys and trainers alike, and if you don't think you can handle it, then you better not be in this business."

Claire nodded as she looked at the floor. She remembered Colin was somewhere on the front side, waiting for her to return, so she excused herself and said she would see them at the farm in the morning.

She walked slowly to the grandstands, where Colin was waiting for her in the same place she had left him 45 minutes earlier, but it felt like a day ago. He approached her, with concern in his eyes. "What happened?" he asked.

"We lost her," was all Claire could manage to say before breaking down again. Her brother held her tightly and let her cry.

When she had regained her composure, they turned to leave, Colin's arm around his sister's shoulders as they exited the grandstands and headed to the parking lot. As they got in the car, Colin paused, clearly trying to collect his thoughts before speaking. "I don't know if this is an appropriate question to ask right now," he said, studying Claire's face, "but, is the jockey alright?"

Claire nodded. The realization dawning on her that human lives were at stake, as well as the lives of the horses. She was so fixated on Melody, she had forgotten about her rider. Fortunately, he was fine, slightly bruised, but none the worse for wear. She remembered he had come to Mandy with his condolences so quickly after the accident, and Claire didn't even remember his name. Is that how it was for a jockey? Were they so expendable that people worried more about the horse than the well being of the human on it's back?

"Are you sure this is what you want to do?" Colin asked his sister.

"Yes, it is," she replied, and they drove home in silence.

CHAPTER 8

In the day's following the loss of Melody, the atmosphere around the farm was somber and quiet. Mandy and Kelly honored the filly with an engraved plaque on the stall which she had occupied, and even with the influx of new horses to the farm, they left her stall empty for a week before moving in a new tenant. Claire kept busy and continued to get stronger. She was consistently galloping 10 to 12 horses a day, and with new horses coming and going regularly, she found it hard to keep track of all the horses she had ridden. Her regulars on the farm were down to Max and Reggie only, as the rest were at Finger Lakes for the summer. There were days when she wouldn't see Kelly or Mandy at all. Kelly was staying at the track and managing the stable there while his dad shipped a load of horses to run in Kentucky, and with the racing at Finger Lakes in full swing, Mandy was spending a lot of time working with numerous trainers to re-home horses that were no longer going to be racing. To Claire's surprise, there were a large number of horses that just weren't suited for the racetrack, and Mandy was on a personal mission to make sure they all went to appropriate homes or retirement facilities. Claire realized just how naive she was when it came to under-standing everything it took to get one single horse ready to run, and she didn't give much thought to what happened to them after their careers were over. At some point, Mandy had explained to her that there were a few trainers and owners out there who cared very little about the long term well being of the horses in their charge, and once their racing careers were over, they would be shipped to the slaughter house, or some other equally horrible end.

Before Mandy ever came to the track, she was active in seeking out exracehorses for careers in jumping, and since coming to the track, she had more resources available to her for re-homing those horses whose racing careers were over. Every single trainer on the track knew and respected her and her mission, and she was the first person that they would contact when they had a horse in need of a new job. Claire admired Mandy's dedication to her cause, and she thought that she might be interested in helping, if she ever had any time!

One morning, about a month after the accident at the main track, Kelly showed up at the farm to watch Claire work Reggie. She handled the big bay with confidence, and finished the work within a tenth of a second of the time that Kelly had asked. As she approached Kelly and William, she noticed that her boss had a serious, yet thoughtful look and she didn't hesitate to ask him what he was thinking.

"I am thinking you're ready to go to the real track," he said with very little emotion.

Claire's mind was racing. Going to the Finger Lakes would mean she was closer to her dream, but she had grown so accustomed to the work at the farm and its more laid back atmosphere, she found she was a little sad.

"Okay. What do I have to do?"

Kelly smiled slightly. "Just show up there instead of here at 6am."

They had reached the barn, and Juan came out to get Reggie. Kelly hopped off of William, walking him back into the barn to take off his saddle. William wasn't ever thrilled to walk on the hot walker, so once

Kelly had him untacked, the groom came to hand walk him for a few minutes before putting him away for the morning.

Kelly motioned Claire into the office with him. She followed and moved the requisite cat from the requisite old sofa, both of which seemed to occupy every single barn office she had ever been in. As she sat, Kelly sat down to his computer and began working on something that Claire couldn't see. She sat silently, waiting for him to open up to her what was on his mind. After a few moments, he did, asking her a question that took her by surprise.

"How's your money situation?"

"Um...fine," Claire said, unsure of what he was digging for. "Why?"

Kelly continued with what he was doing on the computer, not looking at her when he spoke. "Have you been saving what you've earned?"

"Yes. I am trying to save up for a new car," Claire said. Her boss shook his head, still evading her gaze.

"Is that wrong?" Claire enquired. "My car is kind of a clunker, and I was hoping I could save up for something a bit better."

Kelly was still cryptic. "What about your mom and aunt? How are they financially?"

Claire was confused, but she answered his question anyway. "They're alright for a while. Probably not forever though. I was hoping I'd be able to eventually make enough money that I could help them out as well. Why are you asking me these questions?"

Kelly finally stopped what he was doing on the computer and looked directly at Claire. "I'm asking you these questions, because I need to know how prepared you are to support yourself when you begin your apprenticeship. If you're lucky, and have a good agent, you may do well right away, but if not, will you have enough money to pay rent and basic living expenses until things pick up?"

She was even more confused. "What do you mean by paying rent? Why can't I just live at home and ride at Finger Lakes? That's what I was assuming I was going to do."

Kelly sighed and shook his head again. He couldn't blame her, she really didn't know what was going on, but sometimes he felt like he had to explain everything. "Are you really serious about riding, Claire? Do you really want to ride in the Kentucky Derby?"

Claire nodded vigorously.

"Then," he continued, "Finger Lakes is not the place to be. You're talented, I think you could do extremely well, but it would be a shame for you to waste those talents at this track. Where do you suppose the best riders in the country ride? I mean the Ryan Valentins of the business that find themselves with a Derby mount year after year."

Claire shrugged. "I don't know....Kentucky, California maybe."

"Exactly. If you want to ride with the big boys, you have to put yourself in the right place. Mandy and I have been talking, and we came up with a short term plan for you, if you are interested."

She sat up straight, and listened as Kelly spent the next several minutes laying out the details of Claire's new life course according to the Zakarian's. He suggested that she begin working at Finger Lakes immediately. She needed to gain real racetrack experience, as well as gate works and learning the ins and outs of life in the business. The goal was to have her ready to ride her first race by Thanksgiving, allowing her a couple of weeks to earn her first five wins that are required before she is officially able to begin her apprenticeship. After she earned those wins, he told her she should head to Phoenix, where he had an agent contact, and ride there until April, perfecting her skills and winning as many races as possible. If things went according to plan, she could leave Phoenix in mid-April and move her tack to Hollywood Park in L.A., and join the ranks of the top riders in the country. It sounded like a fine plan, with the exception of one small detail.

"Phoenix? Really?" she asked, unable to mask her disappointment.

"I know it wouldn't be your first choice, but I thought it made the most sense. I have an agent contact over there, and he owes me big. He's a good agent when he wants to be, a car salesman and could sell ice to an Eskimo, but it goes without saying that he is probably not the most honest person you will meet in this business. I hate to say it, but honesty is not a virtue that most agents are known for. That's something you're going to have to learn the hard way, there's absolutely no way around it."

Claire just sat, frozen in silence as the thought of leaving her home and family settled itself into her mind. "Isn't there anyplace closer?" she practically begged.

"About 90% of this business is who you know. Your agent is your ticket, and he can make or break you in a matter of weeks. If you're serious, I'm providing you with your first important contact, and he happens to be in Arizona. Your abilities as a rider will speak for themselves, but without an agent, you could be the best rider in the world, and you won't get anywhere. Do you understand what I'm telling you?"

"Yes."

"Does it make sense why I was asking you about money? You will need as much savings as you can, because you're going to be on your own. You'll need a place to live, transportation, money to live, and you will have to pay for your tack and your licensing. Remember also that your agent gets 25% of your paycheck, and your valet gets another 5%. Right off the top, you are taking away 30%. You have to be smart about your money."

Claire nodded, realizing that there was still so much that she didn't know. She felt like a deer in the headlights, but she found her voice, and it seemed the only thing she could say was, "Phoenix?"

Kelly laughed. "Have you ever been there?"

"No," Claire said. "I have seen pictures though. Mostly of cacti."

Her boss just grinned at her. "Yep. Lots of cactus and hotter than the hinges of hell in the summer, but if things go according to plan, you will be out of there by April. It is actually quite pleasant during the winter months, you might enjoy it."

"I like snow," Claire said bluntly.

"Well, you won't be seeing much of it there. Personally, I wouldn't mind spending the winter somewhere I didn't have to shovel out of feet of snow to find my way to the barn every morning, but to each their own I suppose."

Claire was a bit snide in her response. "Why are you here then?"

"Because Mandy loves it here, and wouldn't ever consider leaving. Besides, we're established here. I may bitch about it, but it is still home."

"Exactly."

Kelly realized what she meant. "I'm sorry. I know this is your home, and this is where your family is, but you're still young. This is your opportunity to become a top echelon jockey. Do you think you could live with yourself if you didn't at least try?"

It was Claire's turn for the realization. "You're right. I couldn't." She stroked the cat that had found it's way onto her lap. "I have to speak to my family though, before I commit to anything."

"Of course. And it's not like you're leaving tomorrow. You still have 6 months of work to do," Kelly said as he stood up from his desk. "Let me know what you decide," he walked to the door. "Don't forget to be at the track tomorrow. Same time."

Claire nodded, and remained sitting as Kelly left the office. The orange cat in her lap was purring loudly as she rubbed his belly. Her mind was spinning. Arizona? California? She had never been to either of those places, and now she was being told that she needed to go there by herself, leaving her family and everything she ever knew behind. What would her aunt think? She didn't want to abandon her to care for Claire's mother alone. What about Colin? He would probably be fine without her, but how would she make it without him? Kelly was providing her with an invaluable opportunity, but she was struggling to come to grips with the reality of how her life would change. The one thing that she knew she had to do was go home and talk to Robyn and Colin. If they had any feelings that she shouldn't go, then she wouldn't. She would be a jockey at Finger

Lakes, and she would live with the knowledge of a missed chance. She wouldn't sacrifice her family to chase her own fancies.

The drive home seemed shorter by half as Claire's mind continued to shuffle through the various possibilities of ways to address the topic with her family. She was unsure of how she should approach the subject, and decided the best way would be to just be up front with them. As she pulled up to her house, she noticed Ed looking out the window at her. His favorite perch while at their house was on the back of the recliner that butted up to the main living room window. He had a great vantage point to the street, and he could gaze wistfully at the squirrels who made their home in the giant oak tree in the front yard.

Claire entered the house and called a hello to whoever was there as she was removing her boots.

She heard a muffled greeting from the kitchen, probably Robyn and Colin preparing lunch, and she headed directly to take a shower. When she was through, she put on a pair of shorts and a tank top and found her flip-flops. She decided she was too lazy at that moment to dry her hair with more than just a towel, so she headed into the kitchen with damp hair. The sooner she gets this conversation out of the way, the better.

"Hi Claire! How was your morning?" Robyn asked cheerily. She was always cheerful, and Claire never quite understood why.

"It was fine," Claire replied, as Colin came over to her and gave her a one armed hug. His other hand was holding a table knife covered with mayo.

"Damn, girl! You are looking all muscly and cut! What happened to you?" he laughed, ruffling her hair.

"Riding 10 horses a day that want to pull my guts out, that's what happened," she said, as she pulled away for the millionth time from his annoying brotherly gesture.

Robyn piped up. "Well, I think you look fantastic."

"Thank you," Claire responded, proud of her new physique. "What's for lunch?"

"Turkey sandwiches, Colin style," her brother replied.

Claire smiled as she stole a pickle from the jar. As far as she was concerned, her brother made the best turkey sandwiches on the face of the earth.

Robyn went out to the living room to wheel Cora in to the table for the meal, while Claire and Colin settled themselves down to eat. She was starving, and decided to wait until after lunch was done to begin the conversation. Her brother watched her intently as she ate, it seemed as though he knew something was up, but was going to wait for her to approach the subject. Once she began to slow down, he gave her the opening she needed.

"What's on your mind, sis?" he asked.

She paused for a moment, trying to decide the best way to put her thoughts into words. Finally she just spoke. "Kelly and Mandy think I should go ride in Phoenix this winter to do my apprenticeship."

Colin looked her and smiled. "I know."

Claire startled. That was in no way what she was expecting to hear. She looked over at Robyn, and her aunt just nodded.

"What do you mean 'you know'?"

"Kelly called me yesterday. We talked at great length about our hopes for you as a jockey, and we discussed several options that would give you the best chance for success."

Claire's mouth hung open. She could not believe that Kelly had led her through an entire conversation that morning about what she could do, letting her stress about her family's response, when he had spoken to them before he even spoke to her. "What an ass!" Claire blurted out.

"Now Claire," Robyn said gently "he's a very good man, and he sees the talent you have. He's only trying to do the best for you, and I think he figured by talking to us first, it would take some of the burden off of you."

"He spoke to you too?" Claire was exasperated.

"Well, of course. He wanted to be sure that I'd be all right caring for your mom alone. I assured him that I would be, and besides, Colin will be close by if I need anything."

Claire was simply dumbfounded. All this time she was stressing about this moment, and it was for nothing. "So, you guys are okay with me going to Arizona, and then California, and not coming back for who knows how long?"

Robyn nodded, and Colin spoke. "I can't say it won't be hard. I am going to miss having my little sister to torment, but we'll manage. This is your life Claire, and you need to live it. You can't be making decisions based on what you think everybody else wants. Do what you want. I think Kelly's right on when he says that you have the talent to go all the way. Why not take advantage of the chance he's giving you?"

"I know...you're both right. I guess I'm just scared," Claire finally admitted out loud. "I've never been completely on my own before, and I'm looking at being totally alone in a completely unfamiliar place. You know that I'm not good at making friends, and I am just afraid I won't be able to be the kind of person I need to be in order to succeed."

Colin looked at his sister with admiration, and he thought for a moment before he spoke. "Didn't Amelia Earhart say that if life hands gives you the opportunity for adventure, you must always take it? I think it was Amelia Earhart. Anyway, this is your opportunity for adventure. For God's sake you're 18 years old. Most of your classmates are looking at spending the next four years of their lives with their nose buried in a text book, and you're going to be off touring the country, riding fast horses and making lots of money. Seems like a no-brainer to me!"

Claire giggled. Leave it to her brother to make light of what she anticipated was going to be a heavy situation. "Well, I guess I'm going to Phoenix then."

Colin and her aunt smiled at each other, and they finished their lunch in silence. When their meal was done, Claire wheeled her mother back into the family room while the other two cleaned up the dishes. She wished she had some way of knowing what, if anything, was going on in her mother's head. Leaving mom was going to be the hardest. Not from the fact that she would miss her so much, but in her mother's already fragile state, a bout with pneumonia could kill her. Claire didn't know if she would be able to live with her choice if something happened, and she lost her mother while she was out gallivanting around the country. She sat on the sofa, next to her mom's chair. When she spoke to her mom, she always spoke quietly, hoping that if she were close enough and quiet enough, maybe she could illicit some response from the fragile, yet still beautiful woman whom she had been so close to growing up.

"Mom," she said. "I'm going away. After Christmas, I am going to go be a jockey in Arizona, and then, with a little luck, California. I want to ride in the Kentucky Derby some day, and Kelly says that this is the best thing for me to do. He thinks I'm a really good rider, and I have the ability to ride at the bigger tracks. He's set me up with an agent in Phoenix, and I'll be there by the New Year," Claire paused for a moment, watching her mother's vacant blue eyes. "I'm afraid, but I'm going to treat it like a new adventure. In the mean time, Kelly thinks I'm ready to start working horses in the morning at Finger Lakes. He's going to teach me how to break out of the gate, and I'll get to work with more than just one other horse. It's time I get in at the track and really start learning something. He says I should be ready to ride my first race by Thanksgiving, and he is pretty sure they'll have enough horses for me to ride that I can get my five winners so I can officially begin my apprenticeship the first of the year. He says that would give me an entire year as an apprentice, and put me in the best position to be eligible for any awards. I think he might be getting a little ahead of himself, as I haven't even ridden a race yet, but it is nice to have his support."

Claire stopped talking and watched her mother. Again, nothing, but it felt good to talk to her. She didn't know if anything was understood, or even heard for that matter, but she still always included her mom in her daydreams and fantasies.

The next morning, Claire woke feeling a bit of anxiety. She knew it was unfounded, but she was heading to the "real" racetrack, and she didn't know what to expect. As she headed out the door, the heavy air hit her like a wet cloth. Summertime in upstate New York could be miserably humid, and this day was going to be no exception. Even at 5:30 in the morning, she could tell it was going to be one of those days where she would never feel dry. Maybe a trip to the lake would be in order after the morning's work.

She drove to the track, finding herself a parking place near the backside entrance gate, and headed to the stable area, waving her license at the security guard who was manning the stable gate. He nodded politely as she walked through and made her way toward Kelly's barn. When she arrived, she was greeted by the morning hustle and bustle of the grooms readying their tends for the day's exercise, or grooming those not headed to the track. There were already horses on the walkers, and grooms were actively cleaning stalls and filling hay nets. The pace of life seemed so much faster than at the farm, and Claire found herself watching in wonder as at least 10 grooms maneuvered about the shed row, expertly handling the horses and chatting amongst themselves.

Kelly popped his head out of the tack room door. "You ready?" he asked.

"Yep," Claire replied as she did up the chinstrap on her helmet. Kelly said something in Spanish to the groom nearest to them who nodded and disappeared into a stall about three doors down, emerging moments later with a medium sized, plain bay horse.

"Give this guy a good strong gallop. He shouldn't give you any trouble," Kelly said quickly. "Don't dawdle out there...I have got 12 lined up for you this morning, and we have to account for the track breaks as well."

Claire nodded and got her leg up. As usual, Kelly just tossed her right into the thick of things, and she had to hang on and go with the flow. She remembered him saying when she first started that she needed to stay off the rail and out of the way of the workers, so she backtracked the gelding midway around the turn and then turned him around to begin her gallop. Her mount was steady, but strong, and she forgot any anxiety she had about the morning once she felt the rhythmic strides beneath her and the breeze hitting her face. She pulled the horse up on the backside, after galloping the full perimeter of the track, and jogged him back to the barn. As she was jogging, she took the time to study the activity of the other horses and riders on the track. At the farm it was just her, and sometimes Mandy, but here, there were probably 30 horses on the track at any one time, everything from joggers to gallopers to workers, and she understood the importance of keeping your eyes and ears open. With that many horses on the track, there were bound to be accidents if people weren't careful.

When she returned to the barn, she quickly dismounted, only to be greeted immediately by her next mount. She followed the same routine for her next five horses, and then it was called break time on the track. That was when the track was shut down for training for 30 minutes so that the tractors could be out on the track, turning the dirt and maintaining the surface, keeping safe and even footing for the horses.

During the break, Claire went into the tack room to talk to Kelly. He was deep in conversation with a jockey that Claire recognized to be the one who had ridden Melody when she broke down.

Kelly looked up at her as she entered. "Hey Claire, how'd everybody go?"

"Good," she replied, shifting uncomfortably under the stare of the jockey that was camped out on the sofa.

"Who's this, Kelly?" the rider asked in a voice that seemed a bit more interested than just standard curiosity.

"Glen, this is Claire. Claire...Glen Mason," Kelly introduced them.

Claire held out her hand to the man who stood up from the sofa and shook it firmly.

"So you're the one he's been talking about. I can see why he kept you a secret. When you're up for a real ride, just let me know," he winked slyly, and grinned at Kelly.

"Don't even think about it Mason," Kelly barked. "If you, or any of your pinhead buddies even so much as think about looking at her sideways, I'll put my foot so far up your ass you will be able to read my shoe size!"

Glen deflated slightly. "Fine...you're the boss. We still good for that race on Saturday?"

"Yeah," Kelly said. "Send your agent around."

"Will do," Glen replied and ambled out of the room.

Claire was lost. In a matter of 30 seconds, it seemed like there were three different conversations going on, and she only caught the gist of one of them. "What just happened?" she asked Kelly as he redirected his attention to her.

"That is what you need to expect at the race track. That was pretty mild, some of them won't be so subtle."

"That was subtle?" Claire asked, bemused.

"For those guys, yeah, it was pretty subtle. Don't worry. I've got your back here. Glen will tell his buddies that you are off limits, and they will hopefully respect that. There are perks to being the top barn at the track. Everybody wants to ride for me, so they try not to piss me off!"

"What's happening Saturday?"

Kelly looked at her, initially confused. "Oh, there is a race that we are in, and Glen is supposed to be riding one for me. I told him to send his agent around so we can get the call in the book."

It was Claire's turn to look confused. "The call in the book? What does that mean?"

"Entries for a days races are taken a few days prior to the day of the race. Your agent has the condition book, which lists all of the possible races for that day's entries, and it's his job to get you mounts for the races each day. He will speak to trainers who want you to ride their horses, and mark down in the book, which trainer wants you to ride which horse in a specific race. That is called getting a call, and it is also his job to know the horses on the track and try and hustle you the best horse for each race. A good agent is worth his weight in gold, but unfortunately, the good ones are pretty hard to come by."

Claire could only nod. Yet another thing to put down on her list of things she needs to learn. Every time she thought she could cross something off that list, three more things were added.

"The track is open in a couple of minutes, you better get ready," Kelly said, breaking Claire's train of thought. She headed back out into the shed row, and realized how warm it was getting. She did up her chinstrap again, and prepared to mount her next horse. This one was a worker, going a half a mile. She was excited for her first work on the main track. Kelly told her to keep her eyes open, and if somebody was being stupid and galloping on the rail, she needed to yell. "You have the right of way," he reminded her. "Make sure they know that."

She nodded and headed out to the track. The work was smooth and uneventful. She was beginning to feel confident about the transition from the farm to the racetrack. None of the horses had been too much for her to handle, and she had received some compliments from other riders while she was riding. She wasn't sure if the compliments were genuine, or if people were kissing up to her because she knew Kelly, but she didn't really care. Her life in the race business had reached a turning point and she was progressing faster than anybody had anticipated.

The morning drew to a close, and she finished with her last mount as the track gates were closing for the day. She was one of the first ones on the track, and one of the last ones off, and she was on a high. Her last horse of the day was Wolf, and she was glad to have the opportunity to ride him again. He was one of the ones she had really missed at the farm, and although he was just jogging that morning, she was happy to be up on his back once more.

As she dismounted the big, gray gelding, and handed him off to his groom, Kelly appeared. "Nice job today, Claire. You handled it perfectly"

Claire beamed at the compliment. "Thank you. I felt good, the horses felt good...it was a good day."

Kelly nodded his assent. "Your days aren't always going to go this well, but I am glad your first day here was a success. I tell you what, people noticed you."

"Really?" Claire asked, raising an eyebrow.

"Really. I was standing at the fence with a couple of other trainers watching you work, and they all wanted to know who you were and where you learned to ride. I think you may find yourself with some calls from other trainers when it comes time for you to get your first races in. They were all impressed."

Claire smiled. It was more than she could have ever hoped for, and she still had several months to go before she could race. She could really take this opportunity to show the people around here what she could do....assuming she learned how to do it all first.

Kelly saw the dreamy look in her eyes and brought her back to earth. "Don't let it go to your head though. I told you that today was good, but they won't all be like this. You are going to have days where it feels like you can't do anything right and you are going to want to throw in the towel. On those days, you have to remember the good days and move on."

"I know," Claire said. "But couldn't you have just let me have a few seconds of bliss?"

Kelly grinned and slapped her lightly on the shoulder. "You'll be fine. You're a great rider, and with a little coaching, you will be a great jockey. What we need to work on is your people skills."

"What do you mean?"

"Being a jockey isn't just about riding. You have to be able to talk to trainers and owners. A certain amount of ass kissing is required and you have to learn to not take things personally. You will get taken off horses, people will talk smack about you, guys will come on to you, and you are going to have to learn how to deflect the shit, listen when you need to listen, and above all, know when to tell people to piss off."

"I assume you are going to teach me all of that?" Claire asked Kelly, slightly amused, but also realizing that he was being completely truthful.

"There are some things I can teach you, but a lot of the interpersonal stuff you are going to have to learn by trial and error. The only way for you to know how to respond to a situation is to have been in that situation before. It will take a lot of mistakes, and as long as you are able to learn from those mistakes, you will be fine. Now go home. You have another early day tomorrow, and it looks like today is going to be steamy."

Claire said goodbye and headed to her car. She figured she would be on cloud nine for the rest of the day, and the lake was calling her for a swim. Her brother agreed to join her, and when she got home, they packed a picnic lunch and headed out. While they enjoyed the cool water of the Canandaigua, Claire thought about the previous fall, in this exact same place, where she decided that she wanted to pursue a career as a jockey. It seemed like so long ago, and she tried not to think about how much she would miss her favorite place, because at that moment, her life was perfect.

CHAPTER 9

Autumn in upstate New York was Claire's favorite time of year. She loved the colors of the changing leaves, and even though she had traveled with her family to New England for some prime leaf peeping, she was still convinced that where she lived could rival Vermont's best foliage.

Her work at the track was steady, and she was beginning to pick up on the lingo and the life style. Kelly had been right about her having good days and bad days. Most of her days went off without a hitch, but periodically she would struggle. Some days it felt like every horse had it in for her. She had been dumped more than once, and run off with a couple of times. On those days, she felt like she was making a mistake in her choice of career. She didn't seem to notice any of the other jockeys getting run off with, but Kelly said that it happened to everybody at some point.

One crisp, October morning, Claire arrived at the track, ready on time, as usual. She took out her first several mounts of the morning, and at break time, Kelly called her into the tack room.

"What's up?" she asked, not surprised to see the jockey, Glen, parked on the sofa once again. It seemed to be his favorite hang out at break time.

Kelly was reading the racing form, and barely looked up at her when she entered. "Are you ready for your gate okay?"

Claire was surprised. "You mean today? I thought..." her voice trailed off, as she was not entirely sure what she did think.

"Yes, today," Kelly said. "Glen here says you are, and he'll give you your okay. You need to be cleared by the gate crew, but they have been watching you, and everyone says you're ready, so are you ready?"

"Um...yeah, I guess," Claire replied, nervously. She had been to the gates several times, and had worked out of the gates on her own, but she had a feeling this would be different. "What do I have to do?"

"I am sending out a set of four to break from the gate. You will be on one, Glen on another, and we are waiting for a couple other jocks to show up," Kelly continued. "Just break sharp and work in a group for a half mile. You'll be fine."

Claire nodded, unable to speak. She was about to take on yet another milestone in her quest to be a jockey, and this was a big one. She knew that with the approval of a journeyman jockey, and the gate crew, she could be officially cleared to ride her first race.

Kelly stood and headed out the door, calling orders to the grooms and greeting the two other riders that strolled into the barn. The horses began emerging from their stalls, and within moments, all four riders were mounted and heading towards the track. Claire was thrilled to see she was going to be riding Blue...one of her other favorites from spring at the farm. She knew her mount was experienced from the gate, and all she really had to do was hang on and not hit his mouth or his back when the gates popped open. He would take care of the rest.

As the foursome arrived at the gates, the crew, who had been bantering amongst themselves, came to handle the horses. Claire had watched these men work, and while they may be somewhat crass and obnoxious at times, they knew their business with the horses, and performed their job like professionals. She remembered her first time to the gate. She was nervous and that was transferring to her horse. Her gate man walked her through what she needed to do in order to have a successful break. He showed her how to grab a handful of her horse's mane, and give a bit with her reins so she didn't hit the horse in the mouth when the gates opened and the horse bolted out. That also involved being forwardly balanced in her saddle, making sure she didn't bounce her butt on the horse's back upon leaving the gate. At the time, it seemed like a lot to remember, but after a few times out of the gates, she grew more confident, and proceeded to do well. This, however, would be her first time breaking from the gates with more than just one other horse for company.

As she expected, the men of the gate crew put her second in line. That meant she had a horse on either side of her, and she would be forced to keep her mount straight. A little bit of bumping coming out of the gates could be expected, but as a jockey, you couldn't be taking out half the field by not steering your horse on a straight course.

Blue entered the gates and stood quietly as any professional racehorse would do. Claire pulled her goggles down over her eyes and grabbed a handful of chestnut mane. She kept her eyes forward, but was aware of the loading of the other horses. Glen was on her outside, and he gave her a few words of encouragement. She smiled, remembering her first actual meeting with the man. Since that time, she had actually taken a liking to him. He wasn't as crude as he initially made out to be, and he had helped her out by giving her some valuable pointers from a professional's point of view.

The four horses were loaded, and Claire loved that moment of stillness before the gates sprung and the bell sounded. They were off! Blue leaped out of the gate, straight as an arrow, and Claire moved with him with no interference to her mount at all. To her outside, Glen allowed his horse to drift in slightly coming out of the gate, bumping Claire from the outside and pushing Blue in. It wasn't dangerous, but clearly deliberate on the part of the other jockey. He wasn't endangering her, but he wanted to make her think on her feet. Claire responded by steading her mount and giving him a smooch to move forward quickly. After the initial scuffle from the gates, the foursome sprinted down the track on even terms. Glen kept his mount close to Claire, clearly pressuring her towards the horse on her inside, but she wouldn't be intimidated. She eased Blue out ever so slightly, putting the pressure right back onto her rival. It felt natural to her, and her mount continued to respond to her every asking.

When the work was over, all four horses were eased back to a jog and headed back to the barn. Glen caught up to Claire. "Hey girl, nice job," he said.

"Thanks," she replied, not sure if he was being completely genuine.

He sensed her misgivings. "No, I mean it. You did good. You didn't back away from the pressure, and that is great. Not only that, but you pressured right back. Don't be afraid to do that in a race. These guys will try to intimidate you by putting you in tight, and you have to hold your ground. Don't let them take advantage of you, because if they see they can do it once, they'll just keep on doing it."

Claire nodded. "Thanks, I'll remember that," she said, as they came off the track and headed to the barn.

The grooms came out to retrieve the horses, and Claire and Glen walked over to where Kelly was standing.

"You got your okay," Kelly said to Claire, with a smile.

"Awesome!" Claire said, getting a high five from Glen.

"You found yourself a good little rider," Glen nodded to Kelly. "I don't usually say this about girl riders, but she is talented, and she's fearless. I bet she does well."

Kelly agreed, and motioned Claire to her next mount. No time to celebrate a success when there was more work to be done.

Her next mount was a leggy bay filly that she had grown to like. Her barn name was Baby, and although she was only a two year old, she was quiet and well mannered, and Claire had never seen her do anything stupid. They headed down the track, and began to gallop. While Claire liked the filly, she didn't necessarily like the fact that she was so heavy headed. It felt like she was always pulling her down to the ground, and it seemed as though she would face plant if Claire didn't hold her up. She was accustomed to the filly's way of going, and adjusting to the weight in her hands, when suddenly the weight wasn't there. Claire new in an instant that something was wrong, but she didn't figure it out quickly enough. As she pulled up on the reins, the entire bridle came with them. It didn't make any sense! What was happening? In that split second, Baby also became aware that something was off, and she began to pick up speed. Claire realized with dismay what had happened. Her bit had broken in two, and had completely come out of the filly's mouth. She no longer had any control, and no way of stopping the horse who was going faster with every stride. Claire had a moment to make a decision. She looked up and saw the tracks outrider sitting near the rail out of the turn. She yelled for help, and to her great relief, Peggy the outrider was really good at her job. Peggy kicked her horse into a full gallop and allowed Claire's filly to come up on her outside. She kept pace with the bit less runaway, easing her toward the outside fence where she would be safely away from the other horses on the track, before she reached over and grabbed the noseband of the young horse, which was the only remaining piece of equipment on the filly's head.

The entire event took place in about a minute, but to Claire, it had felt like an hour of pure terror. As she was being pulled up, her mind was racing through all of the possible disastrous outcomes that could have happened and didn't, and she said a quick and silent prayer of thanks to whomever, for keeping her safe.

"Are you okay?" Peggy asked, once she had everything under control.

"I think so," Claire responded shakily. "One minute we were galloping along just fine, and the next minute I had nothing in my hands!"

Peggy nodded. "You're lucky you can think on your feet. If you had waited to call me even a few more seconds, I might not have been able to get to you."

Claire could only nod. Her mouth was dry and her hands were beginning to shake.

They jogged back down the stretch of the track, and Claire was greeted by congratulatory cheers from other riders who had witnessed the ordeal. Many of them saying how gutsy she was just to stay on, as they would have bailed off.

Peggy led the filly off the track, and Kelly came running over. He had watched from his spot on the rail, and was also amazed that both horse and rider had come away unscathed.

"My God Claire. Are you alright?" he asked as he took ahold of the filly, leaving Peggy to go back to the track.

"She's fine," Peggy said as she turned her horse away. "But your grooms need to do a better job of checking your equipment. That could've ended badly."

Kelly nodded to the outrider and thanked her for keeping everybody safe before turning his attention back to Claire and his filly.

"What happened?" he asked, although he saw remains of the bridle and knew before Claire even spoke.

"The bit broke. How does a bit break?" Claire's voice had really begun to shake.

As they reached the barn, Baby's groom came out to collect the filly. Kelly began yelling at the man in Spanish, showing him the broken equipment and carrying on further in the language that Claire still didn't understand. She simply excused herself to the tack room where she sat on the sofa, next to a black and white barn cat, and tried not to throw up. Her whole body shook. The realization that she could have been killed was just settling in, and she wasn't sure how to handle it.

Kelly burst in, obviously angry and flustered. Claire wasn't sure who was more upset, herself or her boss.

"God, Claire, I am so sorry. That was a copper mouth bit, and the problem with copper is that it can be worn down. That filly is so heavy in the bridle, I shouldn't have had that bit in her mouth."

Claire realized just how much Kelly cared about her, and she felt better. "It wasn't your fault," she said. "Nobody could have known. Shit happens, and I am all right. Baby is all right, and if it is any consolation, it will never happen again. Right now, your grooms are checking all of the bits, and I bet you will be getting rid of anything copper. Am I right?"

Kelly looked at her and smiled. "You're right. I just felt so helpless. I could see what was happening, and I couldn't do a damn thing about it!"

Claire laughed. "You felt helpless? Try being in my shoes out there!"

They both laughed. It was cathartic, and Claire began to relax.

Kelly had been leaning against the desk, and he stood abruptly. "Better get out there. Wolf needs to go work a half."

After the last incident, she was not looking forward to getting back up on a horse. She also realized Kelly knew that, and he was making her go back out there and get over it. He understood it was the same concept as if you had been bucked off. You don't go home, you get right back on. So that is what Claire did. She took Wolf out for his work, and he went beautifully. It was just the distraction that she needed from her scare, to return her confidence.

When she returned to the barn after the work, Kelly was waiting for her again. "I know that you didn't really want to do that, but you had to."

"Yes, I know. He went great, and I am feeling better," Claire said.

"Good. Now you can be done for the day. I had a couple more lined up, but you can take a break. You probably need to go home and change your underwear anyway....I know I do."

Claire laughed at the image. "Are you sure you don't need me to get anymore?" she asked.   "Yeah, I'm sure. Go home and relax. You earned it today."

"Alright," she replied, and headed toward the exit.

*

The leaves were nearly off the trees, and the morning workouts were getting colder. Claire had to bundled herself up against the frosty morning air, and there were several times that it was so cold that her fingers were cramping against the reins. She was getting antsy for her first race, and she felt like she was in a holding pattern. Trainers were approaching her, asking when she would be riding, and she could only be vague with her response. Kelly and Mandy were making sure that everything was in order, and she knew they were looking ahead to what horses she could ride in what races, but she was growing impatient.

Finally, the week before Thanksgiving, Kelly called her into the tack room after the morning works. She flopped down on the sofa and removed her helmet, hoping that this was the day, but not wanting to get too excited.

Kelly, in his usual style, didn't waste any time. "I'm naming you on two horses for Saturday." Claire jumped up with a shout. She couldn't help it, and grabbed Kelly and hugged him tightly.

"Thank you!" she practically screamed as he escaped from her hug and forced her to sit back down.

"I want you to listen to me," he continued, seriously. "I'm your agent while you're here. I don't want you winning more than five, and I will make sure I put you on the ones that will get you there. In the mean time, I don't have a problem with you riding a few for other people, but I'm not going to let you ride just anything. I'll be choosing your mounts for a few reasons. One, I know the crap that some of these trainers want to run, and you don't need to be getting on any three legged donkeys just yet. Number two, it is imperative that you don't win too many. I want you to be have one full year of eligibility for the Eclipse awards. I know that may sound lofty, but you have what it takes to get there. I'll get you on a few other horses for experience, but you'll be winning on mine."

Claire could only nod. Kelly was on one of his soapboxes, and she knew better than to interrupt.

"Furthermore," he continued, "I'm being incredibly selfish. Mandy and I have done a lot to get you to this place, and I want my share of the accolades," he smiled at this, and that gave Claire the opening that she needed.

"You guys have done so much for me, and there's no way I'm ever going to be able to repay you. I understand what you said that it's about who you know, and I never would have made it if Jürgen hadn't put me in contact with you."

Kelly smiled at her. "There is one thing you can do," he said.

"What's that?"

"Win the damn Derby."

Claire grinned, and at that moment, she thought she just might.

*

In the few days leading up to her first race, Claire could do little to settle her nerves. She continued her morning work, and went for runs in the evening, for no other reason than to kill time. She found herself fidgety around the clock, and was driving her family crazy. Colin promised that he would come to watch her ride, but her aunt didn't think that the cold weather would be suitable for her mother, so she was going to stay at home and wait for updates from Colin. The racing form became Claire's reading material every evening, and she had memorized every horse in both of her races. In her first race, she was riding a horse named

Open Harbor. He was a nice, gray gelding who had been consistently in the top four, but in his most recent race, he was in traffic trouble the entire way and ran sixth. Kelly told her that the jockey was to blame, and he also told her that the jockey was almost always blamed if the horse didn't win. A trainer doesn't want to admit to the owner that the horse wasn't good enough, or not ready for the race, so the jockey is the immediate scapegoat. That didn't always mean that the jock did anything particularly wrong, but it was easier to blame the rider than admit fault. Unfortunately, jockeys took the brunt of the blame, since only one horse could ever win, jockey's seemed to be blamed a lot. Kelly had told Claire to develop selective hearing when it came to what owners and trainers said after the race. Usually, by the following morning, everything had been forgotten and sights were set on the next run.

Based on what Claire had learned from the form, Open Harbor liked to run mid-pack, and had about a quarter mile burst at the end. He preferred to be on the outside of horses, and in his last race, he broke from the one position, and was never able to get out to his favored part of the track. On Saturday, he would be breaking out of the number seven post going six furlongs, and Claire knew she would have the perfect opportunity to position him where he liked to be in order to run his best race.

Her second mount of the day was a mare that she had galloped and worked regularly at the track. She was a flashy chestnut mare, tall and leggy, with four white socks and a big blaze down her face. Claire liked her, but the mare could be a little flaky during gallops, and tended to be spooky. Her name was Lady Cardinal, and Claire had a feeling that Kelly had set it up just for her. Unless Claire screwed up royally, the mare should win for fun.

When Saturday finally arrived, Claire was beside herself with nervous excitement. She went and did her usual work in the morning, and then Kelly took her to the jockey's room and showed her around.

He had provided her with one of his old saddles, and helped her in the selection of her jockey pants and girths. She was connected with a supplier of goggles and whips and the rest would be provided for her. Kelly introduced her to her valet, whose name was Al, and he promised to take good care of her. She was taken to her 'box', which is where she would keep her things. The ladies room was pretty run down. Apparently there weren't very many female jockeys that came through Finger Lakes, so she had the space to herself. Check in time for the races was an hour before the first post. She told the clerk of scales that her weight was good...she was required to ride at 111 pounds, given her ten pound weight allowance for being an apprentice rider, and then it was a waiting game. Her first race was the third on the afternoon, so she got her gear on and then just sat in the common room, waiting and shaking. She studied the silks that she was wearing. They were the Zakarian farm silks, bright turquoise body, with white sleeves that had three black bars on the upper arms, and on the back, a large black 'Z' with wings. They were familiar to her, as she had seen them on many riders of Kelly and Mandy's horses during the year, but she felt a particular pride in wearing them herself. She sincerely hoped that she could do them justice.

The clerk of scales called the jocks out for the third race, and it was finally time. Claire got her nerves under control, and headed out to the paddock.

"You alright?" Glen asked, as they were walking out.

"Yes....a little nervous though," she replied quickly.

"You'll be great....Listen, I know I can be an ass sometimes, but don't worry, I'm looking out for you out there. I won't let anything happen to you."

Claire smiled stiffly and nodded. "Thanks."

She walked up to Kelly and he held his hand out professionally to shake hers. She took it, but couldn't even force a smile.

"Claire, you'll do fine. Don't worry. This guy will take care of you. I want your first race to be a good experience, and while you may not win, you will learn a lot."

Claire could only nod, as Open Harbor was brought out by Mandy. She approached the horse, as she had seen the other jockey's do, and Kelly legged up effortlessly. While she was gathering her irons and tying her reins, she saw her brother standing by the fence. He gave her a huge smile and a thumbs up. She couldn't help but smile back, in spite of her butterflies. As Mandy walked her through the short tunnel, she stroked her mounts mane in an effort to calm herself, more than her horse.

"You're gonna be awesome," Mandy said encouragingly, and patted Claire on the leg as she handed her off to the pony rider.

From that moment, she was truly on her own. Her pony girl knew the routine, but she was also aware that Claire was a bundle of nerves, and decided against the small talk. They warmed up sufficiently, and before Claire knew it, they were being called to the gates. In a matter of minutes, she was in the hands of the gate crew, and her new career was mere seconds away from a start.

Her horse entered the gate easily, and she was as ready as she was going to be. She tightened her goggles down over her eyes and grabbed a handful of gray mane. Looking down the long expanse of brown dirt of the backstretch, her mind settled. This is what she was meant to do, and she was ready. The gates flew open, and they were off! The gray gelding broke cleanly, but not incredibly sharp. She allowed him to settle into his stride, about mid-pack, and she found herself beginning to relax. In seconds, she had gone from a bundle of nerves, to a confident jockey, expertly handling her steed at 35 miles per hour down the backstretch of a racetrack. She could hear the smack talk of the jockeys around her, but she tuned it out. Her path was clear, and her horse felt strong.

As the field made their way through the turn, she smooched to her horse, asking him to pick up his pace and chase after the frontrunners. She heard Glen next to her, telling her to go for it, and she did just that. They came out of the turn, heading for home, and she was in the clear, asking her horse for more speed. Open Harbor was slow to respond, so she chose to give him a crack with the whip as a little added encouragement. He quickened his stride, and she could hear the noise of the crowd as they moved closer to the finish line. There was one horse in front of her, and while she pushed as hard as she could, she knew they was not going to catch the rival. They swept passed the finish line, solidly in second place, and Claire was elated.

She eased her mount to a stop, and turned him to canter back toward the grandstand area where Kelly and Mandy would be waiting. As she pulled up in front of her mentors, she couldn't stop smiling. They greeted her with cheers, but Kelly reminded her to salute the stewards before she dismounted. She tipped her whip to her helmet, and then tossed it to her valet and swung off her horse.

Kelly grabbed her in a hug, as Mandy grabbed the horse's bridle. "Fantastic job!" Kelly exclaimed. "You did perfect!"

"Thanks.....that was amazing!" she replied, and knew that she couldn't wait until her next mount.

Claire took off her saddle, and Kelly guided her over to the scales. The first four finishers in every race had to weigh in after the race was concluded, so she hopped up on the scale and got the okay from the clerk, before handing her saddle off to her valet and heading back to the jockey's room. She was going over the last race in her head; trying to think of things she could have done differently in order to win. Kelly would be able to provide her with the best insight, but she knew she'd have to wait until the end of the races to speak to him about it. In the mean time, she simply had to dust herself off to be ready for her next ride Her silks weren't changing, so again, it was hurry up and wait. In the meantime, she watched the replay of her first race, hoping to see if she had made a mistake, but she was in awe, watching herself on television. Not too bad for a first timer, she thought.

Glen came into the common room, as he wasn't riding the fifth, and sat down next to her on the sofa. "You did pretty good out there."

"Yeah, thanks," she replied, taking some gratification in knowing that he had run third.

"You should win the next one," he said casually.

"I will," she said, almost regretting her confidence, but not quite.

He smiled at her. "Don't get too cocky. You're only just beginning. I'm not going to burst your bubble just yet, but come talk to me in a week or so, when reality sets in, and you'll know what I mean."

Claire wouldn't let him deflate her spirits and she shrugged it off. Here and now, she was good. Within a few minutes, the riders were called for the sixth race, and she headed back out to the saddling paddock. After the first time, now it was easy, and she walked out to greet Kelly with confidence.

Mandy was there to meet her this time, as Kelly had taken over the saddling duties, and just like her husband had, she reached out to shake Claire's hand. It was a true gesture of professionalism; probably more for the spectators than anything else, but it made her feel comfortable.

"You got this," Mandy said.

Claire smiled, feeling relaxed and ready.

Mandy legged her up, and Claire gathered her irons and tied her reins for the second time that day. She found her brother on the rail again, and he gave her another big smile and thumbs up.

The same pony rider picked her up, and again, they headed off toward the starting gate in the six-furlong chute. Claire found it comforting that the pre-race routine was the same time after time, and she felt more at ease during her warm up, transferring her confidence to her mount.

This time around, Claire would be breaking from the number three position. It would be tighter quarters, but she wasn't concerned. She had found her niche out there on the racetrack, and had discovered that she truly was a fearless rider.

The horses made their way to the gate, and Claire once again readied herself....pulling down her goggles, and grabbing some mane. The gates popped open, and once again, they were off.

Her mare broke more sharply than her previous mount, and she found herself on the front end, only strides out of the gate. According to the form, this horse liked to be on or near the front end, and she was in the perfect position. The field cruised down the backstretch, and Claire sat comfortably on her mount, not needing to be concerned about traffic, but regulating the mare's speed so that she didn't use it all up too soon. As they entered the turn, Claire glanced under her inside elbow, the way Kelly had taught her to look behind her for the competition, and saw that she was at least four lengths in the lead. She still felt good, her mare was tugging at the bridle, and she let her out another notch down the stretch. Aware of what was going on around her, she couldn't hear any competition, but she took out her whip anyway, and gave the mare a slight tap on the shoulder, just to keep her on task. The finish wire approached quickly, and Claire was never threatened for the win. She gave a bit of a fist pump as she crossed the finish line, and looked back, only to see the rest of the field a good ten lengths behind.

Her emotions were a whirlwind as it dawned on her that she had just won her first race. Easing back to a jog, she turned the mare around and returned to the people who had made this opportunity possible.

Kelly and Mandy were both there waiting for her, with ear-to-ear grins on their faces. Claire couldn't help but smile at her bosses as they grabbed the mare's bridle.

"Awesome!" Mandy exclaimed.

Claire couldn't even speak, and Kelly didn't say a word. He just smiled at her and patted her on the knee as he circled the mare, waiting for the necessary people, including Colin, to take their place in the winner's circle for the photo.

After the picture was taken, she jumped off her horse, only to be enveloped in a bear hug by both Kelly and his wife. They couldn't find the words to congratulate her, and when she finally escaped their clutches, her brother grabbed her.

"You were amazing!" he said.

Claire stepped away from him, only to notice that he actually had tears in his eyes.

"Are you crying?" she asked, slightly amused, as she had never seen such emotion from her brother.

"Only a little bit," he replied, and hugged her once again. "I don't care if you ever win the Kentucky Derby...this was good enough for me!"

Claire had to get on the scale, so she gave Colin one last quick hug, and went to finalize her win. The clerk of scales congratulated her, and on her way back into the jockey's room, Glen emerged, and before she even realized what was happening, she was doused with a bucket of ice water. She screamed, and ran into the ladies room, listening to the laughing and cheers of her fellow riders after her initiation into the world of professional jockeys.

A hot shower was enough to calm and warm her, and she stood under the stream of water, reflecting on the excitement of the day. Her first two mounts as a jockey, one resulting in a win, was more than she had ever imagined. Six months ago, she would have told anybody that they were crazy if they had predicted such, but now it was reality. She emerged from the room to cheers from the people who had helped her along the way.... Kelly and Mandy, and most importantly, Colin. He was so proud of his baby sister, and she could see it in his eyes as he grabbed her and hugged her again.

"Did you make any money?" she asked, assuming he had made a bet.
"Nope."

She looked at him quizzically. "Why not? Didn't you bet on me?"

"Of course I did," he replied casually. "But I am not going to cash my ticket. This is going to be worth something someday!"

They all laughed at that, and headed home. The day was over for Claire. She had Sunday off, but she would ride three races on Monday, and it would be Thanksgiving week, and she had a years worth of things for which she was thankful.

CHAPTER 10

In the two weeks after Thanksgiving, before the Finger Lakes meet ended for the year, Claire rode in several races, and she discovered that Glen was right when he told her things would get harder.

After her initial win, she sat down with Kelly and Mandy and discussed the two races, and what the strategy was from there. She discovered that the plan for those first two races was to get her on the track and have a couple of uneventful and confidence building races. The problem was, those races did not prepare her for the reality of daily racing. Very rarely would things go so smoothly in a race, and she soon realized that guiding a mount through traffic was no easy task. She rode horses that tired, and failed to give her anything to work with. After a few races, the other jockeys stopped making things easy as well. She found herself being pressured at times, or being swung wide in the turns, thus losing valuable ground. Every single race was different, and every race was a learning experience. Ultimately, Kelly had planned things beautifully, and she won her five races. The final win was a $50k stakes race on Reggie. The talk around the track was that she was spoiled...Kelly and Mandy were handing her life on a silver platter, and she wouldn't do as well when she had to fend for herself. Probably, there was some truth to the talk. She did feel like the Zakarian's had given her everything she needed to get where she wanted to be, because without them, she would never have made it as far as she had.

With her impending move to Phoenix, she was grateful for the racing experience she had gained. She would be able to go to the new track and focus on refining her skills and winning as many races as possible. Kelly had contacted the man that would be her agent, John Greene, and he was incredibly enthusiastic about having her book. He guaranteed wins, and had already begun spreading the word to the local trainers that he had an awesome new 'bug girl' coming to town.

Almost on cue, the day after the race meet ended, the snow began to fall. Claire loved the snow, and that part of New York got quite a bit of accumulation every winter. For as long as she could remember, they had enjoyed a white Christmas, and this year would be no different. Christmas in the Durham household was always over the top. Claire's mother had been crazy about the holiday, and she would decorate the house from top to bottom. So much so, that their father had likened it to an explosion in Santa's workshop. Cora had been teased about her enthusiasm with the decorations, but after the accident, Claire, Colin and Robyn continued her tradition of extravagant decorating and elaborate Christmas Eve and Christmas Day meal preparations. Colin took over the cooking, while Robyn and Claire were left to do the decorating, and in two years, they had their holiday preparations down to a science.

With a few weeks left before Claire was due to leave for Phoenix, the snow on the ground had brought any thought of riding to a standstill, so she turned to a treadmill, and Kelly's mechanical horse, to keep fit. The mechanical horse was exactly what it sounded like....a large, horse shaped mechanism that held a jockey's saddle and had a horse 'head and neck' that moved up and down, simulating the motion of a real horse. It was primarily a tool used by jockeys to maintain condition, and get in a bit of extra practice when they weren't riding the real horses. She used it to maintain her leg strength and to practice her skills with the whip. Watching the journeymen twirl their whips around their fingers, and expertly switch their stick from one hand to the other in one fluid motion, all the while pushing their mounts without any interference, was something that Claire knew she had to be able to do, and quickly. Kelly spent hours going through the motions with her, critiquing her form and giving her any extra pointers that she required.

During one particular session, Claire was feeling confident with her stick skills and got a bit too aggressive. Kelly stopped her immediately.

"What are you doing?" he asked, somewhat exasperated.

"I'm whipping. What does it look like I am doing?"

Kelly shook his head. "If this were a real horse, he would leave the race with welts. Do you really want to hit that hard?"

Claire was mortified. "Welts? I had no idea. I didn't think I could hit that hard."

"It really doesn't take much, and you're a lot stronger than you think. Leaving welts on a horse can buy you a hefty fine and nice vacation from racing, as you could be suspended. Remember, Claire, your whip is just a tool. You use it to encourage your horse to run faster, but never to punish. If you have a horse that is tired down the stretch, whipping and whipping isn't going to accomplish anything. There are rules as to the number of times that you can hit a horse, and it is up to you to use good judgment with your stick. Does that make sense?"

Claire nodded, and Kelly continued. "I've seen young jockeys continue to hit a horse that is 10 lengths ahead of the field...why? These are all things you're going to have to learn. Use some common sense. When I was a rider, I was fined $500 and suspended for three days because I made a horse bleed. Don't let your desire to win override your better judgment."

"Okay," Claire said. "What am I going to do without you guys when I leave?"

Kelly smiled, but shook his head. "You're going to be fine. It'll be good for you to learn from other people. You can still always call Mandy or I if you need to, but I think you will find you need us less and less. Your agent will have some insight, and if you can find a few journeymen who are willing to help you, you'll be great. I think there are three or four other women riders in Arizona, so that will be helpful too, although you'll be able to ride circles around those girls."

Claire felt grateful for the advice and confidence, and she proceeded to practice her stick handling with slightly less vigor.

As Christmas drew closer, Claire rushed to finalize all of the details of her move. She was going to be flying to Phoenix, and she had enough money to buy a cheap car when she arrived. Colin said that he would sell her Honda and send her some extra cash. She had been contacting apartment complexes, and thought she had found something that would work. There was a fairly large complex, just across the main street from the racetrack where she would be able to get a one-bedroom apartment pretty cheap. She had been studying the city of Phoenix itself, and found it was just a giant, sprawling metro, with the suburbs blending into each other. The layout of the streets seemed pretty straightforward, and she didn't anticipate having any trouble finding her way around.

In spite of all her preparation, she was still terrified. She was less scared of the riding aspect of things than she was about the idea of being alone. All her life she had been close to her family, and her brother had always been by her side. Even when he went away to college, he was still close enough to her that she could see him if she needed to. Now, she was going to be thousands of miles away from everything she had ever known, and she was more than a little apprehensive.

Colin had found himself a perfect job in a suburb of Rochester, teaching and coaching hockey....just what he wanted. He was going to stay living at home with their mom and Robyn. This was comforting to Claire. At least things wouldn't be too different for everybody at home.

Colin and Robyn were busy preparing for what was going to be a Christmas and going away party for Claire. Mandy and Kelly would be coming, as well as Jürgen, whom Claire hadn't seen in months. She was embarrassed about the fact that she seemed to forget about her life at the barn of the man who gave her the contact to get in to the racing business in the first place.

Christmas morning dawned white and beautiful. Claire was still a giddy little girl when it came to opening presents, and the four of them gathered around the tree to exchange gifts. There wasn't much, they needed to be conservative financially, but there was always something special for everybody, and this year was no exception. Colin and Robyn had pooled their resources and gotten Claire a sizable gift card to a department store. Since she was going to Phoenix with only a suitcase full of clothes, she would need almost everything for apartment living. It wasn't a fancy gift, but Claire was thrilled. It was perfect, and it wouldn't take up any space in her suitcase.

When the exchanging of gifts was over, they all moved into the kitchen to prepare the evenings meal, but Claire was more a hindrance than helpful.

"How on earth are you going to live on your own?" Colin joked. "You can't do shit in the kitchen!"

"Colin!" Robyn exclaimed. "Don't curse your sister!"

Claire giggled, but Colin didn't exactly back off.

"She can't boil water. What's she going to eat?"

Claire pushed right back. "I'll eat stuff I don't have to cook!"

Her brother began to laugh. "You going to live on peanut butter sandwiches?"

"If I have to," she replied, stubbornly. "I can do macaroni and cheese, and I'm a pro at ordering pizza!"

"Oooh, health food," Colin jeered. "You'll get fat, and you won't be able to ride."

"You're a jerk."

At that moment, the doorbell rang, and Claire took off to greet her guests, grateful for the opportunity to get out of the kitchen.

She opened the front door to Kelly, Mandy and Jürgen. They all exchanged greetings and she showed them into the family room. Claire had positioned her mother's wheel chair next to the Christmas tree, allowing for enough space for the guests. Mandy didn't hesitate to approach Cora and introduce herself, even though she understood that there would be no response. Kelly hung back, clearly not as comfortable out of the barn as his wife. Claire was excited to have the opportunity to spend time with these amazing people, away from the barn. People tended to look different out of grubby track clothes, and both Mandy and Kelly cleaned up nicely.

Robyn and Colin came in the room, and further introductions were made. Mandy hustled into the kitchen, and Kelly handed Claire a large wrapped box that he was holding, before sitting down on the sofa.

"Merry Christmas," he said.

Claire wasn't sure how to respond. She wasn't expecting a gift, and was kicking herself for not having purchased anything to exchange. "Thank you," she said graciously, and sat down to open the box. To her surprise, the box contained a beautiful, expertly crafted, brand new racing saddle. She knew this was an incredibly expensive gift, and she was not sure how to proceed.

Kelly broke her silence, anticipating her response. "Don't even think about saying you can't accept it. You have done so much work for us, and this is the least we can do. Besides, you'll need at least one or two more saddles, so this is just a starter."

Claire could feel herself choking up, and she didn't want to start crying just then...she knew she wouldn't be able to stop. "Thanks." It was all she could manage as she stood to give Kelly a hug.

Jürgen took that moment to hand her a small wrapped box. "This isn't as fancy as what you just got," he said.

She shook her head, and casually waved him off, sitting once again to open the gift.

Inside the box was a small gold medallion, about the size of a quarter, on a beautiful gold chain. Claire was quiet, but Jürgen spoke quickly.

"It is a Saint Christopher medallion," he said, knowing that Claire was not religious, he continued. "He is our patron saint of travelers, and he will protect you on your journeys."

Claire's eyes welled up again. She had never been much for religion, and she wasn't sure what she believed, but she knew Jürgen was a devoted Catholic, and his gift to her was a testimony to his faith and his feelings for her, and she was touched. "Thank you so much. It's beautiful." She proceeded to remove the medallion from the box and put it around her neck. Some deep part of her knew she would never take it off as long as she was riding the race horses, and she found she was comforted, although wasn't sure why.

Colin called them all into the dining area. It was a tight squeeze, but they all sat at the table and shared a fantastic meal. Robyn spooned food to Claire's mother in between bites of her own meal. Everybody was happy and content, and Claire didn't think that a movie could make a better picture of the group of family and friends that Christmas evening.

As the meal began to wrap up, the appropriate compliments were given to the cooks. Everybody was stuffed, but Robyn then produced her signature cranberry apple pie, and they all indulged one more time in the sweet delight of dessert. Claire looked out the window, and saw that it was still snowing...big, fat fairy tale snowflakes, adding to the already significant accumulation of snow on the ground. For a fleeting moment, she hoped that it would snow forever, and she wouldn't be able to fly out in two days time. She was just so happy in that moment, that she couldn't even think about Arizona, but she guessed that moments like this were what the best memories were made of, and she would take this evening with her no matter where she found herself living.

Dinner was officially over, and people began to make their way up from the table. The men stayed in the kitchen and did the dishes, while Claire, Mandy and Robyn moved out into the family room, positioning Claire's mom again by the Christmas tree.

Mandy was the first to speak. "I want to thank you for an amazing evening. Christmas at our house is usually Chinese take out, so this was a lovely change," she was directing her statement more at Robyn than Claire.

Robyn replied. "You're most welcome. It is nice to have guests...usually it is just the four of us."

The women sat in silence, gazing at the lights of the Christmas tree, lost in their individual thoughts. Claire could hear the banter of the men in the kitchen and suddenly and without any warning, she began to cry. The more she tried to control it, the harder she sobbed, and after a startled moment, Mandy moved in and embraced her in a hug.

"What's the matter girl?" she asked quietly.

Claire continued to cry, and once she was able to get herself under some sort of control, she answered. "I am just going to miss you all so much. I couldn't have asked for a more perfect evening, and now you're all going to leave, and I don't know when I'll see you again. I'm so afraid to go, but I know I couldn't live with myself if I stayed."

Mandy released her hold on Claire and looked at her seriously. "You know that we will always be here for you, no matter what. Call us anytime. I know it's going to be hard, but this is something you have to do. You have such amazing talent, and I really think you could be one of the top riders in the country. I'm not just saying that to make you feel good. We wouldn't have made these arrangements for you if we thought otherwise."

Claire nodded, and wiped her eyes with the tissue her aunt had handed her. She sat quietly for a moment before looking up at Robyn, who was holding onto her sister's hand.

"What do you really think about my plans?" she asked.

Robyn paused for a moment, trying to collect her thoughts, before she finally spoke. "You know we support you, no matter what. If these professionals think you can be a top jockey, and if it 's what you want to do, then you need to do it. You are young and talented and you need to take advantage of it while you can. No regrets, remember?"

Claire nodded, and steadied her resolve. She would go to Arizona, and her primary goal would be to be the best that she possibly could, and whatever happened, happened.

The men finished in the kitchen, and came back out into the family room, where it was time for everybody to say their goodbyes. Kelly and Mandy would be coming to the airport to see Claire off, but this was the last time she was going to see Jürgen for what could be a very long time. In all the years Claire had known the old German, she had never seen him display any more affection than a handshake, and that evening was no different, although he held her hand for a moment, before letting her go.

"Keep Saint Christopher close to you," he said quietly and continued. "I know you're unsure of your faith, but will you do it for me?"

Claire nodded, seeing the affection in his eyes that he did not show through his actions. "Goodbye," she said. "I promise if I ever get to come home, I'll come see you."

He smiled gently as he stepped out the door into the night. "I know," he said, placing his hat on his head as he walked out into the snow.

Kelly and Mandy were right behind him, although they promised to meet Claire at the airport in two days time to see her off. Goodbyes were said, as well as the obligatory safe drive home, and Claire closed the door to the night.

She was exhausted from the day's excitement, so she excused herself to her room where she went to bed, slipping into a quiet and contented sleep.

The next day was spent doing last minute packing and preparations. Her brother teased her constantly. That seemed to be his way of dealing with her impending departure. She became short tempered and irritated, only because she knew he wouldn't be teasing her for much longer. He obliged her request for spaghetti as her going away dinner, and that night, the foursome ate in relative silence. There was not much more that could be said, and Claire thought if she tried to start a conversation, she might break down again, so she simply kept quiet.

Not surprisingly, sleep didn't come easily on the night before she left. She had to be to the airport by nine o'clock, and finally fell into a restless, dream filled sleep around four. A few short hours later, her she awoke to the sound of her alarm clock, jumped out of bed and hurried to get ready. Colin had made breakfast, but nobody had much of an appetite, and soon after, they were all piled into the van, her mother included, and on their way down the snowplowed roads, to the Rochester airport.

Kelly and Mandy, who were there as promised, greeted them inside. Claire went to the ticket counter and checked her bags, paying extra because they were overweight with all of the clothes and riding gear she was going to need. They walked toward the security checkpoint, Claire pushing her mother's wheelchair, and Colin carrying her backpack, while Kelly, Mandy and Robyn were chatting a little too loudly about how excited they were for her. Goodbyes were short. Claire knew she was going to cry, so she tried to hurry, but her friends and family wanted to hold on. Robyn hugged and kissed her, and told her she was going to be fine. Mandy and Kelly both hugged her at the same time, making her promise to call them with updates, and assuring her they'd watch every single race on television. Colin was the hardest to say goodbye to. He held her tightly, squeezing her until she couldn't breathe.

When he finally released her and she caught her breath, he said, "I'm not going to tell you it isn't going to be hard, or you're going to do awesome. We both know that. Just know if you ever need me, I can be on the next plane out, no questions asked. I love you so much, and I only want you to be safe."

Claire nodded, unable to look him in the eyes. She bent to kiss her mom, and then headed through the security line and on an airplane bound for Phoenix.

CHAPTER 11

Several hours after leaving Rochester, Claire's plane landed at Sky Harbor International airport in Phoenix, Arizona. There had been a brief moment in Chicago, where she had to change planes, that she thought about just turning around and going back home, but she didn't. She boarded her next flight, and kept going.

As she got off of her plane, she thought about what Kelly had told her about her new agent. He had described John Green as a giant surfer dude. Claire didn't really know what to make of the description, but she guessed that if she didn't find him, he would find her. It didn't take long, once in the main terminal building, to pick out the man that Kelly had described. He was indeed a giant, and as he approached her, she further understood what her boss meant. John had to be at least 6 foot 5, and roughly 300 pounds. He had bleach blonde hair, that was slightly unkempt, but the most amazing thing to Claire was the fact that he was almost unnaturally tan. She assumed it had to do with hours in the Arizona sun, and was grateful that she was devoted to her sunscreen.

"You must be Claire," John said, holding out his hand in greeting.

"You must be John," Claire said in return, unable to take her eyes off the gaudy Hawaiian style Bermuda shorts and pink, button up semi-dress shirt that was large enough to be a tent. Her new agent's outfit was completed by a pair of over polished brown loafers and no socks. The entire ensemble was enough to make Claire a little queasy, especially on a 40 something year old man, but she was in Arizona. Maybe that was the way people dressed.

"Yep," he replied. "Let's go get your bags and get to the track. You need to get licensed....I've got six workers lined up for you tomorrow morning, and if everything goes well, you'll be on horses for the races on Friday."

Claire nodded as they headed towards baggage claim. She had gotten used to being thrown right into the thick of things, and she took this as a good sign from her new agent. At least he was optimistic. As she collected her luggage, John went to get his car, and she waited by the curb, shocked by the 65-degree temperature and sunshine. After leaving New York, this weather change would be an adjustment. Most people would be happy with the warmer temperatures, but it wouldn't be long before she missed the snow.

John pulled up to the curb, and Claire was again surprised. He was driving a flashy, and very expensive looking gold Mercedes. The trunk popped open, and Claire heaved her bags in, John not bothering to get out of the car and help her, but she managed. She closed the trunk and climbed into the front seat of the luxury sedan. The car smelled new, almost too new, and its leather interior was spotless. She didn't know if he was trying to impress her, but it was working. He was obviously a good enough agent to afford this kind of car off 25% of his rider's earnings at a track that wasn't known for big purse money.

Her mind began to wander as they left the airport. John was talking on the phone, business of some kind, and Claire looked out the window at the desert scenery. She couldn't get over how red everything seemed. The rocks, mountains, dirt, everything seemed to be a varying shade of reddish brown, with the exception of the cactus, which she also found intriguing.

She had only ever seen the giant Saguaro cactus in books, and now they were everywhere. Her first order of business, when she got a little time, was to go and investigate one of those prickly monstrosities up close.

John finished his phone call, and turned his attention to Claire. "I saw that you won a stake closing day there at Finger Lakes. How'd you pull that off?" he seemed skeptical of her limited, but successful race record thus far.

"Kelly put me on the horse. I had a good rapport with that particular horse, and he had worked well for me. Kelly was confident, and he gave me the call. It was pretty easy really; Reggie did nothing wrong, and was way the best. I basically just had to sit there," Claire explained.

"That must have pissed off the other jocks royally," John said. "It's unheard of for a bug, especially a girl, to win a stake before her apprenticeship even officially starts."

Claire just shrugged. "Kelly took care of me all summer, and he got me ready. I think he just wanted to build my confidence and give me a good start."

John nodded. "Yeah...he's a pretty good guy."

Claire took that moment to ask the question that had been nagging her since she had heard Kelly mention that John owed him a favor. "So, what exactly happened, that you owe Kelly the favor of taking my book?"

"Nothing major. I had his book for a while I was working for another guy in West Virginia. He didn't stick around too long, Kelly I mean, but we kept in contact. He was a good jock to have...won a bunch of races, but he couldn't keep his weight under control. We parted ways just before he retired...he was going to go back to Finger Lakes and I had an offer from a guy to come over here, so that was that."

Claire pondered the vague, lack of explanation, and decided she'd ask Kelly for the story some other time.

About 45 minutes after they left the airport, John turned into the racetrack. The left side of the road was a fairly large, horseman's parking lot, and the right of the narrow roadway was lined with palm trees, and some desert loving shrub, of which kind, Claire had no idea. John parked the car, and they headed to a small outbuilding that Claire assumed was the licensing office. They walked into the office area, which was narrow and cramped, allowing for people to approach the counter, or just scoot to one side and have a seat. Claire went through the motions of getting her license while her agent spoke to what appeared to be a couple of trainers. He was already touting her as a rider to the two men, who seemed to have differing opinions about the new 'bug girl.'

Once she was finished, she left the tight quarters of the building and met her agent outside the door. He was still having what seemed to be an animated conversation with one of the trainers, but stopped when she arrived, and proceeded to make introductions.

"Claire, this is George. I am trying to get you on some of his horses," John said heartily.

Claire held out her hand, and the trainer, a thin, leathery man, shook it, but shook his head as well. "I'll not be puttin' any girl on my horses," he said plainly.

Claire was offended. "Why not?" she asked. "You haven't even seen me ride."

George turned and spat around the wad of tobacco in his mouth, and wiped it with the back of his hand, before he replied. "I aint never seen a girl jock that looked like any more than a monkey humpin' a football on a horse. You won't be no different."

"We'll see," Claire replied, deciding that she wasn't going to let this man's backward attitude deter her. George just shrugged and ambled through the gate leading back to the barn area.

She and John followed a ways behind, and her agent gave her the tour of the barn area. They wandered through the expansive rows of stalls, and Claire was introduced to more people than she could possibly remember at one time. After walking for what seemed like forever, they had covered the entire barn area and headed up to have a look at the track itself. Claire looked at the brownish red soil of the main track, and then at the infield, which was decorated with a large pond full of geese, and again, more palm trees. The grass of the infield was beautifully green, and Claire started at the vision of the turf course. She realized that she had no idea how to ride on the grass. Finger Lakes didn't have a turf track, and it didn't even occur to her to ask about the differences. She decided that she would call Kelly right away and ask about racing on the lawn.

"Hey. You need a car?" her agent asked, snapping her out of her thoughts.

"Yes. I don't know where I'm going to find one though," she replied.

"Don't worry, I know one of the trainers here has a car for cheap...I will give him a call and get you hooked up."

"Thanks," she said quietly. She hadn't been in Phoenix for three hours, and she was already meeting people, getting a car, and stressing about riding on the turf, and the day wasn't even done. She still needed to get to her apartment and get checked in, although she didn't even have a bed to sleep on. Perhaps she would just stay at the hotel near the track for a night or two so she could get things organized.

John drove her to the apartment complex, which was actually within walking distance of the track, and she went to the office to get officially checked in. She had done the initial application and paid her deposit over the phone, so all she had to do was get her keys. As she entered her ground floor apartment of the building that looked like it had been built in the 1960's, she decided that every single one-bedroom apartment was the same. The floor plan was very similar to her brother's place in Syracuse, probably only about 500 square feet with a small kitchen, one bathroom and a small bedroom and living area. It was nothing fancy, but it would do, since she wasn't planning on staying for long. Her goal was to be in California by April, and the dumpy apartment was just a temporary bump in the road.

John left, and she was alone with no bed, no furniture and nothing to eat. He had promised that he would speak to the trainer with the car, and hopefully she would have it after morning work. In the mean time, she unpacked her suitcases as much as she could, got what she would need for a night in a hotel, and headed on foot, across the street to her lodging until morning. Standing on the corner, waiting for the traffic signal to change, she was struck with the realization of how alone she was. She immediately took out her phone and called her brother.

"You made it!" he answered, without even saying hello.

"Yes. I'm here," she replied, trying to sound upbeat.

"What's it like?" Colin asked.

"Brown....sunny....not too bad. My agent thinks he can get me a car by tomorrow, so that's good."

"Good," Colin replied. "What are you doing now?"

"I'm heading to the hotel. I have my apartment, but I don't have a bed to sleep on yet, so I am going to the hotel across the street. If I get a car tomorrow, I'll go do some shopping. Maybe just buy an air bed for now."

"It sounds like you have got it all figured out," Colin said.

"Yeah. Just a little lonely is all," Claire said, walking across the parking lot to the hotel lobby. Claire could hear her brother sigh.

"You just got there," he said. "Give it some time."

"I know. I'll be fine. I've got to go check in, so I'll just call you tomorrow," she said.

"You better."

Claire could hear the smile in her brother's voice, and was immediately comforted. Things might not be so bad. The people that mattered were only a phone call away, and she was all right with that.

*

She awoke in the morning and hurried to get ready to go to the track. Fortunately, it was a short walk to the track from her hotel, so she half jogged across the lot to the entrance of the barn area, where her agent was waiting for her. John directed her to her workers for the morning, and she was pleasantly surprised at how busy she was. The hustle and bustle of the track was just like Finger Lakes, and she fell into her comfort zone once she got on her first horse. Her agent had been doing his job, and Claire was happy to know that every horse she was to ride that morning was a worker. She asked John if there were any to just gallop, and he told her to get that thought out of her head. She was a jockey now, not a gallop girl. Let some other gallop boy get paid for that, she was going to be getting paid to win.

When the morning work was over, she met up with her agent in the parking lot, as they were going to meet the trainer with the car. She was surprised to find out that the man was one she had worked a couple of horses for that morning. His name was Dale, and he walked them to the truck, not car, that he was offering for sale. Claire was a bit dismayed at the vehicle. It was an older model Ford pick up, with slightly oxidized, olive drab green and white paint. But, she figured, beggars can't be choosers, and the price was right.

"I'll take it. Thank you," she told Dale.

He nodded casually. "You're welcome. It'll serve its purpose," he gave her a good once over, and spoke again. "You look pretty good out there on the horses. I'm not the only one who noticed."

Claire smiled. "Thank you," she replied politely, not sure what else to say.

Dale continued. "I hear that you got your start with the Zakarian's, is that right?"

She nodded quickly.

"Well, in that case, you're on the right track. Kelly was a phenomenal rider in his day, if you learned from him, you're ahead of the game."

Claire looked at the trainer, surprised at the fact that everybody she talked to knew Kelly. "Why does everybody seem to know Kelly?" she asked, to either man who would answer.

Dale looked at her quizzically. "You must not really know much about him, do you?"

She shook her head, a little embarrassed. Kelly rarely talked about himself, and Mandy didn't offer many details either.

"Kelly Zakarian was an Eclipse award winning apprentice about 12 years ago. Everybody in the industry knew him. Unfortunately, he struggled too much with his weight and only was able to ride for a couple of years after that, but he was an incredible talent. Everybody thought he'd be the top rider in the country."

Claire was surprised. She knew Kelly had been good, but she didn't know how good.

Dale continued. "Then, there was that incident with his friend....it really shook him up, and he just kind of faded away. I'm glad he is doing well training. Often times, good jockeys don't make the best trainers. I should know...I was a crappy jockey but I can train okay," he laughed, and then handed Claire the keys to her new wheels.

She handed him the wad of cash that she brought, and decided to hold her question about Kelly and the incident with his friend, although it seemed like everybody knew more than she.

As Dale was turning to walk away, another man, obviously a jockey, greeted Dale with a handshake while passing, and approached Claire and John casually.

"Is this your new girl?" he asked John, without so much as an introduction of himself.

"Yep. Eddie Gomez, Claire Durham," John completed the intro and Claire shook hands with Eddie.

John furthered his introduction for Claire's benefit. "Eddie's the leading rider here, has been for years."

Claire nodded, unsure of what to say.

Eddie looked her over, and then broke the silence. "I hear you came in from New York, is that right?"

"Yes."

"What do you think of Phoenix so far?" he questioned.

"It's warm....and brown," she replied.

Eddie laughed. "You got that right...you think it's warm now, wait until July!"

Claire decided it was best not to tell him that she didn't plan on staying until July, so she just nodded and smiled.

"John says you moved into an apartment across the street, is that right?"

"Yes, why?"

"I am guessing you don't have any furnishings, considering you flew in, and your agent can't think past the end of his nose when it comes to things like that."

Claire raised an eyebrow at that statement. "No, I don't have anything...just some my clothes, but now that I have a car, I'm going to go get some stuff. Why do you ask?"

Eddie glanced over at John, who was again on the phone, which seemed to be permanently attached to his ear.

"Well, if you're interested, I have some things you can use....an old sofa, and even older TV, and a full size bed that used to belong to one of my kids. It's not much, but it will give you someplace to sleep. I can bring it over if you like."

Claire was thrilled. "Yes, thank you!" she hesitated. "I can't pay you for it right now though. I haven't ridden yet, and I what I had in hand, I just spent on a car."

Eddie waved her off. "Don't worry about it...we were going to donate it anyway. When you're done with it, give it to someone else."

"Thank you," Claire said again, and then had a thought. "Why are you doing this for me...you don't even know me?"

Eddie smiled kindly. "Because I was in your shoes once; a new rider at a new track with nothing but the clothes on my back. I had somebody help me out, and it's time to pay it forward. I'll see if my wife can dig up any more stuff that might come in handy, and I'll swing by your place this afternoon."

Claire felt that all she said was thank you, but she said it again and Eddie left. As he walked away, he studied him, thinking that all jockeys were built the same...small and slight, but strong as an ox, pound for pound. Eddie had a Hispanic last name, and he looked like he might have some Hispanic heritage somewhere, but he spoke without the slightest of an accent, if anything, he had a bit of a drawl, like he might be from Texas, or somewhere else south.

Shortly after Claire returned to her apartment, Eddie called and said he was on his way, and that his wife had thrown a few more things in for her. He arrived soon after, and they began unloading his truck, assisted by his son Alex, who appeared to be about 15. Claire was ecstatic as the guys brought things into her place. A decent television, an old, but well cared for sofa, a full size mattress, box and frame, a semi-beat up night stand and a small table with two chairs that she could use for meals.

As they were finishing up, Eddie brought in a box, with a few odds and ends of things, that he dropped on the kitchen counter.

"I hope this all works for you. My wife insisted on sending all this extra stuff. If you don't want it, just pass it on," he said, as he was leaving.

"Thank you again, and say thanks to your wife. I appreciate it all," Claire said, with genuine gratitude. Eddie nodded and let himself out, saying that he would see her in the morning, and Claire proceeded to look through the box of goodies. It would seem that Eddie's wife had given some thought to what she was putting in the box, and for that, Claire was grateful. She pulled out several pots and pans, some basic cooking utensils and a small bedside lamp, perfect for reading.

Claire began to feel quite confident. People, for the most part, were kind and helpful. She had a truck and a bed and a couple of live mounts for her upcoming first day of racing. Things were looking good, so she decided to call her brother with the news, and then maybe it was time to go grocery shopping.

*

Claire's first days in Phoenix were pleasant and productive. She began to learn her way around the backside of the track, and got a good feel as to who the trainers were and where they were located. Her agent gave her some tips as to what trainers to pursue for mounts and which ones to stay away from, but all in all, she felt she was getting along just fine. She had gotten on some nice horses, and had received mostly positive feedback from several trainers and a few riders.

Her first race was a mile on a cheap claimer. She was excited to be back racing...three weeks off was too much, now that she had found her passion. Kelly had called her the morning of her first race and they spoke at length. She had told him about all the people she had met, and he was optimistic about her chances on both of her horses that day.

"The sooner you get your first win there, the better. Win right away, and people will begin to notice," he told her.

Claire remembered what else she had wanted to ask him about. "There's a turf track here....I don't know how to ride on the turf. What do I do?"

She heard Kelly laugh before he spoke. "Riding on the turf is no different than riding on the dirt. The grass tends to favor closers, and there are some horses who really love it, and some who hate it, but it really is no big deal. You may find that you like riding on one surface better than another, and the form will tell you about how your horse should run on the given surface, but don't worry about it. Just ride your race. Oh, and one other thing," he continued. "Don't let those guys intimidate you. You are a new apprentice, and nobody knows anything about you. Those jocks are going to do their best to get your measure...they are going to put you in tight, and probably float you out. They need to see what you know and how much of a threat you are going to be. If you let them intimidate you right away, you'll never earn any respect. This is where all of the things that we have talked about over the last few months will come into play. You have to be tough and fearless, but smart. Make good decisions and always know where you are and who is around you. You only have a few months to make a good impression and win as many races as possible if you want to get to California and ride with the big boys."

Claire thanked her old boss for his insight, and promised she would do what he said. He reminded her that he'd be watching every race on television, and he would let her know if she screwed up.

She was quietly confident as she was legged up onto her first mount, feeling instantly at ease when her butt touched the saddle. Her horse was fidgety and ready to run, and she was just as eager to get going. The race went well, she positioned herself appropriately, and took an opening on the rail turning for home. As unbelievable as it was, that ten to one shot won going away, and she instantly became a target to the other riders. Nobody had anticipated that she would be confident enough to move her horse through a tight spot on the rail, and the other jocks were especially amazed at her strength down the lane. She never wavered, was confident with her stick handling, and her weight allowance was a significant benefit.

Her agent was thrilled; as she ran third on her next mount that day. Once the races were over, John approached her, grinning from ear to ear.

"You did great!" he said. "I've got trainers asking about you left and right. You'll be riding the card before you know it!"

Claire knew that meant she would ride every race, and while it sounded nice at first, it also sounded exhausting. She only hoped her agent was right and she could get more and more live mounts.

As she was walking to her truck, Eddie called to her, jogging to catch up. "Nice day today," he said.

"Thanks, but I expected you guys to be a little tougher on me," she said, with just a touch of arrogance in her voice.

"Don't worry, we will be," he said smiling. "We just had to see what you are made of. If you keep winning races like that though, you won't be making many friends in the jock's room. A lot of these guys struggle to win enough races every week to make a living, and the last thing they want to see is some 18 year old girl come in and take over."

She nodded, understanding what he was talking about, but not really seriously considering herself a threat to anybody just yet.

Eddie continued. "Just watch yourself out there. They....I mean we... are going to start riding you a bit tighter. There are a couple of guys, and I am not going to name names, that will put you in some down right scary spots. Don't be afraid to claim foul if you have to. Show them that they can't intimidate you."

"Ok, but can I ask you a question?" she looked at Eddie seriously.

"Of course," he replied.

"Why are you being so helpful? I mean, I understand giving me some stuff for my apartment, but if I'm competition, why are you helping me?"

Eddie looked at her for a moment before responding. "Here's the deal," he said. "At the end of the day, we are all out there together. At any given time, there are ten other horses and riders around you, including myself. Some people think that it is every man for himself, but we have to look out for each other, and if I am riding with somebody with less experience, I need to know that I'm still safe out on the track. There are a lot of journeymen out there who ignore the bugs, but I'm of the opinion that the more I can help you, assuming you take the advice, the safer we all are out there. This is a sport where people can be killed; it shouldn't be because somebody makes a bad decision. Nobody wants to live with that guilt."

"I understand," Claire said. "And thank you for that. I guess I never thought of it that way before."

"Just remember that you will be a journeyman too someday, and you will be in a position to help somebody out that is just starting. Use what you know to your advantage and help keep people safe."

"I will," Claire promised, thanking the jockey again as she got into her truck. She had a lot to think about, and she was glad that Eddie chose to be honest with her and share some valuable insight.

That evening, she received a phone call from both Colin and Kelly, congratulating her on her win, and wishing her luck for the rest of the weekend. She spoke to her agent briefly, and he told her he had so many phone calls from trainers wanting her to work horses, he was having to turn people away. It was a good sign that Kelly might have been right, and this was the place for her, for the time being.

*

A few weeks went by, and her business, by all accounts was booming. She was riding 6 to 9 mounts a day on race days, and she was so busy in the mornings that she rarely had time to take a break.

One morning in particular, she was heading down the shed row at break time, wanting to go into the kitchen and get herself a cup of coffee, when she overheard bits of a conversation that stopped her in her tracks. She waited where she was, listening to the two male voices around the corner of the barn.

The talk was about her and she knew it, but she was frozen by what she heard.

"That new bug girl," the first voice was saying. "I heard she was in New York with Kelly Z."

The second voice chimed in. "Yep, that's what I heard. She is a good rider, but I heard she was sleeping with Kelly, that's how she got that stakes horse before she even started her bug."

Claire stood still, listening, as the first voice sounded again. "I wouldn't doubt it...she is probably sleeping with her agent too, you know that guy will do anything that walks. How else could she be winning so many races so soon?"

"I know," voice number two concurred. "Maybe I can get her in the sack...she looks pretty nimble." They both laughed, then Claire could hear them walking away.

She was stunned, and her stomach was suddenly in knots. At that moment, coffee was the last thing on her mind, as she immediately reached for her phone to call the one person she knew would tell her how to handle the situation.

Kelly answered his phone on the first ring. "Hey girl, what's up?"

"People are saying that I slept with you to get such good mounts?" Claire blurted out, nearly in tears.

She could hear Kelly sigh on the other end of the line, and there was a long silence as he gathered his thoughts.

"I don't doubt it," he said. "What did you hear exactly?"

Claire proceeded to tell him the conversation she had overheard. When she was finished, the response she got from Kelly was not what she had been expecting.

"Welcome to horse racing," he said, bluntly. "I'm only surprised it's taken this long for the rumors to start."

"Doesn't it make you angry?"

"Claire, do you remember when I talked to you about hearing what was important, and letting everything else roll off?"

"Yes."

"Well, this is one of those times you have to just let it roll off. The plain fact is, you are a woman in what is still a male dominated industry, and there's going to be talk. The small minds think the only way a woman can be successful in horse racing is to sleep her way to the top. That mentality is probably never going to change, and unfortunately, it does happen, probably more times than anybody would like to think about."

Claire sighed, and sat down on the bench next to the little chapel near the track. It was one of the few places where she knew she was alone. "It's just not fair! I don't want people thinking all of my success has come because I am sleeping with the right people!"

"Can I ask you a question then?" Kelly said.

"Of course."

"Did you and I ever sleep together?"

"Come on Kelly," Claire said. "You know we didn't."

"Okay," he continued. "Have you slept with your agent, or any of the people they're talking about?"

"No way," Claire responded.

"Then, what difference does it make?"

Claire understood what Kelly was saying. "None, I guess. I just don't like the rumors."

"Neither do I, but there's absolutely nothing you can do about it. Those guys are just trying to get under your skin, and you can't let them do it. The racetrack is like a small town, and the rumors fly, no matter what. What it means is you have to grow some thick skin, and turn a deaf ear when necessary."

"Ok...you're right. I'm sorry; I just got upset is all. I'm not used to this kind of thing."

"I know," Kelly said. "The really unfortunate thing is that you get used to it. Doesn't seem right to me, but it is what it is."

Claire thought of something else she had heard. "They also said John sleeps with anything that walks. Is that true?"

Kelly snorted out a half laugh. "Yep. That isn't a rumor; it's the plain truth! I swear to God, Claire, if he ever makes any advance on you, you call me immediately! Is that clear?"

She was startled. "Yes...Do you really think he would?"

"I wouldn't put it past him. That guy has the morals of a tomcat, and I told him not even to think about it, but he doesn't usually think further than the end of his dick. You call me if he even so much as makes a suggestion, you got it?"

"I got it. Thanks Kelly." They said their goodbyes.

Claire sat quietly, pondering the conversation she just had. She wasn't sure she liked the new perspective that she got about the racetrack life. She wasn't fooling herself, she knew the rumors weren't going to go away, but she also knew she was going to have to toughen up. Since she'd begun working with the race horses, she just never even considered seeking out any relationships. It would only get in the way of her ultimate goals, and now that she had started on that path, she wouldn't be stopped. Sex just complicated things, and she didn't need it. Aside from her minor crush on Kelly, which she never, ever revealed, she just didn't find anybody at the race track that appealing....yet.

Her thoughts were continuing to churn when she was startled by a voice behind her.

"Claire?"

She turned to see whom the voice belonged to, and saw a slight, kindly looking older man, with salt and pepper hair and weathered skin. She had seen him around the track several times, but she didn't know who he was.

"Yes?" she said, standing to greet the man.

"I'm Father Mike," he said, and she realized he was the track Chaplain.

She shook his hand. "I'm sorry, I don't really know you," she said. He knew her name, but she was sure they'd never actually met.

He smiled at her. "But everybody knows you, young lady."

She sighed again. "Clearly," she mumbled, thinking about the two jockeys she had overheard.

Father Mike motioned her inside the little, white, non-denominational chapel. She followed reluctantly and he patted the seat next to him on the well-worn pew.

He looked at her a moment, as if to try and read her thoughts, before speaking. "I didn't mean to be eavesdropping, but I heard some of your phone conversation. You are upset by the rumors you're hearing?"

She nodded, not knowing what to say.

"The person you were talking to on the phone told you that is the way things are at the track. Am I right?"

Claire nodded again, and then began to rehash all of the morning's events leading her to where she was at the moment.

Father Mike listened intently, and when she was finished, he spoke again. "The key to making it in this business is to have faith in yourself. Only you know your own heart, and nothing anybody else says matters at all. The gossip you hear is going to be a difficult burden to bear, but remember that the Lord never gives us more than we can handle, and He knows the truth as well."

Claire was uncomfortable with the direction that the conversation was headed, and decided to speak up while she had the moment. "I don't want to offend you Father, but I am not really sure if I believe in all that God stuff," she knew it sounded ignorant, but she didn't know how else to address her lack of religious convictions with a man who had dedicated his life to his faith in God.

The chaplain smiled and patted Claire's knee. "I am not offended. But I am going to tell you something that I would like you to consider. You are in a profession where you're riding 40 miles per hour on a thousand pound animal with a brain the size of a chicken egg, who may one day decide to go right instead of left. Perhaps you better have faith in something."

Claire looked at the chaplain, considering what he had just said. "What do I have faith in? I don't know if I believe in God, or anything else for that matter, so what do I do?"

Father Mike looked at her again. "Is that a Saint Christopher around your neck?"

Claire nodded, reaching up to finger the medallion that had somehow found it's way out from under her shirt.

"I would say you have faith in something then," he said.

Claire shook her head. "No, this was given to me by a friend back home. He asked me to wear it, and I told him I would. That's all."

It was the chaplain's turn to shake his head. "It was important to this friend, right? Hence it is now important to you. If it really didn't matter, you could have simply tossed it aside, but you put it around your neck, and I bet you haven't taken it off, have you?"

Again, Claire shook her head.

"You may not even be aware, but that is faith. No matter how small a gesture you think it might be, you have faith…in yourself, in your friend, in the choices that you have made up to this point. It may not be the true faith in God as you are led to believe, but faith in something is better than no faith at all. Just something to think about," he rose from his seat. "I have things to do, but if you ever want to talk about anything, know that my door is always open." With that, he walked out of the small building, leaving Claire to ponder their conversation.

CHAPTER 12

Weeks turned into months, and Claire was doing better than she had ever dreamed. She was winning at least two races every day, and had several days where she logged three of four. On one amazing day, she won six of the seven races she rode, setting a record for most wins in a single day for a female jockey, and tying the record for most wins in a day by any rider. Her confidence was through the stratosphere, and she felt invincible. She had turned into a fan favorite and found she had a knack for interviews. The Daily Racing Form had interviewed her on a number of occasions, and the local newspaper was doing a running piece on her and her day-to-day life. On the outside, her life was perfect, but on the inside, she was in turmoil. While she was confident in her riding, and thrilled with her success, she found that she was incredibly lonely. The racetrack consumed her days, but when she got home every night, she was alone. She had discovered that true friendships were nearly impossible at the track. The other women jockeys were irritated with her success, and it seemed like the majority of the men only wanted to get into her pants. Eddie had stopped helping her; in fact, most of the jockeys were deliberately trying to make things harder. They seemed to forget that the more difficult situations they put her in, the better she got. She was getting opportunities to make split second decisions and improve her overall skills in a race. School had never been her strong suit, but she was an incredibly fast learner on the racetrack, learning from her mistakes and the mistakes of others. She had become consumed with studying the tendencies of other jockeys and trying to use their personal preferences to her advantage. When it came to pure strength, she was still not where she wanted to be, but as far as track smarts, she was as savvy as many of the journeymen, and had absolutely no fear. She wouldn't hesitate to navigate her mount through an opening that many riders would be too intimidated to go for, and there was more than one instance when she would come back to the jockey's room with white paint on her left boot, left there from her scraping her foot on the rail while scooting through a particularly tight spot.

Her time in Phoenix was limited, and she knew it. California was where she wanted to be, and she had many trainers telling her she could do well there with the right agent. Her own agent, she had come to realize, was not going to be accompanying her west. John was a good agent, initially, but as time had gone on, she found she was doing most of the legwork for him, and he spent his mornings standing on the rail drinking coffee and gossiping. Even with the money she was making, he always seemed to be short of cash at the end of the week, and had begun asking her for and advance on his paycheck fairly regularly. He was forgetful, not telling her about morning workers, and trainers were getting angry. Most were loyal to her regardless, but many didn't want to deal with her agent at all. They tolerated him because he was representing her, but very few of them held their tongue when he consistently left them hanging. The rumor was that he was doing drugs. She didn't want to believe it, but she had heard from another jockey who had had him once as an agent, whenever he had a top rider and was making decent money, he got back on the drugs. He was already a heavy drinker, and Claire was amazed that he could function at all sometimes. His behavior was becoming more and more erratic; he would fail to show up on race days, claiming to be watching the races from home, but clearly having no idea what had gone on in each race. It was time for her to move on, and she knew it, but she didn't have any contacts in California yet, and she was just going to have to deal with the situation for the time being.

*

April was hot, and Claire wasn't used to the sweltering heat. With only three weeks left before the start of the Hollywood Park meet in Los Angeles, she was starting to get worried that she wouldn't

be able to find an agent to take her book, and she might be stuck in Phoenix with John.

One particular Saturday, the temperatures were in the high 90's, and Claire had seven mounts on the day. She found herself sucking down the water, and dunking her head in a bucket in between races, just to keep cool. Her mounts were live, and she'd already won three races before the last of the day. All she wanted to do was get done and get back to her air conditioned apartment, and she blamed her lack of focus due to the heat, on what happened in the last race of the day.

Things were going as usual. Her horse was the favorite, and she knew she should win. She was positioned behind the two front-runners turning for home, and she made the decision to save ground and drop down to the inside, rather than swing wide. She waited for the hole to open up, and when it did, she dropped down and shot through. There was some yelling behind her, but she didn't look back to see what was going on, pushing her mare forward to the finish and winning the race by a length.

As she was galloping out, Eddie pulled his horse up next to her and began cursing her with an unending string of expletives.

"You could have killed me out there! What the hell were you thinking?!" he screamed.

Claire was unfazed; her success had made her somewhat arrogant. "You're fine...I didn't do anything to you," she yelled back.

Eddie's face was nearly purple. "Don't you look where you are going? I was in there, and you dropped down without so much as a look over your shoulder! Do you have any idea how close I came to clipping your heels? It is a bloody miracle my horse stayed up!"

Claire just shrugged as she turned her horse and headed back to the grandstand area. "You know I was on the best horse. You shouldn't have been in there In the first place," she said casually.

Eddie shook his head. "Get ready for a vacation," he said, and smooched his horse past her.

Claire neared the trainer of her horse, but before she dismounted, she noticed that he was shaking his head as he grabbed his mare's bridle.

"That was pretty stupid," he said as she dismounted.

"What's the problem? I won didn't I?"

He looked at her incredulously. "Go get on the phone...the stewards want to talk to you."

Claire glanced at the tote board, and realized that there was a steward's inquiry against her. Her stomach lurched. She had never been on the receiving end of an inquiry before. She had instances where she was moved up a placing due to somebody else's infraction, but never her own. Suddenly she began to doubt herself. Maybe she had made the wrong decision. She knew she didn't look, and she should have.....always look, Kelly had told her, even if you are sure you are clear. She hadn't, and easily could have caused a major accident.

She waited for Eddie to be done talking on the phone near the scale, and when he was finished, he handed it to her without saying a word.

"Yes," she said firmly, not wanting to seem intimidated by the authorities.

"Claire, what happened out there?" the head steward asked, in a voice that was more than slightly accusatory.

Claire rehashed the events of the race as she recalled them, being careful not to place any of the blame on herself and instead saying that Eddie was trying to go through a hole where there wasn't one, and it was his fault. Unfortunately, they didn't seem to agree with her, and she noticed that mere seconds after she hung up the phone, she had been disqualified from first and placed sixth. Suddenly she was furious. She stormed into the jockey's room and threw her helmet down, cursing Eddie and the stewards. Fortunately, with so few women riders, she was alone in the ladies room, and didn't have to share her spectacle with any other eyes.

Still seething, she took her shower, and decided she was going to confront Eddie outside of the room. Dressing quickly, she rushed out the door to find him, and she spotted him waiting by her own truck. She was livid. Not only did he cost her a win, but she had lost the element of surprise, hoping that she could catch him off guard; he was waiting on her instead.

Claire quickened her pace as she approached him, preparing to let out a string of expletives matching his, but he spoke first.

"Are you okay?" he asked.

"What?" she said, completely taken off guard. She was prepared for him to yell at her again, and she was ready for a hostile exchange of words, but he asked her again if she was all right.

She stuttered, trying to find her voice, as she wasn't prepared for civilized talk. "Um...I'm fine." She caught her breath, and swallowed her pride for a moment. "Are you alright?"

"I'm fine. Thanks for asking," he replied, immediately diffusing the situation, and Claire lost the focus of her anger. "I know you're angry," he continued. "But that call had to be made. You could have caused a serious accident out there Claire."

"It wasn't that bad," she said sulkily.

"No, it wasn't, but it could've been. You're a great rider, and everybody loves you, but the only way to learn from your mistakes is to make the mistakes. There isn't a bug out there who hasn't had their number taken down...its all part of the process."

Claire glared at Eddie, but she could feel her anger abating, being replaced with shame. "I'm sorry. It won't happen again."

Eddie placed his hand on her shoulder and smiled. "Oh, it probably will happen again. Even us journeymen get our numbers taken down from time to time. Just don't let your confidence replace common sense."

Claire nodded as Eddie left her standing alone next to her old truck. Within moments, her phone rang. She looked to see who it was, and for the first time since she had known him, she didn't want to talk to Kelly. She answered anyway, resigning herself to the fact that she was about to get a major ass chewing, and she might as well get it over with.

"Hey Kelly," she said quickly. "How's New York?"

"Not as interesting as Arizona I see," he said. "What happened?"

She wasn't in the mood for games or another big explanation, and she found her response a bit snippy. "You saw what happened. I came down on Eddie and got my number taken down. It wasn't as bad as it could have been, but Eddie and I talked, and it's all good."

"Fine. I am glad to hear that you're taking some responsibility."

"What happens now? What do I need to do?"

Kelly spoke directly. "Go into see the stewards tomorrow and watch the films of the races. Eddie will be there too. Talk to them about what happened. You're still learning, so they might go a bit easier on you, although maybe not. You're probably going to get the standard three days suspension. Take it graciously and keep your cool. The last thing the stewards want is attitude."

"Ok. What do I do during my suspension? Just sit around and do nothing?"

"Pretty much. Take a break, but be prepared to watch some of your horses win with other riders. That's the worst part, and probably the reason why suspensions are effective."

"Alright, thanks," she said, missing her old boss, and her old life. "Kelly," she said, and paused. "It's really hard here."

Kelly seemed surprised by her statement. "What do you mean it's hard? You're doing so well. Better than even I expected. You're winning a ton of races, and the money has to be pretty good, isn't it?"

"That's not what I mean. I know I'm doing well, and I love the racing part, but I am really lonely. There just isn't anybody here that I feel I can be friends with. I guess I'm just missing home....missing people that I trust. And, it's bloody hot!"

She could hear Kelly sigh on the other end of the line. "It'll get easier. I know what you're going through, but remember that your situation there is only temporary. You're only about three weeks away from heading to California, and once you get there and get more settled, you'll meet people. It's life Claire, and it will get better. Look at the bright side....you're doing really well riding, and you are enjoying your job. Imagine how much harder it would be if you were struggling to make a living."

"You're right, and I know. I guess I am just feeling sorry for myself after what happened today."

Kelly changed the subject. "Do you have any contacts in California yet?"

Another thing that Claire had been stressing about was brought to light. "No. John keeps telling me that everybody is watching, but I don't want him as my agent over there, and if people are supposedly watching, nobody is saying anything."

"You're right about John...he's best when he's temporary, but don't worry...somebody will call, you can bet on it."

"Even after my major screw up today?"

"Yes Claire. One suspension as a bug doesn't make you a bad rider. What you gained today was experience, and everybody gets days once in a while."

The next day, Claire went in front of the stewards to plead her case, and as Kelly predicted, she was served a three-day suspension. Watching the race on video was an eye opener, as she saw the extent of what she had done, and how she'd so nearly caused Eddie to fall. It could have been disastrous, and she was grateful it ended the way it did. She probably deserved her three days, and she would take them without argument.

While serving her suspension, she watched several of her mounts win with other jockeys. The week that had started out bad, had just gotten worse. It made sense what Kelly had told her. Watching somebody else win on mounts that should have been hers was heartbreaking. She knew in the grand scheme of things, those mounts really didn't matter, and she would continue to win races after her suspension was over, but it still hurt nonetheless.

She was angry and frustrated, and had nothing to vent her frustrations on, so she sat in her apartment and sulked. Her phone rang, and she didn't recognize the number. Part of her wanted to ignore the call, as she didn't think she was in the mood to be gracious to anybody, but she knew that was being childish, so she answered. "Hello?"

"Claire!" a loud voice bellowed through the line. "How the hell are you? I see you got yourself some days...doesn't matter. When can you get to Hollywood?"

Claire was startled, and somewhat terrified by the booming voice she was hearing that she didn't recognize in the least. "Who is this?" she asked, not as forcefully as she would have liked.

"Oh, shit...sorry! I'm Frank...Frank Rossi. I'm going to have your book over here. I've been watching you, but I didn't have an opening. My top kid just lost his bug and wants to go to Texas for crying out loud, and I want your book. You are better than he ever will be, to be honest, he couldn't ride a stick horse, and I have got trainers lining up for you. Everybody knows you young lady."

"I've never talked to you before,"Claire said, not wanting to be too hopeful of this boisterous stranger. "We've never met...how is it you are taking my book?"

"Oh, don't tell me you are bringing that asshole John Greene over here? He'll bury you!"

"No, but I still don't know you."

"No worries, Kelly called me, although he really didn't have to.....like I said, we've been watching you over here, and I want your book, before somebody else gets it. What'd you say?"

Claire was stunned. She wanted to believe she was getting her shot, but it seemed too good to be true. "Um, okay, but I have to talk to Kelly first. Can I call you back tomorrow?"

"Fine, but don't take forever. I have a ton of jocks wanting me to represent them, and if you say no, I have to let one of these other pinheads know. But you aren't going to say no, so I'll see you here in a couple of weeks."

He hung up just like that, and left Claire sitting, staring at her phone. It was late in New York, but she called Kelly anyway to verify the story of this strange Frank Rossi.

Kelly said that he had indeed spoken to Frank, and there wasn't a better agent in all of California, maybe even in the country. Yes he was outspoken and somewhat arrogant, but everybody loved him, and underneath his boisterous demeanor, he was the kind of guy who would give you the shirt off his back.

Claire hung up the phone with Kelly, and could barely contain her excitement. This was it, her chance to ride with the big boys, and in spite of what she had heard, she was excited to experience Los Angeles. Living on her own wasn't as bad as she thought, and she was ready for a new challenge.

*

Once her suspension was satisfied, she got right back into her winning ways, which included a sizable stakes win on the turf. She had come to enjoy riding on the grass, and found she looked forward to the turf races.

John wouldn't be going with her to California, and she would be glad to leave him behind. While she knew that she owed a certain amount of her success to his early work, the majority of her accomplishments had come from her own hard work and her ability to diffuse situations he had created by lying and cheating the trainers and owners. In her mind, she knew Frank Rossi was probably a more dependable character than John, he would have to be if he was one of the top agents in the country, but she couldn't help but worry. Her observations of the agents in Arizona led her to believe that most of them were of more than questionable morality, and they were the worst gossips on the track. Any rumor that was started about anybody could be traced back to one of the agents who were perpetually clustered around the race office or the track kitchen. It was as if they had nothing better to do than tell stories, regardless of whether or not they were true.

The week before Claire was due to leave for California, John disappeared completely. She went to the track for her morning work, and he was nowhere to be found. She went to check with her usual trainers who gave her work for the morning, but nobody had heard anything from John. When she went to Dale Johnson's barn, the man who sold her the truck, she got a bit of info as to the reason her agent was MIA.

"John heard you were going to L.A.," Dale told her, when she asked.

"How did he hear that? I haven't even told him yet...I was going to wait until he had finished working the last weekend."

Dale shook his head. "Haven't you learned anything about the racetrack kid? Everybody knows everything all the time. What you may think is a secret is known by everybody within days, sometimes even hours."

Claire was baffled. "But how...? I haven't said anything to anybody!"

"Frank called me asking if I would be willing to put you on some of my horses over in California. I wasn't the only trainer he called. A lot of these guys have a barn over there, so Frank is doing the right thing in asking us. Word got to John that you are going to be at Hollywood opening day, and Frank has your book."

"Crap," Claire sighed, and sat down on a nearby bale of hay. "Does this mean I'm not going to see my agent for an entire week?"

"Oh, no...he'll wander back through in a couple of days. John doesn't like confrontation, and he has lied to enough people about everything that nobody particularly misses him. I've known the guy for a long time, and he's never changed. Did Kelly ever tell you why he fired John?"

Claire shook her head. She had been wondering what the actual story was behind their parting of ways, but John's explanation was vague, and she just hadn't had the opportunity to ask Kelly.

Dale proceeded with the brief tale. "It was in West Virginia. Kelly had gone with a trainer who had a nice string of horses; one in particular was on track to being a multiple stakes winner. He won a nice allowance race, and then a $50K stakes race. There was a big race coming up, a $150k I think, and Kelly was set to ride that horse, but when entries came out, somebody else was named on the horse, and he was riding a much lesser mount. He was livid and went to the trainer asking why she had taken him off, and she said she didn't, his agent spun her at the draws, and she had to scramble for a rider at the last minute. She was mad at Kelly, thinking he chose another mount after winning on her horse, but he hadn't....it was John. Come to find out, the trainer of the horse Kelly ended up riding paid John $400 to put Kelly on his horse. John, being all about instant gratification, took the cash, thereby costing Kelly thousands of dollars in earnings. The other horse went on to win seven stakes races and was named horse of the year at the meet, and Kelly didn't get a sniff of any of that money all because John wanted a quick fix. The stupid thing is that John would have made more money in agent fees if he had kept Kelly on the horse and just waited for the paychecks, but he isn't capable of thinking that far ahead. I think Kelly would have killed him, but realized he wasn't worth the effort. That was when he fired John and left West Virginia."

Claire couldn't believe what she had heard. It was heartbreaking, but made her angry with Kelly at the same time. "Why would Kelly set me up with him, knowing what the guy was like?"

Dale was gazing out at his horses on the hot walker, and took a minute to speak. "I think he was hoping that maybe John had found some responsibility. John will never be able to repay the debt he owes, and Kelly knows that, so he took advantage of the situation. You needed a contact, and John can be a great agent when he wants to be. Kelly knew your stay here was only temporary, and John has been a good, temporary agent."

Claire nodded slightly, but she had another question. "How do you know all of this? You've been training here for 20 years, and it all took place in West Virginia? I know race trackers talk, but that's a pretty long distance conversation."

Dale never looked away from his horses as he answered her. "Kelly's my nephew. His mother was my younger sister. She died from breast cancer about five years ago."

"I'm sorry. I didn't know any of this," Claire said, trying to get her head around everything she had just heard. Nobody ever said anything to her, and she had known Dale for three months, and Kelly for a year.

"You wouldn't be expected to. Kelly's dad and I never really got a long, and after Joan died, we just didn't speak much."

Claire just stared blankly out at the horses walking in their endless circles. The track life was a hard business for everybody, and what she had known before her conversation with Dale had only really been the tip of the iceberg. She decided to change the subject. "Will you have any horses for me to ride in California?"

Dale laughed heartily. "Of course! You're my go to girl! Frank knows my number, and we'll get you on some live horses soon enough."

"Thanks," she said, standing from her hay bale and getting herself ready to take out her next worker. Break time was over, and it was time to get back to the horses.

Dale had been right. John strolled in one morning a few days later. When Claire confronted him with where he had been, he said he decided to go on vacation. He and his new girlfriend had gone to Vegas, where, of course, he had lost all of his money, and had no qualms about asking her for an advance on his last paycheck. She had reached the end of her patience with him, and refused his request. As far as she was concerned, she couldn't be on her way to California soon enough.

There were things to get in order before she left. As Eddie suggested, she arranged to donate all of her large furniture, and Father Mike had been elated when she offered it to the chapel. He worked with many of the grooms on track, and there was always need.

Her biggest order of business before leaving was to buy a new car. She had been saving her money, sending some home to her aunt and mom, but there was plenty left over to buy a decent car. Driving the old truck into Los Angeles wasn't too appealing, and she knew she'd need something more conservative on gas given the amount of driving between tracks. She found herself a nice, used hybrid that was only a couple of years old. It would suit her perfectly, and it got great gas mileage. Just what she would need for navigating the Los Angeles traffic scene.

Her new agent, Frank, had called her from time to time. The conversations were always short, and very one sided. He talked, she listened. She was pleased to know he'd made living arrangements for her, and it seemed like he knew everybody everywhere. Claire was impressed. He had a confidence that was catching, and as she drove out of Phoenix, she was giddy with excitement. In spite of a few minor bumps in the road, her life was going according to plan.

CHAPTER 13

Claire drove to Los Angeles, and was grateful that she paid a little extra money for the car with a GPS, assuming that she would spend the better part of her time in California desperately lost.

Even the faceless voice of the navigation system seemed annoyed as Claire made more than one wrong turn trying to find her new apartment.

The apartment complex was old, but well maintained, certainly better than the place she had stayed in Phoenix. She checked in at the office and got her keys. Her unit was on the second floor, and she let herself in, bracing for what could potentially be a dump. The apartment itself was slightly larger than where she had stayed previously, and she was pleasantly surprised at how clean and well maintained it was.

She began making trips up and down the stairs, unpacking her car. While she was able to bring most of the small things, kitchen supplies etc., she still didn't have a place to sleep. After she was unpacked, she decided to head to the nearest store for supplies and an airbed. It would have to do, and she'd buy some furnishings later in the week.

Her phone rang as she was getting in the car. It was her agent, telling her she needed to meet him in the backside kitchen at Hollywood park at 7:00 the next morning.

She left to do some shopping, and returned to her apartment where she was overcome with mind numbing loneliness, so she called Colin.

"Hey girl," he answered. "Did you make it to smog city?"

Claire was amused at the disdain her brother held for California. Slightly ironic, given that he had never actually been there. "Yes, I'm here. Alone."

She could hear Colin shuffling around in the background, and then she heard Ed's unmistakable squall, which he emitted every time he thought something wasn't going exactly the way he thought it should.

"You know what you need," Colin stated, rather than questioned.

"Don't say a boyfriend...I don't need the drama right now. I'm in a new city, and judging from what I've learned about the racetrack, I don't think I'm going to be actively seeking out a relationship."

"Relax, I wasn't even going to suggest it. What I was going to say is that you need a cat."

Claire groaned. "Seriously, I think I'd rather have a boyfriend."

"You're funny, but hear me out. I know that you and Ed don't get along so well, but I am sure you could find a nice cat at the shelter. Cats are low maintenance, and it doesn't matter if you're gone for long stretches of time. It would be a companion with out the worry of needing to take it out for walks. They're perfectly happy to lounge around in an apartment all day, and litter boxes are easier than outdoor potty trips for a dog. Just think about it. You might find you enjoy the company of someone who doesn't talk back."

"Ed talks back."

"You know what I mean."

"Alright. I'm going to get settled here, and get into my work routine, and then I might consider it."

After hanging up the phone with her brother, she pondered the idea of a pet. She had never considered herself a cat person, but on the track and at the farms, they were everywhere, and perhaps there was something to having a four-legged companion. The more she thought about it, the more she liked the idea. As soon as she was settled, at least with a bed and a sofa, she would go to the local shelter and see if she could find a feline that was the opposite of Ed. She got her airbed ready, and tried to sleep. The excitement of being in a new city and a new track kept her awake much longer than she would have liked.

Morning came quickly, and according to the map, the trip was about 35 miles, so she figured that leaving at six would give her more than enough time to get to Hollywood Park, even with a wrong turn or two. Unfortunately, Claire had no experience with L.A. traffic, and very shortly after getting on the freeway, she was at a dead stop. Six lanes of traffic, and not one was moving any faster than the others. She began to panic. The traffic gridlock had her moving at a crawl, and there was no way she was going to make it to the track on time. Not the best first impression, and she was sure that her agent would take one look at her hour late arrival and tell her to get lost. Maybe Colin was right in his musings of L.A. She was not off to a great start.

She pulled into the parking lot at Hollywood Park, over an hour late. The security guard checked her in and told her where to find the kitchen. She immediately felt like a small fish in a very big pond. The track and its surroundings were more than double the size of Phoenix, and she was in complete awe at the expanse of everything. Making her way to the kitchen, she summoned her courage and opened the door. She had not made it two steps inside the building when she heard a familiar booming voice calling her name, and instantly silencing the chatter of the patrons of the backside cafe.

"There she is! It's about time girl! Where the hell have you been?" Frank hollered, as he was walking toward her.

Claire immediately blushed, as all eyes were upon her. She dropped her eyes to the floor, studying her well-worn boots. "I was stuck in traffic," she said quietly.

Frank stood in front of her and laughed heartily. "Welcome to California!" he said, and grabbed her in a bear hug. Claire gasped for air. Her new agent was a big man, although not as big as John. He was very classically Italian, with dark hair that was graying slightly and a bit of a belly indicative of an indulgence in pasta and red wine. She couldn't help but take an instant liking to him, even as he turned her around to face the people in the room. He had his hands on her shoulders and uttered a shrill whistle, redirecting everybody's attention to Claire.

"People, listen up. Right here, you are looking at the next Eclipse award-winning apprentice. I shit you not, this girl can ride, and y'all have my number."

Claire was mortified, but she offered a halfhearted wave to the dozens of eyes that were fixed on her alone. For what seemed like an hour, but was certainly only a few seconds, people stared at her, some shaking their heads, and others nodding as they scrutinized Frank Rossi's new acquisition.

In an instant, Frank turned her and ushered her out of the kitchen. Once she was outside and away from the embarrassment of her introduction, she turned to her new agent.

"Do you mean what you said....about me being the next Eclipse award winner?"

Frank looked at her seriously for a moment. "Claire, I know we just met, but you're going to learn that I always mean what I say. I'm going to tell you the truth, even though it may not be what you want to hear at the time. You are a bug, and while you may think you know everything, I'm here to tell you that you don't. If you trust me to do my job, then we'll do just fine. There are things I'm going to do that might not make much sense to you right now, but my goal is long term. What's your goal?"

"To win the Kentucky Derby," Claire said without hesitation.

"Well, welcome to the frigging club. Do you think that every single jock out there doesn't have the exact same goal?"

"I am sure they do, but none of them are going to work as hard as I am."

Frank looked at her and a huge smile broke on his face. "That's exactly what I want to hear!" he bellowed. "We're going to do just fine together."

Claire decided that if he was going to be completely honest with her, she should be with him, and so she decided to head off any ill intentions. "I am willing to do what I need to, within reason. I won't be sleeping with anybody for mounts, so don't even ask."

Frank smiled again. "I like you Claire, but I am your agent, not your pimp. I don't give two shits about your sex life. I'll get you the best mounts that I can based on your skill as a jockey, nothing else. What you chose to do with yourself otherwise is your business."

"Thanks," she said, and meant it.

They walked around the backside; it was bustling, as there were only a few days before the official beginning of the meet. She was once again introduced to what seemed like hundreds of people she would never remember, but Frank new everybody, and she felt good about her morning. Many trainers had told her they'd been watching her, and she would be getting mounts. Frank was busy setting up workers for the next morning, and she observed the activities on the track. Everything seemed to be on a different level from where she had come from. The horses all looked bigger and faster and better turned out. The stable areas were perfectly manicured with potted flowers and pruned shrubbery, and at every turn she saw something else to remind her that she was now in the big time.

"It's so beautiful.....and big," she said, to nobody in particular.

"This is nothing girl...wait until we get to Del Mar," Frank said in response. "That's where the surf meets the turf, and in my humble opinion, the most beautiful track in the world!"

Claire nodded in response. She had seen pictures of the track at Del Mar, but she really had no idea what to expect. The meet there didn't begin until July, so she had to wait a while, but she was excited nonetheless.

"Do you want me to buy you lunch?" he asked as they were wrapping up for the morning. "Excuse me?"

"You hungry? Pretty simple question. We need to discuss our strategy. You need to know what the routine is here, and I need to know what you expect of me. This is a business meeting, not a date. Tax write-off for me anyway," he said with a grin.

Claire relaxed, remembering she was not with John anymore, and this guy was a professional.

"In that case, what's good around here?" she smiled in reply.

They left the track, and she rode with Frank to a trendy little cafe. Claire was famished, and ordered herself a plate of seafood pasta. Her agent was watching her every move, and she began to feel uncomfortable.

"What?" she finally asked, around a mouthful of food.

"I am going to send you to the track nutritionist."

She was slightly offended. Her weight was still well under what she needed to be to ride, so she didn't know what his motives were. "Why?"

"Because you need it. The track guy is fantastic, and he will get you exactly where you need to be."

Still annoyed, she got defensive. "My weight is fine....better than fine. What's the problem?"

Frank just smiled at her. "No problem, if you want to stay where you are. You need to be stronger, and this guy will tell you how. I don't know much about it myself, but Ryan swears by the guy, and look where he is?"

"Ryan?" Claire asked, feeling stupid.

"Valentin. Top jock in the country, won the Derby last year? Have you been living under a rock for God's sake?"

The light bulb went on, and it dawned on Claire that she was going to be riding at the same track as the jockey she admired from last year's Derby. "Oh, yeah. Sorry, I just wasn't sure. He uses the nutritionist?"

"Yep...says he's the reason he has done so well. Improved his strength ten fold."

Claire was suddenly very interested. "Okay. When can I meet with the guy?"

Frank gave her an amused look. "I'll set you up a meeting tomorrow after works."

They ate in silence for a while, but Frank spoke once again. "What do you expect from me?" he asked plainly.

"What do you mean?" Claire was not used to such blatant honesty.

"Well, you say you want to win the Derby, as does every jock who has ever sat a horse, but what do you want from me as an agent?"

Claire thought for a minute, and she knew the answer, thinking about the agent that she just left. "Honesty. That is all. Don't screw me around. If I mess up, tell me. If I have a choice of mounts, ask me, don't make a decision without talking to me first."

"Good girl," Frank said, meeting her eyes. "I know who you came from, and it is a testament to you that you did as well as you had, given your agent. I told you I'll be honest, and I mean that. This is my living as well, so the better you do, the better I do. You think that I can eat at places like this by being stupid?"

Claire smiled and shook her head. "Kelly told me something once," she said, "and I want to know if it's true."

"Go on."

"He said that an agent isn't my friend, he is my employee. I pay you to do the work, and you do your job, that's where the relationship ends. Is that the best way to work this business?"

"Yes and no. I know what Kelly's saying, he spent his entire, albeit short, career with shitty agents, and he did well in spite of it. However, if you can have a friendship with your agent, as well as a business relationship, you could be even more successful. A business relationship is based on money; a friendship is built on trust. If you and I trust each other, we will make the money. It is a win-win for both of us, and I would hope you'll be able to come to me as a friend, rather than my boss from time to time."

Again, Claire nodded, more than happy with the answer she had received. "I guess I didn't think that was possible. I had watched the agents at the other track, and there isn't one of them that I'd like to be friends with."

"You are playing in the big leagues now. We don't get where we are by being like everybody else. You and I, we'll be fine. I know how good you are, and with a little help, and a lot of luck, I think you just might get to the top."

Claire was still used to people telling her what she wants to hear, so she wasn't convinced.

"Yeah, you probably say that to all your jocks."

"No, I don't. I told you, I tell the truth. My last jock went to Texas because he wasn't going to make it here once he lost the bug. Trainers are all over a good apprentice until they lose their bug, and then it is like starting over again. That five pound allowance is a pretty big deal, and when you lose it, either you can hang with the big guys on your own, or you can't, and my last kid couldn't." He took a drink of his wine, and continued. "You, on the other hand, will make it. Being a woman has its advantages and disadvantages. Some guys won't ever use a girl, but some trainers are quick to jump on the bandwagon, and if you're good enough, they'll love you, especially if you start getting national recognition. Give me four years, and I will have you riding for James Imler in the Derby."

Claire smiled, knowing that James Imler was one of the top trainers in the country, and if Frank was promising that she would ride for him, then she knew she would. Things were certainly different here in California, and she was beginning to like it. Finally, some commitment from somebody.

Her mind wandered, when the events of the morning snapped back to her. "One more question."

Frank gave her the come on with his hand, as his mouth was full.

"Why on earth do I have an apartment in Arcadia, which seems to be about 35 miles away from Hollywood Park? Shouldn't I be living in Inglewood?"

Frank nearly spit his mouthful of food. "Are you crazy girl? Inglewood? No, you're fine in Arcadia. You are just around the corner from Santa Anita, and that's where you want to be. Nobody wants to live in Inglewood. You had better learn the lay of the land here in So Cal, there are some places you really don't want to find yourself lost."

"Oh," she was still incredibly naive when it came to geography. Life was so much simpler in upstate New York, quiet and laid back, and she always felt safe, no matter what time she was out and about.

Frank continued. "It'll be good anyway. By next week, you'll be working horses early at Santa

Anita before coming here to work some more. Most days, you will just be at Hollywood all day, save the early morning works at Santa Anita. Fortunately, Del Mar starts in July, and then you'll get a break from the commute for a couple of months while you hang out on the beach in San Diego. I bet you find life is pretty good here in So Cal."

They finished their meal, and before they parted ways, Frank gave her a list of her next mornings works, and where they could be found, reminding her to leave home an hour earlier if she wanted to get there on time.

As Claire got into her car, she became aware of how she was no longer a big fish in a small pond. California was going to be a whole different ballgame and she couldn't help but feel small and insignificant…and lonely. In that second, she decided that she couldn't wait for her furry companion.

She found her way back to the vicinity of her apartment, and then went to the store to get some basic supplies for a cat. After a few texts to her brother regarding the things she might need, she was prepared. Her GPS lady gave her instructions to the nearest animal shelter, and she found her way easily.

As she entered the shelter, she approached the main desk and said she was interested in adopting a cat. One of the shelter technicians guided her down a narrow corridor to where she would find the available animals. When she entered the room, her heart sank. There were rows and rows of cages, every single one of them occupied. She was overcome with the desire to adopt every single cast off cat in the room, but she guessed her new landlord wouldn't approve of a crazy cat lady in a one-bedroom apartment. It took all the courage she could muster to begin looking in the cages for a prospective companion. Every cat tugged at her heart, and she thought maybe she would try and find a kitten....something that could grow up with her. She asked the technician if there were any kittens available.

"Unfortunately, no. Kittens adopt out really quickly, everybody wants the cute, cuddly kitten, so they are never in the shelter for more than a few days."

Claire nodded. It made sense. She decided that she would just adopt an older cat...maybe give one a second chance.

As she strolled through the room, looking in the cages, her attention was captured by a single brown paw poking out of the grating a couple of rows down from where she was. She approached the cage, and looked inside. What she saw was slightly scary, but intriguing at the same time. The little cat looking back at her was anything but cute and cuddly. He was a small, plain brownish tabby, with no white at all. His head was small, and oddly shaped, almost like a pear, with a long pointy nose. His ears were about three sizes too big for his head, and one seemed to be slightly deformed, angling off to one side, rather than straight ahead. Claire noticed that his tail was about half the length of a normal cat's tail, and to top it all off, he had extra toes on his front feet!

"What's wrong with this one?" Claire asked the technician, who had come back to see how she was doing.

"Technically, nothing. He is healthy, but nobody wants him. We figure he is about 6 months old, but he had obviously had some hard times."

"What's the deal with his feet?"

"He is what is called a polydactyl. It means many toes. It is a common genetic defect in cats, usually strays that have been subject to inbreeding."

"What about his tail?"

The tech glanced at the cat, who was now lying on his back, with both of his paws clinging to the bars of his cage. "We don't know for sure how he lost it...he came in that way."

Claire was about to move on, but she couldn't. "Can I see him?" she asked the tech.

The young technician looked at her strangely. "Yes. Nobody's ever even asked about him before, and I have to warn you, he is pretty ornery. I think he would just as soon scratch your face as sit in your lap."

Claire shrugged. "I don't mind, I just want to see him up close."

The technician took the little cat out of his cage and guided Claire into a small, completely in closed room, where she could have some time alone with the odd creature.

As soon as the door closed behind the woman, the little cat began his show, chasing the toys

around the room, and climbing his way up Claire's pant leg, only to leap down when she reached to pet him. She couldn't help but smile at the little misfit, and she knew he was the cat for her. How she would explain this to her brother, she had no idea, but she was smitten.

She sat in the room with the cat for a few more minutes before the tech came back in and asked what she thought.

"I'll take him."

The technician smiled, and sighed with relief. "If you go up front, they'll have all the necessary paperwork for you to fill out. I'll get him ready."

Claire nodded and smiled. "Thank you," she said, as she handed the fractious kitty back over to the tech.

Legalities were attended to at the front desk, and in a matter of minutes, she was handed her new cat in a cardboard carrier. He was protesting his confinement at great volume, but she wasn't about to let him out until they were home.

On her drive, she was thinking about her new friend, and what his name should be. Small, ugly and ornery. It reminded her of something, and she remembered. John Henry. Her favorite racehorse, and her new cat was a feline replica. Claire didn't know if she believed in fate, but there was certainly something cosmic about the events of the afternoon, and her cat had now had a name.

Once at home, she let John Henry out of his box to explore his surroundings. He seemed at ease, which was unusual. She anticipated that he would find somewhere to hide for a while, but he didn't. He wandered around, found his food and his litter box, and then began to pounce around at play. Claire bounced the feather string toy idly as she watched the ugly little cat entertain himself, and she knew she'd done the right thing. She decided to send her brother a picture of John Henry first, before calling him with the news. Let him call her.

Within seconds of hitting send on her phone, it began to ring. Colin didn't even bother to say hello.

"What the hell is that?" he asked.

"John Henry. My new cat."

"You couldn't find something that actually looked like a cat?"

Claire giggled. "Hey, he just fits."

"Yeah, you're right....you always had a knack for the difficult ones, horses, cats, whatever."

Claire was still watching John Henry as she spoke. "He doesn't seem to be too upset about his new digs. I thought cats were supposed to be more sensitive to change."

"Some are, but not all. Do you want to know what Emily thinks?"

Claire didn't think she did, but she wouldn't say that to her brother. "What does Emily think?" she asked, with a touch of snideness to her tone.

"Emily says that rescue animals know they've been given a second chance. She believes, in many instances, the animals can sense a new opportunity at life and they're grateful. I don't know if I believe it or not, but it's a nice thought anyway."

It was a nice thought, and for as much as Claire didn't really want to give her brother's girlfriend credit for anything, she began to think a little bit better of Emily Clark, soon to be D.V.M.

Colin broke her train of thought. "I am going to show this picture to Emily. She'll love it." Claire was quiet as her brother continued. "She likes you Claire. I know that you've never met, and I know how you feel about her, but she really does care. She's been following your races, and she really admires your talent. Will you just give her a chance?"

Claire sighed. She knew she was being unreasonable about Emily, especially since she had always seemed to just miss meeting her for one reason or another, but it was difficult. "I'm sorry Colin. I know I've been difficult, but I'll try. It might help if I actually got to meet her someday. I am beginning to think she might just be a figment of your imagination. She seemed to be conveniently gone every time I might have had a chance to meet her. Do you keep her in the closet or something?"

"Funny," Colin said, and the conversation lightened significantly.

Dinner was done in the microwave, and she sat on the floor of her unfurnished apartment, eating her meal and watching John Henry, who had worn himself out and was asleep next to her, purring loudly. Even his purr was different. Most cats sounded like a motor, but he sounded like a rusty chainsaw with the hiccups. He was perfect.

The next morning, Claire woke early and made sure that she got to the track on time. Traffic wasn't as bad an hour earlier, and she got in with time to spare.

Frank met her in the kitchen and they headed together to the first barn. It was still dark, and several of Claire's first works were done under the big lights of the racetrack, which gave an eerie illumination to the horses training.

She worked until the break, and as the light of dawn was bringing color to her surroundings, her agent gave her some news that she wasn't ready for.

"You're working in company with Ryan, first after the break."

Claire's stomach did a summersault. She knew she was going to meet the nation's leading rider sometime, she just didn't know if she was ready yet. Her mouth was dry, and all she could do was nod.

Frank looked bemused. "Don't worry. Just don't let him intimidate you. He's going to try it from the get go. He is the smartest jock on the track, and he wants to get your measure....oh, and he hates bugs.....and girl jocks. You'll be fine," he laughed.

Claire nodded again, although she was sure she might die, and they headed to the barn where her next mount was to be found.

The break was not quite over when they arrived, and Claire waited by the entrance to the shed row after being introduced to the trainer. There was no sign of the country's leading jockey. Maybe he would be a no show, and Claire's palms would stop sweating, but she doubted it. Leading rider's don't get that way by not showing up for work.

Frank was standing next to her, browsing through his condition book when Ryan came strolling down the shed row, twirling his whip in his fingers and looking the epitome of cool.

As he approached, Claire couldn't take her eyes off of him. She had seen him on television, but in real life, he was magnetic. He was built like a typical jockey, lean and strong, with a picture perfect physique. She found him incredibly attractive, his chiseled jaw and sharp features made him stand out from any of the other riders she had seen, and his steely blue eyes seemed to look right through her as he came closer.

He stopped short of Claire and her agent, leaning up against the railing of the shed row.

"Ryan," Frank said, nodding curtly.

"Frank," Ryan replied, with the same coolness.

Frank decided on an introduction. "This is Claire. She's my new bug girl, and your company for this work."

Ryan nodded at her, but didn't speak, continuing to twirl his whip casually around his fingers, never really looking at her. She decided not to say anything, which wasn't difficult, as she was tongue tied anyway.

The duo of horses was brought out for them, and Frank gave Claire her leg up. They were instructed to work the horses 5/8 of a mile, the trainer wanted it solid, and the horses to finish together. Claire kept quiet as they walked their mounts together to the track, wishing for Ryan to break the silence, but he never did.

Once they reached the track, they broke off together, side by side around the turn as they reached the starting point. Claire was positioned on the inside, and looked over her shoulder before dropping down towards the rail to begin the work. They picked up speed and continued to match strides down the backside. Claire's horse was nice, and was working easily. She felt like she had a ton of horse underneath her, and knew that all she had to do was ask, and the gelding would give her more. As they entered the turn, Ryan began to let his horse drift in slightly. It wasn't much, but he was putting pressure on her mount, easing them closer to the fence. Claire was alert, and noticed that he was beginning to push her even harder. She didn't think he would actually be stupid enough to put her over the rail in a morning work, but he was definitely trying to intimidate her, as Frank said he would. She wasn't going to take it, even if he was the leading rider in the country. "Hey! Back the hell off. It's just a work!" she said to him as her inside boot was hitting the rail, and her outside boot was pushed tight against Ryan's own.

To her amazement, Ryan eased his horse off of her, not saying a word, and they finished the work strong, head and head past the wire.

Idol or not, Claire was prepared to have words with the country's leading jockey, but by the time she got her horse pulled up and turned around, he was already well ahead of her on the track heading back to the barn. It wouldn't be a good idea to chase after him, not after her horse had just worked five eighths of a mile, so she let her mount settle into a comfortable jog. There would be another time for conversation with Ryan, of that she was sure.

As she got to the barn, the veteran jockey had already untacked his horse and was leaving. Maybe he was avoiding her, but she didn't think he was the type to avoid confrontation. She dismounted, and began to take off her horse's saddle. Frank was standing nearby talking to the trainer, and after she had put down her tack, he motioned her over to them.

"Nice work young lady," the trainer said. His name was Charlie. He looked to be in his fifties, but Claire came to realize that life on the race-track aged people dramatically. He could have been much younger.

"Thank you. That's a really nice horse," she replied honestly.

Frank chimed in, not being one to be quiet for any length of time. "Looked like Ryan was riding you pretty tight, but he backed off. What'd you say to him?"

"I told him to back off, it's only a work....and he did."

"Good girl," Charlie said. "Don't take any crap from these guys. I think you'll be able to hold your own just fine."

Claire smiled. Her morning was going well, and the remainder of her workers were all nice horses. She was beginning to sense a major difference in the horses from Phoenix to California. Every horse she got on seemed to be well trained, well mannered and knew exactly what they were doing on the racetrack. She had yet to encounter anything stupid or crazy, and while she guessed that there were some of those around, California horses seemed to be a much higher class than where she had just been.

When Claire's morning work was finished, Frank reminded her that she was to meet with the track nutritionist/personal trainer. The man's name was Shane Winters, and he was going to meet her in the common area of the jock's room.

She went into the common room and sat down on the nice leather sofa, waiting for Shane. Within moments, a man walked into the room, she assumed it was him, so she stood for a proper greeting.

"Claire?" he said, approaching her.

"Yes. You must be Shane. Nice to meet you," she said, holding out her hand.

"Likewise," he said, and then took as step back away from her. "Let's have a look at you."

Claire felt immediately uncomfortable, as he seemed to be looking over every inch of her body.

Shane was a man of average height, but had a very strong, lean build which was accentuated by the well-fitted designer jeans and expensive looking shirt, that was just tight enough to be vain without being distracting. He was shaved completely bald, which gave him an air of authority in Claire's mind, and his light brown eyes had a very intense and focused look. He actually reminded her of some actor she had seen in action movies, but she just couldn't place it.

"Not bad," he said, after what seemed like an hour, but was probably only about 5 minutes. "But we still have some work to do."

Claire felt stupid. "What do you mean?"

Shane motioned for her to sit, and he joined her on the sofa. "You have a great foundation, and you are undoubtedly strong, but you need to be stronger."

"Why? I've been riding for months now, and I've held my own. What's different?"

Shane looked at her with an intensity that made her squirm slightly. "What's different is you are about to start riding with the best jockeys in the world. Do you think they got to a certain point and then said 'that's good enough?' No, they are always pushing themselves, just like any other professional athlete. Your job keeps you fit, that's true, but if you want to be the best you can be, it's going to take work outside of the track as well. Do you understand?"

"Yes," she had actually given very little thought to her own conditioning. She'd just kind of gone with the flow, knowing that she was strong, but taking it for granted.

"I've watched you on television, and you're a great rider, but I want you to be strong, and I don't mean strong for a girl, I mean strong enough to outride any one of these guys if you have to. You have a God given talent, and that, combined with the strength to enhance it, will put you right up there at the top with the Ryan Valentins of the industry."

Claire sat up a bit straighter with the mention of her idol slash adversary. "Does Ryan work with you?"

Shane smiled ever so slightly, noticing Claire's sudden interest. "You're damn right he does. Three strength and cardio sessions per week, and his diet is impeccable. Gone are the days of binge and purge. These guys know that the best way to be strong is to properly fuel the body. With the proper fuel, they can maintain their weight and their strength. It take's a lot of dedication on their part, but the proof is in the pudding."

"Alright then, what do I have to do?" Claire asked. She knew she was up for the challenge, and if it would make her stronger, then it would be worth any sacrifice.

"I want you to meet with me on the two off racing days for strength work, and as long as you can commit to the cardio on your own, we won't have to do that too. There are some great hills to run around here, and I am sure you can find some running trails you'll enjoy."

Claire nodded, taking notes in her head while Shane carried on for about 25 minutes, hammering home the importance of a healthy and balanced diet and all of the nuances to go with it.

"Do all of the jockey's work with you?" Claire asked, when he finally drew breath, knowing that this whole lifestyle change might be easier if she could observe others at the same time.

"No, not all of them, but I can tell you right now, my guys are six of the top ten at the track, and in the top 20 in the nation. Does that help?"

"Yes," Claire had one more question she was afraid to ask, but had no choice. "It sounds fantastic and all, but I am pretty sure I can't afford you, can I?"

Shane smiled and shook his head. "Right now, probably not, but your agent has covered your first month. If, after a month, you aren't satisfied, and want to stop, that's fine, I completely respect it, but I can promise you, if you stick with me, and do the things I tell you, after a month of riding, you won't have any problem affording my services. Sound like a deal?"

"Yes...deal." She said with a sudden and overwhelming urge to cry. Frank had arranged everything. He was nothing like her old agent. John never paid for anything if he could help it, and here was Frank, shelling out what was probably a good chunk of money for a rider who hadn't even won her first race for him yet. She was aware of just how much faith he was putting in her to be a winner, and she could only hope she could live up to everybody's expectations.

CHAPTER 14

Opening day at Hollywood Park brought a new level of excitement. She was the only woman in the ladies jocks room, so she had the entire place to herself as she went through her pre-race routine.

Once ready, she went to the common area, where a young jockey came in, one she had recognized from watching the races on TV. His name was Travis Browning, and he used to be one of the top riders in the country. Claire never really knew what happened to him. He was an award-winning apprentice, and had great success, but then he began to fall apart. Now his mounts were few and far between, and while he was still an incredibly talented rider, people just didn't want to put him on horses.

He came in and plopped down on the sofa next to Claire. "You the new bug girl?" he asked, knowing full well who she was.

"Yes. I'm Claire," she said as she held out her hand.

"Travis," he said, shaking her hand in return. "What race you in?"

"I ride the fourth and last," she said, trying not to sound disheartened that she only had two mounts on the day. Frank had told her to expect it to be slow the first week, but he was confident, simply because she was getting on a lot of horses in the morning, and said the mounts will pick up.

Travis picked at something on his boot. "Good for you. I'm in the fourth only. Good luck." "Thanks," Claire responded, not sure what else to say.

Travis looked at her for a second before asking her his next question. "Do you want to go out sometime?"

Claire was shocked at how forward he was, but subtlety seemed to be a lost art at the track. She studied him carefully. He was a few years older than she, but he looked like he had had a hard life. He just looked tired. She hoped he wouldn't end up looking ten years older in three years time, but the track life seemed to age everybody. Time to head him off at the pass. "No, thank you. I'm not really interested in dating anybody right now."

"You a dyke?" he asked plainly.

Again, Claire was taken aback. "No. I just have other priorities."

"Whatever," he said, looking somewhere else. "Just thought I'd ask."

Claire was about to try and make some sort of small talk when she looked up and saw Ryan enter the room and her breath stopped. He was half dressed, wearing only his jock pants and boots, and his body was like none that she had ever seen in her life. He was the absolutely perfect specimen of a man. Sculpted to precision, with every muscle and sinew visible under his tanned skin. His abs gave a new meaning to the term 'six-pack', and his back and shoulders were cut unlike anybody she had ever seen. But, what caught her attention the most was the tattoo. His entire back was covered in what could be described as a tribal design. It extended around both sides of his rib cage, and over his shoulders, stopping about mid-way down each arm. She stared unabashedly, trying to decide if it was one large tattoo, or several joined together. There was no color to the design, it was strictly black line drawing that appeared to contain various images, but Claire wasn't sure she could identify anything specific. She thought she saw a horse head intertwined within the lines, but when she looked again, it was gone. The only word she could come up with was beautiful, but she didn't dare speak it. He was watching her, and she knew it, but she couldn't take her eyes off of him. It would seem her sofa companion had a different idea.

"For God's sake Valentin, put a damn shirt on.....nobody wants to see that," Travis said, with more than a little hostility.

Ryan's cocky smile stirred something deep inside of Claire as he replied. "Oh, I think somebody does," he gave her a wink, and as quickly as he entered, he left.

The first words she had ever hear him speak in person, and she knew that they were directed at her. Her face flushed, and she tried to look away, but Travis sensed what was going on.

"What an arrogant prick. You're not actually into that guy are you?" he asked.

Claire didn't know what to say. She hadn't been. He didn't even acknowledge her presence the day they worked together, and he had never spoken directly to her, but she was feeling something for him she couldn't explain. "No," she lied. "I've just never seen a tattoo like that before."

"Hmmph," Travis grunted. "Whatever floats your boat. I hope it hurt like hell."

Claire chose to ignore that last statement as the call for the jockey's for the fourth race came, and none too soon. She was preoccupied, thinking about Ryan, and what Travis had said about him. Travis was probably jealous. He had been a contender against Ryan for a few years, but now, Ryan was still on top of his game, and Travis had fallen by the wayside. As Claire waited to go out to the paddock, her mind was wandering to the tattoos. Her brother had some sort of Celtic band tattooed around his bicep, and she always gave him a hard time about it, but never really thought about men with extensive tat work. She found that she was incredibly turned on by the artistry on Ryan's body, and secretly hoped she could get a closer look someday.

She forced herself to focus on the task at hand. It would be very poor form for her to be distracted going into her first race at a track of this magnitude. The trainer legged her up onto her mount, and all thoughts of Ryan left her mind. Her horse was an older mare, cheap by California's standards, but the purse money was still about four times that of Arizona. Her earning potential was enormous, and she had spent some time daydreaming about what she could do with her wealth should she begin winning races the way her agent predicted.

The field of horses made it to the starting gate, and she entered the number three stall. Her gate handler greeted her and then focused on her horse, who was standing quietly but alert. Claire had studied the racing form, and knew her mare didn't have much of a shot in the race, but her goal was to ride a clean race and try and place in the top four. The gates popped open, and her horse sprung forward. Claire was ready, and she settled the mare mid pack down the backstretch. She saw Travis on the lead, and the other riders surrounding her. They were riding her tight, and she knew that she was going to have to work hard to get a clear run in the stretch. These guys weren't going to cut her any slack, so she would have to make her own way. Her horse felt good, but she didn't feel like she had a ton of horse underneath of her as they were midway through the turn. She asked the mare for more speed, and she gave it. Travis's horse was tiring badly, and she could see another horse coming up on her outside. The field came down the stretch for home, and Claire rode hard, knowing that her mount was giving everything she had, but it wasn't going to be enough to win. They passed under the finish line in second, which pleased Claire. She rode a solid race, not making any mistakes, and the mare significantly outran her odds of 12:1.

She brought her horse back to the front of the grandstands, where her trainer was waiting, saluted the stewards and dismounted. The trainer was elated with the race, and promised Claire some better mounts. She thanked him and went to the scales to weigh out. As she was headed back to the jockey's room, Travis approached her.

"Nice work out there," he said. "You look good on a horse, and I don't mean for a girl."

"Thanks. The mare ran big," she replied.

She went in to clean up a bit, and then play the waiting game, as her next race wasn't until the last of the day. The common room was quiet, with a few other riders in there, doing their own thing, and while she secretly hoped that she would see Ryan, she knew that he rode all the rest of the races that day, so she would just have to make do by watching him on the television. It couldn't hurt anything....he was the best rider in the country, she might learn something.

After watching him win three of the next four races, what she learned was that he never made a mistake. He sat as still as a statue on his mounts, and when the time came to start pushing, his motions were subtle and fluid, and the horses responded. He rarely had to whip more than once or twice. His strength down the lane was unmatched, as often times he could push a horse ahead just by hand riding.

Emotionally, she was in turmoil. Watching him ride, she was starstruck. He was amazing, and she idolized his talent, but she wanted to see him off of the horses. The image of him walking into the common room would be forever seared into her brain, and she knew he was going to be the subject of many fantasies. He was 34 to her 19, but that didn't matter. She knew she couldn't be in love, but she was definitely in lust.

The last race of the day finally arrived. This mount had even less of a shot than her first, but that didn't deter her. The race was a mile, and she was starting from the outside post. When the gates popped, her horse left a step slowly, which allowed her to guide him down to the rail in an effort to save the most ground. They stayed near the rear of the field, in front of one other horse only, until the second turn, and she began to ask her horse for more run. He responded slowly, and she had no choice but to take him wide around the other horses. She found that these riders hugged the rail like nobody's business, and the chances of slipping through on the inside were nil. Mid way through the turn, her mount was still passing horses when she came up on Ryan's outside. He looked over at her, and gave his horse a smooch. His mount responded, and as he was keeping pace with Claire, he began to push her further to the outside. She tried to hold her ground, but her horse was intimidated, and continued to move away from his rival, increasing the amount of ground he had to cover with every step, just to get to the finish. Ryan pushed his horse forward, leaving Claire hung much wider than she wanted to be, and without enough horse to make up the lost ground. She ended up finishing mid pack, and Ryan won yet another race.

She was furious as she walked back to the room. She'd allowed herself to be manipulated on the track, and it had probably cost her a top four finish. It was coming to her attention that Ryan was going to make her life difficult every opportunity that he could. Even more frustrating to her was the fact that he was so damn good-looking, and so arrogant, and Claire had no business feeling anything but loathing, but she couldn't stop the butterflies she had when his tattooed body would invade her mind.

She showered and dressed hurriedly, knowing that her agent was waiting for her. As she left the jockeys room, she looked around for Ryan, but didn't see him. Frank was waiting for her by the paddock gate, and he wasn't alone. Ryan was with him, and they seemed to be having a rather heated discussion. Claire gathered herself, trying to will away the butterflies as she approached. They saw her coming, and Ryan immediately turned to leave.

"Watch it Valentin, that's all I am saying," Frank said as Ryan turned to walk away.

"Then tell your girl to stay out of my way, and we won't have any problems," he responded rudely, not so much as giving a backward glance.

"I need to stay out of his way? What the hell?" Claire said angrily as her butterflies immediately vanished.

Frank grunted. "I told you, he hates bugs, but he hates girl riders even more. He ain't gonna make your life easy out there, that's for sure."

"Lovely," Claire said. "What do I do?"

"Nothing. Ride your races, but know where he is on the track every second. I don't think he's going to look for trouble, he's smarter than that, but if he has an opportunity to screw you, he will. Don't trust him for a second."

Claire nodded. She didn't like what she was hearing, but if that was how it was going to be, then she'd adjust accordingly.

*

In the following weeks, Claire settled herself into a routine. She would wake early to work horses at Santa Anita for a few hours before heading to Hollywood to work more horses, and then on race days, she would just stay the day at the track. With only two days off of racing a week, she didn't get much of a break, as on those two days she was meeting with Shane for her workout sessions. Her time at home was limited, but she enjoyed her evenings alone with John Henry. He was an ornery little cat, but he loved Claire, and as much as she hated to admit it, she was quite taken with her feline friend. They would play all evening, and then at bedtime, he would curl up right next to her and not move all night. She felt guilty leaving him alone every day, but he seemed to be happy just to have his own place, and he never much objected to her absence.

At the racetrack, Claire was beginning to make a name for herself. She was starting to win races, and the mounts were getting better by the day. Ryan had not spoken to her since her first day in the room, but he made it a point to wander through the common room, shirtless, as if just to tease Claire with the constant reminder of his perfection.

Opposite of Ryan was Travis, and he and Claire had become friends. Periodically, he would ask her out, but she always refused. Their conversations were limited to the jockey's room, and the kitchen at break time in the mornings, but it was good to have somebody to talk to. Travis was a nice enough guy, but he was struggling. He had no support from family, and had been on his own at the track since he was sixteen. Claire could tell he had a drinking problem, as she rarely saw him without a beer, even early in the morning. It made her nervous, given her own family history, but she kept her mouth closed, which was something she would regret in the days to come.

A few days later, Claire was in the track kitchen, getting herself a cup of coffee during break time when Travis came up next to her.

"Hey girl, what's up?" he asked, same as always.

"Nothing....just need my morning pick me up. You?"

"I got mine," he said, raising a can of cheap beer to his mouth.

Claire shuddered. How on earth he could drink beer at eight o'clock in the morning was beyond her. They went and sat down at one of the tables for their usual chat. She was worried about her friend. He seemed to be losing touch with the day-to-day life, riding fewer and fewer horses in the afternoon, and he spent most of his mornings in the kitchen.

The door opened, and a group of trainers and riders came in, bantering loudly, and Claire noticed that Ryan was amongst them. He looked over at her table, and excused himself from his companions, heading her way. Her stomach immediately began to flip flop, but she kept her cool, wondering why he was coming to speak to her now. It turned out he wasn't.

"Hey, Browning," Ryan said, hitting Travis's helmet with his whip a little harder than necessary.

Travis flinched and tried to grab Ryan's stick, but Ryan was far too quick, getting it out of his reach with one fluid motion. "What the hell? Asshole. What do you want?" Travis said bitterly.

"You do remember that you have to work one in company after the break? Given your tendency to forget shit, I just wanted to give you a reminder. Unlike you, I have workers lined up all morning, and I can't afford to miss one on account of your drunk ass." Ryan flicked his stick at Travis, then tucked it into his back pocket as he left, not acknowledging Claire's presence, again. She may have had some feelings of lust for Ryan, but in that moment she felt sorry for Travis.

"I hate that guy," Travis said, crunching his beer can in his hand.

Claire looked at her friend, trying to hide her concern. "Has he always been like that?"

Travis nodded. "He's been on top for too long. There hasn't been a rider come through here that can outride him, and he knows it. All the trainers are so far up his ass it isn't even funny. He runs the show. I gave him a run once, but it didn't last long," he stood. "I'd better get going... don't want to piss off the king." He walked away, tossing his empty can in the trash as he went out the door, and that was the last time Claire ever saw him.

At the races that afternoon, Travis was a no show. Didn't even bother calling in that he wasn't coming. Claire was worried, but everybody said he was fine, probably just drunk and, since he had shown up one too many times to ride with a blood alcohol level through the roof, the stewards were keeping a much closer eye on him. Better for him if he just didn't bother coming in.

Claire rode her races, having her first multi win day, where she won two races, and had three seconds in five mounts. She was beginning to feel more confident amongst these super talented riders, and while she was getting respect from most of them, there were a few who still didn't take her seriously. Ryan had not done anything blatant, but she didn't give him much opportunity. She tried to stay away from him on the track if at all possible, and she was usually relieved when they weren't even in the same race together.

After the races, she was eager to get home. The traffic, as usual, was terrible, but she finally made it, and was greeted with enthusiasm by John Henry. She made herself some dinner, and began her evening ritual of play with her cat. It was near bedtime, when she heard a knock on her door. She was apprehensive, she never had visitors, and at night, being a woman alone, wasn't sure if she wanted to answer.

"Who is it?"

"Claire, it's Frank."

She unbolted the door quickly. Something was wrong; otherwise her agent would have simply called. He had never come to her place before.

Frank walked through the door, and Claire could immediately tell that something terrible had happened. This was, after all, not the first time she had received late night bad news.

"Frank? What is it? What's wrong?" she asked, her voice shaking.

"Travis Browning is dead."

Claire gasped. It couldn't be. She had just been talking to him that morning. "No....not possible," she was shaking her head, as her body was beginning to tremble.

"I'm so sorry Claire. I know you two were friends. His agent found him at his house a couple of hours ago. He'd been trying to call, but Travis never answered, so he just went over. Travis was dead in his living room."

Claire was struggling to keep her composure. "How?"

Frank shook his head. "Drugs. Booze. A combination of the two. As horrible as it sounds, everybody could see it coming."

Claire couldn't keep it together any longer, and she broke down in tears. Frank hugged her. He wasn't comfortable, but held onto her anyway, letting her cry. She finally moved away from him and sat down. John Henry jumped up in her lap and begun to rub his head against her.

Doing what he could to console his master. She ran her hands over his soft brown coat as she waited for Frank to speak.

"I know you were talking to him this morning, did he give any indication anything was wrong? Anything other than normal?"

Claire shook her head. "No, he was fine," she paused for a moment, going over the events of the morning in her head. "Ryan came to talk to him, and he got a little flustered." She remembered Ryan's treatment of Travis that morning, and hoped desperately that his actions hadn't caused Travis to take his own life.

Frank didn't seem concerned about the information he'd received.

"Have....had Ryan and Travis always disliked each other?" she asked.

Frank nodded. "They were fierce competitors when Travis was at his peak. People thought Travis might be the one to give Ryan the most run for his money in the standings, and he did, for a while, but he couldn't lay off the booze, and started his skid. Ryan didn't cause Travis to kill himself. He hates everybody, and he pretty much treats them all with the same disdain. No...Travis made his own choices, and unfortunately, they were mostly wrong."

Claire sat in silence. Her mind was reeling, and she couldn't believe she'd lost her friend. "I wish there was something I could've done." .

"You did do something."

"What? He's dead," Claire said flatly.

Frank looked at her steadily. "You gave Travis something that he hasn't had in a long time...a friend. It was the best you could do, unfortunately, it was never going to be enough."

Claire nodded. Frank let himself out, and she sat quietly, listening to John Henry purr on her lap. It was late, even later in New York, but she had to talk to Kelly.

"Hello? Claire?" Kelly said sleepily. "Is everything Ok?"

"No," Claire blurted. "Travis Browning is dead. He killed himself...I just found out. I'm sorry to call you so late, but I had to talk to somebody."

She could hear Kelly rustling around. She heard Mandy's voice in the background, and Kelly told her what had happened. "It's fine. You know you can call me at any time. What happened?"

"They think it was an overdose. Drugs and alcohol. He was a no show at the races today, and his agent found him tonight."

Kelly sighed, and was quiet for so long that Claire thought they had been disconnected. "I'm so sorry, Claire. I know you were friends."

Claire remembered that Kelly had been involved in a similar situation. Now was as good a time as any to ask. "Kelly, what happened to your friend? I have heard bits and pieces of the story, but I don't know the details. Will you tell me?"

Kelly was quiet again for a moment, but when he spoke, his voice had changed. There was a sorrow in it that Claire had never heard before. "Steve was my best friend in the world. We grew up together on the racetrack, we started our apprenticeships about the same time, and we were basically inseparable. We were both doing well, and the money was coming in. He was riding in Philadelphia, and I was in New York. I had my parents supporting me, as well as a lot of other good people, but Steve had nobody. He had no one to guide him, or help him make the right choices. He started drinking, and I had heard he was doing drugs. His business started falling, but mine was climbing, and we began to grow apart. It seemed like the better I did, the more he drank, and the worse he did. He blamed me for his fall from grace, and I guess I blame myself too. He was always more suggestible, more likely to cave to the pressures. I should have been there....kept him closer, but I didn't. I was young and selfish, riding high on my own success," Kelly paused, and Claire heard him take a deep breath. "He called me one night, he didn't sound right, and asked if I could come and see him. I didn't want to, it was late, and it was a long drive from where I lived in New Jersey to his place in Philly, but he insisted, so I went. When I got to his apartment, the door was open, so I let myself in. He was there. Standing in the middle of the room in just his boxers. God he was thin, gaunt looking. He had a gun. I don't know where he got it, but it was in his hand. Part of me wanted to think it was just a toy, and he was playing some joke on me, but I knew that wasn't true. I was sure he was going to kill me, and I tried to talk to him, but he was raving. There were empty bottles everywhere, and it is amazing that he was even standing. I didn't know what to do. He was carrying on about how this was all he deserved, and I was the golden boy. He said that it was my fault that he was in this position, and he was the better rider, but didn't get the breaks that I did. I was frozen Claire. I was afraid to reach for my phone, and I didn't know what words to use. He had begun to cry, and I thought I might be able to get to him and get the gun away, but I couldn't. He put the gun in his mouth and pulled the trigger. There was nothing I could do. The police told me later that he was so high on coke and booze it was amazing he didn't kill me too."

Claire had begun to cry again. She had no idea what Kelly had gone through, and it was far worse than she ever imagined. No wonder he just faded out of the riding scene. It made her own problems seem small.

"I'm so sorry Kelly. That must have been awful."

"It was, but it was a long time ago. I am sorry to say Claire, it's an all too common occurrence in this industry. So many of these young kids are talented riders and have a ton of success right away. They have no positive role models, and they don't have any idea how to deal with the sudden influx of money, girls, and all the other temptations. Keep your head Claire. You know you can call Mandy or myself at any time. Talk to your agent. Frank is a great guy, and he won't let you go the wrong way. Remember your family, your mom, your brother, your aunt. They all care about you, and even though they can't be there looking over your shoulder when you encounter the difficult situation, remember what they stand for."

Claire nodded her head, and wiped her tears. "Thank you, Kelly. You guys mean more to me than you know."

"You're welcome. Call whenever you need."

Claire sat quietly well into the night. Her mind was hazy, and she wondered if there was truly anything she could have done to save her friend. They weren't incredibly close, but she did consider him a friend, and had looked forward to their conversations.

The next morning, life went on as usual at the racetrack. Horses need-ed to be worked, and the races would go on. The atmosphere was subdued, and there was a moment of silence in honor of Travis between the third and fourth races. Claire was unsure how she was going to focus to ride, but found that being on the horses helped ease her sorrow, and she won two races in honor of her friend.

As she was leaving the jockeys room at the end of the day, her name was called from behind. She stopped as Ryan approached her. Even in light of everything that had happened, her breath still caught in her chest when she looked at him.

"Yes," she said, trying not to give away her emotions.

Ryan looked at her, his blue eyes piercing hers. "I'm sorry....about Travis. I know you two were friends."

Claire nodded her acceptance of his condolences, but still found her-self angry. "You didn't have to be so hard on him, you know. He said that's just the way you are, but I don't think it was right."

Ryan dropped his gaze for a moment, and for the first time, Claire didn't see the arrogance to which she had become so accustomed. "I know. I've been thinking about it since I heard the news last night. I know you probably don't think I'm capable of the emotion, but I do feel bad. He was a good kid, but he made some bad choices. Anyway, I just wanted to say I'm sorry."

"Thank you," Claire said, and he walked away, leaving her standing alone and more confused than ever.

CHAPTER 15

Spring turned to summer, and before Claire knew it, Hollywood had ended, and it was time to go to Del Mar in San Diego. She had finished the meet at Hollywood, fourth in the jockey standings,

having a major surge of wins toward the end, but she was still better than 20 wins behind Ryan. Regardless, she was incredibly happy, and in light of Travis's death, she kept her wits, sending half of her paycheck, no matter how large or small, home to her aunt and mother, every single week.

Del Mar was one of the elite meets in the country. It ran for a short period of time, only about six weeks, but it was comparable only to the meet at Saratoga in New York. The purses were huge and the crowds were even bigger. It was the meet where the surf meets the turf, and when Claire walked onto the apron of the grandstands, she could actually see the ocean from her vantage point, but even better, she could smell it. The entire venue was a sight to behold, from the lush green of the turf course, to the sandy colored surface of the main track. Every square inch of the palatial grounds was perfectly manicured, catering to the elite of the industry, and for the first time, she really loved California.

She had found a one-bedroom apartment, fully furnished and quite pricy for the short amount of time she would be there, but she didn't want to share with anybody else, and she needed a place that would accept John Henry. The complex was home to some of the other riders, so she did have people nearby if she wanted. This meet would be much more laid back than her life in L.A., if only that she was working horses in one place, near her temporary home, and she wouldn't be leaving her cat home alone for so long during the day.

Frank had gotten even more maniacal. There were times that she was embarrassed to be seen with him, the better she did, the louder he got, doing everything at the top of his voice, and he had developed an arrogance that could only be rivaled by Ryan's.

Del Mar was Ryan Valentin's meet. The previous year, he had won 50 races, and earned over $300k in six weeks. Claire could only dream of that kind of success, especially as a bug, but with Frank's confidence in her, it would only be a matter of time.

Her days were spent riding, and she would head to the beach after the races, mostly to relax and people watch. The surfers were out in force, and Claire admired their skills and precision on their boards. Her idea of enjoying the ocean was walking in the surf, and she did that daily. She was happy and content, but she was also lonely. While she didn't want to deal with the complications of a romantic relationship, she craved companionship, but not the kind that most of her fellow jockeys had to offer. She still had her fantasies about Ryan, and he still succeeded at feeding them, showing up in the common area shirtless, as usual, just to get her heart racing, or brushing up against her at random moments, making her whole body tingle. He hadn't spoken to her since Travis's death, and he was riding her just as tough as ever. Things with him weren't likely to change anytime soon. She would continue to fantasize, until it got old, and he would continue to tease, until he got bored.

Claire won races. More than she could have hoped for, and the flow of cash tempted her beyond belief. She kept her senses, and rather than keep it to spend, she sent it away. A few days after her second large check, she did what she had wanted, and waited for the call. It came, as she expected.

"Claire.....What have you done?" Colin asked, without so much as a hello.

"Why, whatever do you mean?" she replied, feigning innocence.

"You know exactly what I mean. You know I can't accept this."

She smiled to herself. The conversation was going exactly as she scripted. "Of course you can.

Don't argue with me. It's my earnings, and I can do with it what I want."

Colin calmed slightly, and she could hear his gratitude in his voice. "It's too much though. I am going to send some back."

"No you're not. You're going to put a down payment on a house, and if you absolutely have to get rid of the leftovers, you will give it to Aunt Robyn for Mom's care."

"Okay then. Thank you. You're amazing you know," he said, slightly choked up.

"I know. Buy yourself a nice place....a place for two, and I don't mean you and Ed," she said, suggesting that Emily would be joining him sometime.

"I will. And thank you again." He changed the subject. "I'm thinking about coming out to see you in a couple weeks, is that fine?"

Claire was excited. "Of course! Just come to San Diego. We're at Del Mar now. It's beautiful here, I know you will love it!"

Colin was happily skeptical. "We'll see about that...but I would love to see the beach. Thanks again. I love you sis."

Claire reciprocated, and said her goodbyes. She went to bed that night feeling good about herself and what she had done. The knowledge of the money that she could make was hitting home, and she understood how some of these young jocks went overboard. Her experiences early would never let her get stupid, and she would always remember Travis, and Kelly's situation, and keep her success in check.

A week before Colin arrived, Claire experience the true roller coaster of the racing industry. She won her first graded stakes race, a $150k race on a horse that she had come to love, and two races later, she was cut off abruptly by another rider, clipped heels, and went down. She hit the ground hard, but she was unhurt, and got into the ambulance under her own power. The ride back to the jockey's room seemed a lot further than a half a mile, as she was asked a multitude of questions trying to determine if she had any sort of head injury, but she said that she was fine, and was released to the room to ride her final race.

For the first time in weeks, Ryan approached her. "You okay? You hit the ground pretty hard," he said casually.

"I'm fine. I have to ride the last. I'll be fine," she said, slightly flustered.

"You'll be sore tomorrow," he said. "You are still on the adrenaline high, but tomorrow morning, you're gonna hurt."

Claire nodded, knowing that he was probably right. "I'll be fine."

He smiled at her, and her knees went weak. After weeks and weeks of riding against him, and knowing his attitude, he still gave her the butterflies. He left to get ready for the last race, and she did the same. He beat her, as usual, but she rode a good race, finishing second. She had gotten used to looking at his backside on the racetrack, but it was a view she didn't mind.

It was early evening when the races ended, and she showered quickly, looking forward to going home and resting her body, which was growing noticeably more sore. She exited the jocks room, and ran straight into Ryan, who seemed to be waiting for somebody. That somebody turned out to be her.

"How do you feel?" he asked.

"A little sore."

"Okay, I know I've been kind of an asshole to you, but I was wondering if you wanted to join me tonight for some dinner...kind of a truce, if you'll have it?"

Claire's stomach did flip-flops. Her mouth was dry, and she knew that she should say no. Every ounce of common sense said she should refuse, but her body was screaming yes.

Against her better judgment, she replied. "Alright, what's the plan?" she inquired, faking the smoothness of a woman who had found herself in these situations regularly.

Ryan smiled at her easily. "There's a nice restaurant just down the road, in La Jolla. Go home and get changed and I'll pick you up in an hour."

All she could do was nod as he walked away. She watched him go, appreciating the view even more, in his designer jeans and tailored sport coat.

She hurried home, grateful for the fact that she had packed every woman's obligatory little black dress. It had been an impulse purchase during a sightseeing trip to Beverly Hills, and despite its hefty price tag, she had bought it anyway, not thinking she would ever have the chance to wear it. The chance had come, and she put it on, admiring her beautiful and strong physique in the mirror. She'd taken advantage of Shane's services, and he was right. With the proper diet and exercise program, her body was as solid as a rock, not an ounce of fat, and toned to absolute perfection. She pictured herself walking next to Ryan. He was a jockey, and not statuesque according to the traditional standards of a man, but he was taller than she, and perfect in every way. She chose to ignore their age difference as she paced nervously, wishing she were more comfortable in the 4-inch heels that were also an impulse purchase. John Henry sensed something different, and he was meowing repeatedly, expressing his displeasure at the change in his routine.

Ryan arrived right on time, and she didn't want to seem over excited, so she took a moment to calm herself.

"Hi," she said when she opened the door, trying not to sound nervous.

"Wow. You clean up nice."

Claire giggled like a child. "Thanks, so do you."

He smiled at her, making her knees go weak. "You ready?"

"Yes," she said, pulling the door closed behind her.

They walked to the parking area, and Claire was beginning to feel like she might be about ready to step into a life that was light years out of her comfort zone. Ryan's car was a very expensive looking, European sports car. He was wearing a perfectly tailored, custom suit that probably cost more than her entire wardrobe, little black dress included. The amount of money that he was able to spend on things, riding horses for a living, was absolutely mind bending.

The restaurant that he took her to was incredibly posh. They walked in and were greeted by the host, who addressed Ryan by name.

"Good evening, Mr. Valentin. I have a table ready for you and your lovely guest out on the terrace, if that is acceptable."

Ryan nodded, and motioned Claire to follow the host, while ever so slightly brushing his hand against the small of her back, giving her goose bumps. The entire situation was surreal. Never in her wildest dreams would she have imagined dining at a five star restaurant with one of the best riders in the world, but here she was, and walking on air. They were seated outside, on the terrace, overlooking the endless blue Pacific and the setting sun which cast a golden sparkle over the surface of the water. It was a beautiful evening, with the smell of the ocean mixing with the sweet aroma of the flowers growing up the hillside underneath of them overwhelming the senses.

Their waiter approached immediately, and Ryan proceeded to order a bottle of wine for the table. Claire's mind was racing. He had to know that she wasn't old enough to drink, but the waiter didn't ask any questions. She had never so much as had a drop of alcohol, and since her parents accident, she swore that she never would. But, this situation was different. She didn't want to seem like a child, after all, she was riding with the big boys now, so she chose not to say anything, promising herself that she would only have one glass of wine. She began to look at the menu, and again, realized just how far out of her realm she actually was. There were no prices next to any of the entrees, and her brother always told her that if you have to ask, then you probably couldn't afford it. The atmosphere had an air of wealth that she had no way to grasp. A fancy dinner for her family was The Olive Garden, but she was pretty sure that none of the patrons of this facility would be caught dead at such a place.

"What do you feel like eating?" Ryan asked, bringing her attention back to him.

"I'm not sure. Everything looks so good.....and expensive."

He gave her a half grin. "Don't worry about it. Order what you want."

She was about to protest when the waiter arrived with the bottle of wine. He went through the motions with Ryan, and when her date nodded his approval, he poured the rich, burgundy liquid into Claire's glass.

"Cheers. Here's to a good day for both of us," Ryan said, holding up his glass.

She toasted her date, and took a sip of the wine. It was better than she had anticipated, and even though she had no basis for comparison, she was pretty sure it was a very expensive bottle.

Claire took the opportunity to go with that line of conversation. "Better for you. You didn't hit the ground."

"True. How you feeling after that?"

"A little sore, but not too bad. I was pretty lucky."

"You were. Several years ago, I was in a similar spill. My horse clipped heels and I went down, but I wasn't clear of the field and I was run over."

"Oh my God!" Claire said, not thinking that her idol had ever tasted dirt. "Were you alright?" "No. I broke my back.....transverse process L1 through L5. It took me eight months to get back on a horse, and to this day my back still hurts."

Claire didn't really know how to respond. She had been lucky so far, and had never been seriously hurt, but her time could come.

They ordered their meal, and continued to chat about the racing. Ryan asked about Claire's family, and she gave him the story. The wine had made her chatty, and she did most of the talking, telling him more than she should, and not letting him get in a word. She was happy he didn't seem uncomfortable with her tale, and even happier that he didn't shower her with pity. He just nodded and listened.

Claire drank her glass of wine, and not having any experience with alcohol, all it took was one and she could feel her head start to get fuzzy. She refused Ryan's offer to pour her a second class, he didn't question her, but finished the bottle himself, not seeming to be feeling any ill effects of the alcohol.

At the conclusion of the meal, the waiter brought out the bill, and Claire didn't even want to think about it. Ryan paid with a credit card, but as they were standing to leave, he dropped three, crisp hundred dollar bills on the table.

"You just gave our waiter a $300 tip?" Claire asked incredulously.

Ryan put his hand on her back again, guiding her away from the table. "You're not old enough to drink, are you?" It was a statement, rather than a question, and in Claire's slightly intoxicated state, she understood he had bought the waiter's silence on the matter. It occurred to her that it probably wasn't the first time he had done something to that effect, but her head was foggy, and she couldn't stay focused on the thought for very long.

Once the sun had set, the sea breeze was cool, and Claire shivered, partially against the chill, but mostly because Ryan had his arm around her shoulders, and she could feel the heat of his body against hers. He helped her into the car, and she knew immediately what the night was going to bring. The glass of wine had loosened her inhibitions, and she was overcome with the desire to see Ryan's tattoos up close and personal.

"Where too?" he asked.

Claire didn't hesitate. "My place."

"Yes ma'am." he said with a hint of a smile that Claire couldn't see in the dark of the car. The drive was fast, but not fast enough for Claire's liking. Every fiber of her body was aching to be touched by him, and she hoped that she had the self-restraint to not just tear his clothes off when they got to her place.

She fumbled with her keys when they reached her apartment, and he steadied her hand with his own. She was sure that she wasn't drunk, but she now knew what people meant when they said 'tipsy.'

Ryan came in and closed the door behind him, taking time to secure the deadbolt. He took off his suit coat and hung it carefully over the chair before turning to Claire.

She stepped out of her shoes and approached him, reaching out to touch his hand. He touched her face, tucking her hair behind her ear as he leaned in to kiss her. Her body melted into his touch and as their mouths met her knees immediately buckled. He wrapped both of his arms around her, and kept her on her feet, his embrace was strong, and she felt as though she were being clutched in a vise.

Their kiss was interrupted by a third party, one whom she had completely forgotten about. Ryan pulled away from her suddenly, when John Henry let out his wail of unhappiness.

"What the hell is that?" he asked, looking at the cat, who was giving him the stare down.

Claire laughed. "That's just John Henry....my cat. I don't think he is too happy with me." "Hmmm. If you say so. He kind of looks like a giant ferret."

She laughed again, giving Ryan a playful punch to the chest. "Hey, that's my pet you are talking about."

"Fine. I'm sorry. Now where were we?"

Claire picked up where she had left off, taking his hand and leading him to the bedroom. With the door closed behind them, and John Henry safely on the other side, Claire turned to Ryan, running her hands over his chest as he kissed her. She began to unbutton his shirt, one button at a time, tracking her fingers down his torso. Slowly, she removed his shirt, taking the time to run her hands over his shoulders and down the length of his sinewy arms, her fingers skimming the defined ridges of his abs. With his shirt off, Claire began to run her fingers over the lines of his tattoo, lightly following every curve, wanting to ask him about it, but choosing not to break the silence. She continued to trace the lines of the ink, moving around behind him, caressing his body lightly while her fingers made their way over the muscles of his back. His breath quickened, and Claire's body was screaming for him as he turned to face her again, kissing her with greater intensity. He ran his hands over her back, gently unzipping her dress and letting it fall to the floor. With one fluid motion, he picked her up, and laid her on the bed.

He was an experienced lover, and Claire found herself reaching the heights of pure ecstasy more times than she thought possible. Twice during the night, he had awoken her, and with the effects of the wine faded away, she discovered an even greater passion to their encounters and her own levels of bliss.

In the pre-dawn hours, she finally fell asleep in his arms, her body exhausted and completely spent.

Several hours later she awoke, with light streaming into her room, and John Henry laying near her face, purring loudly. For a moment, she wanted to reach over to touch Ryan, but the cat's presence in the bed was enough for her to know that he was gone.

She got up, hoping that he was awake and had just gone into another room, but her gut told her he wasn't there, anywhere. As she walked into the kitchen, she prayed for a scene from the movies, perhaps a romantic note taped to the coffee pot, anything to indicate he was just out and would be coming back, but there was nothing. No sign, other than her own aching body, that he had ever even been in the apartment.

John Henry was meowing, demanding breakfast, and she gave it to him before dropping herself on to the sofa. How could she have been so stupid? There was absolutely no reason for him to want anything to do with her, and she had let herself believe that he was interested. In the weeks that she had known him, he had never really treated her with anything other than loathing, so why had she allowed herself to be fooled into thinking he actually cared about her. Clearly, all he wanted was sex, and she gave it to him, oh so willingly. She was disappointed in herself, knowing that she'd promised people that she wouldn't allow herself to get into this position, but her body had overridden her brain. It wasn't even possible to blame the wine. It wasn't an excuse; she had only had one glass. All it had done was remove her inhibitions, and apparently, her common sense.

She felt that she had to talk to somebody, but she couldn't tell Colin, and she especially couldn't tell Kelly.

"Hey, Claire. What's up?" Mandy said, picking up after only one ring.

"I think I did a really stupid thing...colossally stupid."

"Oh God, who'd you sleep with?" Mandy asked, somewhat exasperated.

"Ryan Valentin," Claire mumbled.

"Oh. Wow, I was only jok...Ryan, seriously? What the hell were you thinking?!"

"I don't know! I wasn't thinking...I had some wine, and one thing lead to another, and, well...." Claire tailed off.

Mandy sighed on the line. "Wine? Claire, you aren't even old enough to drink. What happened?"

Claire rehashed most of the details of the evening, leaving out the more private ones, and she waited for Mandy's response.

"Ok. I'm not going to give you a lecture. You know what I think. Yes, I am disappointed in your actions, but at least you're now aware of the consequences. I'm guessing that he was long gone this morning."

"Yes," Claire said, not trying to hide her disappointment.

"You didn't actually expect him to stick around, did you? You only have one thing that he wanted, and you gave it up all too easily. Please tell me that you were smart about it, that you used protection."

"Yes, of course," Claire continued. "I just couldn't help it. Have you actually seen him, I mean, other than on television?"

"I can't say that I have," Mandy said. "He's all that and more from the sounds of it?"

Claire admitted that he was. "I had no control of my actions. I haven't been able to take my eyes off of him since I got to California, and there was no way I could say no."

"Alright. But is it going to happen again?" Mandy asked.

"Probably not. I'm sure he won't ever speak to me again."

"Probably not," Mandy agreed.

"What do I do now?" Claire pleaded. "Everybody's going to know that I slept with him. How am I going to go into the jocks room and face them all?"

"You just have to. You don't have a choice. Hold your head up, and don't let anybody know he hurt you...especially him! It's all you can do."

Claire knew she was right, but those first steps into the jockey's room in a day's time were going to be the hardest she would ever take.

Mandy spoke again. "Can I ask you something, woman to woman?"

"Of course," Claire said.

"Was it good?"

Claire smiled, thinking about just how good it had been. "Amazing beyond words."

"That's my girl," Mandy laughed. "Look at it this way....you needed it, you got it out of your system, and now you can focus on beating him on the racetrack. Maybe it wasn't such a bad thing after all, but don't make it a habit."

Claire laughed, feeling better about her situation, but still apprehensive about her next meeting with Ryan. "I won't," she said and hung up the phone.

The next day, she worked her horses as usual, with no sight of Ryan. She summoned her courage when it was time to go to the room for the races, and did exactly what Mandy had told her, walking into the common room with an air of confidence that she hoped was convincing to the other riders. The other men in the room treated her the same as always, and she relaxed. She didn't feel like every set of eyes was on her, and maybe they didn't know. Ryan never showed up in the common room, and she only saw him going to and from the paddock for their respective races. At one point, she had tried to make eye contact, but he avoided her. She couldn't help but feel like he had been watching her a moment before, but he gave no indication that she even existed.

For the rest of the week, they ignored each other. Claire put on a brave face at the track, but she couldn't deny the fact she was hurt. She wasn't used to the way this world worked, and was angry with herself for allowing Ryan to treat her as though she were disposable. Under any other circumstances, she had thought more of herself, but in this instance she felt undeserving of any man. She should have never given herself up so easily. There was no way Ryan would have offered her any kind of commitment, and she knew that, part of her knew it before she even allowed him into her bed, but she still hated herself.

Colin arrived the following week, and she was grateful for the distraction her brother offered. They did a lot of sightseeing, and walked on the beach almost every night. He watched her ride, and was thrilled to get in several win photos, as well as pad his wallet with a little extra cash that he had made from betting. Ryan continued to ignore her, and she gradually began to allow herself to relax in his presence.

The last day of Colin's stay, they headed to the beach after the races, for one last stroll through the sand. The sun was warm, and the breeze was pleasant as they chatted idly about nothing in particular. Claire was going to miss her brother terribly. It seemed like he had only just arrived, and he was already leaving. The cool water of the surf was playing around her ankles as the waves broke nearing the shore. She was looking at her toes as they would disappear in the sand, and Colin was rambling on about how nice it was, and how he was wrong in his opinions of the California life. The beach was busy, so when Claire heard someone coming towards them from the water, she paid no attention, continuing to be mesmerized by the sand in her toes.

An all to familiar voice brought her out of her trance, and she looked up to see Ryan, soaking wet from a swim in the ocean, wearing only swim trunks, and looking as amazing as ever. "Hey Claire," he said, shaking some of the water out of his sandy brown hair as he stopped in front of her and Colin. "Who's your friend?"

Claire was angry for a moment, until she understood. Ryan was jealous. He hadn't spoken a word to her, but now that there was another man with her, he was interested again. She thought of playing him by saying that Colin was somebody other than her brother, but she didn't think Colin would get it, and in the end, the truth won out as she went ahead with introductions.

"Ryan, this is my brother, Colin. Colin, Ryan Valentin."

The men shook hands, sizing each other up.

"Good to meet you," Ryan said. "Claire didn't say anything about you coming into town."

Colin only nodded, never taking his eyes off the jockey. "So.....I guess I am just going to tell you right now. I don't give a shit who you are, I want you to stay away from my sister, or I will personally make your life miserable."

Ryan never even flinched in his response. "Well, I guess that's up to her now, isn't it?" And with that, he walked away, leaving Claire standing stunned, and Colin furious.

"What a jackass. I can't believe you actually slept with that guy!" Colin said, turning away from Ryan as he left.

Claire was startled; sure she'd never told Colin about her tryst with Ryan. "How'd you know I slept with him?"

"Mandy told me. I know you told her not to, but she was worried about you Claire, and I am now too, judging by your choice."

"I'm so sorry. I really am. It just happened. Do you know that this, just now, is the first time he's talked to me since that night?"

Colin shook his head. "Yeah, nothing like another man in the picture to draw his attention back to you," her brother ran his hand through his hair, and looked out at the water. "You're better than that guy, Claire. I hope you know that. I don't care how much money he has, it doesn't give him the right to treat people badly."

Claire nodded. "I know. I made a mistake, and it won't happen again."

"I think I'm more disappointed in the drinking Claire. Given the way you chewed my ass about having one beer in the privacy of my own home, here you are not even old enough to drink, and you're drinking in public. You have to be smarter than that. The sex isn't my biggest concern. Mandy said you were smart about it, and we all give in to our desires once in a while, but you could have gotten in serious trouble over the wine. Didn't you think about that at all? You're a talented rider, and in the public eye. What do you suppose would have happened if you had been caught?"

"I don't know. I'm sorry, that's all I can say. I'm sorry." It really was all she could say. She hadn't realized how much she had hurt her brother until now. She had only been thinking about herself. Colin hugged her, as only a brother could, and they headed off the beach.

"That is one badass tattoo though," Colin mused.

Claire smiled. "Yes, it is."

*

Colin left, and Claire was alone once again. Ryan was back to not speaking to her, and she was back to being almost used to it. The Del Mar meet was nearing a close, and she found herself not wanting to go back to L.A., but she had to focus her efforts on winning and have a strong finish.

One morning, during break time from the works, her agent approached her, and he looked livid. "Claire...what did you do to Ryan?" he asked sharply.

Her mind began to race. It had been over two weeks since her night with him, and, aside from the confrontation with her brother, she hadn't spoken to him at all. "Nothing. Why, what's going on?"

"Well, apparently he's on a personal mission to take every single one of your live mounts for the remainder of the meet. Thank God most of these trainers are loyal to us, and I've done my job well, otherwise you could be seriously screwed. Most trainers and owners would jump at the chance to have him on their horses," Frank was flustered, and shaking his head. "What on earth did you do to the guy? I didn't think you two even spoke?" He looked at her long and hard, and then it was like a light bulb clicked on. "Mother of God, you slept with him, didn't you? You know what, I don't want to know, never mind. You just made my job harder, but I'm not the best for nothing. You really could've picked somebody other than the leading rider in the country to....you know.....dammit Claire. I have to go work now. If I do my job right, you have nothing to worry about, and I always do my job right, but just don't do it again. Hear me?"

Claire nodded, thankful that Frank's tirade was over as he stormed out of the kitchen and off to the barns.

It was time for her to do something. Ryan was counting on her to just sit idly by and allow herself to be manipulated, but she wasn't going to let him run the show any longer. She managed to track him down, finding out who his last worker of the morning would be for, and making sure she was close by when he was done. She waited quietly out of sight, feeling like some sort of stalker, but not knowing any other way to confront him, since he had been avoiding her like the plague. As he left his last mount, she emerged from her hiding place and fell into step next to him.

For a split second, she thought that he tensed, but just as quickly, he regained his casual composure. "What's up Claire?"

"I know what you're doing, and I'm going to tell you one time to back off. I don't appreciate you badmouthing me around the track. I didn't do anything to you, so why don't you mind your own damn business, and leave mine alone."

"Whatever," he said casually, indicating that he had participated in the conversation beyond his desire.

Claire grabbed his arm, turning him towards her, forcing him to look her in the eye. "What is your problem? You think just because you have everybody here kissing your ass, and you can wave cash around like it were nothing, that you have the right to treat people like shit?"

"Let go of me, Claire," he warned.

"What....you embarrassed now? I was just another conquest, and now you don't want anything to do with me? That's fine. I had no expectations of you, but this is my business, my livelihood, and I am not going to stand by and let you try and bury me."

Ryan had broken free of her grip, but he was angry. It was likely the first time that anybody had the nerve to confront him about anything, and he hated it. "Fine. You just stay out of my way, and I'll stay out of yours," he snapped. "And tell your brother he has nothing to worry about."

With that, he walked away, leaving her hurt once again.

CHAPTER 16

Summer turned to fall, and Claire was on fire. She had become somewhat of a celebrity on the racetrack, and had done several interviews with the racing presses. There was talk that she was the top contender for an Eclipse award for leading apprentice in the country, but she wasn't going to get her hopes up just yet. Frank was pushing her hard, with her mornings full of workers, and afternoons with a minimum of seven mounts every day. He had his eye on the Eclipse award, and it seemed like he was more excited about the potential than she was.

Fall in California meant racing at Santa Anita, and Claire loved it. The track was beautiful, with every inch of the grounds perfectly manicured, and the beautiful San Gabriel Mountains in the background. She couldn't think of a better place to ride, except possibly Del Mar, but San Diego would always hold memories for her that she would rather leave buried. Ryan had certainly seemed to forget about her. They never spoke, and in spite of his treatment of her, Claire still found herself looking at him. He was like a Rembrandt that you couldn't tear your eyes away from. She wanted to hate him. She wanted to loathe him with every fiber in her body, but she couldn't. Her memory was like some sick, sadistic record player, skipping back to that night with him at the most inopportune times, making her heart break, but her body lust for him over and over again.

By mid-October, Claire needed a break, and she convinced her agent to allow her a couple of days to go home. She longed for the fall foliage, and missed her family so much that it hurt. For all of her racing success, she felt herself more alone than ever, and she needed to remember why she was there.

Frank was unhappy, reiterating to Claire that they were in their final push for the Eclipse award, but she reminded him that she wasn't going to be missing any actual race days, and people could survive without her working horses for two mornings. She told him that he would just have to work a little harder for a couple of days, and with his usual flair for the dramatic, he told her to go get on a plane.

New York was beautiful. Crisp and cool, with the leaves in full color. Claire was happy to be home, if only for a couple of days. Kelly and Mandy had come to the house for a big dinner that first night, which Colin had prepared in honor of her visit. Emily was in Ithaca, and couldn't make the drive, so once again, Claire didn't get to meet her brother's girlfriend.

They all talked well into the early hours of the morning, Mandy and Kelly staying, despite the fact that they had an early morning at the race-track. Claire felt at ease, and loved once again. These people were her whole life, and yet she had begun to lose touch during her time away.

Kelly was thrilled with her success, telling her I told you so more times than she could count. He was convinced that she was going to win the Eclipse award, although he said there was a kid back east who had been winning a ton as well. Mandy was more interested in life in California, although she deliberately skirted around the subject of Claire's love life, or lack there of. Claire went to bed that night the happiest she had been in a long time, and fell into a deep and contented sleep in her own bedroom.

The next morning, she woke early, still on California time, and just lay in bed looking at her surroundings. It was her room, but Colin had moved in for a while after she left, and things were different. It looked more like a guest room now, than the young girl's room that she had remembered. She was not yet 20, but she felt like she had grown years since leaving home the previous December. The responsibilities of life on her own had given her a new perspective on things. While most of her classmates from high school were attending college parties, or frantically studying for exams, Claire was riding horses for a living, and making a good living at that. She felt more grown up, and while she still wasn't really considered an adult, she knew the life she had been leading, and the decisions she had to make in that day to day life, made her more grown up than the majority of 20 year old women she knew.

She continued to lie in bed, staring at the ceiling, lost in her thoughts. It was at quiet times like this her mind would wander back to Ryan. There had to be some way to forget him, to forget that night and wipe the slate clean, but she just didn't know how to do it. How did he do it? Was it such a common occurrence for him that he'd never even given it a second thought? Probably, but a part of her still wanted to believe he'd felt something. So many times, she would feel like he was watching her, but when she would look at him, he would be looking away. Was that just her own mind wishing, playing tricks, or had he in fact been watching her? She'd probably never know. Maybe, after enough time passed, she would be able to look at him without feeling that stir deep inside, but how much time, she had no idea.

There was the sound of footsteps in the hall, and Claire decided it was time to get up and help her aunt with her mom, so they could have breakfast. Colin had found his own place, with a little help from Claire on the cash front, and he was now living about 10 miles north of Robyn and mom. He was teaching, so she wouldn't see him until that afternoon, but they had agreed to meet at her favorite spot by the lake. Claire couldn't wait, as the lake was most beautiful that time of year.

She wandered into the kitchen, pausing to give her mother a kiss on the cheek.

"Good morning Mom....Aunt Robyn."

"Morning, beautiful. How'd you sleep?" Robyn chimed, cheerful as ever.

"Like the dead. I haven't slept like that in a really long time," Claire said, as she poured herself a cup of coffee, and sat down at the table.

"Good. You needed that quality of rest. I'm guessing you don't get much out West."

Claire just shook her head, staring into her coffee cup as Robyn bustled about the kitchen, preparing a simple breakfast, and telling Claire to stay put.

Her aunt set out breakfast and finally sat down. Claire took over the duties of feeding her mother, and Robyn watched her for a moment in silence.

"You look older, Claire. You've really grown up," Robyn said.

Claire pondered the statement, realizing how many people she had seen on the racetrack who looked years older than they actually were. She didn't want to become like that, but after 10 months on the track, she was changing, hardening to the life, and she wasn't sure how she was supposed to feel about it.

Robyn could sense her discontent. "It's not a bad thing you know. I didn't mean that you look old; I just mean you've changed. You've become a beautiful young woman, not the little girl that I remember. I guess you have the guys lining up down there, don't you?"

Claire shook her head. She usually told her aunt everything, but she just didn't want to bring up the subject of Ryan, so she told half of the truth. "No.....I don't have a whole lot of time for a relationship. Frank, my agent, has got me working so hard that I barely have time to eat, much less date."

Robyn shook her head. "I'm going to have to have a talk with this agent of yours. A woman is entitled to have some fun once in a while."

Claire smiled, and turned her attention back to her mother, not wanting her face to give anything away to her aunt, who seemed to be highly tuned to Claire's emotional state.

Robyn changed the subject anyway. "We've been watching you, every single day. It used to be the home and garden network, now we are watching the horseracing network. I never thought I would say this, but I have found it fascinating, and I have learned a ton. I love it when you win....we get to see you in the interviews."

Claire hadn't even thought about her family watching her races so frequently. It had just never occurred to her that they would be watching, and she knew she'd been doing a ton of interviews. "Do I sound like a complete idiot?" Claire laughed.

"Heavens no! You're fabulous! Most of those guys can't string together three coherent words, but you are so well spoken and poised on camera. It's like you have been doing it your whole life." Robyn paused a moment to take a sip of her coffee. "There is one guy though....what's his name.....Ryan something...he does a good interview. And he isn't hard on the eyes either. Do you know him? Are you friends?"

Claire should have known that she wouldn't be able to steer the conversation away from him forever, but she was going to nip it in the bud. "No. We aren't friends. He's arrogant, and pretty much keeps to himself."

Her aunt looked at her for a moment, and if she sensed anything, she decided to keep it to herself, for which Claire was grateful.

They all had a lazy day, Claire never even getting out of her pajamas until it was time to go meet Colin. She had forgotten what it was like to just sit around and do nothing, and while she enjoyed it for the day, she

knew that she couldn't get used to it. Her work may have been emotionally and physically exhausting, but she loved it, and she didn't think she
would ever be able to go back to a normal life.

Come mid-afternoon, she was heading out to meet her brother. She
drove the all too familiar route to her spot by the lake, knowing that she
was a bit early, but that was by design. She wanted to have some time
alone. The lake was quiet, and more beautiful than Claire had remembered. The water was still and the sky was clear. Autumn colors burst
from the surrounding trees, creating a kaleidoscope of reflection on the
mirrored water. She sat on the rock wall; in the same place she had nearly
two years before. This was the exact place that she had made the decision
to become a jockey, and so much had happened since that November day.
Aunt Robyn was right, she had grown up. She was no longer just a silly
little girl with a dream. She had made it work, with the help of a lot of
people, and was realizing that dream.

Colin arrived, and sat next to her. Neither spoke for quite a while,
simply enjoying the silence of each other's company.

Her brother was the first to speak. "You alright?"

Claire nodded. She was all right, better than all right. "Yes. I feel
good. Colin, I'm happy, and I love my work. I just forgot how much I miss
everything over here."

Colin nodded. "We miss you too kid, but this is how life works. We
grow up and move on. I just didn't think that you would move to the
other side of the country.....but it doesn't matter. You're doing awesome.
We're all so proud of you."

"Thanks," Claire said, staring out at the water.

Her brother was looking at her, and she finally turned to face him.
"What? Don't tell me I've gotten old."

"No. Grown up, but not old," he sighed. "That guy really did a number on you didn't he?"

It was Claire's turn to sigh. She knew she had to talk about it, and she knew Colin would listen, but she didn't know how to begin. "Yes, he did... he still does...but you need to hear me as a friend, not my big brother, alright?"

"Fine. Just spare me the graphic details. You're still my baby sister, and I don't care how grown up you look, I don't want the mental picture, alright?"

Claire smiled. "Of course." She was quiet for a moment. "I was stupid. I let my body override my brain, but the thing is, I as much as I try, I can't get him out of my head. He doesn't speak to me...doesn't even acknowledge that I exist, but I can't make him go away."

"Claire, you were stupid, but that doesn't excuse his behavior. I am sure you've come to learn how some people just think they can have whatever they want because they have money or fame or whatever, regardless of what it costs others. He may be one of the best jockey's in the world, but he is still just an obnoxious little punk. His ego is overcompensating for his lack of size, so to speak." Colin seemed to be taking great pleasure in voicing his opinion of Ryan. "You know what you really need to do? And I am saying this as a friend, because as a brother, it kind of creeps me out."

"What?"

"Go shag somebody else. Find yourself a one night fling and do what you need to do to get rid of this guy."

Claire laughed. "You're awful, you know. I'm going to tell Aunt Robyn what you just said to your sweet, innocent little sister."

Colin gave her a shove. "Sweet and innocent my ass," he said, and they both laughed. The conversation moved on, and they stayed at the lake far longer than they had planned.

Claire had to leave the next morning, and she was already missing her family and friends.

"So," Colin said, "you're going to be back for Christmas?"

Claire shook her head. "I can't, I'm sorry. Santa Anita starts the day after Christmas, and we will be in the final week push for the Eclipse awards. I can't afford to miss any time. My agent was in apoplexy when I came this time, and I'm not even missing a day of racing."

"He's working you too hard. He need's to back off, or you are going to burn out."

"This is what it takes. These guys don't get to the Kentucky Derby by backing off. It's a constant battle for the best mounts, and if I don't ride them, somebody else will."

Colin shrugged. "Just be careful, okay. Don't forget how to have fun."

"I won't...don't worry."

Her stay was over almost as quickly as it had begun, and she was headed back to California. John Henry greeted her with enthusiasm when she got home, and she settled back into her routine.

*

The fall meet at Hollywood Park brought a new level of intensity to her life. Frank was on the brink of a heart attack almost daily, and Claire pushed herself to the edge of her physical limits in every race she rode. It was her meet...almost. She and Ryan had been playing leapfrog in the jockey's standings, each winning multiple races a day, and there were times that she thought she might actually have a shot at winning the title.

The race for the riding title came down to the very last day of the meet. It was mid-December, but still fairly pleasant, as it never got very cold. Claire had 7 mounts on the day, and she felt good about her chances on all of them. Ryan had 8 mounts, and they looked just as good as hers. She was finding some pleasure in knowing that he must be furious that she was giving him such a run, and she really believed she could beat him. After her first race, and win of the day, she was one ahead, but by her fourth mount, he had pulled ahead of her by one. She won her next, pulling even again, and with only two more races left, she was confident she could eek out one more win to beat him, assuming he didn't win any more. Neither of them won the next race, and it came down to the last. There was a huge crowd at the track, and the hype of the race for the jockey's title was at its peak. It was Claire, the female apprentice, versus Ryan, the seasoned veteran with over 3,000 career wins. The crowd had their favorites, and Claire could hear people calling her name and cheering her on during the post parade.

The field settled in the starting gate, and then they were off. Claire maneuvered her mount into the perfect position, right on the outside of Ryan's flank, keeping him close, while the two speed horses were killing each other off up front. They came into the turn, and Claire kept her horse glued to Ryan's hip. She had a ton of horse under her, and it was looking like Ryan's mount might be tiring. The speed horses faded back, leaving her and Ryan in the ultimate stretch dual. Stride for stride, head and head, they surged down the lane. Claire could hear the roar of the crowd as she pushed her horse with every ounce of her strength, and he gave her all he had. Ryan was riding equally as hard, determined not to be beaten by the girl, and they crossed the finish line nose and nose.

Claire had no idea who had won. Usually, even in close photos, she knew which way it would go, but not this time. She allowed her horse to gallop out, pulling up on the backside, and trying to catch her own breath. Ryan had already turned back to the grandstands, so she smooched her mount forward and went back to the huge crowd still awaiting the results of the photo.

She had just arrived at the trainer, when the results of the photo were posted on the infield tote board. She had the crowd on her side, and she could tell by the collective 'ooh's that she had been beaten.

She quickly took off her saddle and went to the scales, getting cheers and condolences from everybody around her. Determined not to look at Ryan, she headed back to the jockey's room, but was held up by a little girl asking for an autograph. She obliged the young horse lover, but the delay had allowed her rival to catch up to her. She tried to ignore his presence, knowing he was beside her, but refusing to say anything.

He never spoke, and she went into the room, furious. She usually was able to check her temper, but she forgot her self-control and threw her helmet across the room, watching it bounce harmlessly off the far wall and settle into a spin on the floor. This business had taught her sportsmanship, and losing with grace, but at that moment she abandoned any hope of losing with dignity. In that very second, she hated Ryan. His skill on a horse was unmatched, and she must have been crazy to think that she could actually outride him.

As she left the jockey's room, any hopes of a quick escape were dashed. Frank was waiting for her. She was sure he was going to be angry, but instead he grabbed her in a huge bear hug, squeezing her until she couldn't breathe.

"You were unbelievable! Did you hear that crowd? That's what I'm talking about! This is what this game is all about Claire! Can you feel it?!"

"But I didn't win," she said flatly.

"Doesn't matter! These people love you! Claire, you're still a bug, and a girl, and you just gave Ryan his closest finish yet. He was sweating it, and that thrills me to no end. You think he isn't scared shitless that you are going to beat him at Santa Anita? It's more of a possibility now than ever! Way to go girl!" Frank paused to draw a breath and then continued. "Dinner on me tonight, wherever you want to go!"

Claire sighed. She was in no mood to go out to dinner with her agent, but she felt she owed it to him. After all, she would have never gotten this far without all of his hard work. "Okay. I'll think of something."

"Uh oh...your friend is coming," Frank said, still overly gleeful.

Claire turned to see Ryan approaching her. She forgot to hate him as he neared, looking as cool and sexy as ever.

He looked right at her, but any hope that she had for civility vanished when he spoke. "Sucks, doesn't it? Well, maybe next time you'll beat me." Worse than his words was his audacity as he smacked Claire on the rear end with his stick as he was walking away.

Claire couldn't help herself. As soon as he was far enough away, she let out a scream of rage.

Frank said exactly what she was thinking. "Check out the balls on that guy. Wow. Not so much as a 'hey, nice ride', he just rubs your face in it. I mean, I knew he was an ass; I've been working around him for 15 years now, but damn. How in the hell did you sleep with that guy?"

"I have no idea," she said. "I'm hungry, let's go eat."

Dinner was nice, and she and Frank spent the evening discussing the strategy for the last two weeks of the year. She was to work horses every morning at Santa Anita, and he told her she was likely to be the first one on the track in the morning, and the last one off when the track closed for training. It was exciting, and she was trying not to think about the very real possibility that she could end the year as the leading apprentice in the country. Frank was pushing hard, but his efforts were appreciated. Kelly had told her that her agent was her employee, not her friend, but she felt she and Frank were, in fact, friends. He was like a father figure, keeping her in line when she would get attitude. He was crazy, and there were times Claire was embarrassed to be around him when he was off on one of his tirades, but it was just Frank, and the trainers and owners really did love and respect him. His job was hard, even harder as women jockeys seemed to be a tougher sell than their male counterparts, but he never faltered, and she guessed she was so successful because he didn't consider her a 'girl rider'. To him, she was a rider, and a good one, and that was all that mattered.

She followed his guidance to a T, and when Santa Anita started, the day after Christmas, she got off to a strong start, winning three races the first day. With only a week to go, she rode hard, and went home completely exhausted every night. Part of her couldn't wait until New Years, if only that Frank would stop stressing about awards, and maybe relax a bit.

Claire spent New Year's Eve at home with John Henry, and she was asleep by 9pm. The next morning, she saw Frank first thing.

"Well, we did what we could. Now we just have to wait and see if you get nominated. We'll know in a week or so. I can't see any reason why not, so I am going to go ahead and get our plane tickets."

"Plane tickets? To where?"

"The awards banquet is in Vegas this year," he said, sounding far more excited than she felt he should.

"Lovely. What am I going to do in Vegas?"

"Win an Eclipse award, and go to bed, since you aren't old enough to be partying with the rest of us old men."

"Sounds like fun," Claire said sarcastically, although she had never been to Vegas, and was more excited than she let on.

Two weeks later, nominations were announced, and Frank called Claire the minute he heard. "We're going to Vegas!" he screamed into the phone. "I knew you would get it!"

Claire couldn't pretend to be calm about it anymore. She had worked so hard all year, and this was like the Oscar's of the racing world. Frank felt obliged to tell her that Ryan would be going, as he was nominated for top rider in the country for something like the 10th year in a row. She wasn't concerned. She had found it easier to avoid him, and she was pretty sure he would be hitting the town in Vegas, while she would be hitting her pillow.

*

Three weeks later, she was in Las Vegas, getting ready to experience the over the top, elaborate party that was the Eclipse Awards. The ceremony was all pomp and circumstance, with everybody dressed to the nines. Claire was fascinated watching the people. So many of them she had seen on the racetrack in boots and jeans, and here they were, in tuxedos and dresses. It didn't seem possible that these were all the same people who were at the track before the sun rose. Her dress for the evening had made the little black dress of Del Mar fame seem cheap. It was a beautiful, floor length, fitted blue chiffon with the back cut out completely, showing off her well-defined physique. Just putting it on made her feel like a movie star. The color perfectly complemented her eyes, and she finished the look with a pair of silver stilettos that gave her an added five inches of height. It was a rather shameless display, and she knew it, but she felt like a million dollars, and, even if she didn't win the award, nobody was going to forget her anytime soon.

Frank came to her room to escort her to the banquet hall. She was ready to go, and opened the door quickly.

"Holy shit," he said, not even trying to hide his amazement. "You look fantastic. If I wasn't old enough to be your father...," he tailed off, smiling at her.

She laughed, and took his arm as he escorted her down to the banquet hall.

They entered the hall, and Claire was taken with how elaborate the setting was. She had never even dreamed of being a part of something so big, and it was so far out of her realm of comfort that she almost turned around to go back to her room. Instead, they found their way to their table. They were seated with the two other riders who were up for apprentice awards, and as she approached, the young men both stood, greeting her respectfully, but were clearly entranced by her appearance.

The banquet hall began to fill, and Claire, in spite of her better judgment, found herself looking for Ryan. She wasn't sure if she really wanted to see him, or if she just wanted him to see her. She got her opportunity when Frank motioned her to a table to introduce her to trainer James

Imler, who was nominated for top trainer in the country, and was moving a stable of horses from New York to California. Frank wanted her in his barn, and she wanted to ride for him, so she collected herself, and walked with confidence to his table, where, of course, Ryan was sitting as well.

Frank approached the trainer, who stood to greet him, and shake Claire's hand. He was tall and lean, with slightly receding, salt and pepper hair, and he smiled at Claire immediately, guessing that he had probably been a very attractive man in his younger years, but the racetrack had taken it's toll, as it did with everybody.

Frank and James were speaking, and Claire stood, listening intently, but knowing that Ryan's eyes were fixed on her in her over the top sexy dress. She smiled to herself, and said the appropriate things when asked. The temptation was too great, and she finally looked at Ryan. He was looking back at her, and never attempted to avert his gaze. She felt her stomach flutter, and she willed herself calm, looking away from him casually. Frank had finished his conversation, and they turned to go back to their table. Claire stood a little straighter, and walked with a little more confidence, knowing that Ryan was watching her every move.

The meal was served, and after the appropriate amount of time, the awards presentation began. The top horses in their respective divisions were honored. James Imler took the award for top trainer, and then it was time for the apprentice award to be given. Claire couldn't calm her stomach, and the top three were named, followed by the obligatory, respectful applause. A moment of hesitation, and the leading apprentice in the country award goes to....Nate Tomlinson.

She didn't win. It was the rider from New York; the other kid that everybody had been talking about. She tried not to seem disappointed, and clapped for the winner, but felt that she had let people down. Frank sensed her unhappiness and he patted her hand.

"It's alright. You had a fantastic year, and everybody knows it. Don't be too hard on yourself. We'll see where that kid is come summer, and I guarantee you'll be doing better than he will."

Claire smiled, appreciating his confidence. It came as no surprised that Ryan won the award for overall outstanding jockey. He was very gracious in his acceptance speech, but Claire couldn't help feeling a little bitter. It seemed like he was looking right at her, prodding and gloating subtly at the fact that he, once again, was the winner, and she was second.

At the conclusion of the night, Frank walked Claire back to her room. He was planning on hitting the town for some Blackjack and he wished her a good night before leaving.

Claire walked around her room, still wound from the events of the night, when she heard a knock on her door. She smiled to herself, assuming that it was her agent with one last offering of support before he headed off to gamble.

She was still smiling as she opened the door, but her smile faded when she saw Ryan. He was standing in front of her, still in his tux, although it was no longer buttoned, and his tie was hanging loosely around his neck. His look was always effortless, he knew exactly what he wanted and how to achieve it. Claire could feel the heat rising through her body. She was furious with herself for still having such a reaction to him, but it was far beyond her control.

"What do you want?" she asked, trying to sound blasé.

"I just wanted to say congrats. You had a great year. I think you should've won, but it was going to be close either way."

Claire wanted to be annoyed, but her voice betrayed her. "Thank you." It was all she could say. She wanted to yell at him, tell him that he was an ass, and didn't deserve the time of day from her, but she couldn't, and knew she never would.

He smiled at her, inching his way closer. "You look beautiful, you know," he said, as he reached to touch her hand, letting his fingers move slowly up the length of her arm.

She had to pull away, say no, tell him to leave, but she was frozen. She was going to let him into her room, and once again, he was going to hurt her. Her mind was fuzzy, and she hadn't had anything to drink. It was him. He was intoxicating, and she would never be able to refuse. He leaned in closer. If she took a step back, they would be in her room. For a split second she held her ground, as he got so close she could feel his breath on her cheek and his lips brushing the side of her face.

"VALENTIN! WHAT IN THE NAME OF ALL THAT IS HOLY DO YOU THINK YOU'RE

DOING?" Frank screamed from the far end of the hall.

Ryan startled and took a step back, and looked at Frank who was striding toward them quickly. "Nothing," Ryan said, dropping his hand from her arm, severing the connection between them.

"I was just leaving."

Frank's face was purple and he lowered his voice only slightly. "Your goddamn right you are leaving. I swear Valentin, if I see you back here I won't hesitate to cut your dick off!"

Ryan looked unfazed and he walked away.

Frank turned to Claire. Her face was flushed, and she tried to look anywhere else. "Where's your head girl? It's a damn good thing that I showed up when I did. I don't think you can say no to that guy, can you?"

Claire was ashamed. Frank was right, and they both knew it.

"I'm staying here tonight. Don't even try to say no, because you know full well if he sees me leave, he'll be right back."

Claire shook her head. "You don't need to do that. Don't ruin your evening on my account. I'll be fine."

"Forget it. I'm crashing on your other bed."

CHAPTER 17

The day after the awards, Claire returned to Los Angles and returned to work. Now that her apprenticeship was over, the break that she hoped was coming was just a fantasy. Frank had told her that things would be harder now that she no longer had the five pound weight allowance of an apprentice. Trainers had to be convinced to put her on their horses because of her riding ability, not just to get the extra five pounds off of their horse's backs. Basically, what it came down to was convincing them that she was just as capable as any journeyman on the track and deserved an equal shot even without the weight allowance. From a trainer's perspective, why should they put her on their horse, with only one year of experience, when they could put on someone like Ryan who had better than 15 years experience? Frank had his work cut out for him, but he was still confident, determined to push her harder than ever.

After her morning work, that first day back, she decided to get her beach fix, so she drove the 45 minutes from her Arcadia apartment to Santa Monica. It wasn't a quiet beach, in fact it was bustling, but she chose to find a place to sit and just watch the comings and goings of the people. It was time for her to get over Ryan. Her experience in Vegas had scared her. She realized that she had no control over herself when he decided he wanted her, but she also understood that he only wanted her when she was at her most vulnerable. He was clever that way, and it was time for this little game to come to an end. The problem was, she had no idea how to go about making things change. She got up from her seat in the sand and began to walk down to the surf. It was cool but pleasant, and she took off her shoes and walked into the water. She continued to stroll down the beach, the wind blowing her hair around her face.

"Stop....don't move," avoice said to her, from a few steps away.

She stopped abruptly and looked up into the lens of a camera. The man behind it was clicking the shutter rapidly, and she felt mildly irritated. "What are you doing?"

"Hang on," he said, pausing to look at the photos he had just taken. "Perfect."

"Excuse me? What are you doing?" she asked, slightly amused, now that she had seen the cameraman's face.

"Taking pictures. Our assignment for our photography class was to take a picture of the most beautiful thing we could find. I just finished my homework,." he smiled.

"Wow. Nice line. Do you do this every day?" she asked, smiling as she studied his face. He was young, probably in his early twenties. His brown hair was slightly unkempt, and, in typical college student fashion he was a few days into needing a shave. He was tall, taller than most of the men Claire had grown accustomed to in the last year, and he had an athletic, but not overly muscular build. She found his appearance pleasing, and non-threatening in the fact that he was the polar opposite of Ryan's clean cut, designer look.

He laughed at her, and he had an infectious smile, she couldn't help but smile back. "Yes, I do take pictures every day, I have to for my class, but no, I'm not a pick up artist. I'm Jeremy...Jeremy Hurst," he held out her hand for a proper greeting.

"Claire Durham. Nice to meet you."

"You a student?" he asked.

"No. I'm a jockey," she said, curious to see what his reaction would be.

"You mean like a disc jockey....on the radio?" he asked, believing that he was making a reasonable assumption.

"No, horses," she responded with a little laugh. She couldn't picture herself jamming tunes on the radio.

"No shit!" Jeremy said. "I've never met a jockey before. How old are you? You look awfully young to be a pro."

"I'll be 20 in March, and I've been riding for a little over a year."

"Are you here, at Santa Anita?"

She nodded.

Jeremy was almost giddy. He went on to explain how he was a television and communications major at UCLA, and he really wanted to work in television, primarily sports TV.

They sat on the beach and talked, and Claire found she was happy to talk about something other than the racetrack. Jeremy knew horses had four feet, and that was about it. He asked her questions about racing, but was more interested in her life before the track. He was easy to talk to, and Claire told him most of her life story and then listened to his.

Jeremy Hurst was 21 and a junior at UCLA on a scholarship. He was originally from Idaho, somewhere near Boise, but he wanted to get out of the small town environment and hit the city. Los Angeles was his home for now, but his goal was to work in New York City with some professional sports teams. She listened to him ramble on about his hopes and dreams, and was relaxed in his company. They chatted for hours, and she was startled that she had lost track of time. She was going to hit traffic on the drive home, but she needed to get back, as she had an early morning, and John Henry would be upset if she didn't give him his due attention.

She stood up to leave, shaking the feeling back into her legs. "Thank you for a nice afternoon," she said. "I had a great time doing nothing."

Jeremy smiled at her. "I know we just met and all, but I'd like to ask you for your phone number."

Claire thought hard. Here was the perfect distraction to her problem with Ryan, but she didn't think she was really ready for a serious relationship. Her career was about ready to really take off, and she didn't need the complications of a romance. She decided if he were really interested, he would make it a point to find her...after all, he knew where she worked, so she shook her head. "No. I don't think so. You know where to find me," she said, walking away and leaving him mildly flustered.

Two days later, Claire went back to racing, and she was pleasantly surprised to see Jeremy standing by the rail of the paddock. He smiled at her, and she tipped her stick to acknowledge him. She was happy that he was there, and had been hoping that he might be interested enough to show up.

Of her five mounts on the day, she won two races, and she could hear Jeremy screaming like she had just won the Derby. It was a little embarrassing, but it felt nice having someone there that was cheering just for her, and not for a big cash payout.

After her last race, she told him to give her a few minutes and she would come out to meet him. As she was showering, she realized that she hadn't thought about Ryan all afternoon. She had wanted a distraction, and she had found it, and maybe it would be a little more than just something to take her mind off of her current situation.

She left the jocks room, and found Jeremy waiting. "Now can I have your number?" he asked, his infectious smile getting her again.

"Yes," she said, and proceeded to give it to him.

"Ok, I am way out of my element out here in Arcadia, and I don't really want to drive home right now. Is there anyplace good to eat around here?"

Claire laughed. "Of course, let's go."

They were leaving the track, heading toward the parking lot, when Ryan showed up. Claire couldn't say she was surprised. He seemed to have a knack for appearing when she had another man present.

"Hey Claire, good day today," he said, acting like they were the best of friends, having a casual conversation.

"Thanks," she said, looking at him as he was studying Jeremy.

She introduced the two, and to her dismay, Jeremy was over the moon about meeting the top rider at the track. So much so that he asked Ryan to sign his program, to which Ryan readily obliged.

Claire got him away from the other jockey, who appeared to be quite pleased with himself as he went to his own car. "You really didn't have to do that you know," she said to Jeremy, who was oogling Ryan's wheels.

"What?" he asked, completely oblivious to having done anything wrong.

"Ask for his autograph. His head is big enough already, he doesn't need any more encouragement."

"Sorry," Jeremy said, "I didn't realize. You two don't get along?"

"Not really." It was clear Jeremy didn't need to know anything about her relationship with Ryan, and she intended to keep it that way, at least for the time being.

They went to dinner, and Claire had a fantastic evening. They talked about books and travel and their dreams, and, while her work was the topic of some of the conversation, it was not the focus of their evening. She had forgotten what it was like to talk to somebody about something other than horse racing, and she loved it.

When dinner was over, Jeremy drove her back to Santa Anita where she had left her car. It was cold, but she felt warm. She hadn't laughed so much in as long as she could remember, and she was at ease. Jeremy's comedic timing was impeccable, and that, combined with his fairly dry sense of humor had Claire in stitches at the most random moments. She was still laughing when she reached her car, but Jeremy was not. He was looking at her and smiling, and she knew he was going to kiss her, and she also knew that she wanted him to. His kiss was soft and gentle, the perfect first kiss, and while her body did not completely dissolve the way it had with Ryan, it was still exciting, and she found herself wanting more. Jeremy, however, was a perfect gentleman. He opened her car door and wished her a safe drive home and a good night's sleep.

In the weeks that followed, Claire's relationship with Jeremy blossomed. He was dedicated to his schoolwork, but he was at the races every weekend, and she looked forward to seeing him. Mostly, given the distance, and the L.A. traffic, they just talked on the phone. Claire felt like a 15-year-old girl, waiting for his call every night. They never seemed to run out of things to talk about, and Claire discovered that being a part of such an easy and enjoyable relationship had done wonders for her days at work. She was riding with much more focus, but she was also more relaxed, and her horses responded. The wins were coming regularly, and she was beginning to feel like she was really a part of the scene, being accepted by her peers in the jocks room, and gaining the attention of the public as well as the media. Ryan's demeanor was icy, and mostly he ignored her. Claire could guess that he was put out by her relationship with Jeremy, but it no longer mattered. She was happy.

Jeremy was an attentive lover, and although he didn't have Ryan's intensity or experience, he was always in tune with her desires, he was always there in the morning when she woke up. They were good together, and Claire found herself in a situation that she had never been in before. She was falling in love.

*

That summer, Jeremy decided not to go back to Idaho in order to stay with Claire. Del Mar came around and they went together. With nowhere to be, other than the races, their evenings were spent on the beach and their nights were passionate. It was hard to believe, that only a year ago, Claire was an emotional disaster, trying to deal with Ryan and their situation. This was completely different, and wonderfully amazing. Colin came to see her again, and this time he brought Emily. The four of them had a fantastic time, and Claire was thrilled with her brother's acceptance of Jeremy. With her own romance in full swing, she found it easy to accept Emily. She was tall, with long blond hair and fair skin, classically beautiful, and Claire truly expected nothing less for her brother. They were a picture perfect couple, the four of them spending their time talking, or not talking, just enjoying being together.

The day before Colin and Emily were set to leave, they all headed for the beach again, and Claire was allowed some time alone with her brother, as Jeremy and Emily were involved in a fairly competitive game of Frisbee.

Colin stood in the surf, looking out at the ocean. "It's a whole lot different than last year, isn't it?"

"Yes, it is," she said, smiling.

"Jeremy's a good guy. It is nice to see you so happy."

Claire nodded. "It's nice to be happy."

"It's probably not appropriate to ask this, but how are things with Ryan? I mean, it's not like he isn't present in your daily life, you work together. How's it been?"

Claire shrugged. "It's fine. We don't speak, other than a few words on the track from time to time. It's the way he usually is, and it makes it pretty easy to ignore him."

"Good. I like Jeremy better anyway. Although that was one cool tattoo."

Claire smiled. "I know. That's the one thing he reminds me of daily."

She thought about her days in the jocks room, and, in spite of Ryan's chilly demeanor, he still would amble into the common room shirtless, from time to time. Claire would like to think that she was over it, and that she had gotten bored with his shameless display, but seeing him like that still make her heart beat just a little faster.

Colin and Emily left, and Claire and Jeremy enjoyed the remainder of the meet on their own, moving back to L.A. in September, where she had a significant amount of momentum going into the start of the Santa Anita fall meeting.

TWO YEARS LATER

CHAPTER 18

Two years had passed, and Claire's life had become almost a fairy tale. Her career as a jockey was solid, making her a top contender in every meet that she rode, including winning her first riding title at the Hollywood Park fall meet, beating Ryan by a good five wins.

Her relationship with Jeremy was perfect. He had become her rock, always there supporting her through the emotional roller coaster ride of the horse racing industry and eventually, they had moved in together, to a modest house that Claire had purchased. It was modest by anybody's standards, but it still boasted a heft price tag, being in Los Angeles. Jeremy had graduated from UCLA, and had found himself a paid internship working with the press in the local minor league hockey team's marketing department. He was thrilled, and while it wasn't the Rangers, he had his foot in the door. Colin was euphoric, after all, hockey was hockey, and east coast versus west coast didn't matter. Jeremy was a keeper.

Claire was impressed with Jeremy's attitude. Most men would be threatened by the income gap. She was making more money than she ever thought imaginable, but Jeremy was unperturbed. He still supported her, attending the races as often as he could, and his rational was that Claire couldn't be a jockey forever, and his time would come to be the primary income source, and even if it never did, he said he was enough of a man to appreciate a woman footing the bill. She was secretly happy he was thinking so long term. Their relationship had been easy and they had progressed with very little conflict, other than the minor argument about where to go for dinner. She was in love with him, and he with her, and while she wasn't sure about the idea of marriage, she couldn't imagine her future without him.

Finally, after two years, Claire almost decided that she was over Ryan. Almost, however, was the key. He had perfected the art of completely ignoring her most of the time, but occasionally he would brush up against her, or touch her in passing, and she would have to catch her breath. She knew he was fully aware of his actions, and she was pretty sure he knew the affect he still had on her, which is obviously why he would never stop those random touches. On the racetrack, she was relieved when another bug boy showed up and became the new target of Ryan's on track aggressions. She remembered when she was the one the other riders were testing, trying to intimidate, but no longer. In the time that had passed, she was as strong as any other rider in the colony, and they all treated her with the respect that was usually reserved for only the top journeymen.

Life as Claire knew it took a dramatic turn that March. She was leading the standings at Santa Anita for the first time, with a six win cushion on Ryan, and a meet full of potential with live mounts on every race day. It was her 22nd birthday, and she was looking forward to being done with work. Jeremy had planned a romantic evening, with dinner and the beach, and for the first time in her entire career as a jockey, she couldn't wait for the races to be done. She went into the jocks room and went through her usual pre-race routine. The reflection in the mirror was that of a woman, no longer a girl. She was strong, and beautiful, and more confident than she had ever been. Her Saint Christopher was still around her neck. In all the years, she had never taken it off. It had become a part of her, and she usually was unaware that she was even wearing it, but it was showing signs of wear and tear. She bent over to adjust one of her boots, and the medallion fell to the floor. The clasp had finally broken.

"Dammit," she said, under her breath, as she scooped it up. She had been thinking of replacing the chain for some time, but just never made it a priority. She dropped it in her box, determined to go and pick up a chain the next day.

Her next race was called, and she headed out to the paddock, walking right next to Ryan, but they ignored each other. The race was on Santa Anita's unique, downhill turf course. Claire had come to love that particular course, as it felt like the horses were flying as they hit the turn for home. Her mount was a nice gelding, but he had a tendency to be a bit stupid. It was his first time on this course, but she thought he would do well, as it suited his close to the front running style.

The field entered the gate, and she settled herself in the number two post position and waited. The gates sprung, and Claire's mount broke sharply. She allowed him to quicken his pace as they went down the hill, making the slight right bend before again easing to the left in preparation for the turn home. Her horse was steady as she maintained her position, on the rail, near the front of the pack. They crossed over the dirt of the main track and entered the stretch for home. She got down to riding, and was aware of Ryan coming up on her outside. He pulled up next to her, and they were once again in a stretch dual. Her competitive drive took over, and she wasn't going to let him beat her. She switched her whip to her right hand and went to hit right handed. In the seconds that followed, time seemed to slow down. Her horse ducked from her right handed whip and went straight into the inside rail, trying to jump, but with his speed, angle to the fence, he missed the jump, getting his legs tangled in the posts and he fell. Claire had no time to react and could feel her body being driven into the ground as the 1,000 pound animal fell on top of her.

For a few seconds, everything went black. She lay completely still, trying to get her bearings, when a couple of the guys from the gate crew were suddenly standing over her.

"Claire? Hang on. The doctor is coming," she heard a voice say.

"Don't move okay, just lay still," another voice spoke.

She did as she was told, and within a few more seconds, the pain became intense. Her leg was searing with an agony she had never before experienced, and she began to writhe.

"Just be still, the doc is almost here."

Claire tried to look at the man who was speaking to her, but he was looking at her leg. "How bad is it?" she gasped.

The two men looked at each other, but neither answered.

A second later, the track doctor, Dr. Botha arrived by her side. "Claire. Lay still. Let me look." He said. His kindly, soft voice was soothing, but at that moment, the pain was so intense that she thought she might lose consciousness.

People began to swarm around her. The track paramedics and the rest of the gate crew, and she could hear Jeremy's voice above all the others. It seemed like an eternity, but he found her and took her hand. She looked into his eyes and saw the horror and anguish on his face.

"Jeremy," she said, still trying to catch her breath, but not seeming to be able to. "Nobody is telling me what's wrong. Tell me what's wrong."

He shook his head, looking like he might actually be sick, but he found his composure long enough to tell her. "Your leg is broken. Badly."

She was hit with a wave of pain and she tried to fight against it, but she could feel herself begin to fade out of consciousness. She was aware of the flurry around her, and could hear bits of conversations something about a bone through the boot, but then she was gone.

The next several hours were a haze of pain and blackness. She was taken to the hospital, but in the time that followed, her mind was a tangled web of agony, disconnecting from her immediate situation.

*

There were voices, and she was aware of a dull throb of pain, but she couldn't pinpoint an exact location. She lay with her eyes closed, gradually becoming more aware of her surroundings, but confused, as the voices that she was hearing didn't belong. She tried to recall what had happened, but could only remember being in a stretch dual with Ryan, and then fragments after. Her horse had fallen, and there were people all around her. She could remember the cool, sweet smell of the grass of the turf course, but then there was the pain.

She tried to refocus her mind on where she was, and the voices she heard still didn't make any sense. It sounded like her brother and Kelly, and Jeremy, but it couldn't be. With great effort, she opened her eyes to her surroundings. She had heard right. Colin and Kelly and Jeremy were all there, sitting in chairs in the large, private hospital room, talking amongst themselves. Even in her hazy state, she was overcome with emotion.

"How did you get here so fast?" she croaked, her throat terribly sore, and her ribs aching when she spoke.

They all jumped up and rushed around her bed, Jeremy grabbing one hand and Colin grabbing another, the worry on their tired faces being replaced with smiles.

"Believe me, it wasn't fast," Colin spoke first. "That was the longest plane ride of my life." Claire was still confused. "How long have I been here? What day is it?"

Jeremy spoke next. "It's Sunday afternoon. You came in yesterday around 3:00."

She looked at Kelly, whose face looked haggard. "You came too?"

He smiled at her gently. She hadn't seen him in so long, and as she grew as a rider, their phone conversations had become more and more infrequent. "Of course," he said. "We always watch your races, and Mandy and I saw the accident. God, Claire...I thought you were dead," he ran his hand through his hair, shaking his head. "I called Colin immediately. He'd seen it too. He booked us two tickets on the next flight to L.A."

Claire could feel the tears welling in her eyes. Her brother had lost some of his composure, and had begun to shake slightly. "It was so bad, Claire. We thought you were dead. Jeremy called as soon as he could and told me you were so badly hurt, but alive. I've never been so relieved."

For a moment, the room was silent, nobody sure of what to say next.

Jeremy broke the silence. "Um, this might not be the right time, but Happy Birthday." He handed her a small box. It was too big to be a ring, for which Claire was grateful, so she opened it carefully. Inside was a beautiful gold chain.

"I got it to hold your Saint Christopher. Your other one was looking a little worn."

Claire gasped. Was it purely a coincidence, or some sick twist of fate that the first time she rode without her medallion was when she has a horrible spill.

Jeremy was somewhat oblivious as he continued. "I couldn't find it in your things though. The hospital gave me all of your belongings, but it wasn't there. Did they lose it?"

Claire shook her head. "The clasp broke, just before the race. I put it in my box in the jocks room."

The three men stood quietly for a moment, and Claire decided to ease the discomfort with a change of subject. "What happened exactly? How badly am I hurt?"

Colin and Jeremy looked at each other, and Jeremy decided to be the one to speak. "You have three broken ribs....the laceration on your face.....a broken tail bone, and your leg."

Claire thought about it all. Her cheek was sore, and felt tight, she knew why it hurt to breathe and speak, and a tail bone couldn't have much done with it anyway, but what about her leg? "What about my leg, Jeremy? tell me."

He couldn't contain his shudder before he responded. "It's bad. You have a compound fracture of both the tibia and fibula. It was the most horrible thing I have ever seen. Your bones were visible...they had punctured through your boot."

Jeremy had to sit, as just the replay in his head had made him nauseous, but Colin continued. "You had surgery. They put in a rod and several screws."

The reality of the situation suddenly hit home. Claire's career as a jockey was potentially over. The ribs and tailbone would mend, but with a fracture that severe, she may never even walk properly again, much less ride. She turned her attention to Kelly.

"Am I going to be able to ride again?" she asked him.

He shook his head, looking at her sadly. "I don't know. I'd been in spills in my day, but nothing like this Claire. I just don't know."

She felt like she wanted to cry, but was also overcome with anger. How could this have happened? Crying hurt, and she tried to contain herself, but in a matter of seconds, everything that she had been working for was torn away.

Jeremy held her hand tightly, and Colin got emotional. Kelly looked slightly uncomfortable, but Claire motioned him to her. "I never said a proper thank you."

"For what?" Kelly asked.

"For everything. My entire career would never have happened without you, and if this is the end, then so be it, but you are the reason I got this far."

Kelly nodded, unable to speak, and quickly excused himself from the room, saying he needed a coffee and would bring some back for everybody else.

Claire was in and out of narcotic induced sleep for the rest of the day. When she was awake, Colin and Jeremy were always there. Kelly was in and out. He had taken the opportunity, while in California, to go and see about some horses he and his dad might be interested in buying and shipping back to New York.

By noon on Monday, Claire was feeling more awake, but also more aware of the pain. She had a bit to eat as her guests entertained themselves. Kelly was reading the racing form, and Jeremy and Colin were playing cribbage. In spite of it all, Claire was feeling all right. She was with the people that cared about her, it was just under unfortunate circumstances. There was some kind of ruckus going on outside of her room, and she could hear shouting. She had a split second to realize who was coming in before he made is usual grand entrance.

"Dammit Claire! You are taking years off my life girl!" Frank said, at a volume that was enough to shake the entire room.

Kelly, Colin and Jeremy all stood, Colin was somewhat startled, not having experienced Frank at his finest, but Kelly and Jeremy were simply amused.

"Kelly Z! How's it hangin' man! Long time, no see!" Frank continued, shaking Kelly's hand vigorously.

"Frank," Kelly said, in a much more subdued manner, but Frank had already turned his attention to Claire.

"How you holding up?" he asked, lowering his voice only slightly.

"I hurt, but I'm alive."

"No kidding. I thought you were a goner. You know you're killing me?! Don't ever do that again," he said, his voice elevating once more.

"There may not be an opportunity Frank...the doctor says I might not ride again."

"Bullshit! Those doctors don't know jack. Do you think that Ryan Valentin just gave up when he broke his back, and everybody told him that he would never ride again? No, he was back eight months later. You have a broken leg, you're not paralyzed. Six months, and you'll be back in the saddle."

The mention of Ryan's name irritated her, given the circumstances, but Claire was cautiously optimistic after Frank's outburst. "You think so?"

"Damn right, and just in time to get ready for the Derby next year." He headed out the door in just as dramatic a fashion as he had entered, and he was well down the hall before his shouts about the Kentucky Derby could no longer be heard.

There was a silence in the room, before they all burst out laughing. It hurt Claire to laugh, but felt good just the same. The tension had been eased.

"Is he always that crazy?" Colin asked.

Claire and Jeremy both nodded in unison.

Kelly chimed in. "I haven't seen him in years. I was thinking he might have mellowed a bit, but obviously not."

They all smiled again, and settled back down to what they had been doing before her agent had made his entrance. Claire watched the men in her room. Kelly was once again absorbed in the racing form, and Colin and Jeremy were dickering about an extra peg here and there in their cribbage game, when there was a quiet knock on the door, and Ryan walked in.

In an instant, the atmosphere had changed, and the tension was so thick it could be cut with a knife. Colin looked at Claire anxiously, and all three men quickly stood.

"Kelly...Colin...Jeremy," Ryan said, acknowledging the three men.

"Ryan. It's been a long time. Good to see you again," Kelly stepped forward, the only one to offer his hand. Ryan shook it, nodding his greeting, but they all stood in silence.

"Can I have a minute with you Claire?" Ryan asked quietly.

She wanted to say no, and she could see Colin shaking his head vehemently, but she nodded anyway.

Kelly picked up his form and left the room, followed directly by Jeremy. Her brother, however, came to her side. "Are you sure about this?" he asked quietly, but making sure that Ryan could hear him.

Claire nodded again, and Colin left the room, saying that they would be right outside if she needed anything, pulling the door closed behind him.

Ryan pulled up the chair that Kelly had been sitting in and sat next to the bed. He was quiet for a moment, studying her face. She was uncomfortable, but she could still feel the stir in her stomach, even so many years and so many icy looks later.

"You really gave us a scare," he said, finally. "You were still so long, and there was so much commotion. We thought you might have been killed."

"We?" Claire asked.

"Myself, the other jocks, you are one of us now Claire, and we look out for each other. Everybody was concerned."

Claire sighed. "Thanks. I'm going to be fine though."

Ryan never took his eyes off of hers. "I know. You'll come back better than ever," he said, and he reached up to touch her face. She pulled away. He wasn't going to do this to her again, and she was angry, but she had the control, and wasn't going to keep her mouth closed any longer.

"Don't. Don't touch me," she said softly, trying to keep her voice steady. "Why do you always do this Ryan? You just waltz in, every time I am at my weakest, my most vulnerable, and you rip out my heart. Why?"

For the first time since she had known him, he looked deflated, and remained silent.

"Can I ask you something?" she said.

"Yes."

"Why me? You could have any woman you wanted, so why me?"

"Because I wanted you," he said honestly. "And come on, Claire. You didn't exactly make it much of a chase."

"I was 19 years old! I was a kid! On my own for the first time, you knew I idolized you, that I would never have said no! You had to know it wasn't right, but you went ahead and did it anyway, didn't you?" Claire tried to shout, but she couldn't muster the strength, her ribs hurt so badly she couldn't take a deep breath.

"I'm so sorry Claire. I never meant to hurt you."

"Liar. You came back again. Or did you forget Vegas?"

Ryan looked away, and Claire couldn't believe that she might have actually seen tears in his eyes.

"No," he said. "I didn't forget. Maybe, the first time, you were just a conquest, but something happened. You did something to me, and I wasn't used to not having control. I reacted the only way that I knew how, and that was by pushing you away....and I'm so sorry, for everything."

Claire was angry. Angry about it all, and she once again, asserted herself. "I think that you need to go. Please go," she said quietly, not wanting to show any more emotion.

Ryan nodded and stood, suddenly looking all of his 37 years. He reached out and grabbed her hand. His eyes glistened, but he spoke with out so much as a waver. "You remember that night in Vegas?"

Claire could only nod.

"If you had let me in, I never would've left." He leaned over her, lightly kissing her forehead, and walked out of the room.

She watched him leave, and her throat began to tighten. Her ribs hurt with every inhale, and she was getting dizzy. There were hushed voices outside of the room, and in a moment, Jeremy came in, alone.

"Claire?" he said, quietly.

She lost all control and started to sob. It hurt so badly, everything hurt, but she couldn't stop crying. Part of her wanted to believe that Ryan had been lying to her, after all, he was a pro at it, and it was just one more way for him to get to her. But, another part of her believed he had actually been telling the truth.

Jeremy sat, holding her hand, until she was able to get herself under control.

Once she was finally quiet, he spoke. "Will you tell me what happened with him? Colin said that I need to know, but it isn't up to him to tell. Will you tell me now?"

Claire nodded, knowing that the tale might send Jeremy running. She had kept it from him for so long, and up until now, it had never really been an issue, just a part of her past that she chose not to divulge. So she told the story, from the beginning, leaving out only bits that her boyfriend didn't really need to hear.

When she was done, they sat in silence, Jeremy looking at her as if he was trying to make a decision.

"Is it over? Are you really done with him?" he finally asked.

"Yes."

"Ok, then. Let's worry about getting you back in the saddle."

Claire smiled at him. He was right. Life goes on, and he would be by her side through it all.

"He's kind of a little guy...do you want me to kick his ass?" he said, the humor coming back into his voice.

Claire laughed in spite of the pain. "No. I'm pretty sure I can handle things now."

"Good. Cause I'm a lover, not a fighter." He winked at her, causing her ribs to hurt again.

CHAPTER 19

The first six weeks of Claire's recovery were brutal. She was always in pain, and not accustomed to being idle, she began to slip into a depression. Her days were tedious, trying to maneuver through her home on her crutches, basically going from her bed to the sofa, as her leg had to be elevated constantly, or it would begin to throb unbearably. The doctor from the track, Dr. Botha, came by her home to change the dressings on her legs, and was constantly on the look out for signs of infection. He was a kind man, tall and thin with curly red hair and glasses. His voice was soft and soothing, and he had an accent that was hard for Claire to place. It turned out that he was originally from South Africa, and had come to the states to study medicine. He was a casual horseman, and he loved his work at the racetrack. She found out from her agent that Dr. Botha was personally responsible for saving the life of a jockey, who would have died on the track if the doctor hadn't been so quick to respond. Claire knew that she was in good hands, and everybody said the Doc was the best. Even after Claire's open wounds had healed, he would still stop by and check on her occasionally, asking her about her emotional state, and expressing genuine concern when she said that she was not doing well.

Jeremy took all the time off work that he could, but he did eventually have to leave her alone at home, where she would sit in front of the television, usually with John Henry in her lap, and contemplate whether or not she would ever be able to get back on a horse.

The first Saturday in May arrived, and Claire and Jeremy were glued to the TV. She was of mixed emotions while watching all the hype leading up to the Kentucky Derby. On one hand, she loved the spectacle and the overall atmosphere, enjoying the back-stories of the horses and their various connections, but this time was different. There was a buzz about Ryan, and it seemed like every other story had something to do with him. She forced herself to watch, although neither she nor Jeremy spoke much during the broadcast.

She had picked her favorite horse, a nice colt from Florida, with a jockey she had never met, and they watched the horses come onto the track for the post parade. The horses all looked beautiful, and she studied the riders, taking note as to which ones looked nervous, which were obviously overwhelmed by the entire experience, and which ones remained completely calm. Ryan looked like cool perfection, an obvious veteran of the Derby, going for a win that would put him in the record books with some of the best riders in history.

The Derby gates opened, and she watched the race...cheering for her horse, while secretly hoping that Ryan would find himself in traffic trouble and not get a clean race. Alas, it was not to be. Riders of his caliber made their own luck, and he had a perfect trip, winning yet another Derby.

The post race festivities and interviews began, and the winning jockey was the hero of the day. Claire couldn't take it anymore.

"Turn it off," she said to Jeremy, who willingly obliged. He could tell she was upset, so they sat and watched some mindless landscaping show in silence.

*

The next several months were grueling. She was off of her crutches, but still had to wear a boot. Physical therapy was in full swing, and between Shane's intense workouts to help her maintain some of her condition, and therapy to strengthen her leg, she was coming home exhausted every day.

Shane was impressed with her strength, and her therapist was thrilled with her progress. He attributed her rapid recovery to the fact that she was still young and she was in such good physical shape. He explained that he had worked with many jockeys after similar accidents, and he said that, for the most part, they all healed much quicker than the hospital doctors said they would, simply because they were in such excellent condition.

She pushed hard, determined to be riding by the Santa Anita meet that started the end of September. Her progress was frustrating. One day she would be feeling good, thinking she could start getting on horses in the mornings, and then she would have several bad days, where she was constantly hurting, and didn't even want to get out of bed, much less do her therapy and conditioning.

By the end of the summer, she was ready to start getting on horses in the morning. Frank was neurotic. His girl was coming back, and there were times when Claire thought he would spontaneously combust. She took it slow, only getting on one or two horses a day for the first week, and then gradually began building up, finding her riding strength again as she began to work horses, starting with short, three furlong works, and gradually building up her distances. Her leg hurt, but it wasn't unbearable, or distracting. Nights were the worst, when it was time to go to bed. After a hard day of work, it always had a dull throb.

One morning, Claire had finished her workers, and went to find Frank, who had told he to come to James Imler's barn. She arrived at the immaculately kept shed row, and sought out her agent, who was in the tack room, deep in conversation with the trainer. She remembered the first time she had met James, at the gala for the Eclipse Awards, and since then, he had given her some nice mounts. They had a good rapport together, and their win percentage was high, although he still wasn't giving her his best stock. Those were reserved for Ryan.

Frank turned to greet Claire as she entered the tack room, and told her to come out to the shed row. The trio walked down the long aisle of the barn, Claire was looking at the horses, who had their heads hanging over the stall guards, curious of the onlookers. Their coats all glistened, and every one looked the picture of perfect health and conditioning. About half way down the row, James walked ahead of them and clucked to an occupant in a stall. Claire watched as a big, beautifully dappled, gray head poked over the guard.

"This is one of my two year olds," James said. "He hasn't run yet, but I've been given strict orders by his owners that they want you to ride him."

Claire stepped forward, allowing the big colt to sniff her hand, before she rubbed his face. He was enjoying the attention, and leaned into Claire's touch, demanding more. He was one of the most beautiful horses that she had ever seen, and in her three years racing, she'd seen a lot of horses. The thought saddened her. She remembered a time when she had formed close bonds with her horses, remembering their every quirk, but after a thousand mounts a year, many of her charges had faded from her memory. Horses come and go, and there were times when she would only ride a horse once or twice before it was gone, or switched to another rider.

There was a feeling that Claire had while standing by the big gray, and she was not sure what it was. The horse was gently mouthing the zipper on her flak jacket, and she was grabbing at his lips with her fingers. They played like that for a few moments, before he turned his attention to his trainer, who was rattling something in his pocket. Claire was surprised when James pulled out a package of M&M's. The crinkling sound of the package had the horse's undivided attention, and he pushed the trainer with his nose, demanding the snack.

"He eats chocolate?" Claire asked, not believing what she was seeing.

"His favorite," James said, pouring some of the candy into his hand and allowing the horse to munch it down. "I have to be careful though. Can't give him too much...don't want to rot the teeth," he laughed as he scratched the horse's ears as the colt was nudging around for more.

They left the horse, and Claire and Frank thanked James for the introduction to the colt and headed away from the barn.

"That's the horse," Claire said, not sure as to why she was feeling so strongly about a horse she had never even been on.

Frank nodded. "Yes it is."

They walked in silence for a few moments before her agent spoke again. "This is our shot, Claire. I don't know that James would have given him to you if it weren't for the owners, but we're going to take it. The pressure's on. He'll be ready to race about the middle of October, so you better be 100%. One screw up, and he'll go to Ryan. You got it."

"Yes. I'll be ready," she said. There was no way that she was going to lose that horse, especially not to Ryan.

"I know you will be. This is our time, Claire. It's our time." Frank said, and they headed their separate ways.

*

The day before her first race back, Claire and Jeremy were at home, she was having a hard time relaxing, and he was worse. She could tell that he didn't want to seem overly concerned, but he couldn't hide his anxiety about her getting back to the races. He was sure he had lost her once, and he didn't want to experience anything like that again. After dinner, they were trying to relax by finding something mind numbing to watch on television, when the doorbell rang. Jeremy got up to answer it, and Claire was unconcerned, assuming it was just one of the missionaries that would periodically show up, and Jeremy would send him on his way.

"Claire, you have a visitor," Jeremy said, with obvious tension in his voice.

She looked around to see Ryan standing at the entry of the family room. What was he thinking showing up at her home? She didn't stand, but motioned him to the chair, while Jeremy came and sat next to her on the sofa, immediately taking Claire's hand in his own. He had never been possessive, or even remotely jealous, but this was different. Ryan's presence in their home had the green monster lurking in the periphery of Jeremy's consciousness.

Ryan spoke first. "Hey, Claire. How are you doing?"

Claire was wondering what his motives were, but she played along. "I'm fine. Thank you. And yourself?"

"Good. I see you are riding your first back tomorrow."

"Yes," she said, still unsure of the direction of the conversation. "What do you want Ryan?"

He looked at her. "I know you probably don't want me here, but I just wanted to tell you that you'll be okay."

"What do you mean?"

"I know what you are going through right now. I am talking to you as a fellow rider who has gone through the same thing. You're nervous, not sure if you are going to be able to do it, right?"

She nodded, knowing he was dead on.

"Well, you can. My first ride back after my spill, I was a mess...it took every ounce of courage that I had to walk into those starting gates, but I did it. You are going to be nervous, but push it aside...don't let your horse sense that you're scared, or it won't work. Force yourself calm, and remember what you are there to do. It is going to be a tough race, and you're going to be happy to just finish, but once you do, all of the fears will be gone, and you'll be fine again. Trust me on this, I'm speaking from experience."

Claire nodded again, trying to not look into his eyes, not wanting to feel any of the butterflies ready to invade her stomach any time she met that steely gaze. "Thanks for that. You're right, I am nervous, but I'll be fine."

"I know," Ryan said, standing. "I'll see myself out. Good to see you again, Jeremy."

Jeremy nodded in his direction, and Ryan left.

"Do you suppose he's being sincere?" Jeremy asked when the front door closed.

"I think so. He was just trying to help. He has, after all, been hurt badly and knows what I'm going through."

Jeremy grunted. "I'm sure a lot of jocks do, but I don't see any of them showing up at the front door."

Claire shook her head and kissed Jeremy lightly. "It's fine. Will you please stop worrying."

Jeremy kissed her back, and then pulled away. "You know, I don't think I will stop worrying until you retire from racing all together. I never realized how dangerous it is until I saw you laying there on the track, and I was completely helpless. It was the worst feeling in the world, and every time you go into those gates, I am going to say a prayer, even if you don't."

She smiled, and he kissed her again. They headed for the bedroom, and for a little while that evening, she was able to take her mind off her upcoming race.

*

It was race time, and she went through her routine in the jockey's room, it all coming back to hear easily. The Saint Christopher was back around her neck, with the shiny new chain in stark contrast to the worn, tarnished look of the medallion itself.

With time to kill before the fifth race, she wandered into the common room, thinking that she would just watch some of the races as they occurred, on television, and try to get her head where it needed to be.

The room was empty, and she stood for a few minutes, too nervous to sit. She was staring at the television, not really aware of what was on the screen. Her anxiety was getting the best of her, and she couldn't focus on anything, so she retreated back to the ladies room and put on her headphones, trying to lose herself in the music.

The time for her race had arrived, and she went out to the paddock. Her nerves were like live wires, and she almost overshot the saddle as she was legged up onto her horse. Once in the saddle, she began to relax. Being on a horse was still her favorite place on earth, and it was the one place she could always clear her mind.

As the field approached the gate, Claire was beginning to feel the anxiety return. The memory of her accident was again fresh, but she pushed it away, not wanting her horse to sense a change in her emotions.

She entered the gates, and her filly stood quietly.

"You good?" her gate handler asked, knowing it was her first mount back.

"Yep," she replied, hoping her confidence was believable.

The gates sprung, and her filly broke sharply. It was a short race, only five and a half furlongs, and she was well positioned, allowing the speed horses lose on the front, and sitting nicely in third. As she came out of the turn, into the stretch for home, she gave her mount a smooch, and the filly responded, surging forward, catching the tiring front runners in the final strides and winning the race going away. All of the worries of the previous months were gone; she was back where she belonged.

Claire's confidence on the track returned and she found her way into the winner's circle regularly again. Frank quickly decided that vacation was over, and he began working her harder than ever. She enjoyed being back, and things fell into her normal racetrack routine.

After few weeks back riding, Frank called her late, as usual, to go over the next morning's works.

"Big day tomorrow," he said. "It's your time to shine."

Claire was confused. "What do you mean?"

"James Imler wants you to come work that gray colt. It will be his last work before he runs, and he wants to make sure you're up."

Claire was thrilled. She had been waiting for her shot to ride the colt, and she was giddy with excitement.

Frank continued. "Also, the owners are going to be there to watch. No pressure or anything, just bring your A game."

"I always do."

"I know. Just be there on time."

"Frank, relax. I'm always on time. I'll be there on time, ready to ride. Stop stressing."

Her agent laughed nervously and hung up the phone.

The next morning, Claire was busy, but took the time to stick her head into James' barn to get a peek at the colt. She looked in the stall, and was immediately concerned. The colt was laying flat on his side, making loud, and groaning sounds. She clicked her tongue at him, but he didn't so much as twitch an ear. Her Derby dreams were vanishing before they had even begun, so she hurried to find the trainer.

"James. Something's wrong with the colt," Claire said as soon as she found him, in a stall with another horse.

"What do you mean?" he asked, not seeming particularly concerned.

"He's flat on his side, and he is making this funny groaning noise....I think it might be colic!" James laughed, which was not at all the response that Claire expected from a world-class trainer. "What?" she asked.

"It's nap time. He's sleeping, and that funny noise.... he's snoring."

"You're joking?" Claire said, somewhat embarrassed.

"Nope. Claire, that colt is more human than any horse I have ever trained. If he doesn't get his mid-morning nap, he trains like crap. If he doesn't get his daily dose of M&M's, he sulks. Every single day is the same routine. I tried to train him early one day, and he was crabby all the way around the track. He is not a morning person."

Claire laughed, and relaxed. James was one of the top trainers in the country, and he knew his horses well. She left to go work her other horses, and would return at the scheduled time.

When she returned, Frank was waiting, talking to an elderly couple that Claire could only guess were the gray colt's owners. She approached, and Frank made the introductions.

"Claire, this is Walter and Marianne Spencer. They are the colt's owners."

She greeted the couple courteously. They appeared to be in their 70's, both impeccably dressed and quite classy looking. Walter was white haired and portly, yet still carried a distinguished air. His wife, Marianne, was classically dressed, and the picture of wealth and elegance, but she had a kind expression, and took Claire's hand with both of hers. Claire was slightly embarrassed, her dirty, calloused hands contrasting with the woman's ivory skin and perfectly manicured fingernails.

"I am so pleased that you are going to be riding my baby. We have been following your career, and Walter and I both decided that you are the rider for Penfield."

"Excuse me...what's the horse's name?" Claire asked, not sure that she heard correctly. "Penfield," Marianne said again. "I named him after the little town I grew up in, in upstate New
York."

Claire took it as a sign, explaining to Marianne that she knew exactly where the town of Penfield was, given that she grew up right down the road. The old woman was like a schoolgirl when she heard Claire's story, and she couldn't stop talking about how things were meant to be.

The big, gray colt was lead out for Claire, and her breath caught in her chest. She had only ever seen him in the dark of his stall, and in the morning light, he was even more magnificent. He stood about 17 hands tall, and his dapple-gray coat glistened like crystals of ice. James came to give her a leg up, and she headed toward the track. She was taken by the colt's strength, every muscle of his shoulders rippling under her legs.

James gave her instructions. "Four furlongs, easy. He is quirky, won't start his gallop until he stands for a few minutes and watches the other horses on the track. Don't push him to go, he'll pick it up when he is ready."

Claire nodded, and James left her alone with the colt, who did exactly as the trainer said he would. Once on the track, Penfield simply stood, quiet, but alert, watching the activity. He never twitched or trembled, and when he was ready, he turned himself and began to jog, then broke into an easy gallop on his own. He was relaxed, and let Claire maintain a soft hold on his mouth, without pulling. As the half-mile pole approached, she allowed him to ease down to the rail, and he began to pick up speed. She was sitting perfectly still, allowing the big gray colt to lengthen his stride, and suddenly they were flying. It was like no other feeling she had ever had on a horse. His strength and power, combined with his natural speed gave the illusion of floating above the ground. Claire never moved a muscle as they came out of the turn into the stretch. Penfield changed leads smoothly, and continued to cruise down the track across the finish line.

Claire stood in her stirrups, and eased the colt back. It was the first time that he actually took a hold of the bit, and she had to really work at getting him to pull up. She was able to bring him down to a walk, and noticed that the colt had not so much as drawn a deep breath. He was calm, and had expended very little effort in a work that Claire knew was fast. She hoped that James wouldn't be angry, but she never so much as pushed her mount to run, he had done it all on his own, and she wouldn't be surprised if it was the fastest half mile work of the day.

She brought Penfield back to the barn and dismounted, listening to Walter and Marianne gush about how beautifully she had ridden, and how she was made for their horse. James pulled her aside for a moment as the groom took the colt to be cooled down.

"That was good, but a little fast, don't you think?"

Claire was afraid he would say that. "I know it was fast, but I never asked him to run. He was going easy, not fighting me, and I swear I didn't push him. He did it all on his own, and he never even took a deep breath."

James smiled at her. "I know. I just wanted to hear what you had to say. Great job. There's a race for him this coming weekend."

"Thank you. Thank you for letting me ride him," Claire said.

Frank found her quickly, and they began to walk together to her last work of the day.

"I swear Frank, if I am not on that horse this weekend, you're fired."

Her agent laughed. "You're on him. Already got the call. That good, is he?"

Claire couldn't think of another word. "Orgasmic."

Frank laughed so hard that Claire thought he may actually have a heart attack, but there was truly no other word for the feeling she had when she was on that horse's back. This was her Derby horse, and they both knew it.

*

The day for Penfield's first race arrived, and Claire was the most excited she had been in a long time. She had a horse that she was sure would be good enough to take her to the Derby, and she couldn't wait to see what he could really do. His morning work was unbelievable, but, with the competition of other horses in the race, he was bound to be even better. Claire had never been so confident about a horse, and she knew that if she didn't win the race, it would be because of a major mistake on her part.

The saddling paddock was bustling, and Claire made her way to where James was standing with Walter and Marianne. She shook everybody's hands, maintaining her professionalism, and watched her big, gray colt walk calmly around the paddock. He was a perfect picture of fitness and composure, which was unusual for horses in their very first race. Often, the excitement of the crowd and the change in routine could make even the most mellow horses edgy, but not Penfield. He never turned a hair, and continued his walk around the paddock with the air of a seasoned veteran.

"Don't try and get fancy out there," James said. "He should win for fun, just keep him out of trouble."

Claire nodded, as her mount approached, and James legged her up on to the tall colt. She picked up her stirrups, and gathered her reins, giving her colt a pat on the neck as she did so. Both horse and rider were calm, and after a brief warm up, they headed to the gates. With out so much as hesitation, the colt went in, again standing quietly. Claire was ready when the gates popped, but her colt broke a step slow. She wasn't worried, and settled him in position toward the rear of the field. The dirt was coming back into her face, and she knew that some kick back was good for her mount. Getting him used to various scenarios in a race would only make him better, and more relaxed in the long run. She maneuvered him to an outside path, not wanting to get boxed in, and as they entered the turn, gave him a tap on the shoulder with her whip. The resulting acceleration nearly put her off balance as the big colt shot forward, his stride lengthening with every step, and by the time they came out of the turn for home, she was in the clear, and increasing her lead by lengths. She glanced back, and was shocked to see how far they were ahead. The big colt had done it all on his own, and she had never had to use her stick.

They came back to the winner's circle to have the picture taken, and when she dismounted, she received hugs all around from James, Walter and Marianne. On her way back to the jockey's room, she was stopped for an interview. It would seem that other people just saw what she had known for a few days now, and the reporter bombarded her with questions about the colt, and whether or not he was a Derby contender. She answered appropriately, not wanting to give too much away, and then made her way to the jocks room. Ryan was waiting for her, and for the first time, she really didn't want to speak to him.

"Nice horse," he said.

"I know."

"What'd you do to get that one?"

Claire was furious. "I am not sure that I like what you're implying."

Ryan shrugged. "I'm not implying anything," he responded, with noticeable touch of sarcasm. "Nobody knew anything about that horse, and all of a sudden you have the mount and win by 15 lengths. It just seems a little convenient is all."

She shook with anger. "Convenient? That I have been busting my ass here for the last three years, and somebody finally took notice? I suppose you think you should have had the mount? Maybe, my agent is better than yours, or maybe people are finally sick of your attitude of entitlement? Maybe you're just getting old."

Claire knew that what she said was cruel, but she couldn't help it. Ryan was once again trying to rain on her parade, but this time it was business.

Ryan never flinched. "You really think I'm worried about it? I'll have my choice of any horse I want for the Derby, and you have only one. Just remember that it is a long road to Kentucky, and a lot can happen between now and then. Your colt just broke his maiden. It will be interesting to see if he does as well against some real competition." With that, he left her alone, and fuming.

*

The meet moved to Hollywood Park in November, and Claire fell just short of another riding title, losing to Ryan by three wins. Penfield won his next race in the same fashion as his first, the final stakes race of the year for two year olds, who would be turning three at the turn of the New Year. In spite of her agent's protests, she said that she was going home during the break in December, but she would be back to ride the day after Christmas. She and Jeremy left for New York, and Claire was happy to be going home. It had been too long; she missed her family and her friends, and the snow.

She was not disappointed, as there was a blanket of fresh, white powder on the ground when they landed in Rochester. With the money that Claire had been earning, Aunt Robyn had been able to buy a larger, more handicapped friendly home than where they had been living. It was a beautiful house, and had everything that Robyn needed to care for Claire's mom, but it didn't feel like home. So many things had changed while she had been away, and she felt like a guest, in spite of being surrounded by her family.

Kelly and Mandy had been around, and they told Claire that they had been watching every race, and they were particularly impressed with Penfield. Kelly was as confident as Claire that he was her Derby horse, and Mandy promised that if she made it to Kentucky, they would be there to cheer her on.

The thing that Claire loved the most was the fact that she was able to relax. Life in California was constantly on the go; during a week in New York, she barely made it out of her sweats.

One morning, a few days before Christmas, Colin and Jeremy headed out to play hockey, leaving Claire, Robyn and Emily working on holiday preparations. They were all three busy in the kitchen, which was now big enough for everybody to move without constantly bumping into each other, and conversation was easy, until Emily dropped somewhat of a bomb.

"I think Colin is going to propose at Christmas," she said, not looking up from her cookie making.

Claire was stunned, but Robyn seemed to take it without surprise. "I think you're right," Robyn said. "But it's obviously supposed to be a surprise. How'd you guess?"

Emily laughed. "Because he has been acting strange for weeks. Men are quite transparent when it comes to things out of the norm."

Claire was happy. Colin hadn't said anything to her about it, perhaps he wanted it to be a surprise to everybody, but she was happy for her brother. As it turned out, Emily was a nice person, and they were perfect together. "I assume you are going to accept," Claire said.

"Of course!" Emily smiled. "And I will be happy to be a part of your family....just make sure there is room for us in Kentucky in May!"

Claire smiled again. She had so much support from her friends and family, and couldn't help but get excited about the possibility of sharing such a huge day with all of the people who had made the journey possible.

Robyn turned the focus to Claire. "Since we are on the topic of relationships, Jeremy seems like a good man. Do you guys have any plans for anything more permanent."

"You mean marriage?" Claire asked, knowing full well what her aunt meant.

"Well, yes."

Claire shook her head. "Not right now. We are happy with the way things are going. I really need to focus on my work, and Jeremy isn't convinced that he wants to stay in California, so we are just going to see what happens."

Robyn seemed satisfied with the answer, but asked her next question anyway. "What about Ryan? Have you got that situation sorted out?"

Claire knew that Colin had told their aunt about her constant battles with Ryan, and everything that had been happening, so she felt she needed to be honest. "I think that it's as 'sorted out' as it will ever be. He is an asshole about 97% of the time, which is making it easier to deal with him now, but..." Claire paused for a minute, wondering if she should tell these women about her true feelings. "He still gets to me. There is still something about him that makes me hate myself a little bit every time he looks at me. I love Jeremy more than anything, and he and I are perfect together, but there is still that little bit of something that shows up in me every time Ryan is around."

Emily nodded. "Don't beat yourself up Claire. You and he had an incredibly passionate physical experience and you were young. As a woman, I am here to tell you that those kind of white hot, super intense sexual encounters are nearly impossible to get over."

"I am starting to realize that," Claire said, sighing.

Emily continued. "Here's the thing though. You're more mature, and more in control now. You're more than capable of handling yourself around him, and he knows that. If it's any consolation, you probably messed him up as much as he did you, but the way he chose to deal with it has been his undoing. Men can be stupid like that, especially ones like him, who are used to having everything go their way. You've handled it well, and you're in the driver's seat. Unfortunately, you're never going to forget, but you've done a good job of doing what you need to do to move on."

Claire nodded. She knew that Emily was right, and a thought was stirring around in her mind, but she wouldn't entertain it, not now. She needed to wait until after the Derby, and then maybe it would work.

They celebrated Christmas, and as Emily had predicted, Colin proposed. Everybody was overjoyed, and Emily had done a brilliant job at acting surprised. Jeremy got a glimmer in his eye, and Claire told him to not even think about it. Not yet.

Claire spent time with her mom, hoping that the last few years would have brought about some kind of change, but they hadn't. She was exactly the same, although Claire thought she looked older.

Christmas Day was subdued with the knowledge that Claire and Jeremy would be leaving well before dawn the next day so that Claire

could make it back in time to ride. Dinner was fabulous. With Colin and
Jeremy in charge of the meal, it was the best meal Claire had had in a long
time, making her feel nostalgic about the years at home, when her family
would gather around the table.

"It's a darn good thing you found a guy that could cook," Colin jibbed
at his sister.

"I know. I got lucky," she said, smiling at Jeremy. He and Colin had
become quite close, and Claire was pretty sure Colin spoke to him more
than her.

Morning came early, and everybody said their goodbyes. Claire was
sad, but eager to get back to work. The horses were waiting, and her agent's
anxiety level was through the roof, as he was sure that Claire was going to
miss her plane, or some other disaster was going to befall and she wouldn't
make it back in time to ride.

CHAPTER 20

Just when Claire thought that Frank couldn't work her any harder, he managed to find a way to drive her to her physical and emotional limits. He had taken on the duties of personal manager, as well as jockey agent, coordinating her interviews and dealing with the various press people. Penfield was suddenly on everybody's radar, and so was Claire. She found herself doing interviews almost weekly, and as the big, gray colt continued to win, she was getting more and more attention. There was a buzz around the idea that she might be a serious contender in the Derby, and being a woman made the hype even greater. She dealt with it, although it pushed her far out of her comfort zone. Over the years, she had tried to get used to the cameras, but they still made her slightly uncomfortable, and at every opportunity, she tried to turn the attention to the horse, after all, if it weren't for Penfield, she'd never have been in this position.

They won their first major Derby prep, and the next stop would be the Santa Anita Derby. It was a huge race, with all the major implications of Derby contention. If they won, they'd be one of the favorites going into Kentucky. Claire had been studying the competition going into the race, and knew that her major rival would be Ryan's horse. He, as expected, had found a live mount with Derby potential, and up until this point, the two horses had never met, as Ryan's horse had been running elsewhere, and was shipping in to California for the race.

As the Santa Anita Derby approached, Claire found herself increasingly nervous. She had been riding for a few years now, and had encountered every different racing scenario imaginable. She had ridden in stakes races, and big money purses, but nothing compared to the anticipation of the upcoming race.

Derby day was one of the biggest days at Santa Anita Park. Everybody was dressed to the nines, and Claire saw how it was a precursor for Kentucky. A win in this race would guarantee her a trip to the Derby, and the stakes could never be higher.

She was ready, and the riders were called to the paddock, which was brimming with people, friends and family of the connections of every horse in the race. Claire approached Walter and Marianne, greeting them and their guests, and waited for James who was doing some last minute adjustments to Penfield's equipment. He finished and approached her, shaking her hand as usual. "Just do what you do," he said, completely trusting her skills and knowledge of her mount.

"Will do," she said, trying to remain calm as she was legged up. Once in the saddle, she was relaxed, and was lead to the track. They were breaking out of the inside post, number one, and she was listening to the cheers as the announcer called her name. She had developed quite the following amongst the fans, and had been told numerous times that she was the reason the track attendance had been going up. Everybody wanted to see the girl who would beat the boys.

The field approached the starting gate, and her horse moved in quietly, standing at the ready, waiting for the rest of the field to be loaded.

They're off! Penfield broke more sharply than usual, and Claire found herself closer to the front than she would have liked. The speed horses to her outside dropped down in front of her, and the rest of the 12 horse field collapsed around her, angling for the best position going into the first turn. She was in tight, being squeezed from all sides, and trying not to run up on the heels of the horses in front of her. The big colt was pulling hard, not happy about being so contained, but Claire did her best to relax him. The horses moved onto the backstretch and very little had changed. She was boxed in on the rail, and all she could do was wait. Penfield was moving easily, but she knew that if she didn't get an opening, it would be difficult for him to make up distance. The field moved into the second turn, and Claire could see the speed in front beginning to fade. She had to get racing room, but there was still nowhere to go. Her horse was tugging hard, knowing that it was time for the running to begin, but she had to maintain her hold. Her peripheral vision caught a glimpse of Ryan's bright yellow and blue silks as his horse was moving forward on the outside of the horse holding her on the rail. Midway down the stretch, Ryan had clear running, Penfield was fighting, and Claire was still waiting. The horse in front of her began to tire and drift to the outside, opening up the rail. It was a tight squeeze, but Claire angled her colt for the hole and released her hold on the reins. He was ready, and responded instantly, shooting through the space, which was so tight that Claire's boot scraped on the rail. They were finally clear, but Ryan had the jump on her, and was about two lengths ahead, an insurmountable lead with such a short distance to the wire, and even though her mount gave 100%, he was unable to bridge the gap, and they were beaten, running second by a half a length.

Claire felt like crying. She had let down Walter and Marianne, she had let down James and the pubic, but most of all, she had failed her horse. He had done everything right, and she was the one in the wrong. They jogged back to meet the trainer, and Claire quickly dismounted. James was silent, and she knew he was upset. She avoided the interviews, and practically ran back to the jocks room. The tears that she was expecting never came. She was just angry. James Imler had every right to take her off of the horse for Kentucky, and she guessed that he probably would.

She had proven that she was not the best when it came to maneuvering through heavy traffic, and the 20 horse field of the Kentucky Derby would be nothing short of a two-minute traffic jam.

She waited in the jockey's room, long after the races were over, hoping that she would be able to get out alone. She was not in the mood to talk to anybody, and wanted to head to the stable area for a few minutes. Jeremy knew when to leave her alone, and she would appreciate the fact that he'd be waiting for her at home when she was able to pull herself together.

The track was more or less cleared out, and she made her way to the backside alone. She went directly to James Imler's barn, which was quiet after the excitement of the day, with just a couple of grooms going about their business, not paying any attention to Claire. Penfield was in his stall, polishing off his dinner as Claire looked in on him, giving a little cluck of her tongue. He came to her, nuzzling around in her pocket for the treat that he knew was there. She pulled out her stash of M&M's, and gave the colt a handful, which he munched happily, allowing Claire to rub his ears.

"I'm so sorry big guy," she said to the horse, who was still pushing around for more snacks. "It was all my fault. I let you down. You're so much better than that, and we should have won. I screwed up, and it won't happen next time....assuming there is a next time." Penfield bobbed his head up and down, as if in agreement, and then continued his search for his favorite treat. She stood quietly, stroking the big horse's neck, pondering whether or not this might have been her last ride on the horse she had fallen in love with.

"There will be a next time."

Claire jumped as she heard James' voice. "How long have you been standing there?" she asked, turning around.

"Since you got here. I thought I'd let you have your conversation."

Claire didn't respond, rather waited for the lecture that she was sure was coming. James knew she was waiting for him, so he spoke. "It was a tough beat, wasn't it?"

She nodded.

"But, not the end of the world. It's horse racing Claire. Shit happens. You rode a good race, but the circumstances weren't in our favor today. That hole you took on the rail was unbelievable. So many people have been talking about what a gutsy move that was, and how there are a lot of more experienced riders who wouldn't have taken that opening. You did good. So, we lost today, but that doesn't mean I don't trust you as a rider." He reached over to give the horse a pat. "This guy loves you, and he runs for you. I am not going to take you off. Walter and Marianne love you, and they wouldn't even hear of it. We're going to Kentucky, and you are going with us."

Suddenly, the tears came; tears of relief and joy, and Claire was embarrassed. She didn't want

James to see her cry like that, emotional outbursts were not generally approved of in the racetrack environment, but she couldn't help herself. The trainer gave her a squeeze, but indicated that she needed to pull it together. Penfield was curious as to her sudden change in demeanor, and he nuzzled her face, as if to tell her that everything was fine. She smiled and laughed, saying goodbye to James and deciding that it was time to head home. She had big news to share with everybody she knew.

*

The weeks leading up to the Derby were chaotic, and Claire was sure that her agent would rupture something. The buzz around her had reached epic levels, and she was constantly being asked for interviews and photo opportunities. One of the news channels wanted an hour-long piece on her, including her family and early days at the track, and she was more stressed than she thought possible. Jeremy was solid, there for her every second that she needed it, and, more importantly, putting the brakes on Frank periodically, making sure that she always had a little time to herself.

Even poor John Henry was feeling the effects of the pandemonium, and he spent most of his days underfoot, demanding attention that nobody seemed to have time to give.

The hardest part of it all was that Claire still had to do her daily work. She still had horses to ride, and business to conduct on the track. It seemed like the days flew by, and before she knew it, it was nearly time for her to leave for Louisville. Penfield was already there, as James had flown him over a few weeks prior in order to get him acclimated and training over the new track. Claire had been apprehensive. Never having ridden over the Churchill Downs race track, she was concerned that she wouldn't be able to have a ride over the course before the big race, but Frank, being the super agent that he was, had scored her two mounts before the Derby, one being one of Kelly's horses that he had decided to ship down for the big day. Kelly had told Claire that his horse probably wasn't a winner, but it would give her a trip over the track, and it was a good excuse for he and Mandy to be there anyway.

The Wednesday before the Derby was the post position draw. Always a big deal, Claire watched it on television, hoping for the best draw possible. There were to be twenty horses in the race, so many that the gates used for everyday racing weren't big enough, and an auxiliary gate would be attached, adding an additional six positions. The consensus amongst Penfield's connections was that they would be happy with anything from about post 12 to 17. Any of those positions would enable Claire to position her horse outside of the speed, and away from potential traffic trouble. Reason would dictate that an inside post would be more favorable, as to allow the shortest distance around the course, however, in a race with 20 horses, an inside post could mean disaster, especially if your mount wasn't quick leaving the gate. There would be guaranteed traffic, and trying to establish any kind of position on the track could be nearly impossible.

Claire was in the jocks room, in between races, glued to the television, praying for a good draw. About half of the field had been drawn, and

Penfield's name still had not come up. With the inside and far outside posts still open, Claire began to get nervous. Post number nine was drawn, and the horse for post nine was Penfield. She was happy, knowing that it was an excellent draw, not exactly what they had hoped, but she didn't think it would matter. Her heart sank when she heard that Ryan had drawn number ten, right on her outside. Of all the other riders in the race, she knew he was her main competition, and he would never allow her any breathing room.

"Perfect," he said from behind. "That's exactly where I want to be."

Claire glared at him, and without a word, she went to get ready for her next race.

*

When it came time to leave for Kentucky, she and Jeremy were both bundles of nervous energy, which resulted in then snipping at each other most of the morning before their flight left. Once in Louisville, she was not allowed to relax, as Frank had arranged several interviews and photo sessions for her on Friday, followed by a must attend pre-Derby party where all of the participants in the race would mingle. Frank shuffled her and Jeremy out of the party early, saying that she needed to get her rest, although she knew it was futile...there was no way she was going to sleep. In their hotel room, she paced nervously, and Jeremy, who was usually the calm one, was just as on edge. She tried to study the racing form, but found that she couldn't focus. She knew every horse in the race, and every jockey's strengths and weaknesses, and looking over it again would accomplish nothing. It was early into the morning before she finally fell into a restless sleep, with fragments of dreams weaving in and out of her subconscious.

Early in the morning, Claire arose, and began her pacing again. She showered, but couldn't decide on what to wear, as she had packed several different dresses for the day, but none of them seemed appealing.

"Claire, you have got to calm down," Jeremy said finally. "You're going to drive me crazy."

Claire wanted to shout at Jeremy, but she knew he had a point. "I'm trying. I just can't handle the wait. There is still 12 more hours, I didn't sleep for shit, I have to ride the first and second races, and then I get to sit, in the jocks room for the rest of the day. What am I supposed to do? I'm going out of my mind."

Jeremy shrugged. "I hate myself for saying this, but why don't you talk to Ryan?"

"What? Why?"

"Because he's ridden this race a dozen times, and he knows what to do. He had his first Derby once too, and he might have some tips on how to keep your cool."

Claire knew he was right, and she also knew that it took a lot for Jeremy to say that to her. "Alright. I'll talk to him when I get in there but he may not speak to me. He isn't about to make things easy. I'm his primary competition."

"Maybe not, but it doesn't hurt to ask. There are a bunch of other jocks in there too, so if he won't speak to you, ask one of them."

Claire nodded, and then continued to fret about her wardrobe.

After what seemed like an eternity, she was able to leave. Jeremy would follow shortly with Colin and Emily, allowing her some time completely to herself before the chaos began. All she wanted to see was the twin spires of the historic venue, but she was whisked into the jockeys quarters, with a security escort, not able to do any sightseeing. It was times like this that she was grateful to be a woman. There was not another female jockey on the card, and she had complete privacy to get ready for the first race of the day.

Once in the room, she found she was able to relax slightly. She had to be ready for her first mount, Kelly's horse, and she didn't want to make a fool of herself. This was the real deal, and if she couldn't put forth a good performance in a minor race, how could people expect her to pull it together for the biggest race in the world.

She put on Kelly's familiar black and turquoise silks, thinking about the last time she had worn them, her final race at Finger Lakes on Reggie. It seemed like a century ago, as she thought about how far she had come, as both a woman and a jockey, since that time. The riders were called for the first race of the day, and as she took the escalator down to the paddock, she was greeted with cheers from the fans. She had no idea how well known she had become, and there were people clustered around the paddock fence, calling out well wishes as she made her way over to the covered saddling box where Kelly and Mandy were standing with her mount. All professionalism was forgotten, and she received a hug from each of them. Mandy was giddy with excitement. "Do you see all of these people here for you Claire? Isn't it just unreal?"

Claire nodded.

"You made it girl. We are so proud of you!" Mandy gushed, hugging her again.

Kelly, however, still had business to attend to, and his horse was his priority at that moment. "This guy is probably outclassed in here. Just let him break and run his race. He'll be good, just get yourself around the track, and pay attention. Look around you, and familiarize yourself with everything. This is a much bigger track than you are used to, so get your bearings. You'll be fine."

Claire nodded again, as Kelly legged her up onto the big chestnut gelding who reminded her slightly of Max. She listened to the familiar bugle of the trumpet as the horses made their way through the tunnel from the paddock to the track, and Claire had to catch her breath. She was there. The apron of the grandstand was packed with people, and the Derby was still six hours away. There was an electric buzz through the crowd, and it sent a chill down her spine. Her horse was anxious, unaccustomed to such a huge crowd and the noise that it brought, and

Claire was happy to be through the post parade and moving away from the grandstands over to the backside, where things were quieter, and her horse could relax. Once there, she looked across the infield at the spectacle. The twin spires of the grandstands were piercing the sky, and she still couldn't believe that she had finally made it.

The field made their way to the starting gates for the one-mile race. Unlike the other tracks that Claire had been riding, Churchill Downs was significantly larger, and a mile would be completed with only one turn. It was another thing that she wasn't used to, but she was just going to ride her best and let her horse take care of the rest.

In the starting gate, the gelding was restless, but her handler calmed him, and they were off.

Claire could feel right away, that her mount wasn't of the highest quality, but he was trying, and she allowed him to settle about mid-pack down the backstretch. As they turned for home, she asked for more run, and he gave it, but it was never going to be enough to win. They crossed under the wire in third, which was better than anybody had expected. Her horse had given her everything he had, and she was pleased with him.

Back at the grandstands, Kelly and Mandy were elated, hugging Claire as she dismounted. "That is the best this guy has ever run. You sure you don't want to come back to Finger Lakes?" Kelly said, laughing.

"Maybe someday," Claire said.

Mandy smiled at her. "You'd better not. You belong here with the big boys."

Claire thanked them and headed back to the jockeys room. She had to ride the next race, and then it was the waiting game.

Her next mount was a colt who was rank, and difficult to handle. She had her hands full the entire race, and he had worn himself out by the time the real running began, fading down the stretch, beating only two other horses. Claire was slightly disappointed, but this was not her home track, and she had to take what she could get. The experience over the track was what she wanted, and she was feeling more confident about being out there for the Derby.

She sought out Ryan. He had several mounts on the day, most of the stakes on the undercard, but he was in the common area when she entered. Her fears that he wouldn't speak to her were eased when he initiated the conversation.

"How you holding up kid?"

"Terrible. How do you do it?" she asked, getting straight to the point. "How did you keep it together in the hours before your first Derby?"

He smiled at her, and her knees weakened, only slightly. "What choice have you got?"

"Don't be an ass. I know I don't have a choice, but what can I do to make it easier?"

Ryan looked at her for a moment, as if trying to decide what to say. "Do you want to know something? I still get nervous. This is my twelfth derby, and I still get a bit jittery."

Claire was annoyed. "Right. I didn't think you got nervous about anything. You're as cool as a cucumber every single time you are on a horse. What's the secret?"

"No secret, but you just said it. The instant I am up on the horse, everything goes away. I'm there to do a job, and that's what I do. You'll get there, it just takes time."

"Ugh....you're no help at all!" Claire exclaimed with exasperation. "I don't have time! I'm riding in the Derby today!"

"Don't worry, I'm right next to you, and I'll be keeping you close the whole way," Ryan said, a touch of sarcasm coming into his voice.

"I bet you will, for about a mile, and then you better be ready to ride," Claire said, hoping she sounded as cocky and arrogant as he was. He gave her a slightly amused look and left her alone.

The hours drug by, and she spent them watching the races as they were taking place, on the television in the room. Ryan, in his usual form, won two of the races on the undercard, and the buzz around him was almost comparable to the hype surrounding her. He was one Derby win away from being the winningest jockey in Kentucky Derby history, and he was determined to make that happen. They were both looking to make their marks the racing record books, and this race would truly be the race of a lifetime.

With an hour left to post, it was time for Claire to get ready. Any hopes of being still had long since vanished, and she paced nervously. Trying to sit just made her knees shake, so she stood and walked. She fingered her Saint Christopher for a moment, and then tucked it into her undershirt, making sure the clasp was firm, before reaching for the silks of Walter and Marianne Spencer. They were beautiful, with the body being a rich, crimson red, with white sleeves. On the back was a large white circle, centered with a red and black ladybug. Marianne had told Claire that she had loved ladybugs since she was a little girl, and when she designed the silks, she knew they would have a ladybug. Claire found it fitting, as she had heard that ladybugs always find their way home. She hoped that she would be getting that ladybug home first.

The jockeys of the Derby all gathered for a photograph, and the time had nearly come. As the twenty riders left the jocks room, with their security escort, and they were all silent, making their way down the escalator, with camera's in their faces, moving toward the paddock. With several of the spectators screaming her name, Claire was feeling like she might vomit, but she was hoping that she looked as calm as the other jocks. Ryan was next to her, and as usual, he was the picture of cool, giving her a tap with his stick as the group of riders, in their brightly colored silks, moved into the saddling paddock.

Claire's stomach turned over as she entered the paddock, seeing the massive crowd, shoulder to shoulder, in the enclosure. She could hear people shouting her name from the fence, and she scanned the crowd, trying to find Jeremy, or her brother, or any familiar face, but it was futile. The crowd was so huge that there was little hope of picking out an individual in the sea of humanity.

She found Walter and Marianne in the paddock, and greeted them, trying to keep her voice from shaking, and then made her way to the saddling box where James was waiting with Penfield.

He shook her hand. "How are you doing?"

"Nervous," Claire admitted.

"You'll be fine. It's just another horse race, and you know how to ride."

Claire nodded and turned her attention to her horse. He looked fantastic. His dapple-gray coat was glistening and he was turned out to perfection. She thought that he never looked better, remaining calm amongst the chaos, and her anxiety level dropped a notch. The call for riders up was made, and Claire waited until it was their turn, and then she was legged up as Penfield was led out to circle the paddock, before heading through the tunnel and out onto the main track.

James gave her a pat on the leg and moved away, leaving Claire alone on her horse, with only his groom at his head. Once on her horse's back, she discovered that Ryan was right, and she immediately began to relax. Her colt was quiet and alert, paying attention to the crowd, but not getting too riled up like some of the others in the race. She could hear her name being called, and as she looked across the mass of people, she felt overwhelmed. They were beautiful, with the women all dressed to impress, with their obligatory Derby hats, and the men were equally well turned out. It was a sight that was unmatched anywhere, but the thing that got to Claire the most was all of the support for her. There were signs with her name, and people screaming for her attention. In the weeks leading up to the Derby, she had done interviews by the dozen, but the implications of them had never really hit home. The eyes of the entire country were on her, and she couldn't let them down.

The horses made their way through the tunnel and out to the track, the bugler sounding the familiar call, and then it began, My Old Kentucky

Home came over the PA system, and Claire's throat caught. The crowd of over 100 thousand people was singing the words, and she couldn't stop the wave of emotion, quickly wiping the tears, and taking a deep breath. The air was sweet with the smell of roses and perfume, and heavy with humidity. Claire had forgotten about the humidity, and felt her skin begin to prickle with sweat. It was a beautiful evening, pleasantly warm, with the sun dipping slowly in the western sky, and she took a second to soak in her surroundings.

They turned, passing the grandstands again, as they broke into a jog and began an easy warm up. Penfield was traveling well, and Claire found herself calm. Ryan was right. She was here to ride, it was what she loved to do and she was ready. Her pony rider eased them to a walk, and she looked around at the other horses in the race. Some were calm, and others were clearly agitated, and she began to feel even more confident. Penfield was cool and relaxed, and she spoke to him quietly, stroking his mane. His ears swiveled as he listened to her voice and she continued to talk, as much to keep herself calm as her horse.

It was time, and the horses were called to the gates, and Claire took a deep breath as she pulled her goggles down over her eyes. This was it. In a mile and a quarter, and about two minutes, it would be over. Penfield entered the number nine stall and stood quietly. She was aware of the activity around her, and heard Ryan speak.

"You ready to ride?" he asked, without taking his eyes off the long stretch of dirt in front of them.

"Yes I am," she said, also not diverting her attention from the track.

The field was almost loaded, and Claire was remotely aware of a hush that had come over the giant crowd. She was ready, and the field was in. The horses were all quiet for a split second.....

.......And They're Off!

CHAPTER 21

Penfield broke on even terms with the field, Ryan's horse broke slightly inward, and bounced off of Claire, but she was able to hold her colt steady, and he found his stride quickly. The run down the stretch to the first turn was long, and Claire worked on easing her mount closer to the rail. Horses on both sides of her were jostling for position, and the speed had gone quickly to the lead, leaving room for Claire to drop down slightly to save ground going into the turn. She was wary about getting right on the rail, as she wanted to leave herself a clear path. Ryan was glued to her outside, matching strides as they went into the first turn, not giving her an inch.

Through the turn, Claire had her hands full. Penfield was tugging at the bit, but she was surrounded by horses as the rest of the huge field was tying to settle into their desired positions without losing too much ground or running up on heels. With twenty horses, there was a significant amount of bumping and cursing from the other riders, but Claire kept her cool and maintained her position, not allowing any of the other jocks to push her around.

As the horses left the first turn and moved into the backstretch, her horse switched leads smoothly and relaxed into the bridle. The rest of the

field was beginning to settle into their positions, as the key for the moment was to just relax and wait for the right time to make the finishing
move. Her big, gray colt was steady, and Claire talked to him softly. They
were positioned mid-field, about seven lengths off the front-runners, and
her mount was moving easily. She glanced over at Ryan, who was not
moving a muscle, and she knew that he had a ton of horse under him. He
looked over at her briefly.

"How you doing?" he asked. Trying to gauge the competition.

"Well enough," she responded, not wanting to give anything away,
and hoping she was telling the truth.

As they moved down the backstretch, Claire looked around. She had
two horses on her inside, and Ryan on her outside, with about five horses
in front of her, and the rest of the field behind. She knew that there were
some closers back there, horses who would come flying in the stretch, but
she wasn't worried about anybody but Ryan, and he was going to keep in
her sights until the end, and she knew that he had the horse to do it.

Entering the turn for home, the front-runners began to come back
to the rest of the field. Claire felt like she actually had a shot, her horse
was still traveling smoothly, and she had yet to ask him for run. She kept
toward the outside, allowing the front speed to come back, blocking off
any inside path for potential late closers. It would be better to force them
to the outside, and get the jump on them from her favorable position. She
gave Penfield a tap on the shoulder, and the colt responded, lengthening
his stride as they came out of the turn and into the final stretch to the
wire. Ryan was still right next to her. He had perfect measure, anticipating
her moves before she even made them, and he was able to keep his horse
right in stride with hers.

The roar of the crowd was deafening. This was the moment that the
entire racing world had been waiting for; would it be the first woman
to win the Derby, or would Ryan become the all time leading Kentucky

Derby jockey? Either way, all one hundred thousand plus people were on their feet, and the roar had reached a crescendo.

Claire was on the inside, and Ryan on the outside, head and head surging down the stretch. Each horse was pushing beyond their limits, and Claire knew that it was do or die. She continued to push her colt, going to her whip, first with her right hand, and then switching to the left. Penfield continued to give, never allowing his rival an inch. Ryan was down and riding as hard as ever, but gradually, bit by bit, her great, gray colt was finding more. Claire continued to push, but instead of whipping, she put her stick away, and rode with her body flat to her horse's neck, asking for everything he had, and her mount gave it. Thirty yards from the wire, Claire was a half-length ahead, and even with the deafening roar of the crowd, she heard Ryan.

"Go on girl, you got this."

She did. Sweeping past the wire, with a single length victory over the best jockey in the world.

Claire's mind became a blur. She reached down and gave her horse a pat on the neck, as she relaxed and let him gallop out, easing up slowly. About half way around the turn, the scarlet-coated outrider moved his horse up next to her, grabbing Penfield's bridle and being the first to offer her congratulations. She was eased up to a walk, and there were shouts and cheers from the other riders as they were returning their mounts to the grandstand area. Throwing her arms around her horse's neck, she whispered a quiet thank you to the magnificent animal. For Claire, the reality had not yet begun to sink in. She was approached by the mounted reporter who asked the question that brought it all home.

"Claire Durham, you just became the first woman to ever win the Kentucky Derby...how does it feel?" the woman asked from astride her pony, holding out a microphone to Claire.

Claire began to get emotional. "I'm not sure.   This horse is just so amazing, and he did everything right. I am so happy to have been given the opportunity to ride him."

The reporter got off another question. "That was a pretty incredible stretch dual. How does it feel to outride the top jockey in the country?"

That was a question that Claire didn't even have to think about. "It feels fantastic," she replied, beaming.

She answered a few more questions, as the outrider took her and Penfield towards the winners circle, where there was an enormous crowd waiting to greet them. The roar from the crowd in the grandstands was at epic levels, and Penfield began to bob his head up and down, in acknowledgement of his own brilliance.

They stepped onto the grass of the turf, making their way toward the winner's enclosure, and James burst forth, closely followed by the grooms. Claire was required to stay mounted, so she leaned over for a hug from the trainer, as the grooms took charge of the colt, sponging cool water over his head and neck.

They stepped into the winner's circle, and Claire heard shouts of congratulations from everybody, including Jeremy, her brother and Emily, Kelly and Mandy, and above all the other voices, she could hear that of her agent, bellowing at the top of his lungs.

The garland of crimson roses was placed over her lap, and she inhaled their sweet aroma, as horse and rider were moved into place for the photograph. She was finally able to dismount, giving Penfield a hug before he was taken back to the barn. As she turned, Colin and Jeremy immediately grabbed her in a huge hug, followed by Emily and Kelly and Mandy. Penfield's owners, Walter and Marianne were slightly more reserved with their enthusiasm, but Frank hugged her so hard she thought he might crush her.

What followed was question after question, as the media was poised after the trophy presentation. Claire answered them all, trying her best to attribute her success to the horse, saying that he was the one who did all the work, and he was truly something special. After what seemed like hours, but was actually probably only about 30 minutes, Claire was able to make her way back to the jockey's room, wanting to stop for autographs, but being ushered along by the two beefy security guards. There was still another race to be run, but Claire was done, and she welcomed the privacy of the ladies room where she sat, trying to wrap her head around what had just happened, and not sure how things were going to change for her from that moment forward.

She took her time changing and gathering her things. There were people waiting for her, but she chose not to hurry. The last race was long over before Claire headed out, and most of the riders were gone, save one.

"I thought you were never going to come out of there," Ryan said.

Claire smiled as he approached her, stopping for a moment before embracing her in a hug. "You were amazing...congratulations, you deserved that," he said, releasing her.

"Thank you. Sorry you didn't get your record breaking win."

Ryan laughed. "No you're not. Besides, there's always next year."

"That's true," Claire said, knowing that Ryan probably had a better shot at another Derby win than she ever would.

"Now, you better get out there and greet your public. Your life's about to get crazy," he said, giving her one more quick hug. "See you back in California."

Claire nodded, taking her courage in hand and walking out of the room, unaware of the fact that he never took his eyes off of her as she left.

The rest of the night was a blur of interviews and parties, she answered question after question, and said thank you more times than she thought possible. Jeremy was at her side the whole time, and it was well after midnight before they were allowed to escape and return to their hotel room, where Claire fell asleep almost instantly, completely drained from the excitement of the day.

*

It seemed like she had only just fallen asleep when there was a pounding on their door. She opened her eyes, realizing that it was in fact morning, as Jeremy stumbled out of bed to see who was clearly ignoring the do not disturb sign. He opened the door, and Frank burst in.

"God, don't you sleep?" Jeremy said, rubbing his eyes and climbing back into bed. Frank ignored him.

"Time to get up!" he boomed. "Places to go, and things to do!"

Claire pulled the covers over her head. "I thought you were going to let me sleep in?" she whined.

Frank laughed. "I did. Come on...you have interviews lined up all day today, and I've had to turn people away. Let's go."

Claire decided that it was as good a time as any to tell Frank about what her plans were for the future. He wasn't going to be happy, but it was something that she had thought long and hard about, and she had made up her mind. "Frank, after this is all over, assuming we get through the Preakness and the Belmont, I want to move my tack to New York."

Frank was horror-stricken. "You're kidding me...right? New York? Why in hell would you want to do that? You are doing great in California! Now is not the time to leave!"

"I know, but I need to be closer to my family. Long Island is a heck of a lot closer to Rochester than Los Angeles, and I've made up my mind. I'd like you to come with me."

Frank was beside himself, as usual. "You're killing me girl, you know that, you're just killing me. I hate New York."

"Ok, suit yourself. I'm sure I won't have a problem finding another agent," Claire smiled, knowing how to push his buttons.

"Hell no! You won't be getting another agent. I'll come to New York, but I don't have to like it!" Frank stood. "You are seriously killing me.

Every day that I'm your agent takes weeks off my life...you know that, don't you?"

Claire laughed, and Frank left the room just as dramatically as he had entered, reminding her that she had approximately 30 seconds to be out the door.

The day was full of media frenzy, and Claire did her best to oblige everybody who asked, but by mid afternoon, she was done. She simply couldn't function any longer, and she told Frank to cancel any interviews for a couple of days, as she was going home. Aunt Robyn and Claire's mother were not able to make the trip to Kentucky, and she had to be with them. In those hours, she was missing her mom terribly, and she craved the peace and quiet of home, even if it was only for a day. She and Jeremy escaped on a plane, and she felt instant relief as she sat down, glad that she could finally take a breath.

When she arrived home, she was greeted by her aunt. They cried and hugged, and cried some more. Colin, Emily and Jeremy were in the kitchen, and Claire went to her mother, and sat down next to her, taking her hand.

"We did it Mom, we won the Derby," she said, looking at her mom for any sign of recognition, and for just a moment, Claire saw a flicker and she was sure that there was the tiniest twitch of a smile on her mom's lips. She began to cry, releasing all of the built up stress and emotions of the last several weeks, and her mom just sat quietly and listened.

In that single day at home, Claire was the happiest she had ever been, but life must go on. There were still horses to ride, and California in all its glory was waiting for her to return. But for just a moment, she was home and things were beautiful.